Loyalty Binds You
TYGARYA SAGA
BOOK TWO
by
ANNETTA LINCOLN

Dedication

*To all those fantasy readers who like a strong female lead,
who swears and drinks a lot, kicks ass and takes no prisoners.
This one is for you.*

WARNING

Set in a medieval dystopian world with magic
Mentioned throughout this series are several triggers
including;
A lot of swearing
Violence
Murder
Intimidation
Gas-lighting
Submission
Suppression
Forced Proximity
Explicit sex scenes
Assault

PART I

Welcome Home

ANTYN'S
PROPHECY COLLECTION

Beware the birth of a daughter
of the three formidable races.
This magic must be sought out and controlled for the
Dragon's blood to rule the world and cannot rule
without it.
Keep the silver-haired one close and control the
power to prevent a catastrophic doom
for she will struggle under pain as the power
writhes up to devour her.
The Dragon's blood will rule absolute, the
entire world held by his omniscient vision.
It must be this way for the world to be free
of its own minds oppression and once more rise
up in prosperity and peace under a ruling
God.

- excerpt from
The Prophecies of the Dragon Born 1623

Map of Tylan Continent

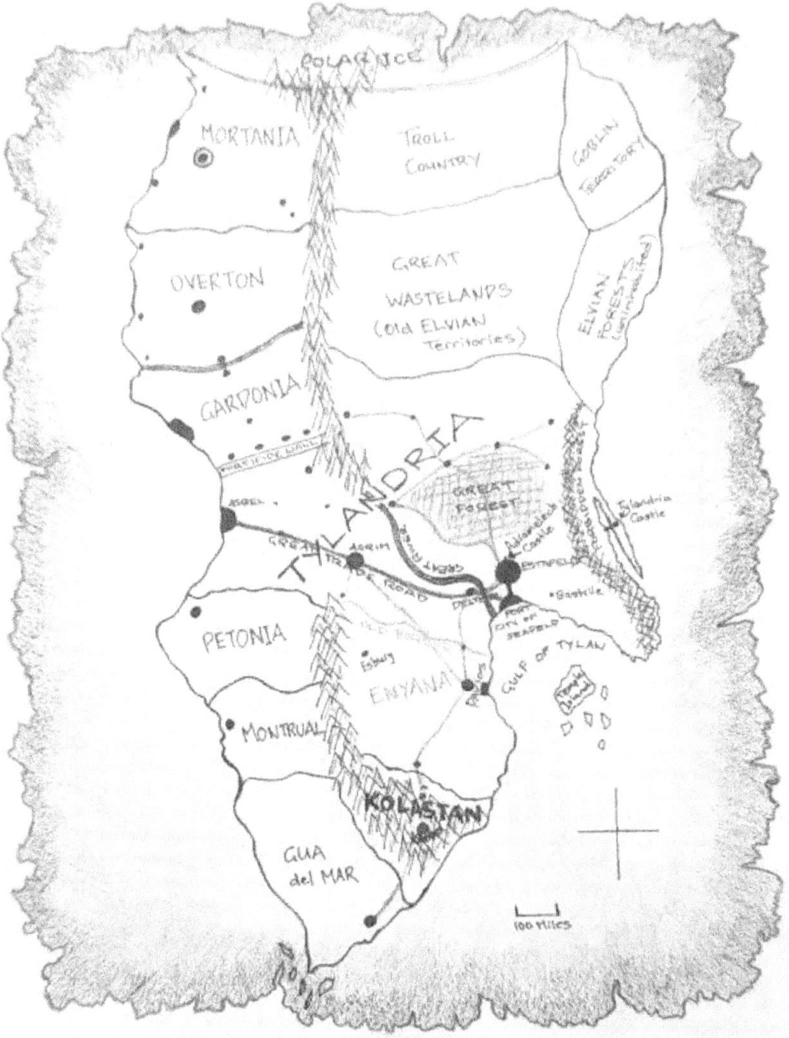

POLAR ICE

MORTANIA

TROLL COUNTRY

GOBLIN TERRITORY

OVERTON

GREAT WASTELANDS (Old ELVIAN Territories)

ELVIAN FOREST (uninhabited)

GARDONIA

THALADRIA

GREAT FOREST

Islandria Castle

GREAT TRADE ROAD

PETONIA

CITY OF SEAFELD

GULF OF TYLAN

ENYANA

MONTRUAL

KOLASTAN

GUA del MAR

100 MILES

Prologue

T he first week on board ship couldn't go fast enough for Tyg. She was sea sick for most of it and wished she could die. Luckily the side effect of her sickness was that Leviathan left her alone. Antyn helped her of course, giving her herbal remedies and magical calming spells to help with the nausea.

By the start of week two she had found her sea legs. She found that keeping to her cabin during the day and coming up on deck for fresh air at night was the trick to keep avoiding Leviathan and the crew, they hardly knew she was there half the time, which was a good thing since they firmly believed, like most sailors, that a woman on board was bad luck.

She knew she couldn't avoid Leviathan forever though and she could feel that his anger and frustration was getting worse by the day, but she enjoyed making him suffer. She figured it had probably been a long time since he had, had no power in a situation and she wasn't feeling like letting him off the hook yet. Although it was now to the point where it was getting beyond either of their control, only Antyn could see that, if it wasn't sorted soon it was going to come to a head and someone was going to get hurt.

There had been a couple of times they had nearly had altercations on board. Leviathan had almost caught her leaving the deck late at night one night. He had come out of his cabin just as she was walking back into hers. She had glanced at him like a terrified rabbit to a wolf and slammed and locked her door as he had growled her name, his cool blue eyes blazing.

Just like at the Manor, he wouldn't enter her room, it seemed. But, her time was running out and Antyn had become more and more insistent that she stop being so childish and patch things up with Leviathan before they reached Tylandria. For the most part she ignored his advice which frustrated him too, besides he was hardly innocent in the whole affair either.

Tyg decided to play a risky game and came up on deck one morning early to see the sunrise after it had been squalling rain for the past two days. Staying in her cabin for two whole days had made her feel nauseous again so the fresh air was welcome. She still had another twelve days on board ship to go, and that was with the assistance of the warlocks using their wind manipulation to keep the sails full and the ships moving at a decent speed. She was standing at the aft of the ship, wrapped in a warm cloak watching as the light increased on the horizon. The Captain was at the wheel and had been watching her strangely as she stood behind him. She was a bit of an enigma since the sailors hardly ever saw her, they knew nothing about her and it was rumoured that she was perhaps the Lord's mistress or whore. They didn't even know Leviathan's real identity, Lord Doven had merely told them he was a special client and to treat him with the upmost respect.

Tyg froze when she heard the Captain suddenly leave the wheel.

"Tygarya." A whisper came from behind her. She grit her teeth, she could never hear that sneaky sorcerer approach.

She turned around slowly to face him. Leviathan was standing by the wheel, he looked like he was trying to approach a wild fawn in the forest. Tyg remembered back to the day in Arial when he had raised a fireball and then come to take her to a banquet afterwards like nothing had even happened, so mercurial it always put her on the back foot.

"I don't want to talk." Tyg muttered.

Leviathan's jaw clenched. "This has gone too far, Tygarya....enough of your childish sulking!" He muttered in that low commanding tone of his. His tone just made her dig her toes in further.

"Really? Because...I don't think so..." Tyg said as she quickly darted round him and took off back to her cabin.

Leviathan growled and shot a fireball over the side of the ship in frustrated rage, down into the frothing waves of their passing. Frustrated he stood at the stern of the ship and looked out at the rising sun not really knowing what to do to get Tygarya back on side.

He couldn't cause a fuss on board, the sailors, given to them by Lord Doven along with the use of the ship, didn't know he was a sorcerer, or an Emperor...only a Lord. It was frustrating...he wanted to just envelope Tyg in his power and make her yield...she had to be made to realise she was his now and it was crucial that she was under his control when they arrived to his homeland.

After killing her boss, who was also her mentor, teacher and benefactor for years he could understand her sulking for a few days, but Palin had known all along what she was and had purposely nurtured that side of her to make her into his own personal killing machine, manipulated and used her for his own gains. Why did she continue to cling to her loyalty?

Leviathan wanted that loyalty for himself.

1

"I'm sick of her avoiding me, Antyn." Leviathan growled as he stalked into the aft cabin.

"Can you blame her, you killed...what's his name...?" Antyn waved his hand around nonchalantly.

"Palin." Leviathan growled under his breath, his fists clenching.

"Yeah him. You killed him right in front of her, but at least she still came with us...freely." Antyn said frustrated. "That means there is still some semblance of trust towards us. Just give her time to take it all in."

"I've given her enough time...what is she trying to prove? I want her back like she was before, when she came to me to get me out of my melancholy."

Antyn wiped his face. "That was before you fought with her."

"I also saved her arse." The growl this time was fierce.

"You also tried to kill her when she killed that assassin..." Antyn sighed and rubbed his eyes. "I don't know Lev, I'm not an expert on human female emotions but..."

"She's not human." Leviathan sneered.

"Been raised human, no matter how psychotically by that asshole, and so still quite inexperienced in relations. She is only nineteen, remember that, you've got decades of experience over her. She probably has no idea how to put things right either and is confused and scared."

"Hmm." Leviathan snorted. "I'm going to talk to her. It's been over a week for fuck's sake, how long can someone carry a grudge?

And I know she's up there now...enjoying the darkness. I can't stand being so close to her, yet so bloody far away!"

Antyn gave Leviathan an exasperated look, it worried him how attached and possessive Leviathan seemed to be over the girl that he also worried it would end up messing with their plans.

"I understand the need to get her under your control, Lev, but be careful. Pushing her could cause the opposite effect, she's extremely headstrong."

Leviathan huffed as he walked to the door and left.

Tyg was standing close to the bow of the ship, her hands rested on the rail, as she looked out at the darkness of the water. The moon was up and shining on the inky black surface. A cool breeze blew against her face, but she didn't care. She loved the night on board ship. It was quiet and peaceful. A time for contemplation. She still hadn't decided whether or not she had made the right decision to return with the brothers. Antyn, of course, seemed nice enough and was helping her learn their language, giving her lessons in her cabin during the day.

Leviathan, on the other hand...

He was so intense. She loathed the way her heart hammered in her chest every time he was nearby, like a silly teenager, infatuated. Was she infatuated with him? That thought just made her want to avoid him even more, knowing who and what he actually was scared her a little and she didn't like the feeling of being scared of anything, or anyone. The fact he was stronger, faster and far more lethal than her definitely scared her...it was a new experience and the way he watched her made her shiver. Her conflicting feelings for Leviathan confused her deeply and she didn't like being confused, and after what he did to Palin just made her even more conflicted. She knew the brothers had some ulterior motive for bringing her to their homeland – her homeland, they had not held that a secret from her, Leviathan admitting more than once that he needed her for something. She just wished she knew what it was.

Tyg was brought out of her reverie by footsteps behind her. She turned to see Leviathan approaching. A spark of warning raced up her body as she saw that same vulture like expression on his face. With nowhere to go she had no choice this time but to face him. He came forward and stood in front of her. An imposing figure, his height and broad shoulders were accentuated by the heavy black coat he wore. He effectively blocked any chance of getting around him to escape this time. Tyg could tell by the way he held himself that he was looking for an argument, she grimaced inwardly...this was it the inevitable clash of wills.

"You have been avoiding me, Tygarya. I won't stand for it any longer." Leviathan said in that low calm voice. His eyes seemed to burn with a strange fire in the moonlight.

Tyg tried to find some way around him, then settled for simply putting her back to him by turning to the rail and looking out to sea.

"Perhaps I have, but can you blame me, after what you did?" Tyg answered.

"What's that supposed to mean?" Leviathan replied, a hard edge coming into his voice. He didn't like the fact that she had turned her back on him. "I saved you...remember what he said."

Tyg took a deep breath. "I'm not stupid..." She turned her head to speak to him without turning around, she heard the growl in his throat at his annoyance. "You said you wouldn't kill him, instead you stuck him like a pig! And enjoyed it! Do you think I enjoyed seeing you do that to my teacher?" Tyg looked back at the sea in the darkness, she could see the twinkling lights of the other ships in the distance. Corvyn was out there on one of those, Leviathan had deliberately put him on a different ship.

"I know you have some ulterior reason for wanting me to return to Tylandria with you than just returning me to my homeland. I don't know what that is, but let me tell you..." She felt him take a step closer, his hulking form looming over her making the hairs on her arms lift. "...I'll not be so easily coerced again by the two of you as I was to get me to come with you. I don't know what magic you used to get me to come with you so easily, but it won't work again. As soon as we reach Tylandria I will be seriously considering getting straight back on the next ship back to Arial."

Tyg bit her lip. Maybe that was too far. She knew Leviathan's terrible temper first hand and didn't want to ever feel that again. The sailors had received his temper in the last nine days, Tyg had heard of him throwing a sailor overboard and striking the first mate for a ripped sail, but luckily these sailors didn't know who or what he actually was or what he was truly capable of, only that he was immensely strong and very quick to anger. The fact that the wind seemed to always be at the tail was only seen as a great luck story as they made great time.

Leviathan laughed. Not the reaction Tyg was expecting, but it never was with him. He leaned towards her, placing his hands on the rail either side of her, effectively trapping her. He pressed himself against her, pinning her to the railing. He lowered his head towards her, grabbing the edge of her hood and pulling it back away from her ear as he brought his mouth close and whispered in a low dangerous tone.

"You think to tell me what I can and can't do in my own Empire? Yet, you say you're not stupid. You have a lot to learn, my dear...especially your place in all of this. When we land you will very quickly realise just how powerful I am. You will need my protection."

Tyg suddenly felt very much out of her depth, his words were threatening yet the smell of him was intoxicating, the warmth of him enveloping her was enthralling, she knew her attraction to him was going to make her relent easily. She tried to break free of his little prison he had created with his body, but he deftly pinned her arms to her sides, by wrapping his arms around her and holding her against his chest. He made her listen as he continued. She wasn't used to anyone being stronger than her and she hated having to yield to him constantly like this so out of control, but she stilled in his arms and closed her eyes, her heart hammering in her chest and her stomach doing strange little flips at having him so near.

"You have journeyed with us at my request, Tygarya. Better for you, because you would still be here, in chains if need be, understand that. You are important to my Empire....and to me. The full extent of which I am yet to fully understand, as I have already told you, so you need to understand this...you will not be going anywhere once you reach Tylandria but to the castle with me. You *will* stay by my side, my dear."

Tyg was on the verge of panic as Leviathan ran his hand up from her hip to under her ribs then against her breast, as he turned his face and kissed her just behind her ear. She gasped and struggled against him causing him to hold her more firmly, painfully. He whispered in her ear again.

"You are mine now, Tygarya. The sooner you accept that fate the better time you will have."

He turned her round forcefully by the shoulders to face him, one hand running to the nape of her neck, his long fingers grabbing into her hair at the base of her skull. He kissed her hard, forcing his tongue into her mouth. His hips pressed against hers as she leaned back against the railing, his hands holding her strongly. Tears started to form in Tyg's eyes as she struggled against him. She didn't want to kiss him like this, but then he trickled power into the kiss. Tyg's eyes widened in surprise, it was like a drug and it made her lose herself as her body betrayed her to the warm sense of pleasure and relaxed, her eyes fluttering closed.

A low steady voice sounded behind Leviathan.

"That's enough, Lev. Let her go." It was Antyn, coming up to check on what was going on. Seeing Tyg struggle then go limp told him exactly what Leviathan was doing.

Leviathan broke off the kiss and raised his arms to the back of his head in mock surrender. A wide grin on his face as he looked down at Tyg. His hips, however, were still pressed firmly against her. She was frozen to the spot, still dazed by his magical kiss, not sure what to do. Their eyes were locked on each other, both of them glowing softly in the darkness.

"Tyg, come away now." Antyn said softly, as he held his hand out to her.

She looked down at where Leviathan's hips were pushed up against her, she placed her hands on his chest and shoved him backwards, her eyes blazing ice blue fire with contempt as her senses came slamming back to her. He staggered back a couple of paces, chuckling to himself. Tyg stared at him a moment then stormed off to her cabin, feeling embarrassed by her reactions to him.

Leviathan put his forearms on the railing, leaning down, and looked out at the black water. He was suddenly no longer amused but quietly contemplative. Antyn watched Tyg retreat then turned and approached Leviathan leaning his hip on the rail sideways, facing him, he folded his arms.

"Was that altogether wise?" Antyn asked, feeling a little mystified by Leviathan's aggressive action.

"It's time she realised she's not here by her own choice. She's figured out that there's something about her that we want. She made it quite clear to me that she intends to resist us every step of the way." Leviathan chuckled. "I think it's time to stop pussy footing around her and let me take over again." Leviathan turned to face Antyn.

Antyn looked over his right shoulder at the water, then over his left shoulder at the couple of night watch sailors who were standing watching the proceedings. Antyn locked eyes with them a moment and they quickly returned to their duties. He turned back to Leviathan who was watching him intently.

"We still have at least another two weeks left on this ship, all going well. I don't think it's wise to let anything about who she...or we...are slip just yet." Antyn glanced back at the sailors meaningfully. Even though they were on Lord Doven's personal ship the crew seemed less than civilised and more like pirates. He wondered if Lord Doven had swapped out the crew or if some of the sailors had refused the contract.

Leviathan followed Antyn's gaze and looked at the sailors, now back checking and tightening ropes, he gave a small snort of disregard.

"Still, a quick lesson in how vulnerable and alone she is out here wouldn't go amiss, besides the pureness of the power radiating from her is intoxicating. It's like a drug, Antyn. I want more, and you know the more I take from her the calmer she will be for the rest of the journey."

Antyn raked a hand through his hair and cursed. "For fuck's sake...just stop feeding her *your* power, it's not fair on her." He looked hard at Leviathan. "If you want to bed her why not do it the normal way and woo her into it with your charms. The attraction is there...just give her time...must you really do this so forcefully...and right now?" Antyn was almost pleading with his brother.

"You're one to talk...besides where's the fun in that? I need her to realise I have full control over her now so she stops this ridiculous charade and submits to my control before we reach shore." Leviathan snorted as he stood up, rubbing his neck.

"Besides, every time we get close something always makes her pull away...you've seen it."

"Yes." Antyn frowned, he had wondered whether it was past trauma that made her freeze up when affections got too raw and real. "So you know she will fight you."

"I know, I'm rather looking forward to it...her weapons are all safely locked away in the hold, I made sure of it." Leviathan said with a grin. "Besides, underneath it all, we both know what she is...a wild Elvian. I want that personality out where I can see it and nurture it." Leviathan turned and strode off back to the aft cabins following Tyg. Antyn watched him go, emotions pulling him in several directions. He sighed, turned and leaned his elbows on the railing staring out at the blackness of the water. He couldn't shift the thought that Leviathan seemed extremely pleased in the fact that Palin had known what Tyg was and had trained her up coaxing some of the worst traits of her race in her. It would have been a lot easier if she had been found still innocent and living with some middle class family, educated and polite. Still the raw power she contained was evidence enough that they had been right to follow the prophecies and search for her. How easy it was going to be to get her to awaken that power under their control was something only the heavens could answer at this stage.

2

Tyg was standing in her cabin, facing the large porthole in the side, looking out at the moon. She was shaking with rage. After fleeing to her cabin she had gone over in her mind what had happened and now she was angry. She didn't like what he did to her, kissing her like that. She lost all control and that scared her wondering how far he would take things if she had no control to resist. It was overwhelming to her senses, and as much as she was attracted to him she did not want to have her body taken without her ability to give her consent. That brought back all the thoughts and feelings of why she allowed Palin to train her as an assassin in the first place. She grabbed her small three inch dagger that she had been hiding under her bed and was now turning it over and over slowly in the palm of her hand, as she stared out the porthole. She would never give anyone that sort of power over her, she would rather die first.

The door banged open and Tyg spun round, hiding the dagger behind her back. Leviathan stepped into the room, dipping his head through the doorway and without even touching it, the door swung shut behind him. Tyg knew that if she tried it, the door would be locked to her efforts. Leviathan had a smug grin on his face which just managed to make Tyg even angrier. He had entered her room...her sanctuary...something had changed between them and she felt it, ever since she had stepped on board this ship and sailed away from Arial. It was that feeling of not being in control of her own decisions anymore and that made her revert back to that wild street urchin that would have done anything to survive and not be abused, triggered by Leviathan's domineering behaviour. The anger burned, her eyes blazing. Leviathan saw it and chuckled a deep rumbling laugh as he approached her. He stopped a couple of yards away from her and held out his hand to her.

"Come to me, Tygarya." Leviathan said softly compelling, using the same tones he had used back in Arial when talking her down.

Tyg caught herself as she was about to take a step forward, the desire to walk into his arms was strong, she grit her teeth and planted her feet firmly against it. What was this strange attraction and desire to do whatever this man told her to do?

"No." She stated firmly.

"Why not? You always have before?" He tilted his head in a curious manner, his eyes narrowing.

"Because, your intention is different this time." Tyg said in a hushed tone, her eyes large and bright.

"My intention?" Leviathan looked amused.

"You mean to harm me...to force me to...I won't let you..."

She took a step backwards, bringing her up against the wall of the cabin. Leviathan raised an eyebrow in surprise, then asked again more firmly this time, that edge coming back into his voice that he was finished with playing.

He smirked on one side of his mouth, beckoning her with his hand. "That's nonsense, Tyg, you're being foolish, come here."

A wave of compulsion overtook Tyg, she shook as she tried to fight it, a faint sweat appeared on her brow a testament to the battle of wills going on. She was attracted to him, but she didn't want this. Why was he doing this?

"You said you would never hurt me." Tyg muttered through gritted teeth.

"I also said this has gone on long enough." Leviathan growled.

Leviathan stretched his hand out a bit further, his mind willing her to obey him. Tyg realised this was about authority, who was in charge here...and as Emperor it should clearly be Leviathan, but that didn't give him the right to demand this of her! Her submission to him would never come that easily.

Tyg's knees were just about buckling under the strain of resisting when, to her dismay, she found herself taking a step towards him, then another. As she moved she noticed that the pressure on her mind lifted slightly with every step. She grinned as she adjusted the grip on her dagger and looked up at Leviathan's smiling face. She would show him the result of messing with her.

"That's right, Tygarya, just take my hand." Leviathan commanded softly.

Tyg locked eyes with him, his eyes were glowing with the power he was using on her. His face twisted in a smug grin. Anger flared up in Tyg as she stepped forward, Leviathan saw her eyes go black, too late.

She brought the dagger round and plunged it into Leviathan's stomach. Her eyes never left Leviathan's and she saw his go wide with surprise as that smug grin slid from his face and went grim.

She looked down at the dagger protruding from his stomach, just above his belt, her firm grip around the handle. Leviathan staggered back a couple of steps, pulling the dagger free as Tyg held it fast. She stared at the dagger, bright red blood dripped down over her hand onto the floor. She grimaced, she hadn't wanted it to come to this but how else could she break his mind hold over her and show him she would not be controlled by anyone.

Suddenly an explosion of pain resounded in her head as she was thrown sideways from a powerful blow to the side of the head by Leviathan's power. Tyg instantly tasted blood in her mouth as she tumbled to the floor. She lost her grip on her dagger and it skittled away. She glanced up through her hair at Leviathan and saw him advancing on her. His eyes blazing, one hand clasped the wound, trying to stifle the bleeding. Leviathan then grinned maniacally at her as he sent his power into her head. Tyg gripped the sides of her head, gritting her teeth, growling against the pain and doubling over.

"Antyn!" Leviathan roared out.

He walked up to Tyg and kicked her hard in the side. Tyg felt the crack of ribs as all the air in her lungs was forced out. As she tried to breathe again she found herself unable to take another breath against the stabbing pain it caused, she started to panic as the pain from her side sent flaring stabs of light behind her closed eyes while the pain in her head continued causing her nose to bleed. Leviathan stepped over her and grabbed her by her hair at the back of her head and lifted her up on her knees as he crouched behind her. He held her head close to his shoulder, breathing in her ear.

"Where the fuck did you get that dagger, you stupid bitch." He muttered through gritted teeth.

Tyg, still fighting for breath was unable to answer, as she struggled against him.

Leviathan turned her round to face him, holding her like a ragdoll. He backhanded her across the face, with the hand covered in his blood. He split her eyebrow with the sharp contact, her head not able to move with the blow. She was starting to see stars and feel faint, but her quick healing was keeping her on the cusp and starting to clear her head.

Just then the door slammed open and Antyn rushed in.

"By the Gods, what are you doing!?" He took in the scene quickly as Leviathan dropped his grip on Tyg's head and stood up. She tumbled to the floor, falling on her hands and knees, her breath rasping in panicked gulps. Antyn stepped up to his brother seeing the wound as Leviathan pressed his hand to it once more.

"My little psycho killer had a dagger." Leviathan chuckled as he winched in pain. "Nothing too deep, I don't think she was trying to kill me..." He had lowered his wards where she was concerned, he wouldn't make that mistake again.

"But you had to retaliate?!" Antyn couldn't help but curse back at his brother and his vicious temper.

Leviathan glared at him then pushed Antyn aside and wrapped his arms round Tyg's waist clearly not finished with her yet, picking her up and throwing her on the bed on her back. Tyg's back arched as her body spasmed with pain and trying to breathe, she couldn't even scream.

Antyn's attention was taken by a couple of sailors passing by the open door, he twisted his wrist and the door banged shut. He stepped quickly between his brother and Tyg, his hands coming up to Leviathan's chest as he braced himself against Leviathan's advancement as Tyg lay prone.

"Stop, Lev, please...let me heal you before you bleed out or something...that blood is dark."

Leviathan looked down at Tyg as she glanced up through her hair at them, still struggling to breathe.

"I just wanted things back the way they were before, for fuck's sake, Tygarya!" He growled at her over Antyn's shoulder. "Did you really think I was going to...?"

"Not now, Lev!" Antyn said crossly. Leviathan clucked his tongue and looked away.

Antyn struggled to manhandle Leviathan out of the room for several minutes until he finally managed to get out of the cabin and across the hall to their own rooms.

Tyg grimaced at Leviathan's parting comment and crawled up the bed, lying propped up on the pillows, having finally got her breath back. She kept her breathing shallow and controlled so as not to aggravate her ribs, she knew they were shattered and would probably take a couple of days to heal properly even with her accelerated healing.

She thought about what Leviathan had said and was fighting remorse. She didn't know what to think anymore and squeezed her eyes shut in frustration. Had she over reacted to him entering her room like that, she had been triggered by strange overwhelming emotions that she just wasn't used to dealing with. Was this what it was like dealing with powerful people...used to getting their way...Lord Kor had been a little bit the same, and she was used to Palin punishing her when she did wrong...had Leviathan really just wanted to call a peaceful truce? If so, why come at her using his power like that to try and coerce her?

After a short while Antyn walked in with a tray of tea in his hands, he placed it down on the table and approached the bed. He looked at Tyg's face. The blood had dried and Antyn grabbed the jug of water from beside the bed and the cloth next to it. He sat down next to her and proceeded to wipe the blood from Tyg's face. He noticed that her eyes were watchful and untrusting, almost feral. No words were offered and Antyn decided that perhaps for the moment silence was best. He checked her injuries and noticed Tyg's split eyebrow was already healed and the black bruising was already out and fading away. It seemed she did indeed heal fast. Finally needing to speak he gave her directions for a salve as he pulled it out of his bag and handed it to her.

"This was to apply twice daily to your cuts and bruising but I see you indeed have accelerated healing like I thought." He poured a cup full of the tea and handed it to her, making her drink.

"This will also help." He said, meaning the tea. He turned his attention to her ribs. "Pull up your shirt and lie on your other side so I can take a look at your ribs."

Tyg looked at him a moment, then did as he asked. Wincing as she rolled over towards him. As she pulled up her shirt Antyn could see a huge area covered in bruising already which should have taken days to come out. He placed his hands over the area, causing Tyg to flinch away.

"It's okay, I can help fix it, make sure they heal back in the right place." Antyn said as he placed his hands over the bottom ribs. He closed his eyes and concentrated. Warmth spread from beneath his hands down through Tyg's skin. At first it was bearable, even pleasant, but after several minutes it started to intensify. Tyg grit her teeth against it.

Just as she was getting to the stage where she couldn't stand it anymore and was just about to pull Antyn's hands away, Antyn opened his eyes and removed his hands. Instantly Tyg could feel the ease in her breathing return. She tried moving and could feel a tightness but not the sharp breath-taking pain. She looked at Antyn and smiled gratefully.

"I told you I could fix it." He said with a weary smile. "It was a punctured lung. If you were a normal human you would have died. Now I need to get some rest myself, you do the same."

Antyn left and Tyg wondered about his words, if you were a normal human, and grimaced. What the hell was she then, really? No one seemed to want to tell her what an Elvian actually was. She rolled off the bed and onto her feet. She wandered over to the chair beside the porthole window and crouched down. She felt under the chair until she grabbed her dagger that had lain hidden underneath. She tucked it under her mattress and climbed back onto the bed too sore and tired to get changed and under the covers, sensing that Antyn must have given her something in her tea to make her sleep. She drifted off to sleep.

3

The next day Tyg woke to find herself tucked into bed with the top bloodied blanket and pillow changed. She grimaced and guessed it must have been Antyn.

"I must tell him not to do that." Tyg muttered to herself under her breath as she sat up. The mere thought of him touching her body even just to move her while she was unconscious made her want to slide a dagger between his ribs.

She winced at the tightness still around her ribs as they were still a little tender. She looked over to the window and saw the sun glinting off the waves, she realised it must be after noon and was suddenly very hungry. She was just about to get up when a small knock sounded at the door.

"Who is it?" Tyg asked, hoping it wasn't Antyn. She really didn't want to face him about last night just yet, especially not on an empty stomach which made her feel every roll of the ship.

The door opened and the cabin boy poked his head in, a wide grin on his face.

"You're awake! Good...I tried before but you were obviously still sleeping. I have some food for you." He said as he pushed the door open using his elbow and carried in a tray containing several sea biscuits, some cheese, dried fruit and a pot of steaming Jasmine tea.

Tyg's mouth started to water at the fragrant smells of the tea as the cabin boy walked up beside the bed and deposited the tray on to her lap. Taking the pot of tea he carefully placed it on the side table. Tyg looked at the tray of food and tucking her hair behind her ears she grabbed a slice of apple and popped it into her mouth. She turned to the cabin boy to thank him and saw him looking at her with his mouth open. Tyg smirked and looked down at her plate.

"It's not polite to stare."

"Sorry, but you're lucky from what I hear." The cabin boy remarked, smiling back, as he poured the tea into a cup for her. "It must have hurt. I heard the commotion...we all did. I thought it was some of the sailors brawling...they do that sometimes. But they've been told to be on their best behaviour with a young girl on board. It wasn't until this morning when I overheard that it was you and the big guy in black....I couldn't believe it! But, looking at you now...I guess it's not true?"

Tyg grimaced, she could just imagine what the rumours were concerning, coming from a bunch of hard up seamen that walked past the door at the most inopportune time, they probably thought she was being raped. "No, whatever they're saying, it didn't happen. Make sure to spread that around."

The cabin boy was only a few years younger than her, she guessed about twelve, and had mainly avoided her since her arrival on board. She guessed now that it was probably nerves. She needed a friend though, and felt that this boy was probably the most genuine person on board. He was relaxed and cheerful and a little roguish.

"What's your name?" Tyg asked, causing the boy to startle with fright at the question.

"Ah, it's Toby, miss." He stuttered in answer, a blush coming to his cheeks.

"Nice to meet you, Toby." Tyg smiled and Toby shyly smiled back. He handed her the cup of tea. She sipped at it gratefully, looking at Toby over the rim as he fidgeted on the spot, not knowing whether to leave or not. "So, why have you been given the chore of serving me, Toby?" Tyg asked patting the bed to indicate he should sit as she drew her knees up, putting the tray on the bed between them.

"Um...well...Lord Antyn said he was too busy and said I should keep an eye on when you wake up and give you something to eat."

"Did he now..." Tyg said in a flat tone.

"Yeah." Toby said as he gingerly sat down on the bed facing Tyg. He watched her as she broke off some cheese and chewed it thoughtfully. "I think it has something to do with his brother, they have both been locked up in their rooms since the fight."

"You don't say?" Tyg replied. "Well I'm glad he sent you, it's nice to have someone to talk to closer to my own age."

"Yeah same." Toby said, a flush returning to his cheeks as he looked down at the blanket, picking at a loose thread. "Although..."

"Although what?"

"Well, we are hardly from the same background, I doubt we would have much in common." Toby said somewhat reluctantly.

"Oh, I doubt that our backgrounds are very different." Tyg remarked, amused.

"Well, you're a lady and...well...I'm just a cabin boy. Where's the sameness in that?" Toby muttered confused.

Tyg laughed. "I'm not a lady...I started out as an orphan and a pickpocket. Worked for the local Thieves' Guild. It just happened that fate put me in touch with a man who helped me to steer away from that life...but a part of me will always be that little thief. Believe me, you don't want to know what I am now." Tyg fell silent thinking about Palin, and what he had said to Leviathan. Just what was she now?

"Wow, I had no idea." Toby said surprised. "I guess we do have things in common after all, I'm an orphan too."

"See, I told you." Tyg grinned as Toby grinned back and nodded. "Toby, could you do me a favour?" Tyg said watching Toby carefully. Toby's expression changed from happy to worry.

"Like what?"

"Well, you would have access to the ship's stores, wouldn't you?"

"Yeah, I suppose? I help the cook prepare the meals." He said a little apprehensive as he rubbed the back of his neck.

"I was hoping maybe you could find your way to getting me a couple of bottles of that red wine I know they have on board."

"Oh, is that all..." Toby grinned mischievously. "I think you deserve it."

"Thanks Toby, you're a real friend."

Toby beamed a toothy grin and flushed. "I'll go and see if I can get them now, if you would like?" Toby got up, relieved to be doing something.

"That would be great, Toby." Tyg said smiling as she watched him leave. She leaned back into the pillows and smiled to herself, it had been a while since she had, had a decent taste of wine with being sea sick, but now she just felt like getting drunk. She popped a piece of dried fruit into her mouth and chewed thoughtfully. Moving the tray to one side she swung her legs off the bed and dug under the mattress with her hand until she felt the cold touch of steel. She smiled to herself and sat in the chair beside the window.

After a couple of hours a light knock sounded on the door. Toby opened it slightly and poked his head in. He saw Tyg sitting in the chair, looking like she just woke up, as she blinked at him trying to focus her eyes.

"It's only me." Toby said as he pushed his way into the room. He held out two bottles of red wine, the grin on his face was full of excitement.

"That was fun I take it?" Tyg asked him as she took the bottles from him and looked down at them.

"Yeah it was." Toby agreed. "I haven't had that much fun for ages."

"Did anyone see you?" Toby looked insulted. "Okay, sorry I asked." Tyg said as she handed a bottle back to him. "Can you open this for me, please?"

"Sure." Toby said taking the bottle and cracking the seal. He pulled a blunt object out of his shirt and pushed the cork down into the bottle. Meanwhile Tyg had grabbed two glasses which were hanging on a frame above the desk. Toby looked at her questioningly.

"You were going to have one with me, weren't you?" Tyg asked as she held the glasses out to him.

He grinned as he poured the wine. "Why not, I'm allowed a glass of ale whenever we reach port, so I don't see why I can't share a wine with a beautiful lady."

"Why not indeed." Tyg said amused at his candour as she sat down in the chair and indicated for Toby to sit on the bed. "Cheers." Tyg said and clinked her glass against his, then took a sip. She watched Toby over the rim of her glass as he took a sip too.

She closed her eyes in ecstasy as she felt the warm liquid flow down her throat and warm her belly. She took another longer sip. She glanced back at Toby and saw him sitting watching her, an empty glass in his hands. She laughed.

"Oh, dear, Toby, you're not supposed to gulp it down like ale, you're supposed to sip it and enjoy the flavour."

"Oh, really?" Toby said confused. "Well, I have to get back to work now anyway...so enjoy your wine, Tyg."

"Thanks again, Toby." Tyg said as he turned to leave. He stopped at the door and looked back. "The pleasure was all mine, believe me." He flashed another grin and left. Tyg drained the glass instantly and refilled it and relaxed back into the chair.

Tyg sat quietly in her room, sipping her wine and nibbling from the tray of food, she noticed the sun going down and wondered just how long she slept. She cursed Antyn for drugging her, but at least neither brother had been back since to give her any grief. She finished her glass and opened the second bottle. She replayed the scene from the night before over and over in her mind. The more she thought about it the more remorseful she became. After a time she became more restless and finished off the second bottle. She grabbed her cloak and wrapped it round her shoulders and headed for fresh air up on deck. She stopped by the door and retraced her steps, retrieving the dagger and concealing it under her cloak on her belt.

Once out on deck she felt a little better. As she stood on the aft deck watching the sunset, breathing in the fresh ocean air, she pulled her hood down and let the breeze run through her hair. She felt eyes on her and turned casually to look. She saw a couple of sailors looking furtively at her, whispering together. 'That can't be good.' She thought to herself, but shrugged and turned back to the view.

She heard footsteps behind her.

"Hey, you." One of the sailors said to her gruffly. She realised then that perhaps Toby had inadvertently let it slip to the sailors that she wasn't some rich lady to avoid but an orphan and a thief and the actions of Leviathan the night before had obviously changed the sailors' view of her. Never before had any of the sailors even spoken to her, something had definitely changed in their perceptions of her. She frowned but didn't reply. She felt a presence by her arm.

"I said 'Hey.'" The sailor repeated as he went to grab her arm, Tyg flinched from his touch and whirled round to face him, her hand going to her dagger.

"What do you want?" Tyg growled.

"Well, now I'm glad you asked see. Because me and my buddies were thinking that perhaps you should be paying us some attention...aye lads?"

The sailor grinned a toothless smile at her as his two mates fanned out either side of her nodding and jeering. She realised that they must definitely think that Leviathan took advantage of her last night, did they now think she had been brought on board by the brothers as their plaything? She wondered why neither brother hadn't been up on deck to set the story straight, were they even aware of this change in circumstance? She rolled her eyes internally. 'Well guess I'm just going to have to fix this myself.'

"What do you mean by that?" Tyg asked calmly as her eyes changed colour. She looked at the sailor that had obviously been appointed spokesman.

"You know what I mean, little lady." The sailor said chuckling at calling her a lady, with great encouragement and lurid comments from his mates. "We wants a bit of what that big guy took last night. We had no idea that's what you were here for...until we saw it with our own eyes."

Tyg thought for a second then grinned viciously. "You want what Lev got from me last night?"

The sailors failed to notice the change in her demeanour and started to get excited.

"Yes, that's what we mean...share and share alike...he won't come up, hasn't been seen at all." The sailor said reaching out to grab her arm again. "We'll be nice...nicer than he was by what we heard, chance to earn a little coin for ya...."

Tyg whacked his hand away, cringing at the last comment. "Does your Captain know you're here asking me this?"

"Of course not." He looked around furtively. "It'll be just between you, me and my buddies here." The sailor indicated his two mates.

"Well...are you really sure you want me to do to you what I did to Lev though?" Tyg asked amused as she acted coy, but gripped her dagger tighter. The sailor took another step closer, putting his hand on her shoulder. Tyg let him this time but recoiled inside to hear the comments from the others.

"Of course, you're a very pretty young thing, unusual."

"Okay..." Tyg shrugged. "If you're sure then, I don't see why not." Tyg replied. As the men hooted and howled in delight the leader of the little group leaned in for a kiss. Tyg watched him intently and just as he was about to touch her lips with his, Tyg's eyes dilated to black and she grabbed his shoulder with one hand while she brought the dagger up with the other and stabbed him in the stomach. As he bent double and staggered back, Tyg put her hand on the back of his neck and stabbed him again and again, with full force, then pushed him forward and jumped up onto a large shipping crate behind her, smiling viciously down at the others. They suddenly realised what was happening when they saw their mate fall and Tyg holding the dripping blade. They tried to grab her but she cut them as she slashed deftly round with the dagger keeping them at bay. The screaming brought more sailors and the others gave a hurried story that she came up on deck and attacked their mate for no reason. This made Tyg furious. She tried to stay calm and concentrate on keeping the sailors away from her as she flipped and twisted back to the deck by the railing. She was surrounded by at least ten men now.

Suddenly the sailors in the centre of the semicircle surrounding her broke away and peeled back, everyone going ominously quiet.

Tyg saw the black clothing of Leviathan coming towards her. As he reached the centre of the circle of sailors Tyg saw that Antyn was also with him as well as the Captain. Antyn bent over the injured sailor as Leviathan turned to face Tyg, putting a hand up for silence as the sailors erupted with their false story again. Once everyone had settled into an uneasy quiet Leviathan spoke.

"Seems that dagger is getting you into all sorts of trouble. Care to tell me what happened?" Tyg looked from Leviathan to the injured sailor then to Antyn who was pressing his hands against the wounds. She turned back to Leviathan who was looking at her amused.

"He got exactly what he asked for." She stated simply, her eyes still a fiery ice blue.

This caused the injured sailor's two mates to start yelling and accusing Tyg of lying. Leviathan swung his vulture gaze in their direction "Quiet!" He turned to the injured sailor. "What's your name?"

"Me names Jock, Sir, and that little bitch is a liar." He replied as he spat in Tyg's direction. She took a step forward, bringing her dagger down towards him menacingly, but Leviathan shoved her back against the railing with a shot of power. He looked at her a moment then turned back to Jock. Everyone stared stunned, not sure what had just happened. Leviathan was over hiding who and what he was.

"What did she say that makes her a liar?" Leviathan asked carefully, knowing how tricky Tyg's words could be.

"She said I asked for this, it's not what I asked for and she knows it."

Leviathan's eyebrows raised slightly as he started to piece things together, he grinned wickedly. "Really, so what was it that you did ask for?" Leviathan asked growling as he stepped forward.

He noticed that Jock and his friends had become very uncomfortable about the situation.

"Ah...just a bit of attention from the wench is all, we offered to pay! She agreed to it! Then stuck me like a pig." He grimaced in pain and started coughing.

Leviathan's face became hard and his eyes glowed. "You're telling me she agreed?" Leviathan turned to face Tyg who was leaning back on the rail with her arms folded, the dagger still in her hand. Leviathan could feel the anger and see the raw power emanating from her. She locked eyes with him as Jock tried to answer the question.

"Yeah, she did..."

"He's the liar, I never agreed to that...why would I? You know what I became, the lengths I went to, just to avoid doing that!" Tyg stated.

An argument started up then between Tyg and the sailors involved. All shouting at each other. Leviathan placed himself in front of Tyg to stop her advancing on the men and locked eyes with her again, as Antyn called for silence once more. Leviathan backed Tyg back to the railing again with a hand pressed intimately to her collar bone. She looked up at him transfixed.

"What exactly did you agree to then?" He asked intently.

Tyg took a deep breath and calmed down again, her head suddenly swooning from the wine, or was it Leviathan's touch? He was gently stroking across her collar bone with his thumb inside the collar of her shirt.

"He asked me to give him the same attention I gave you last night, I agreed and I did." Tyg said flatly her eyes blazing ice blue fire as she stared at Leviathan. She suddenly saw the edges of his mouth turn up slightly in a suppressed grin as he turned to look at Antyn. Antyn was looking at Tyg with a look of bewilderment on his face, then turned to meet his brother's gaze. The two brothers

29

looked at each other for an instant and then Leviathan suddenly started laughing.

"Oh, Tygarya." Leviathan said smiling as they locked eyes again, he brought his hand up and gently stroked her cheek. Tyg smirked as she realised that he understood.

"What's so funny!?" Jock demanded, coughing. Antyn stood up looking down on him with contempt and taking a handkerchief out of his pocket and wiping his hands clean.

"Well, it seems you did get exactly what you asked for." Antyn said to him, then held a hand up for silence as Jock and his mates started arguing again. "Let me explain...what you thought happened between this young lady and my brother did not. She is most definitely not a whore! She is incredibly important to my brother and myself. What did happen was a fight that resulted in my brother being stabbed by her, she is trained to kill." Antyn indicated to Tyg, who was standing with her arms folded looking smugly at all their shocked and mortified faces.

"I hope next time you get your fucking facts straight before approaching anyone to do such a sordid deal." Tyg sneered at them, still holding the dagger, brandishing it at them.

Leviathan held his hand out. "Give me that, it should have been taken off you before."

She reluctantly handed him the dagger. "What am I supposed to do now if one of these other sailors wants a piece of me too?"

"Like you need the dagger." Leviathan snorted and put it on his belt, turning to face the sailors. "It won't happen, don't worry. This will be a lesson to all of them...no one touches my things." His voice was deep and menacing. Leviathan reached out and grabbed her shoulder and pulled her into his side, putting his arm around her shoulders protectively. Antyn looked at him shocked.

"So he just gets away with it." Tyg muttered as she pulled away from his arm but stayed just in front of him as he towered over her, menacing everyone.

Leviathan glanced down at Jock. "You don't think his injuries are lesson enough?"

"No. What's to say once Antyn heals him, they don't try again, out of revenge this time?"

Leviathan looked at Antyn. "He won't be healed, so he won't be able to give you any more grief during this voyage."

"What about his friends?" Tyg asked worried. She didn't what to have to stay in her cabin or have to watch her back every second.

Leviathan straightened as if he had made a decision. "You're right, an example must be made." Triumphant at his subtle manipulation that got Tyg to this point he glanced at Antyn who was watching him with disapproval. Leviathan twisted his mouth sardonically at him and clicked his fingers.

Jock suddenly disappeared from sight and reappeared several yards out to sea, hovering above the waves as Leviathan had flipped his wrist out palm up, he balled his hand into a fist. Jock was suddenly ripped in two with a great spray of blood and dumped into the sea. Leviathan turned to the Captain, his eyes glowing intently. The sailors, all quaking in their boots and muttering about magic, fell to their knees.

"I'm sure you will know how to discipline these others so they don't try anything else?"

"Yes, your Grace, of course." The Captain answered, bowing low, realising suddenly who Leviathan actually was. He had heard the stories before in pubs in the adjacent country's port about the mighty seven foot tall Emperor of Tylandria and his magic, when in dock. He ordered the sailors be taken to the brig. He turned to Tyg. "I apologise for the actions of these men, my lady, and I will personally make sure it doesn't happen again."

"What will you do?" Tyg asked, curiously.

"Twenty lashes for each of them and they will stay in the brig with only stale bread and water until we reach landfall."

"When will you do these lashes?" Tyg asked, as Leviathan smiled down on her.

"Tomorrow...my lady."

"Thank you, Captain." Tyg looked furtively up at Leviathan then heard Antyn cough. He indicated that Tyg should go to her cabin. Tyg looked back at Leviathan as if asking his permission to leave.

"Go." He said quietly and amused, a dark smouldering look in his eyes.

Tyg took the hint and stepped away to leave. She noticed Toby standing by the hatch, looking at her in awe. She smiled to him and as she reached him she whispered. "Guess the excitement isn't over, huh? Do you think you could get me another bottle of that wine?"

Toby grinned and nodded his head, stepping out of the way for Tyg to pass by. "I'll bring it soon okay?"

"That's fine, Toby, thanks."

Tyg went into the great aft cabin area and into her room. She looked around and suddenly felt trapped, not knowing what to expect from the brothers after this. Although it clearly wasn't her fault, she still had to answer for the fight she had with Leviathan.

4

Leviathan turned and stood facing the railing, his arms crossed firmly across his chest, the dagger back in his hand. He turned it over and over, spinning it over his knuckles expertly, as he stared out to sea deep in thought. Antyn walked up to him and leaned on the railing looking down at the water rushing past beneath them. The Captain shouted and gave his orders and the sailors dispersed. Antyn remained silent a moment waiting for Leviathan to speak once the deck was clear. When he didn't Antyn decided he must.

"Well?"

Leviathan breathed in deeply and exhaled very slowly. "She's amazing isn't she?" Leviathan replied in no more than a whisper. "Pure power and she doesn't even realise."

Surprised Antyn looked up at his brother, who met his gaze and chuckled.

"When she's like that she's so dangerous and so damn sexy...I look forward to getting to know her Elvian side better...to nurture it...she is so raw."

"It was only last night that you tried to kill her." Antyn reminded him. "Again..."

"I wasn't going to kill her...I have come to realise just how much she can take...besides she surprised me breaking my compulsion like that...and she is so wild. She needs to be tamed by a firm hand. She wants it, you saw her look to me for permission to leave...don't deny what's plainly in front of us."

"Really?" Antyn said sceptical. "Well, she's going to be a lot harder to get near to now, with everything that's happened between you two over the last few weeks. Both of you have terrible tempers."

"Perhaps." Leviathan replied, looking out at sea again. "But I know, and you know, she feels the same attraction...the same pull...to me as I do to her."

"Destiny?" Antyn scoffed bitterly.

Leviathan turned back to regard Antyn amused, his vulture like gaze settling on him. "Jealous little brother, sick of spending all that time with a girl you can't touch?"

It was Antyn's turn to chuckle. "Jealous of what?" He said. "She doesn't trust you and it's like you said the other day, one step forward, ten steps back every time."

Leviathan scowled. "And you think she trusts you?"

"I think she does, not much, but yes. I have been the one spending time with her teaching her our language and history, like you say."

"Good, then it's up to you to get her to trust me."

"And how am I supposed to do that?"

Leviathan grinned at Antyn's question and clapped him on the back. "You'll think of something, but think of it quickly, I want this angst sorted before we reach home. I need her by my side." Leviathan chuckled again and turned and walked off towards the aft cabin, leaving Antyn watching his retreating back with a confused bitter expression.

After a while Antyn made his way to Tyg's room to find her sitting in her chair looking out the porthole window even though it was now getting to pitch black outside. A glass of red wine in her hand, half empty. On the top of the chest of drawers sat three empty wine bottles. One had fallen over and was rolling back and forth with the rock of the ship.

Tyg turned as the door opened and regarded Antyn with barely suppressed suspicion. She grinned when she saw him notice the wine bottles and deliberately took another sip as he raised an eyebrow in question.

"Don't you think you've had enough?" Antyn asked as he walked into the room and sat down on the edge of the bed.

"No, actually I don't." Tyg replied harshly.

Antyn sighed and rubbed his hand over his face. "You don't have to fight us all the time, you know."

"Is that so?" Tyg spat back with a harsh laugh. "Tell that to your brother then, not me."

"Why?" Antyn asked with another sigh.

"Why? You need to ask why?" Tyg growled leaning forward in the chair. "You know as well as I do how much he tries and tries to start fights with me, he baits me all the time." Antyn chuckled to himself. "What's so funny?" Tyg demanded.

"Leviathan is a bully, yes." Antyn explained. "But I don't see you trying to not react to it, actually from where I sit you seem to enjoy it as much as he does the way you rise to the challenge every time...but you know why he baits you?"

"Why?" Tyg scowled.

"Because he's attracted to you."

"Pah!" Tyg snorted, throwing the empty glass with the intention of smashing it against the wall. "It's a funny way to show it."

Antyn calmly reached up and the wine glass stopped in mid-air, it floated over to him and he casually wrapped his fingers around it, standing up he placed it on the small side table. Tyg looked at him, her temper receding, being replaced by awe. Antyn sat down calmly and continued to explain.

"Lev's never felt like this before, it confuses him...you confuse him. You are not what we expected to find. So he reverts back to what he knows best...how to bully and goad a reaction, he just wants to understand you and knows you feel the same."

"Never felt like what before?" Tyg asked with a hushed tone, still staring at the glass.

"Infatuated, for want of a better word...he is attracted to your wild nature..." He answered with a wry smile as Tyg's head turned at the comment looking at him. "You know what I mean. He's used to women throwing themselves at him, not having to chase them or have them try and kill him."

"Chase...me?"

"Well, yes...what do you think was happening in Arial?"

"So he was trying to impress me...I thought he was joking." Antyn looked strangely at her, she really did have no idea. He smiled to himself. "Well, it doesn't mean I'm going to forgive him for last night."

Antyn sighed again. "You're as bad as each other." He said exasperated.

"What do you mean by that?"

"Never mind, I came here to ask you to join us for dinner, this 'thing' has been going on for long enough, I knew it was going to result in someone getting hurt, can we try and patch things up?"

"What?" Tyg exclaimed. "Why would I want to even be in the same room after what he did?"

"What about what you did, he only retaliated."

Antyn saw Tyg's eyes start to blaze again at that last statement and realised the mistake he made. He grimaced and held up his hands. "Yeah, yeah I know...I shouldn't have said that...I'm sorry...but please join us for dinner? You know he's a prideful man..."

Tyg looked hard at Antyn a moment. "Are you asking or is he asking?"

Antyn replied carefully. "I'm asking you, Tyg, to try and sort this shit out, I know you want to really..." He took her hand. "Will you join me and my brother for dinner in an attempt to get back to some semblance of peace before we reach home?"

"If you're the one asking...then yes alright I will." Tyg muttered.

Antyn smiled to himself and stood to leave. "Thank you, Tyg, I shall return for you in half an hour."

"Very well, I shall be ready." Tyg replied. Antyn noticed a small twitch of a grin on her face.

He bowed slightly with a twinkle in his eye as he wondered what she was up to, as he saw yet another contest of wills about to unfold. She was such a formidable fighting spirit, so damaged by her more than toxic upbringing. If they didn't find some way of getting Tyg to submit to their obvious superiority, he was afraid they might have to forsake their plans and kill her, she was far too dangerous to be kept alive once she realised her full potential, if not controlled by them. And she had no idea how dangerous it would be for her, as an Elvian, to be in Tylandria without Leviathan's Imperial protection. She was last of her kind for a reason, Elvian's had been systematically hunted and slaughtered, because they had been deemed too dangerous of a race to live. A race bred for war and conquest.

He turned and left the room, making his way down the short corridor he entered the brother's rooms and crossed the antechamber towards Leviathan's cabin. He knocked once and entered. He found Leviathan sitting in a chair, studying an ancient looking manuscript. Leviathan didn't even look up as Antyn entered.

"Yes?" He enquired, still reading.

"Just thought you would like to know that Tyg will be joining us for dinner tonight." Antyn stated smugly.

"Really?" Leviathan said as he put aside the manuscript and looked at Antyn, a grin on his face. "Excellent, well done."

"So, you will be on your best behaviour." Antyn stated, causing Leviathan to grin even more.

"Oh, but of course, brother." Leviathan drawled facetiously.

"I mean it, Lev. She basically admitted to me that she doesn't trust you, so this may be your last chance to change that and we *need* to change that."

"And how exactly did she tell you that?" Leviathan frowned.

"By getting me to answer whether it was me asking her to join us for dinner...or you."

Leviathan looked stunned a moment then regarded Antyn. "And you answered that it was you." He scowled, scratching his jaw as he looked away in thought.

"Yes, which turned out to be the right answer, so what does that tell you?"

"That she's extremely devious and has a sharp mind." Leviathan said with a grin.

"That she is, but you will behave at dinner, won't you?" Antyn said it more as a statement than a question. "You both need to stop playing these games, it's getting dangerous."

"Of course, little brother. Don't worry I'll be the perfect gentleman." Leviathan replied, his grin getting wider causing Antyn to grimace.

"Well, I'll meet you, with Tyg, in the fore cabin in half an hour." Antyn stepped out of Leviathan's cabin and wandered across the anteroom to his own to get ready.

5

Tyg smiled to herself as she decided to make an impression at tonight's dinner. She got up and went over to her chest of belongings. Opening it she dug her arms in and took everything out, except for one item that was on the very bottom. She placed everything on the bed and then turned and picked up the dress that Tess had made her especially, as a birthday present. She looked at it, smiling, as she remembered Tess finally giving in and making her a black dress. It was made of the deepest luscious black velvet and would have cost a small fortune to buy the fabric. It had a ground length skirt that came in to hug the hips, a split up one thigh revealing leg as she walked. With a corset style bodice which laced up the front, bare shoulders and long flowing sleeves of the finest silk, making them look like wings. 'It is very daring.' Tyg remembered Tess saying. 'Good' she had replied.

As Tyg slipped it on she felt a change come over her. Something about the colour black just seemed to make her feel strong and confident, but to be clothed in a dress like this...

She walked to the mirror and looked at herself a moment, pleased with what she saw. She reached up and undid the loose braid holding back her wealth of hair, she shook it out letting it fall around her. She looked at it in the mirror, liking the texture the kinks gave it. She grabbed a bunch of silver and black twine from her pile on the bed and twisted two small braids of hair, one from each side of her head and entwined the twine through them as she tied them at the back of her head like a coronet. She then grabbed a large silver chain and buckled it around her waist, the buckle being silver and onyx and hiding a deadly little needle like weapon. She regarded herself in the mirror and smiled.

"Perfect." She said almost purring. She then started to return her clothes back to the chest. As she closed the chest a light knock sounded on the door. She stood, smoothing down her dress and looked towards the door as it opened.

Antyn, wearing his usual grey tunic trimmed with silver brocade stood frozen to the spot looking at her with wide eyes. Tyg smiled at the reaction.

"Oh, my..." Antyn blurted out before recovering. "You are a sight, Tygarya, you really are truly beautiful."

"Thank you." She said, blushing but with an air of confidence, which Antyn picked up on. He regarded her a moment.

"Can I ask why you chose black?" He asked finally.

"Well...it is Leviathan's favourite colour, isn't it?" Tyg said back. "And I am supposed to be trying to mend things, aren't I, that is the mission you seem determined to set as my responsibility rather than the Emperors?" Tyg grinned at Antyn's scathing scowl. "Actually, it's my favourite colour too." She repented, glad her little message had been received.

"Yes, I suppose so..." Antyn said still looking at her questioningly. "Do you actually want to mend things though, because don't just act it for my sake."

Tyg sighed. "Yes, I've thought about it and you're right, I took it too far...I only have myself to blame for what happened...I misread things...I need to talk to him."

Antyn smiled, happy with her answer. "Shall we go then?"

"Certainly." Tyg said as Antyn took her arm and escorted her down the hall to the Master's quarters of Lord Doven's personal vessel.

As they entered Leviathan was standing looking out the window, a glass of wine in his hand. He turned as they entered. He said nothing but Tyg could plainly see the shock on his face as she walked in. She smiled at him smugly. He coughed slightly and glanced at Antyn who inclined his head slightly and shrugged. Tyg didn't miss the movement.

"Is there something wrong?" Tyg asked still smirking.

Leviathan placed his glass down on the table and straightened, his head brushing the roof. He walked towards her purposefully ducking under the low beams. Suddenly she didn't feel quite so confident, the stirring butterflies she felt in his presence flooding back. He took her hand and kissed it, never taking his eyes from her face.

"Nothing is wrong, dearest Tygarya, nothing at all." He said smiling at her. "In fact everything is right...I thank you for coming over tonight...you look absolutely gorgeous, black does suit you."

"Thank you." Tyg said a bit of her confidence returning.

"Come sit." Leviathan showed Tyg to the table and pulled out her chair for her. As she sat down she caught another glance between Leviathan and Antyn. Leviathan bent down and whispered in her ear, causing her to get goose bumps. "Perhaps you would like a drink?"

"Yes, please. A red wine would be nice." Tyg replied as she glanced at Antyn. He had been about to interrupt to say maybe she had already had enough. She looked him full in the face her eyes were ice blue and seemed to be glowing with a strange intensity. He regarded her a moment, then shrugged and sat down at the end of the table, just as Leviathan placed a heavy crystal glass in front of her. Leviathan also sat, at the other end of the table. Picking up his glass, he raised it.

"To better times." He said looking straight at Tyg. She returned the look and raised her glass.

"I suppose so..." She said flippantly then smiled at Antyn waiting for him to raise his glass also.

As he did he was looking at Leviathan. Tyg turned back to Leviathan to find him still staring at her. She noticed something in his eyes she had rarely seen before.

Confusion. She liked it and smiled sweetly at him.

"Cheers then..." She said and took a sip of her wine. She closed her eyes as the smooth dark liquid ran down her throat, savouring the delicious rich woody flavour.

"Better than the stuff that cabin boy has been stealing for you from the galley, isn't it?" Leviathan said with a wicked grin on his face. Tyg opened her eyes and regarded him. She was oozing confidence and power at seeing the confusion still in his eyes.

"Yes, it is...so where do you keep this stuff hidden then?" She said calmly.

She heard Antyn choke on his wine and stifle a laugh as Leviathan's eyes widened slightly in surprise at the comment. Leviathan's gaze slid to Antyn a moment shutting him up, then back to Tyg. He squinted at her in a dark smoulder that made her catch her breath.

"You seem different tonight, Tygarya." Leviathan said to her then, his eyes locking with hers. "More like yourself again...wild and confident."

"Perhaps." She answered, sipping her wine, keeping her gaze locked with his. She placed her glass back onto the table. "Is there a problem with that?"

Antyn chuckled again, trying to cover it with a cough.

"No problem, Tygarya." Leviathan said coolly. "In fact I think I rather like it." His words dripped innuendo and the grin he gave her sent shivers down her spine. "It's about time you let go of what happened in Arial."

Just then the door opened and the cook, followed by Toby, entered carrying plates piled up with cooked chicken and potatoes. Breaking the gaze, Leviathan looked up as they entered. Tyg thankful for the interruption also looked towards them. She smiled and winked at Toby as he entered. He stumbled as he saw her, his mouth dropping open in shock to see her in such finery.

"You stupid boy, watch out!" The cook said to him, he turned from placing his plates of food on the table and cuffed Toby around the back of the head. Tyg was on her feet in a second, she grabbed the cook with amazing strength as she threw him up against the wall.

"Don't you ever lay your hands on Toby again or I'll kill you!" Tyg said through gritted teeth, her lip raised, snarling. Antyn stepped between Tyg and the cook, delicately taking Tyg's hands off him. Facing the cook he talked to him quietly as Tyg felt a firm hand on her shoulder turn her around. She turned and looked up into Leviathan's blazing eyes. She opened her mouth to speak, but Leviathan placed a finger upon her lips to silence her. He gave her a curt shake of his head and firmly sat her down at the table.

Tyg became aware of the fact that Antyn and the cook had left the room, but that Toby was still standing in the room, looking frightened. She turned towards him aware of Leviathan's scathing glare still on her.

"Sorry, Toby." She said quietly. "I suppose I have just made things worse for you."

"Not really." Antyn said as he stepped back into the room. He placed a hand on Toby's shoulder and turned him towards the door. "You had better return to the galley, young man." He said to him as he gently pushed him out the door and firmly closed it behind him. He leaned back on the door and regarded Tyg as she sat at the table. He drank in the power coursing through her, wondering how the hell she could be so unaware of it.

Leviathan was sitting studying her intently too, he placed a hand on her shoulder, making his eyes glow with the power he took from her. Antyn looked away with a scowl.

"What?" Tyg said defensively.

"What do you care for some cabin boy?" Leviathan asked.

"We have a lot in common, I had a similar childhood to him. I know what it's like. I couldn't just sit here and watch him get hit like that."

Leviathan and Antyn stared at each other for a long moment as Leviathan dropped his hand and sank back into his chair. Thoughts seemed to pass between them, finally Leviathan looked back at Tyg as Antyn sat down.

"Very well, I can accept that." Leviathan said sternly. "But you have to realise, that is part of life, you may see it everywhere you go, you can't react like that."

Tyg still felt angry, she grabbed her glass of wine and took a long draft. She placed it down, looking at it. She glanced up at Leviathan and met his gaze, her eyes were still blazing ice blue fire.

"I know, I've seen it just about every day of my life and been on the receiving end but if I ever see that sort of thing directed at someone I know, I will always stop it." She said full of commitment. "I won't change, so don't ask me to." The tone of a challenge in her voice.

"Perhaps we could just forget it for now and continue with our meal?" Antyn said trying to change the subject before things got completely out of hand again.

"The martyr of the downtrodden." Leviathan muttered to himself. He closed his eyes taking a moment then opened them glancing at Antyn. "Perhaps we should."

"Good idea." Tyg said sipping her drink again, her eyes cooling to a pale blue. "I'm starving." She said with a grin.

They ate in relative silence for several minutes, then Leviathan decided to break the silence with a change of subject.

"So, Tygarya." He said turning towards her. "What made you wear that divine black dress tonight?"

"Because black is my favourite colour." Tyg replied. "It is yours too, is it not?"

"Yes, it is...although I must say that seeing you in that dress gives me a whole new reason for black to be *my* favourite colour." Leviathan said with a dark smouldering look, his words again dripping innuendo as he was leaning back casually in his chair.

Tyg faltered and looked down at her plate, which was nearly empty. She pushed it away her appetite suddenly gone as she felt uncomfortable with how to handle Leviathan's outrageous flirting.

"Have you had enough, Tyg?" Antyn asked amused. "There's plenty more."

"No thanks, I guess I wasn't as hungry as I first thought." She said looking down at the table. Leviathan jumped on her words.

"Perhaps we should retire to the couches." He said smugly as he stood up and came round to Tyg's chair, pulling it out for her. She stood hesitantly and Leviathan led her over to the plush seating under the large windows at the very back of the ship. As she sat down Leviathan handed her, her wine glass, now refilled. He sat beside her, facing her, his arm on the back of the couch behind her, his legs crossed over tilting his hips towards her. Tyg took a sip of her wine and looked at Antyn, who was standing looking at Leviathan. Tyg saw that Leviathan was also looking at Antyn. Antyn turned and headed for the door.

"Well, I might leave actually, there's a few things that the sailors still need to do, and I better check that they're being done, I don't really trust this crew or it's Captain anymore, they're a skittish lot since finding out they have a Sorcerer on board."

As he left the room Tyg looked at Leviathan. "You made him leave didn't you? That was a pretty poor excuse he gave." She accused him.

"And if I did is that a bad thing?" Leviathan replied, picking up a lock of her hair and twining it around his finger. "It is supposed to be the two of us that are patching things up...not him."

"I suppose so." Tyg muttered feeling suddenly out of her depth, she really didn't know how to handle this enigmatic man or his obvious experience with seducing women. She had absolutely no experience with this.

Leviathan leaned in to kiss her, causing her to lean away quickly, blushing as he frowned. She stood up and put her drink on the table. "Sorry, I can't do this."

Leviathan, showed his annoyance but quickly covered it up as he stood taking her arms in his hands. "Why, what's wrong?" He asked looking intently at her. "You have kissed me before, you know, and I know we are mutually attracted to each other. Let's put the other night behind us."

"Of course...it's just that...." She faltered, looking at the floor, wishing it would swallow her up.

"What?" Leviathan growled confused. "Why do you do this all the time? This is what is causing all the friction between us, can't you see that?"

She looked up at him, that challenging look in her eyes, as they flashed. "I've been around, I know what this is...you want this to go to the next level...that's what you expect, isn't it?" Tyg looked desperate as Leviathan watched her intently, his eyes slowly widening as understanding dawned on him.

"I can't...I've never...I won't." Tyg spun around and hung her head, squeezing her eyes shut. Leviathan held her back firmly against his chest not allowing her to escape this time and lowered his head to her shoulder.

"You're a virgin?" Leviathan asked in a hushed voice.

Tyg stared at his side profile in shock and embarrassment, it was obvious by his reaction what he had hoped for tonight. She struggled out of his grasp and went to run to the door. He caught her by her arm and swung her round back into his strong embrace.

"Is that why you act like this every time we kiss? It all makes sense now." Leviathan tilted her head up making her look at him. "You should have just said something..."

"It's not an easy topic to bring up..."

He pressed his lips against hers, cutting her off. She fought him a moment, then relaxed and allowed herself to be kissed, it was never an unpleasant experience. Leviathan pulled his head back and whispered to her.

"I promise I will not go further until you want to...you need to trust me, Tygarya. I am a man of my word." She looked into his eyes to try and see the truth of his words. "Trust me, please, Tygarya." He breathed then kissed her again, she opened her mouth to him this time and kissed him back.

"Come back to the couch and at least finish your wine..."

Late that night Leviathan was in an exceptionally good mood as he told Antyn. "How delectable to know she is a virgin." He laughed. "It's like the icing on the cake."

"How so?" Antyn asked uncomfortably.

"To know I will be her first and only." Leviathan looked out the windows dreamily. "Makes things so much easier, her connection to me so much stronger...she'll be mine completely and forever."

"However long that might be..." Antyn muttered causing Leviathan to scowl.

"Ever the pessimist, Antyn." Leviathan growled under his breath.

Antyn shrugged. "We don't know how extracting the power within her is going to affect her, you should prepare for killing her, not getting her in your bed."

Leviathan looked at him with a sour expression. "Enough!"

6

Antyn was sitting in the aft cabin with Tyg, teaching her their language when he suddenly closed the book he had and looked intently at her. Leviathan was seated in a chair at a desk in the corner. Things had settled once again and were more like they had been back in Arial in the days leading up to Leviathan's fight with Palin. Tyg seemed to be in a more relaxed state after her talk with Leviathan and regularly went to seek out his presence and stay beside him, happy to sit silently in the background while he worked then go for romantic little strolls up on deck. She couldn't deny the fact she was drawn to the powerful man and liked knowing he saw her as a woman not an assassin or a freakishly strong monster, because in his eyes she wasn't as strong as him. The following week after confessing she was a virgin to him had gone smoothly with everyone finally understanding and adjusting.

Tyg glanced at Antyn, catching his gaze. "What?" She asked of his serious look.

"As you know we are approaching landfall soon..."

"Yes."

"...there is something I feel I must say to you before we do..."

"What?" Tyg narrowed her eyes.

"I know you have been told this before, but you are now in the company of an Emperor...and well you need to start acting as such."

Tyg noticed Leviathan's head come up slightly, but his eyes stayed looking at his work.

"Yes, yes...behave...I know." Tyg rolled her eyes.

"No, Tyg, I didn't mean that...exactly...more how to act in the company of others."

Tyg stared at him. "I know how to stand there and smile, Antyn."

"You have a tendency to drop people's titles when addressing them, and also...you aren't actually supposed to call Lev, by his name in public either."

Leviathan had stopped reading and had leaned back in his chair, resting his head on his knuckles, watching amused. Tyg's face had darkened to a deep scowl.

"Don't tell me how to 'address' people, Antyn. I'll call people what I like. Always have, always will."

"You are representing the Emperor...you can't do what you want anymore, you are no longer an unlawful assassin who has the privilege of anarchy to do what they want."

"I may not be but I am still my own person..."

"No, Tygarya, you are not." Leviathan interjected in that low tone. "You are mine."

Tyg stared at him, her eyes blazing as her fists clenched but Leviathan merely slow blinked as if daring her to argue the point.

"And that's another thing, Tyg...you can't go full tilt angry every time someone says something you don't like." Antyn continued. "Gods, is there no filter with you? It seems you are either completely unemotional to the point of being psychotic or hell bent crazy letting your emotions run wild."

"Filter?" Tyg growled. "Look, like I have said many times before to many people, you included. I will address a person by their title when they earn the respect to have that title...not just because they were lucky enough to be born an aristocrat or a Lord's son. There are people out there far more entitled to be called Sir than most of the ones who actually are."

"Tyg..." Antyn said frustrated.

"Antyn..." Leviathan said, causing Antyn to turn and look at him. "What's your point to this?"

"My point?" Antyn said more frustrated that Leviathan seemed to be taking Tyg's side. "My point is, as you know...any slight taken in the presence of the Emperor can result in persecution."

"At my discretion..." Leviathan stated calmly.

"Lev, you're really not helping..." Antyn rubbed his eyes with one hand.

"I just don't think you should bother too much with Tyg's deference to Lord's and titles...she is my close companion and so stands above them in my eyes. I don't care what she calls them." Leviathan added that last bit as Antyn was about to say something. Tyg's eyes had gone wide, but then she smiled at Antyn, she was almost going to poke her tongue out at him, but didn't...see I have a filter!

"Fuck's sake, Leviathan..." Tyg looked at Antyn with worry, he seldom said Leviathan's full name and he certainly did not swear at him directly. "I am just trying to make this..." He looked for the right word. "...transition go as smoothly as possible for everyone. You know what they are going to say about her and if she plays up they'll accuse her of...."

Leviathan scowled deeply as Tyg's eyes flew to his face. "Antyn..." His tone held a warning.

"She needs to be warned, and needs to be able to show everyone she's not a fucking savage." Antyn spat in ire.

"What the fuck?" Tyg said. "What are you talking about?"

"I'll sort it, Antyn..." Leviathan growled. "No one is going to dare say anything...trust me."

"So you're just going to let her run rampant through your Empire with no regard to human safety every time someone says something to piss her off?"

"Excuse me? I am right here!" Tyg stood up. "Look I don't give two pieces of copper what anyone thinks of me...if they don't like me...well...fuck, I probably don't like them either." Tyg heard Leviathan snort in amusement. "To be completely honest with you Antyn, I would rather just stay the hell out of the way and not be seen by anyone at all, thank you, so that solves all your problems."

"No, Tygarya." Leviathan said. Tyg heaved a sigh, she knew he was going to say that.

"And why not?" Tyg said. "It sounds like the best option for everyone concerned."

"Because, like I just said...you are mine...and I want everyone to know it."

Tyg stood staring at him. "You, my friend, are a narcissistic asshole."

Leviathan's eyes darkened. "And your Emperor." He beckoned for her with a finger. "Now come here."

Tyg rolled her eyes and walked over to him. He grabbed her around the waist and pulled her down into his lap grabbing her chin and making her lock eyes with him. He could feel the power leech into him calming her down. "Talk to people however you like except me, my dear...just don't maim or kill anyone...and don't ever roll your eyes at me." Tyg's eyes widened as he stared into them, he was exuding a primal dominating force that Tyg couldn't ignore. "Behave, like I know you can when you put your mind to it. You know perfectly well how to act civilised." He bopped her on the nose as her eyes widened even more at the smirk on his lips.

It was Antyn's eyes that rolled this time as he stood up. "You will regret this decision, Lev."

"Don't forget, dear brother..." The way he said it sent chills down Tyg's spine, he felt it and pressed his hand firmly over her thighs to hold her still on his lap and settled his vulture gaze on Antyn. "...I am your Emperor too."

Antyn's eyes went wide as he recognised the tone. He turned and bowed his head at Leviathan, biting his tongue. "Of course, my Liege." Antyn's jaw clenched tight when he did it and he abruptly left the room.

"Leviathan..." Tyg said coolly as he took up a lock of her hair and held it to his nose. "I really don't know if I can stand all the rules and protocols of an Imperial castle. I'll go insane."

"You'll be fine, Tygarya...you will upset a lot of other people...but *you* will be fine...why do I know this?"

Tyg looked at him as he smiled at her, dropping her hair and trailing his fingers up her shoulder and around her neck, pulling her face closer to his as he stared into her eyes with a fathomless stare. "Because you are mine and therefore under my protection as long as you behave and do exactly what I say. I am the only person you ever need to listen to." He kissed her deeply holding her firmly until she relaxed into his kiss and wrapped her arms around his neck. After a minute of kissing he let her sit up, and combed her hair back over her shoulders.

"Tygarya, I do have one request of you?" He asked as he scooped an arm around her and pulled her closer, adjusting her on his lap.

"What?" She asked blinking in a daze of breathlessness.

"When we disembark...I have a small request." He smirked at her losing her senses a little from being kissed by him.

"Yeah, I got that...what?" Tyg asked suspicious now, fully alert.

"That you wear that dress...the black one."

"When we leave the ship, why?"

"Because I want you to make an impression on the people."

Tyg frowned. "Impression? What sort of impression are you going for?"

"A princess come home." Leviathan chuckled.

"What! Are you serious?" Tyg exclaimed.

"Yes." Leviathan said simply.

"But I'm not..."

"Tygarya, you are what I say you are...and I need you to look the part...will you do what I request of you?" Leviathan levelled that vulture gaze at her.

Tyg's face looked thoughtful for a moment. "On one condition."

Leviathan leaned his elbow on the arm of the chair and spiked his fingers to his temple looking amused. "I wasn't aware this was a negotiation...but go ahead..."

"You let the soldiers have their leave."

Leviathan's eyes went wide for a moment, then they narrowed. "One day in a dress for seven days leave...that's hardly comparable."

Tyg raised an eyebrow. "Okay...how long are you staying in this port city?"

"About three days." Leviathan said amused. He loved watching her mind work.

"How about three days of me playing princess in this city for you as you wish, for three days leave for the soldiers."

Leviathan stared at her with a complex look. "I agree, with one term."

"And that is?"

"That you playing at being a princess means you play nice with me...you be at my side, you let me escort you properly...you behave

54

like my...no...like an Emperor's betrothed and do everything required of you to not get into any trouble." Tyg's eyes went wide and she sat back bewildered, he had just snookered her on Antyn's argument. "I will be the perfect gentleman in return, Tygarya, until you cause trouble. Only then will I ever have to step in and control you..." Leviathan smiled at her and grabbed a lock of her hair, bringing it to his face twined around his first two fingers, and looked at her over it, his eyes dancing with exuberance.

Tyg's mind raced, she knew exactly what he was saying. Everything that had happened between them had always been caused by her and her rashness, and quick to violence temper. She knew agreeing to these terms was giving him permission to basically punish her if ever she stepped out of line. Could she give him that sort of control? She felt he could be a harder task master than Palin ever was, especially given the fact he was a sorcerer and could get into her head, but he seemed to understand that what she needed was tight control and structure.

"Then I will try to be the perfect lady, don't be too hard on me." Tyg said as she downcast her eyes and blushed looking at her hands.

Leviathan smiled widely. "The perfect princess, don't worry I will guide you, just stay by my side." He corrected as he leaned in and grabbed her chin, lifting her face. "Demure and blushing...are you acting now?" He asked amused as his vulture gaze settled on her.

Tyg scowled at him and her eyes blazed. "No, but..."

Leviathan chuckled. "Oh, Tyg..." He kissed her lips then looked at her with a dark sultry gaze. Tyg looked into those eyes and he watched as her eyes changed to a pretty sky blue. He kissed her again more forcefully with desire this time. She complied and kissed him back, putting her arms around his neck as she leaned over him, he grabbed her around the waist again, pulling her into him.

He broke off the kiss and pressed his forehead on hers. "Thank you, Tyg."

Tyg shivered hearing him shorten her name, it was weird the effect him saying it had on her, when nearly everyone else called her that all the time, but whenever he said it, it was in a low soft dulcet tone like no one had ever said it before.

"If that's what my Emperor wants me to do, to get the soldiers the leave they deserve."

Leviathan pulled his head back and looked at her suspiciously. "Soldiers...or one in particular?"

Tyg blinked innocently at him. "All of them deserve the leave they were supposed to receive on coming home."

"Hmm." Leviathan snorted. "You're seriously going to have to stop campaigning these underdog dilemmas."

Tyg smiled. "It's only fair."

"Tygarya...stop it now." Leviathan growled.

"Whatever...if it's what my Emperor wants me to do..." Tyg looked up under her lashes at him.

Leviathan smirked and kissed her again, mashing his lips against hers. "Yes, it is!"

Leviathan felt a surge of elation to finally have Tyg exactly where he wanted her, compliantly under his control and giving him the permission to take that control and punish her if needed, knowing full well what he could do to her with his power. She was sublimely naïve.

All he had to do now was maintain and nurture that control, like training a pet, until her power fully awakened by then she would undoubtedly give her power over to him freely.

7

The ships had been docking and being unloaded since dawn as Leviathan waited to dock their own ship until last so all the ore was already unloaded, the soldiers and horses already waiting.

As they were about to disembark Tyg walked up on deck wearing the black dress with a long thick woollen cloak with a large fur lined hood. Leviathan looked at her with a dark smoulder and Antyn smiled at her his eyes twinkling.

"You ready for this, Tyg?" Antyn asked as she approached them.

"No." Tyg said looking at Leviathan and smiling shyly at him.

Antyn looked confused as Leviathan frowned and folded his arms. "Tygarya?" He muttered wearily.

"I just thought perhaps now might be the right time to put this on..." Tyg held up a gold chain on which hung the dragon's head ring that Leviathan had given her in Arial for her birthday. Leviathan dropped his arms and looked at her in surprise. Antyn clenched his jaw and folded his arms.

"Tygarya..." Leviathan breathed and stepped towards her, taking her chin in his hands and lifting her face as he studied her eyes. "Are you sure about this?"

"Trust me I've spent the last few days thinking really hard about this and everything else that has transpired between us." Tyg said and held it up to Leviathan. "I want to show you in some way that I am deferring to you and putting my trust in you as I embark on this new life journey...but I want you to put it on my finger, my Liege."

Leviathan dropped her chin and stepped back and looked at her darkly for a moment. Tyg stopped breathing as he locked that dark smouldering gaze upon her.

"You know what you're doing constitutes a promise to become my consort in the eyes of most?"

Tyg looked a little startled and almost backed up a step. "Ah, I guess so..."

He grabbed the chain and pulled the ring off it then picked up her left hand and slipped the ring onto her ring finger. Tyg felt a strange tightening feeling as the bands seemed to clasp around her finger but before she could look down at it Leviathan kissed her possessively, wrapping his arms around her, one on the small of her back and one on the back of her neck. She forgot about the ring and the strange sensation and kissed him back.

As he raised his head he flicked a glance at Antyn who was watching intently with a smug grin on his face. Leviathan frowned at him in warning and Antyn turned away to hide it.

"Tygarya, you are so full of surprises...but why now?"

"Now seemed like a good time to me..." Tyg shrugged. "If I'm going to play your betrothed I might as well have some sort of symbol to back it up...right? Besides..." Tyg smiled at him and put her hands on his chest. "After our talk and our mutual understanding of the situation I felt like I needed to show you I was on board with it as well. I am willing to try my best if you are willing to wait for me to be ready." Tyg tried to look away shyly but Leviathan grabbed her chin again, demanding her gaze.

"Don't look away...there's nothing to be embarrassed about...I told you that...and this, what you've done now, means more to me than you can ever imagine...you are not playing at being my betrothed, you are now betrothed to me...thank you for trusting yourself to my care, Tygarya." His words made her shudder as he kissed her again then hooked her under his arm to walk to the gangplank.

Tyg suddenly saw the crowd of people who had come to welcome their Emperor home. There were pennons hanging everywhere of black etched with gold with the dragons head on them and flags flying high. Tyg baulked and froze as anxiety filled her with dread.

"Tygarya?" Leviathan asked concerned as he felt her body stiffen against him.

"Sorry, I guess I didn't really realise how much of a big deal your home coming was going to be...I really don't do well with crowds. I'm used to being the one not seen by anyone."

"Don't sweat it, Tyg, just smile and wave..." Antyn said as he walked off down the gangplank and made his way along the avenue made for them by soldiers holding back the throng of people.

Leviathan smiled down at her. "Ready?"

"I don't think I'll ever be ready for this..." As Tyg watched Antyn in the distance lapping up the attention stopping in front of the pretty girls that lined the walkway and taking flowers and cards from them flirting outrageously. He kept it up the whole way until he reached the carriage that was to take them to the large estate owned by Leviathan that was the city chamberlain's seat of power. The crowd seemed to really love their Prince.

Leviathan dropped his arm and pulled her hood down, pulling the cloak off her shoulders. He threw it at a soldier to hold and grabbed her hand. Tyg's eyes blazed at him but he just smirked and pulled her down the gangplank. It was cold and frosty but Leviathan kept them warm using a small trickle of his power. Tyg had the briefest of sightings of Corvyn as they came down the gangplank as he stood to attention and saluted at Leviathan passing by. He gave her a quick acknowledging smile then was gone from her view as Leviathan swept her on. Once they were on the ground, Tyg's legs felt funny. She guessed it was from spending so long at sea, she hoped she wasn't going to get sick again.

She noticed that Leviathan didn't even acknowledge the crowds, even though they all shouted at him to try and get him to look at them, especially all the young women who lined the front, their bosoms pushed up in tight corsets, wearing finely made dresses and plenty of rouge. Tyg's eyes blazed even more. She heard the mutterings and whispers about her...who is that...where has she come from...why is he holding her hand? Tyg looked down at the ground and shrunk into Leviathan's arm not sure how to handle the scrutiny of so many, not trusting herself to stay calm.

"Don't you dare look down, Tygarya." Leviathan muttered under his breath at her in that low commanding voice. "No consort of mine would ever look at the ground so feebly."

Tyg's head snapped up and she glanced up at him, startled. He smiled down at her, which caused a ripple of mutterings from the crowd, then he dropped her hand and put his arm around her shoulders pulling her into his side. This caused an uproar through the crowd and people started shouting out demanding her name and to know who she was.

"Good girl..." Leviathan whispered to her gently. "...we're almost there, you're doing well."

Tyg was relieved when they reached the carriage, but Leviathan turned her round to face back to the crowd holding her by the back of her neck and thrusting her forward. Tyg felt like she was being presented to the crowd and tried to turn around. Leviathan squeezed her neck painfully as he raised a hand for silence making her wince and grit her teeth. Tyg was surprised how quickly the crowd went quiet. Fear, she thought, as much as they all seem to love their Emperor they still fear him greatly, that made her become still in his grip wondering if he would dare to use his power on her if she continued to struggle.

"I am going to address what I keep hearing from the crowd." Leviathan stated in a clear deep voice that travelled over the still crowd with ease. "This is Lady Tygarya Essyndyl, my promised consort. Treat her with respect and stop the infernal muttering." He growled out in a nasty snarl. He turned and pushed her into the carriage, following her in and closed the door as the crowd erupted in cheering and shouting about wedding dates.

Tyg stared at Leviathan with her eyes blazing, as Antyn was sitting in the carriage laughing joyfully.

"Oh, Lev, you do have a way with people...bloody hell..." He said with a slight sarcastic tone.

"That was bloody embarrassing." Tyg muttered and folded her arms defensively.

"You heard the comments...I just put the rumour mill to rest. Besides, by the time we reach the Estate word of you would have already reached them no doubt...so they will be ready for you."

"Oh, they'll never be ready for her." Antyn laughed causing Leviathan to smirk and look out the window.

Tyg scowled at them and shuffled across the seat to look out the other window, looking out at the city...a city she had never seen before. It seemed new, with pale coloured bricks and clean streets. She remembered what Palin had said about Leviathan taking part of Gardonia to break through and make a sea port on this side of the continent.

"Am I going to get to look around?" Tyg asked as she peered through the window.

"Perhaps, let's just let this fervour about you die down a bit first." Leviathan said with a shrug.

"Fervour?" Tyg asked uncomfortably.

"Of course, Tyg, everyone is going to want to get a look at the Emperor's betrothed...to suddenly come back with a promised consort at his side will be quite the news." Antyn mused.

"Okay..." She muttered perturbed by the unwanted attention.

They travelled on for a further couple of minutes as Tyg looked out the window thoughtfully. It was a hilly kind of city that flattened out in a bay like shape towards the harbour, with wide streets bustling with people. They all stopped and bowed and waved and cheered as the entourage of soldiers and the carriage went past. Tyg noticed they seemed to be heading towards a large hill that dominated the southern quarter of the city. On top of it she could clearly see what looked like a limestone palace.

"Is that where we are going?" Tyg asked pointing. Leviathan shuffled across the seat, coming up behind her and leaned over her to look out her window. She was flooded with the smell of him, he smelt strongly of sweat, salty brine and a musk that was clearly male. She found it strange that she didn't find it unpleasant.

"Yes." He murmured close to her ear.

"I thought you said it was an Estate...that's a palace."

Leviathan shrugged. "Whatever you want to call it."

"No...it's a palace..." Tyg thought about it with pursed lips, noticing the block walls encircling it around the hill. "Hmm...it has fortifications...so actually technically it's a castle."

"You read too much." Leviathan snorted.

"And you seriously need a bath." Tyg retorted.

"And you don't?" Leviathan snorted again as he leaned back in the seat.

"Excuse me..." Tyg said insulted, turning to face him. "I at least washed down every day while on ship, did you?"

"So that's where all the fresh water went..." Leviathan muttered as he looked at her amused. Antyn chuckled to himself as he watched the two of them.

"Something amusing you, brother?" Leviathan scowled at him.

"Oh, it's just cute that's all."

"Cute!" Both Leviathan and Tyg growled at him. He stared at them both wide eyed a moment then burst out laughing.

"You can't even see it...that makes it so much cuter." He wiped his eyes and looked at them as they stared at him.

"Shut up, Antyn." Leviathan growled as Tyg's eyes blazed.

"For a scholar your grammar is terrible..." Tyg said sarcastically with a formal tone as she folded her arms with a snooty pout. Leviathan snorted and put his arm around her shoulders pulling her into him, he grinned at Antyn. Antyn had baulked and stared at Tyg with a frown.

"What no smart come back, brother?"

"Hmm." Antyn clucked his tongue and looked out the window.

Leviathan laughed and kissed the top of Tyg's head. "I think you won that round, my dear."

"Ha!" Tyg scoffed. "You still need a bath." She grinned, enjoying the light fun banter, she liked these moments they shared, it showed a different side of Leviathan that she knew was reserved almost exclusively for her and his brother.

Antyn chuckled to himself as he looked out the window. "Oh, they should have seriously been warned at the Estate."

"Castle." Tyg corrected.

"Enough now, Tygarya." Leviathan growled, squeezing her shoulder. She looked up at him smiling sweetly and slow blinked.

"Yes, my Liege." She replied demurely, playing the part she had agreed upon with a cheeky tease.

Leviathan looked down at her darkly making her bite her lip worried she had gone too far.

"Bloody hell, Tygarya, no one can say that like you can." Leviathan bent down and kissed her, pushing her back up against the back of the seat, trapping her in the corner by the window. His hands pressed on to the wall behind and the window to the side. Tyg gasped in surprise and put her hands on his chest, but then relaxed and kissed him back, sliding her hands round to his back, her hands grabbing handfuls of his shirt and she held him strongly. A deep growl came from Leviathan's throat as he deepened the passionate kiss, wanting to ravage this dynamic and wild woman.

"Do you lot mind!" Antyn exclaimed indignantly.

Leviathan stopped kissing her and rested his forehead on hers catching his breath. He glanced out the window and sat back. "We're here..."

8

They entered the large manor on the hill overlooking the city with Leviathan holding tight to Tyg's hand as they exited the carriage.

The custodian of the Estate and law of Asbel city in Leviathan's stead, Lord Chamberlain DuPont of Asbel and the steward of the estate, Master Severn were waiting for them with the staff upon the steps and they all bowed or curtseyed low as Leviathan strode up the steps to stop before the Chamberlain.

"Lord DuPont, I hope we find you in good stead?"

"Yes, my Liege. How was your journey west?"

"Very lucrative." He turned to the steward. "I have a task for you, Master Severn, here..." Leviathan pulled Tyg forward. "...is Lady Tygarya Essyndyl, my betrothed. I wish for you to show her to a suitable room in which she may rest."

Tyg gave him a side eye as Lord DuPont and Master Severn gave their congratulations and bowed their heads to her. Leviathan gave a smirk to her questionable expression.

"I know you're not feeling the best, Tygarya. It will take you a little while to reacclimatise your senses back to walking on solid ground. Just rest, bathe and I will come get you later for dinner."

Tyg smiled. "Thanks, I didn't realise it was so obvious." She put a hand to her stomach and grimaced.

Leviathan laughed and the men smiled in understanding. Leviathan stroked her cheek. "Follow Steward Severn to a room and rest, Tygarya, there is nothing to do and I will be busy with some reports and with the Lord Chamberlain, I have a lot to catch up on so keep yourself out of trouble."

"Okay." She gave him a little pout but wasn't going to press an issue when there really wasn't one. She turned to the steward and he inclined his hand towards the entrance. "This way, please, miss." He clicked his fingers at a maid to accompany them. "Your luggage will be sorted shortly..."

She dutifully followed the steward silently through the halls and up a flight of stairs. He stopped at a closed door and gave Tyg a little prideful smile. "I'm sure this room will be to your liking, my Lady, it has a wonderful view of the harbour and city below."

He threw the doors open dramatically and allowed Tyg to walk in first.

"Honestly, I would be happy with just a room in a public inn at this point." She grumbled. "I'm not used to all this finery, to be honest with you." She commented as she looked at the opulent yet simple room. It was obviously a guest room with neutral tones and no personal effects but the bed looked soft and inviting, although Tyg wasn't really interested in lying down as it would make the room spin. She went to the doors leading to a balcony and looked out at the view.

It was definitely amazing!

She could even see the ships of Lord Doven's anchored in the bay after getting unloaded one by one of its iron ore, soldiers and horses.

"If you require anything please let Lillian here know, my Lady. I will leave you to your rest." Master Severn bowed and left as Tyg looked back at him and nodded, glancing at Lillian the maid.

"Just relax, I don't need anything from you."

Lillian gave Tyg a small smile and cute little bob of a curtsey. "Thank you, miss." However she didn't move from her spot standing and waiting by the door.

Tyg turned away, ignoring the girl and went back to the balcony doors, watching the docks from this distance wasn't easy but she knew Corvyn was out there and hoped he was about to enjoy the news that he was going to get three days leave before having to head on to Enyana with the ore.

She wondered where the garrison was situated when she saw the wagons loaded with ore break from the buildings and look like they were heading out of the city with what looked like Corvyn's black armoured soldiers escorting the long line.

That couldn't be right...

She opened the balcony doors and stepped out to the balustrade, leaning over it and straining her eyes to try and make out what they were doing.

The wagons were being corralled in an area free of buildings not far from the Estate and clearly on the main road that headed east out of the city of Asbel.

Perhaps they intended to send the ore on with a different, fresher lot of soldiers, but it definitely looked like the same ones.

Surely Leviathan didn't lie to her, surely he wouldn't go against their agreement and send Corvyn and his soldiers straight to Enyana?

Her teeth gnashed together in her building ire as she gripped the balustrade in a death grip. "That son of a bitch!"

Lilian almost fainted in fright as Tyg turned and stormed to the door, throwing it open and stalked off down the hall in search of someone to ask where she could find that lying piece of...

She saw a couple of guards near the staircase and approached them.

"Where can I find the Emperor?" She demanded.

The guards both looked her up and down in the tight and revealing dress and one smiled vilely at her. "He's quite busy at the moment, miss. I suggest you return to your room." He sneered the word suggest and his fellow guard snickered.

"I need to speak with him now. Is he down there...?" She went to walk past them but the guard stopped her by putting his arm out and blocking the way.

"No, he's not and I suggest you go back to your room, miss." He repeated more firmly.

Was she being imprisoned?

"Get out of my way." Tyg growled through clenched teeth as she eyed the guard with blazing eyes.

He glared straight back, unafraid. "No, we've been told to..."

Tyg snarled and grabbed the guards arm, twisting it up his back and forcing him face first into the wall with a strong shove to the back of his head, smashing his nose. He cried out startled and the other guard leaped over, grabbing Tyg by the shoulder to pull her back. She grabbed his wrist and twisted around, twisting his arm and forcing him to his knees as he yelled in pain.

"I'm going to go and see Leviathan now and you won't be stopping me!"

Tyg felt the pop as the man's shoulder dislocated and he screamed. Tyg let him go and turned to the sound of the other guard rushing up on her, she hitched her dress up and kicked out at him, getting him in the stomach making him stagger backwards, teeter on the edge of the top step for a moment before falling backwards with a loud crash and clatter as he tumbled down the stairs. His body crashed into a large plinth with a vase on it at the bottom and she saw it crash down onto his arm as he yelled in pain.

As she descended the stairs on her warpath two more guards appeared at the bottom of the stairs along with Master Severn. She stopped by the fallen soldier and picked up his sword, rotating it around showing her skill as she focused on the two guards.

"Stop!" Master Severn yelled.

She gave him a deadly look but threw the sword down. "Where is Leviathan?" Her eyes blazed and she snarled like a wild animal making the steward pale as one of the guards turned tail and ran.

"This way, please calm down..."

"I'll calm down once I've had words with your Emperor about daring to lie to me!"

Leviathan was quickly informed by the guard that ran to find him and he ran through the stone building following the wreckage until he saw her standing in a large formal lounge room growling at the Chamberlain, her eyes blazing as he crouched over terrified. The steward standing by the door baulked at the look on Leviathan's face and dropped to his knees.

"Where the hell is he!?" She screamed.

"Tygarya!" Leviathan yelled. "Calm down this instant!" He could see the power field around her as she innately drew power in, in her ire completely oblivious to it herself.

"Where the fuck are those soldiers going, Leviathan?" Tyg turned and advanced on him, her eyes blazing with ice blue fury.

"What soldiers?" Leviathan asked folding his arms, not afraid of her advancement. "And if you don't stop right now, Tygarya, you will give me no choice but to hurt you." He snarled at her, his eyes glowing in response.

Tyg stopped, but her eyes still blazed. "The soldiers from the ships...I can see the port from my room's balcony, Leviathan....where are they going?"

Leviathan smirked and scratched his jaw. "What's it to you?"

"We had a deal...they were to get leave."

"And they will." His tone dropped as his gaze tightened on her.

"So why are they leaving the city...like they're going to battle?"

Leviathan levelled a cool gaze at her. "Tygarya, this is my army, you seem to forget that..."

"No, of course I don't forget that...but..."

"Our agreement did not state where and when that leave was to take place." Leviathan looked smug now.

"You asshole! Do you even intend on giving them leave?" Tyg's eyes blazed brighter.

"Calm down." Leviathan growled, his tone dropping further in warning.

"I need an answer, Leviathan."

Leviathan sighed. "For fuck's sake, Tygarya...I have issued an order giving them their three days allowed leave once they reach Davios, the capital city of Enyana and safely off load the iron ore." Tyg looked at him a moment unsure, this seemed to make him even more angry as he grit his teeth. "Trust me, Tyg."

"Fine." Tyg said folding her arms and looking away. "But if I find out it's not true..."

Leviathan had finally had enough. He stormed up to her, picked her up by her throat and held her in front of him at eye level. As she struggled against him and tried to pry his hand from her throat he growled low and commanding. "Don't ever fucking threaten me."

"Lev, let her go..." Antyn said calmly coming into the room, followed by the steward, who had run to get him after seeing Leviathan's anger. He waved everyone out of the room.

Leviathan dropped her and turned to Antyn. "You tell her...perhaps she will believe you." Leviathan sneered and stormed from the room, sweeping his arm out and smashing a large urn off a side table in frustration as he went. Tyg was on her knees holding her throat and coughing.

Antyn walked over to her after watching Leviathan walk out. "Are you okay?"

"I'm fine." Tyg spat and stood up. He saw the redness around her neck turning to bruising already.

"Good..." Antyn said coolly, then his eyes glowed. "What the fuck, Tygarya! Why do you always have to test his patience with you? This is exactly the kind of thing I tried to warn against back on the ship!"

"Is it true, Antyn?" She blatantly ignored his berating of her.

"Is what true?" Antyn paced over to a seat and collapsed down in it, raking a hand through his hair in exasperation. "Fuck's sake...how the hell do you two go from mad passionate kissing to trying to kill each other in a matter of fucking minutes?"

"Are the soldiers getting three days leave once they reach Enyana?"

Antyn looked at her strangely and scratched his chin. "Yes...why?"

Tyg looked down at the floor and sat down in a chair opposite him. "No reason." She muttered calmly, all wrath completely gone in an instant making Antyn blink and wonder if he had just dreamed her furious tantrum.

She was feeling more than a little foolish now as she realised she had once again let her wild anger take over and sheepishly looked over at Antyn.

"Is that what this was all about?" He asked incredulously.

Tyg looked up at him. "I thought Leviathan had broken our deal."

"Your deal?" His voice was a little hard.

"He didn't tell you?" Tyg said surprised. "We made a deal that I would play nice and wear a dress if he gave the soldiers some leave."

Antyn stared at her a moment then sat forward, one hand up. "Let me get this straight...you went on a fucking rampage through this place, fighting guards and breaking one man's arm just because you *thought* Lev had broken some deal? Without even asking him first?"

71

"Sorry...I tried to find him, but the guards got in my way..." Tyg muttered and looked down again.

"Fuck, Tyg if I was allowed to even remotely touch you I would fucking have you publically spanked, at the very least for acting like a complete brat!"

"I beg your pardon? What the hell did you just say?" She didn't know what part of that sentence she should be offended by the most.

"Tyg, this isn't funny...you hurt people...you're on Leviathan's soil now...keep a fucking grip on yourself. Everything you do now reflects back on him."

"I suppose I should go and apologise..." She murmured to herself.

"To the soldiers? Probably." Antyn said sitting back in the chair again. "I'm going to have to fix that one guard's arm and Lev is going to have to, probably, pay him some sort of compensation while he's off injured."

"I meant Leviathan." She stared at Antyn perplexed.

Antyn stared back at her. "You really don't feel any remorse for this, do you?"

"He got in my way...I told him to get out of my way...he chose not to." She shrugged. "Were they told to keep me in my room?"

"Bloody hell, of course they weren't, but you were overly aggressive and demanding to see the Emperor..." Antyn muttered, she was worse than even he realised. "I think I'm going to talk to Leviathan myself, make you apologise to the guards and the staff for your behaviour." He said casually leaning his head on his hand and regarding her, already exhausted by her.

Tyg looked at him with a mortified expression. "What the fuck would that achieve? What's done is done."

"The fact that you have to ask that question, tells me it would be very beneficial and humbling for you."

"I fucking hate you." She growled like an animal.

Antyn chuckled. "Sod it Tyg, you are so fucking emotionally led...why say that shit when you don't actually mean it. Yet at the same time you show no emotion or remorse towards taking any responsibility for your actions, you're your own complete shit storm, aren't you?"

"Go through with this Antyn...I'll hate you alright." Her eyes held the truth of her threat.

"I'll tell you what, since you like deals so much..." Antyn said amused. "...if you do a good job of apologising to Lev and putting things straight with him before tonight's dinner, I'll think on whether to make you apologise to the guards and staff."

Tyg stared at him then rolled her eyes. He noticed them cool to a nice sky blue. "Fine." She stood up and walked towards the door. She stopped and turned, pointing at the smashed urn. "Just remember I didn't do that!" She smiled facetiously before turning away and walking off like nothing could touch her.

He smiled at her and shook his head as she smirked and left. "So enigmatically charming..." He raked a hand through his hair and stood up. "How do I always get stuck with cleaning up the mess?"

9

Tyg found Leviathan in the Lord Chamberlain's office, sitting behind the desk with his feet up on it listening with a bored expression as Lord DuPont was talking about her.

They had left the door open, and Tyg was determined to make the Chamberlain regret that action. As she stepped silently into the room she put a finger to her lips as Leviathan scowled at her, his eyes tracking her every move. She saw a shadow of a smirk twerk his lips and grinned back as she walked right up behind the Chamberlain and stood there with her hands behind her back and listened to him.

"She broke a man's arm, dislocated another's shoulder. My Liege, she even threatened you...what are we, your staff, supposed to make of such a thing. Surely you can see that perhaps some warning of her arrival and her nature would have been advisable...I could have got more guards...or something."

"What would that have achieved, Chamberlain?" Leviathan said coyly. "She would have just injured them too, look just stay out of her way, just like you always usually stay out of mine when I'm here."

"My Liege, I assure you, I do not..." The chamberlain bowed his head and Tyg could see he was quaking in his boots. "But...my Liege...some of the staff are terrified of her already and threatening to leave..."

"We're only here for three days, Chamberlain, I'm sure you can sort things, or did I employ the wrong person? Besides what do you want me to do, keep my consort locked in her room?"

"Well..." The Chamberlain was just about to say that wouldn't be a bad idea, when Tyg leaned over him and growled quietly in his ear.

"Boo."

The Chamberlain literally squealed and curled up into a ball sheltering his head as he jumped away. Tyg stood looking at him faintly amused as she smoothed down her dress. Leviathan leaned back and roared with laughter, a very rare occurrence that made Tyg appreciate it more.

"Really Lord Chamberlain, am I that scary?" Tyg said with one eyebrow raised.

Lord DuPont was furious in his embarrassment and turned to Leviathan. "My Imperial Majesty, I don't think this behaviour is acceptable from her...or you." As soon as he said it he went deathly pale and tried to back track as Leviathan dropped his feet off the desk and leaned forward, no longer amused. "I'm so sorry, my Liege. Forgive me." He collapsed to his knees and started babbling. Tyg stared at him with her eyes wide and startled by the change in atmosphere.

"Stand up, man." Tyg growled at him. "Geeze, why is everyone I meet lately so damn serious."

The Chamberlain looked up at her then at Leviathan, who had rested an elbow on the desk and was leaning his head on his fist, looking sideways at them with one eyebrow raised like he was watching a play.

Tyg grabbed the Chamberlain by the shoulder and pulled him up to his feet. "Look I came here to apologise. At least let me do that before you go judging me." She dusted his coat off, noticing the fine embroidery on it, she trailed a hand down his shoulder to his chest as she studied the lapel. "I might have to get the name of your tailor..." She muttered.

"W-what?" He stammered flustered at her touching him, knowing the law and trying to swipe her insistent hands away.

"Tygarya...." Leviathan muttered in a deep breathy tone. She looked over at him with an open curious expression. "Stop touching my man."

Tyg dropped her hands when she saw Leviathan's eyes glow. "Sorry I was just..."

"I know what you were doing...now stop it." His voice held that calmness that was a warning to her.

Tyg pressed her mouth together. "Lord Chamberlain..." Leviathan said in an icy tone causing Lord DuPont to turn and bow his head, down casting his eyes.

"Yes, my Liege?" He voice quavered with nerves.

"Never raise your voice to me again, do you understand?"

Lord DuPont looked surprised and looked back at Tyg. She smiled at him congenially. "I'm sorry, Lord Chamberlain, I hope you can find it in your heart to forgive me for my behaviour earlier and perhaps we can start afresh?"

He bowed his head to her. "Certainly, my Lady...a fresh start sounds like a good idea..." He stammered in his shock, he was sure he would be executed for talking back to the Emperor that way, but he seemed to be in a rather strange ambiguous mood. He looked again at the strange girl standing in front of him, was it because of this girl that the Emperor had possibly become more lenient?

"Oh, and if you could please tell that guard with the broken arm that I'm willing to pay him compensation."

Leviathan sat up, dropping his hand to the desk. "Tygarya..." His tone was deep and warning.

"I'm serious, Lev, please let me do this, I know I did wrong and I've only just arrived on these shores and I don't want to be misunderstood. I have a bit of money I brought with me..."

Lord DuPont nodded. "I will let it be known, thank you, my Lady." He turned to Leviathan. "By your leave, my Liege."

Leviathan waved his hand dismissing him, his eyes fixed on Tyg. "Come here."

"Lev, I'm sorry...really I am." Tyg said nervously as she came round the desk and stood in front of him. He stood up and at the same time pushed her back against the wall with his power, pinning her there at his mercy unable to move. She felt a strange pressure in her head and knew it was his warning. He stepped up as she grit her teeth, struggling against his magical hold with no relief. He slowly and menacingly placed his hands on the wall either side of her and brought his face down level with hers, leaning in.

"Not even an hour here, Tygarya....a fucking hour! And you're threatening *me*!"

"I'm sorry, I just said that...what more do you want me to say?"

"I don't want you to say anything. I want you to shut the fuck up and listen." Leviathan was talking in that calm deep voice. Tyg stared at him wide eyed. She knew that tone and the fact that he was inside her head. "You seriously need to get control of your emotions, Tygarya. I don't know how the fuck you survived back in Arial, when you fly off the handle at every little thing that sparks annoyance in you. But here, you can't be doing that, Tygarya...because here you are dealing with *me*. So unless you want me to keep a leash around your fucking neck and drag you around with me every second of the day...or be locked imprisoned in your room, behave!" Leviathan stared hard into her eyes watching for any reaction while Tyg tried hard to keep her reactionary feelings down. He dropped his arms and stepped back. "There must be something you can do to keep relaxed..."

"Let me train." Tyg said quietly. Leviathan glanced up at her, seeing the power waves still swirling around her.

"Perhaps, that might actually work..." He reached out with one finger and drew a line down her cheek, absorbing the power through that light touch. He watched as she visibly relaxed.

Tyg smiled and leaned her head back on the wall. "It's always worked before."

Leviathan regarded her a moment while he thought about it. "Not until we get to the castle though."

"We are in a castle now." Tyg said tartly, being deliberately obtuse.

Leviathan retracted the hand and rubbed his forehead. "Tyg, for fuck's sake, don't try my patience with you, you really won't like it." His eyes were glowing with the power but Tyg saw it as a warning.

She downcast her eyes. "Sorry, my Liege."

Leviathan's eyes went dark but he walked back to his desk and sat down and looked down at his work. "Leave Tygarya, and behave."

Tyg stood up straight and wandered over to the desk, trailing her fingertips along it as she past it. Leviathan's eyes flicked up and watched the action without lifting his head, then he leaned back in his chair and regarded her coolly when he noticed her fingers stopped directly in front of him.

"That was an order, Tygarya." He said slightly amused with an ironic tone.

"You're still angry with me, what can I do?" Tyg asked then looking at him demurely. "I don't like you angry with me.

Leviathan's lip twerked at the corners and his eyes smouldered as he thought of several things she could do. Tyg caught the expression and frowned. "Oh...really?"

Leviathan shook his head and laughed. "No, Tygarya, I'm too busy, but maybe later, now go away."

Tyg folded her arms and stood there staring at him indignantly. "How fucking rude, who do you think I am, one of your servants? Don't you dare dismiss me like I'm nothing to you. You dragged me over the damn ocean to here!"

Leviathan rubbed his fingers over his eyes and sighed. "Tygarya, you know you are not 'nothing' to me...for fuck's sake I'm busy, that is all. Now I'm back I have an Empire to run."

"Really? So you're not mad?" Her tone accused him of still being mad.

Leviathan stood up and leaned over the desk grabbing Tyg's chin with astonishing speed, making her hands slap the desk as he pulled her over it. "I am fucking furious, Tygarya..."

Tyg looked at him wide eyed, she had to try and make him forgive her before Antyn spoke to him. "I said I'm sorry, I've agreed to make it up...what do you want me to do? Tell me."

Leviathan let her chin go and sighed as he put his hands on the desk and looked up at her as she pulled back, seeing her sincerity. "Seriously Tygarya...I'm mad at myself."

"What?" Tyg was confused.

"I know what you're like, I knew what to expect...yet I left you alone. As soon as we were here I left you to your own devices. I should have known you didn't actually need to rest." Leviathan sat back in the chair and beckoned her round. "I knew better so I blame myself for what happened..." He grabbed her arm as she came to him and pulled her down into his lap. He trailed the back of his hand down her face. "You are so beautiful in that dress and played your part so well, I forgot momentarily what you actually are..."

"And what's that exactly?" Tyg asked her voice hardening.

Leviathan looked into her eyes and gave her such an amazing smile it left her holding her breath. "A girl from another world that couldn't possibly ever fit into this one." He stroked her hair and trailed his fingers through it.

"Oh." Tyg's eyes widened and she chewed on her bottom lip as tears formed behind her eyes. She had a sudden rush of emotions of Stills and the way he had said to her that she was always meant for more. Tyg suddenly crashed down into Leviathan's chest, curling up into him and tucking her head into his neck. He looked surprised for a moment, no one had ever been so openly affectionate with him before, unless they were trying to get in his bed. Yet this felt more expressive of a small child trying to hide from the world. He gathered her in his arms and held her firmly against him, resting his head on top of hers feeling her emotional anguish. His eyes were glowing and dark as he felt the extraordinary power that she held leech into him. He couldn't allow himself to get attached emotionally to this Elvian girl but he found himself becoming more and more so...she was so faceted, and now this vulnerable side which showed itself so rarely, she was indeed like no other in this world. So simple and innocent to his world yet so damn complex and damaged.

But he needed a way to keep her calm and out of trouble...

An hour later Antyn wandered in after a brief knock and looked at Leviathan with complete astonishment. Leviathan was sitting back in his chair, his legs up on the desk as he held out a form he was reading at a strange angle away from himself. The reason for that was because Tyg was curled up on top of him, asleep.

"What the fuck?" Antyn said in a hushed tone as he quickly shut the door. Leviathan regarded him with a smirk and shushed him making Antyn's eyes go wide.

"Quiet, she's asleep." Leviathan whispered.

"You have got to be fucking kidding me, Lev...what the hell are you doing?" Antyn answered in a harsh whisper.

"What?" Leviathan asked confused.

"You don't see a problem with this?"

"No...actually I quite like it." Leviathan grinned as he casually stroked the top of Tyg's head.

"Fuck's sake, Lev, she's not a pet cat."

"No, I know that, Antyn...but look how calm she is." He looked down at her for a moment before his eyes slid up to Antyn, narrowing slightly. "What do you want?"

Antyn sighed and continued to stare at them feeling disturbed. "Did you get a chance to read that list of executions?"

"Yes, I did...they all seem reasonable...go ahead and put my seal to them."

"I was hoping to talk to you about her..."

"Yes, I'm sure you were. Look, Antyn, it's sorted okay. She apologised to the Chamberlain and offered to pay compensation to the soldier for his broken arm...so leave it alone."

Antyn raked a hand through his hair, that damn woman had gotten to Leviathan before him and now look at him...putty in her hands. "Fine...will you attend the executions tomorrow?"

"Yes...I think I will."

"With Tygarya..."

"Of course." Leviathan grinned wickedly.

Antyn rolled his eyes and bowed his head. "Alright, whatever...I'll see you later for dinner." He left the room and shook his head. Seeing Tyg curled up in Leviathan's lap like some pet disturbed him greatly knowing what she truly was.

It was only a few minutes later that Tyg stirred and moaned against him. Leviathan threw the papers down on the desk and held Tyg softly in case she fell off. She lifted her head and looked up at him confused for a moment.

"Did I fall asleep?"

Leviathan smiled. "Yes you did, my dear."

"Oh, Gods...I'm so sorry..." Tyg went to get up feeling embarrassed at having fallen asleep on top of him. How horrifyingly inappropriate!

"Shush, Tyg, it's all okay...I quite liked having you lying on top of me." Leviathan smirked and his eyes sparkled.

"Oh, shit..." Tyg muttered and again tried to get up in her innocent embarrassment. Leviathan held her firmly, amused by her reaction.

"Stop...I was only teasing...although I did enjoy having you so close, I'm not going to lie. Your warmth and that divine scent that lingers around you...I found it quite calming."

Tyg looked at him uneasy and Leviathan could sense her unease. "Don't panic, Tyg, nothing untoward happened, you merely napped."

"How embarrassing..." Tyg muttered. "How many people came in here while I slept on you?"

"Slept on me..." Leviathan's eyes darkened as he repeated her words in a breath.

"Leviathan..." Tyg rolled her eyes and sat up on his lap wiping her face.

Leviathan's eyes went dark. "Don't roll your eyes at me, Tygarya, I've told you before..." Tyg stared at him bewildered as he answered her question like he hadn't just threatened her. "Only Antyn...and the Chamberlain...and the captain of the guard...oh...and the cook with Master Severn." Leviathan chuckled as Tyg groaned. "Did you not sleep well?"

Tyg looked at him and smiled. "Yes I did...your heartbeat is what made me fall asleep."

"You listened to my heartbeat?" Leviathan said softly and ran a finger down Tyg's cheek and across her chin taking in her flawless complexion.

"Yes...it was calming." Tyg lowered her eyes and looked at him under her lashes. Leviathan grabbed her chin and pulled her mouth to his and kissed her, smashing their lips together.

"Might I suggest something...?" Leviathan asked then taking a lock of her hair and twining it round his fingers. Tyg watched him with an eyebrow raised. "I know you are not ready to take the next step but would you consider lying with me at night...fully clothed of course, merely in close proximity."

Tyg's eyes went wide and they shifted to that strange cornflower blue. "I...ah..."

Leviathan kissed her again chastely on the lips. "Think about it...you could sleep listening to my heartbeat every night, curled up in my arms, just like today."

Tyg slipped off his lap and stood up looking at him with a complex expression somewhere between a frown and awe.

"I will think about it." She uttered, barely audible as her voice stuck in her throat.

Leviathan frowned. "Where are you going?"

"I feel that I should bathe before dinner."

Leviathan's eyes widened and he smirked. Tyg went to roll her eyes but stopped herself, Leviathan smirked wider. "Why every time I mention bathing do you do that?"

Leviathan chuckled. "Because one day I hope to be bathing naked with you, my dear." He smouldered at her.

Again Tyg's eyes went wide and her knees went weak as she couldn't help but blush. He leaned forward and caught her by the arm and pulled her back into him. "Do you need me to carry you?" He whispered as he looked at her intensely.

Tyg stood up again, smoothing down her dress. "No, I'll be fine...thank you, my Liege." She said as she stepped away from him.

His eyes darkened and he chuckled. "Tygarya..." She turned at the door. "I do hope we can do this again..." The way his head was tilted with that little smirk made him look so devilishly handsome.

Tyg smiled. "Of course..."

Tyg walked slowly back to her room in almost a dream. She was deep in thought about what he had asked. She had slept with Stills just in the way Leviathan was suggesting and thought nothing of it, but for some reason she felt lying in that way with an Emperor was a much bigger deal. She didn't know what to do, he had completely confused her. She had loved lying curled up on him listening to his heartbeat while he worked. It had definitely calmed her and that was what they had been talking about beforehand. She stopped walking and stared at the floor...am I falling in love with him? That was too dangerous of a thing to even contemplate.

However it made her make up her mind about one thing, no way was she sharing a bed with him, not until she was sure and ready to yield everything to him.

As dinner was called Tyg made her way down to the dining hall to find everyone already there, Lord DuPont was with his wife and daughter making small talk with Leviathan and Antyn, a younger boy sat to the side looking bored. She nervously made her way to Leviathan's side as the steward opened the doors to the dining room and they all entered, Leviathan leading her to a chair beside the head seat, on the left. Antyn took the seat next to her while the Chamberlain sat on Leviathan's right with his wife and children beside him.

Antyn gave Tyg a sideways glance as she turned and smiled up at him as he took his seat. "Seems you won, Tyg...well done." He said facetiously.

"Thank you." She sneered at him.

Antyn chuckled and dinner past with congenial polite small talk until Lord DuPont's wife excused herself and the children before the men retired in the drawing room for cognac and cigars.

Tyg decided to excuse herself as well. "I think I'll retire too, if that's okay?" She looked up at Leviathan expectantly.

His expression hardened a little and he pulled her to the door as Antyn and DuPont said goodnight to her.

"Tygarya..." Leviathan's whispered voice made her turn her head and look up at him. "What I spoke to you about earlier? Is this your decision?"

"I'm sorry, Leviathan, I can't sleep in your room with you...it doesn't feel right."

He nodded his head, the disappointment clear in his eyes. Tyg felt a little thump in her heart and a lump come to her throat.

"Okay, goodnight, Tygarya." He opened the door and indicated for her to leave, suddenly cold.

"Lev...?" She breathed, looking confused.

He placed a hand on her back and pushed her gently but firmly out the door. "I will see you tomorrow, Tygarya, have a good rest."

She stared in disbelief as he closed the door on her, then grit her teeth. Why does he make me feel like I've done something wrong? Why didn't he kiss me?

She turned and made her way silently to her room, tears filling her vision but she refused to let them fall, rubbing at her eyes. Damn him, how does he make me feel so inadequate and frail?

10

Tyg was bored sitting watching the people get their heads chopped off. She was sitting on a dais that was side on to the execution platform so they had a grand view of the axe cutting through people's necks. Tyg was sitting on Leviathan's left, Antyn on his right, soldiers and a couple of strange men in dark green cloaks, surrounded them below the dais keeping the crowds of people away.

She had been surly and pouty all morning after Leviathan's abrupt coldness the night before, what was annoying her was that he was acting like nothing was wrong. He was in his usual controlling and handsie mood, kissing her in front of everyone at breakfast like he was touch starved for her before announcing that they were off to watch some executions.

Tyg was always amazed at the blood thirsty nature of people, and executions seemed to bring out the worst of them, all crowding around shouting insults and throwing things - a final debasement to an already broken individual – then cheering as they watched them die. Tyg took no joy in it, couldn't understand it at all. Yeah sure, kill the guy for his crimes, torture him to confess, but just kill him for fuck's sake...why the need for the crowds. It was hardly a deterrent, like some people said it was. All it seemed to her was entertainment and killing someone should never be for entertainment, killing was serious business. She should know.

"I know you're bored, Tygarya, this is the last one coming up now, then we can go...I have something planned." Leviathan muttered from beside her.

Tyg looked at him. "Something planned?" She smiled. Last time he had something planned they went horse riding in the countryside and he gave her the ring.

...the ring

...the bloody ring that doesn't seem to want to come off!

She had tried to take it off yesterday when she bathed. She hadn't said anything about it...yet...this one she was storing up for the right time. It was obviously enchanted with some sort of spell, the possessive son of a bitch!

Leviathan was looking at her with a frown. "You okay? You seemed a million miles away?"

"Just thinking of the last time you had 'something planned'." Tyg smiled.

Leviathan grinned and his eyes darkened. "Oh yes...that was a good day..."

Their conversation was interrupted by the official calling the last man to the platform and reading out his crimes. Tyg frowned and sat forward slightly.

"Tygarya..." Leviathan muttered. She hadn't taken any interest in the executions up till now.

Tyg turned to him. "Does the executioner look nervous to you?"

Leviathan squinted a bit and shrugged. "Probably because trouble was expected with this one...an escape attempt or something."

"Until the Emperor showed up anyway." Antyn put in. Leviathan snorted in amusement.

"What's so special about this guy?" Tyg asked.

"He's got a bit of notoriety, they say what he steals he gives to those less fortunate." Antyn explained.

"Less fortunate than what?" Tyg asked.

Antyn smiled on one side of his mouth. "Those poor people that live on the streets and struggle to survive."

"You told me everyone here has the opportunity to work."

"If they want to...yes...like I said before some choose not to."

"So then they are in their situation because of themselves...why is he helping them?"

Antyn shrugged. "Unfortunately, there is always going to be people crying out for someone else to save them from their lot in life."

"So he's enabling them?" Tyg said matter-of-factly. This made Leviathan turn and look at her with great interest, a curious smirk on his face.

"Yes in a way I suppose he is." Antyn said with a dark frown.

"So he killed people when he robbed them, that's why he's being executed?"

"Yes."

"Idiot, there was no need to kill...his objective is nullified by his actions."

Antyn stared at her as Leviathan chuckled. "He would still be a criminal..." Leviathan muttered.

"One that could have been rehabilitated to serve his own goals better."

"What the fuck are you going on about, Tygarya?" Leviathan asked rubbing his forehead.

"If he wants to help people, put him to work in an infirmary."

Leviathan sat up and stared at her. "Fucking hell."

Antyn chuckled.

"What?" Tyg looked at them confused.

"I think you may have just changed our judicial system." Antyn muttered.

"Oh..." Tyg said smiling and looked away. "He's going to mess it up."

"What?" Leviathan frowned confused.

"The executioner...he's too nervous...even the people down in the front row can see it...he's not going to do it properly."

Leviathan shrugged and sat back thinking more about Tyg's words before, she certainly had a strange and different view on things.

"Leviathan, aren't these beheadings supposed to be humane and done in one quick stroke?" Tyg asked, curious to his apathetic response.

"Shit, Lev, if the executioner mucks this up it will look like you organised it to happen, public sentiment round this guy is high." Antyn understood what Tyg was getting at.

"Well, I'm not going to go down there and do it, which would be worse...make him a martyr."

"No, you're right." Antyn frowned.

Tyg was watching carefully as the man laid his head on the block and the executioner nervously rubbed his hands together. "I think he may be a supporter of the guy, he's going to regret this..."

"Regret it how?"

"Because he's going to fuck it up and make the guy he idolises suffer."

"Good." Leviathan stated coldly.

Tyg looked at him with a grimace. "You will still get the blame, more so because he'll blame you instead of admitting his feelings for the criminal."

"How the hell do you understand all this, Tyg?" Antyn asked incredulously.

Tyg shrugged. "I don't know…it's like looking in through a window…it's all already laid out in front of me."

Leviathan shot Antyn a strange look and something deep shifted between them.

A scream tore through the silence. "I fucking told you!" Tyg said as she suddenly stood up, pulling her dress up slightly to give her more freedom and jumped the four foot gap from the dais to the platform.

"Tygarya!" Leviathan growled.

Tyg walked up to the astonished executioner as she ripped the axe from his hand and pushed him away, she swung the axe with great accuracy and strength beheading the injured man swiftly as his body jerked and spasmed over the block. Leaving the axe imbedded in the chopping block by several inches. She turned to the executioner her eyes blazing. "Idiot!" She cursed at him. She turned then to look around and noticed Leviathan and Antyn were both on their feet, the guards surrounding them had moved to cover the platform and were shoving the crowd back and the crowd were cheering.

Tyg looked at the crowd confused. The official came up to her.

"My Lady, I think it best if you re-joined his Imperial Majesty and left before the crowd riots."

"But I helped the poor guy?"

"Oh yes, I know…the crowd is cheering you for doing it, my Lady." He said quaking.

"What?" Tyg suddenly saw Leviathan loom up in front of her. She looked up at his face, he was smiling but his eyes were dark and troubled. He reached out and cupped her chin, holding her head up while with the other he had grabbed a handkerchief off the official and wiped her cheek with it. Tyg saw the red colour of blood and realised a splash must have hit her cheek. Tyg blinked and looked at Leviathan shyly.

"Thank you and sorry."

"Nothing to be sorry for, Tygarya...come on let's go..." Leviathan's voice was monotone as he took her hand and led her down the stairs at the back of the platform and through a line of soldiers to a door that lead into the chambers of the magistrate and officials that ran the city.

Once inside however Leviathan's mood changed. He pulled her into an empty room and pushed her up against a wall with a hand around her throat, his thumb pressing against her windpipe.

"Don't ever fucking do that again...do you understand me?" Leviathan growled through gritted teeth. He was raging, the violence that was being held in check clear behind his dark eyes and felt within the formidable aura he emitted.

"I said I was sorry..." Tyg grimaced, taking a short shallow breath.

"You always do! But it has to stop, Tygarya! Your impulsive need to fix a situation, think before you act!"

"But, he was..."

"That doesn't mean *you* had to fix it!"

Leviathan dropped his hand and walked away from her raking a hand through his hair, frustrated. "I don't know how the hell you always manage to come out of these things like the bloody hero, you're just damn lucky..."

"I'm not a hero..." Tyg muttered as she rubbed her throat.

"No, you're not!" Leviathan growled turning back to face her, making her flinch in real fear. He sighed, calming himself with difficulty. "You have an amazing mind, Tygarya, but you are too impulsive..."

"I can't help who I am." Tyg said frowning and looking at the ground.

"So what are you saying to me? Do I put that fucking leash around your neck? You are mine and I demand your loyalty and obedience!"

Tyg looked up at Leviathan with horror. He had threatened that yesterday. "Please don't." She breathed as he strode up and placed his hand upon her throat again, resting it on her collarbone like he had done back in Arial and on board the ship. She felt the sensual heat that touch caused and looked up at him. That dominant power radiated from him as she stared into his eyes. He crashed his other fist into the wall next to her as he leaned down and kissed her, forcing his tongue into her mouth as he swept his hand from her throat to grabbing a fistful of hair at the back of her head and held her firmly. Tyg surrendered to his will and put her arms around him, pulling him in to her and kissing him back just a fiercely.

He broke off the kiss and pressed his forehead to hers. "Why can't you submit your will to me in all situations like you do when we kiss?" Leviathan growled.

Tyg grit her teeth. "Because then I wouldn't be me."

Leviathan stood up letting her go and snorted with a smirk. "I'm saying to submit to *me*, not change who you are."

"How would that have changed today?" Tyg asked confused.

Leviathan gave her a steady controlled look of pure authority that made her knees go weak. "You would have asked my permission before leaping off the dais."

Tyg frowned. "Is that it? You want me to ask your permission?" Leviathan smirked. "Yes."

"Huh..." Tyg said bemused. "Would you have let me?"

Leviathan chuckled. "Probably not."

"Then why are we even having this conversation..." Tyg asked frustrated, she really didn't understand Leviathan at all.

"Because I would have simply sent a soldier up there to deal with it, like I said, Tyg...it doesn't have to be *you.*"

"Oh." She dropped her gaze feeling a little ashamed.

"A calm head, mine...would have sorted the situation out better."

Tyg folded her arms. "Ok, fair enough..." She pouted, conceding the point.

"Now I have to deal with the fallout of the fact that you did it...the Emperor's fucking betrothed jumped over to the platform grabbed the executioners axe and beheaded a man, driving the axe so deep into the stone block they can't get it out...how does one explain that?"

Tyg looked at him concerned. "Oh."

"Yes, Tygarya...oh." Leviathan seemed calmer as he rubbed his forehead with a thumb. "You are an Elvian, Tyg, last of your kind...most humans are terrified of Elvians...I don't need them terrified of you. Understand me?"

Tyg looked at the floor contrite. "Yes." Tyg lifted herself up off the wall and walked over to him, putting her arms around his waist and resting her head on his chest. "I will try harder, my Liege." She muttered against him. Leviathan smiled to himself and rubbed her back.

"Thank you." He heaved a sigh, clearing his thoughts and changing his mood. Mercurial, he focused on being happy and grabbed her hand from around his waist and walked to the door. "Come on then, we have somewhere to be."

"Oh, right...your 'something planned'?" Tyg asked as she allowed herself to be dragged along by Leviathan.

As he stepped out of the room he had accosted for his conversation with Tyg he found Antyn waiting. Antyn gave them a questioning look with his eyebrow raised.

Leviathan's face went flat and stony. "What?"

"All sorted?" Antyn asked with a merry twinkle in his eye.

Tyg groaned. "You don't have to look so smug, just say 'I told you so' and let's move on shall we..."

Antyn chuckled. "I would never be so bold as to say that to the Emperor, Tyg...but thank you for saying it for me."

Leviathan growled. "Cut it out, little brother." The way Leviathan said little brother sent a chill through everyone's blood. "Tyg has acknowledged it and is reviewing her behaviour, let it go."

Antyn's eyes widened slightly at Leviathan's wording. "Okay..." He frowned and bowed his head. "Then enjoy the rest of your day."

"We will." Leviathan growled putting an arm around Tyg's shoulders and walking off down the hall.

Antyn couldn't help but notice Tyg's temperament had been extremely forced. "Like trying to hold back the bloody tide." Antyn muttered and walked off in the opposite direction hoping above hope that Leviathan would work out a way to tame Tyg's wild nature soon.

11

As the carriage moved along the main road heading down the coast, Tyg saw the city scape fall behind and farms take over. Tyg could see people toiling in the fields in the early spring sunshine, tending to their crops.

Leviathan hadn't let go of her hand and seemed to be brooding, leaning back with his long legs up on the seat across from them, his hand holding hers draped across his hard flat stomach, as he jabbed at the horns of the dragon ring with a finger of his other hand, lost in thought.

'Perfect timing then.' Tyg thought. "So do you mind telling me why I can't get that off?" Tyg asked looking at their hands.

Leviathan's eyes slid from the window to hers. "Why would you want to take it off?" Leviathan asked in that low commanding voice.

Tyg's eyes widened and she bit her lip. No, it was the wrong time. "No reason..." Tyg said vaguely.

"Tygarya..." Leviathan warned.

Tyg sighed. "Look, I just wanted to take it off when I bathed last night, that's all...people don't normally wear jewellery in the bath, Leviathan."

"Well, from now on you do." He smirked, but his eyes were dark.

"Yeah, I guess so." Tyg rolled her eyes and looked out the window.

Her chin was suddenly wrenched back round by Leviathan's firm grip as he leaned over her. "Tygarya, you rolled those fucking big beautiful eyes at me." His smirk was triumphant and sultry.

"Ah...did I?" She looked up at him with apprehension at the dark look in his eye.

"You know you did."

"Sorry..." Tyg frowned as he held her gaze, she really didn't like the dark look in his eyes.

"No, Tygarya...no more apologies....punishment." Leviathan growled.

"What the fuck...for what? Rolling my eyes?"

"Yes, it's a pet peeve of mine...and I've warned you at least twice now...it has been driving me crazy since the day I met you."

"Okay...but what...?" Tyg breathed unable to speak any louder under his intense brooding aura.

"I'm not sure what to do...I shall think on it..." Leviathan let her chin go and smirked at her with a deeply sultry look.

"Bloody hell..." Tyg muttered knowing she was going to be walking on eggshells for the rest of the day now, exactly the level of discomfort that he clearly wanted.

He watched her with that vulture glare for a few minutes longer as she folded her arms and chewed on her bottom lip deep in pensive thought.

He was so damn male she really didn't know how to handle it...he seemed so sexually aware and wasn't afraid to let her know it. She knew he was experienced...that was more than obvious just by his age and status...women fell over themselves just to get him to look in their direction, but did he have to say things like that to her...he obviously knew what it did to her, that clenching she felt deep inside her core. She didn't even really know what that feeling was, only that she felt it when they kissed as well so knew it was something to do with sexual attraction...a need...a want for more. She frowned, and he did it deliberately to shock her and tease her. She grit her teeth, she had been letting him do more and more with her every time they kissed on board the ship, his hands felt so good on her, caressing her breasts, squeezing her buttocks, grabbing her thighs. She relinquished control to him because she trusted him, she just knew deep inside herself that he wasn't going to try anything more than what she was ready for...so why did he say these things to her? Punishment...she knew he didn't mean it in the normal sense by that sexy smirk...the worst part about it was something in her wanted to find out exactly what he meant, that deep place...was she actually contemplating that perhaps she was ready to....

"We're here..." Leviathan's voice said quietly, scaring her from her reverie and causing her to jump slightly. She glanced up at Leviathan and met his eyes, they were burning with intense amusement to see the rosy tinge upon her cheeks. "What were you thinking about so intensely, my dear?" He literally purred at her in a husky tone.

Tyg blushed redder causing Leviathan's eyes to widen slightly, his pupils to dilate and he grinned wider. "Oh, I see..." He moved closer to her and put a hand around the back of her neck pulling her to him as he leaned his head down and crashed his lips to hers pushing his tongue into her mouth. He trailed kisses to her neck and then breathed into her ear. "You want to know what I've come up with for your punishment...is that it?"

Tyg gasped and pushed him away firmly, her hands on his chest. She stared at him with blazing ice blue eyes. "Why do you enjoy teasing me like this?"

"Teasing you?" Leviathan questioned, arching an eyebrow as he pushed slightly against her hands making her aware of his muscles straining and bunching. Desire burned in her, she knew she wasn't going to want to hold out against him for much longer. "I'm not teasing you, Tygarya...your punishment will happen..."

"You can't...why do you...?" Her frantic eyes searched his face.

"Say that?" Leviathan finished for her. He broke her defences as her arms buckled, and he pressed into her, a hand going to her breast, the thumb circling her nipple as it stiffened. Using his body he pushed her down on the seat. Her eyes widened as he met her eyes but they were dark and slightly unfocused. "Tygarya, you want this, that's why..."

Leviathan kissed her neck, nibbling and sucking his way down as he popped the front clasps of her dress open and pulled the material aside, he kissed her stiffened nipple causing her to gasp again and clutch his shoulders, grabbing handfuls of his coat as her body arched to his touch.

"See the way you respond...its delectable." Leviathan breathed over her breast, as he pulled the fine lace of her bustier down exposing the nipple to the air of his breath. Tyg moaned digging her fingers into his shoulders, staring at him in a state of desire mixed with fear of stepping over a new line. He lowered his mouth, licking around the nipple and then sucking it gently into his mouth, swirling his tongue around it, flicking it.

"Bloody hell." Tyg moaned as she closed her eyes surrendering to this sweet torture of his mouth. He placed a hand around her, planting it firmly on her back between her shoulder blades and held her up to his mouth as he enjoyed himself lavishing her nipple for several moments. Tyg pressed her thighs together, acutely aware of his other hand now stroking her thigh, his touch burning her as he had swept her dress aside and his skin was touching hers. She heard him growl as he felt her resist him from going that far. He raised his head and looked at her contorted face. She was panting, that deep tightening in her core that she didn't understand screaming to be released. She opened her eyes and he saw her fear as her hand came down hard on his one between her legs.

"Please, no."

"Tyg...you need to trust me..." Leviathan said with a slight frown as he sat up letting her go. He combed his hair back with both hands, calming himself down, feeling a little exasperated.

"I do...I really do...but..." Tyg looked around the inside of the carriage. "Not here..." Tyg sat up tidying herself up and reclasping her dress, and taking a deep breath to steady her beating heart. Things had definitely escalated this time and she knew they would continue to as his desire to have her wasn't being sated.

"Hmm, you are right, Tygarya. Your deflowering should be done properly, slowly...in a bed..." Leviathan shrugged, his vulture gaze returning as Tyg stared at him with a shocked expression. "Come on then..." He opened the carriage door, and Tyg blushed as she stepped out to see three men all standing waiting for them.

"Have they been standing there the whole time?" Tyg whispered to Leviathan as he took her hand.

He grinned wickedly at her. "Probably..."

One man was a servant and held the door open for her once Leviathan had opened it. He had bowed his head and hadn't looked up again even once in Leviathan's presence. One was wearing a fine dress coat and riding pants while the other was wearing a simple linen tunic and brown leather pants. Both men had bowed deeply and straightened, but their eyes were lowered.

Leviathan strode up to the man in the dress coat and took his hand.

"Lord Gravelle, good to see you again." Leviathan said cheerfully making the Lord's eyes nearly pop out of his head as he stammered a greeting back nervously. Leviathan turned to the other man. "And Master Heldon." He inclined his head to him then stepped sideways pulling Tyg up to meet them. "This is Lady Tygarya." They both bowed their heads to her.

"Tygarya, this is Lord Gravelle, he owns this estate, and Master Heldon, he is the master breeder and trainer of the horses."

"Horses?" Tyg said as she smiled at the two men briefly in greeting.

"Your surprise, my dear." Leviathan said.

"Indeed, it is an absolute pleasure to meet you Lady Tygarya, and we are most flattered and humbled by his Imperial Majesty to give us such an honour as allowing us to be the stable of choice."

"Stable of choice?" Tygarya said confused.

Leviathan smirked. "Let's just show her, shall we Lord Gravelle."

"Of course...." He bowed his head again and turned indicating for Leviathan to go first. "This way, my Liege."

Leviathan walked up the path, holding Tyg's hand and flanked by the two soldiers that had travelled on the back of the carriage, one of which had a rucksack over his shoulder. The path went around the side of a fine stone manor house that had climbing roses entwined up frames on both sides of the facing wall, they were all of a pale pink hue, there were trees lining the wide gravel path and Tyg thought the whole place was lovely and pretty. As they rounded the house there was a large corral divided into three distinct circles all fenced off from one another. Each one held a horse...but not just any horse, these horses were as beautiful as the house and gardens, each one was poised and alert, prancing around their respective yards, their manes and tails flowing, their coats shimmering and shiny. Behind them was a line of stables and out further paddocks of lush green grass where other horses grazed.

"Oh my...they are beautiful." Tyg exclaimed as they all approached the corrals.

Lord Gravelle and Master Haldon both beamed with pride as they escorted Leviathan and Tyg along the line so Tyg could see each one of the three horses clearly.

The first one was black and glossy, with rippling muscles, it looked like the horse Leviathan had taken with him to Arial and brought back again. Tyg turned to him.

"Your horse came from here?"

"Yes." Leviathan grinned. "Lord Gravelle owns the most prestigious horse breeding facility on the continent for battle horses."

"Oh, my Liege, I am most gracious of your laudation."

"You know it's true Gravelle, stop being so modest because a woman is present." Leviathan muttered as he folded his arms and watched Tyg as she walked up to the fence and walked along the line looking at the second horse.

It was also black, but had a white blaze down its nose and two white socks on its front feet. The third one was a beautiful fiery chestnut which glimmered and shone in the sun, it too had a white blaze and two white socks but one was on a back leg. They were all stallions, proud, powerful and dangerous in the wrong hands.

Leviathan approached Tyg. "What do you think?"

"They are all beautiful creatures."

"Pick one."

Tyg looked at Leviathan with a curious expression. "What?"

"Pick one, we'll go for a ride."

"Oh." Tyg's eyes lit up as she looked back at the horses. Her eyes fell on the middle one as it had come to the fence and was regarding her curiously. She walked back to it and held her hand out, it placed its chin in her hand and snorted at her as it sniffed her. She raised her hand and stroked her hand down its nose. It bowed its head and shuddered its shoulders, like a pesky fly had landed on its skin. Leviathan frowned slightly at the horse's gentle reaction and stepped over. It raised its head, its nostrils flaring, taking in his scent. It snorted then tensed up and galloped off to the other side of the ring, its tail erect and the hair from it and the long mane streaming out behind it as it trotted around once and came back to Tyg's outstretched hand once again, a wary eye on Leviathan.

"This one." Tyg breathed entranced by the creature.

Leviathan scratched his thumb down his jaw as he watched the interaction. "I agree."

"A most excellent choice, my Liege, I will saddle him up." Master Haldon said as he jumped into the ring and grabbed the saddle that was hanging over the fence ready. He had been unsure about this, had thought it would be too dangerous to have a young maiden so close to these powerful stallions, but after seeing the reactions of them towards her he knew there was something special about this young girl.

Leviathan turned to Lord Gravelle. "Is there somewhere Lady Tygarya can change?"

Tyg turned to look at Leviathan surprised as Lord Gravelle nodded. "Yes, please follow me inside..."

Leviathan held his hand out and the soldier handed him the rucksack, he threw it at Tyg. She looked in it curious and saw her leather pants and black shirt. She looked up at him and smiled before running to catch up to Lord Gravelle, a soldier following behind. Tyg looked back and frowned at the soldier. Leviathan smirked. "Let it go, Tygarya." He called out.

Tyg looked at him briefly then turned away and went inside.

Lord Gravelle showed her through a large living area, into a drawing room that had brown leather seats and a large desk, with books lining the walls. Tyg's eyes went to the books widening with delight. "Does everyone rich have rooms filled with books?"

Lord Gravelle looked at her surprised and smiled. "I suppose they do? You can change in here, I'll wait outside with your guard."

"My guard?" Tyg asked. Lord Gravelle frowned and looked at the soldier standing behind him. "Oh, him....okay."

As Lord Gravelle closed the double doors Tyg changed quickly, rolling the dress up and putting it in the rucksack before quickly braiding her hair back then opened the doors. Lord Gravelle's eyes went wide a moment as he appraised her long legs in the tight black leather pants, her boots that were hidden under her dress now on full display. The guard coughed in warning making him flinch.

Tyg smiled slightly and followed Lord Gravelle back out to find Leviathan waiting, leaning on the fence with his arms and ankles crossed, his shoulders hunched slightly, his head bowed as he looked at the ground in quiet repose. Tyg froze at the sight of him. He was standing the same way that Stills used to and it was sexy as hell. Leviathan looked up as she exited the house and smirked on one side of his mouth almost like he knew. She swallowed hard and walked down to him. He straightened up and held his arm up to her as she walked into him and he wrapped his arms around her, kissing her hair. She noticed that the full black stallion had also been saddled and Master Heldon was holding them both as they stamped and snorted at each other.

"Ready?" Leviathan asked as he let her go again and stepped over to the black stallion and jumped up into the saddle.

"Definitely!" Tyg exclaimed and jumped up into the saddle too.

"Then let's go..." Leviathan kicked his heels into the horse's ribs with just enough pressure to make him dive forward into a gallop. Tyg laughed as her horse responded and jumped into a gallop to catch up, she didn't even need to instruct it. They galloped off up the path and out to where the carriage was waiting and then turned left and galloped off up the road.

Once they had gone a half a mile Leviathan slowed to a walk and Tyg slowed her horse too.

"This is awesome!" Tyg called out into the breeze. They had the ocean cliffs on one side of them and undulating paddocks of green on the other side. Leviathan smiled as he watched her enthusiasm and again reminded himself that she was only nineteen years old. He hoped he wasn't going to have to break that spirit too hard for her to be useful.

"What would you call it?" Leviathan asked her as they walked along.

"What?"

"The horse, what would you name him?" Leviathan rephrased the question.

"Oh...does he not have a name?"

"He has a formal name that is given by the breeder to reflect his breeding stock, but what would you call him?"

"Huh...I don't really know....maybe....Fulminous?"

"What?" Leviathan was surprised to hear that language. "How do you know the language of the gods?"

Tyg shrugged. "I read it somewhere...it means thunderbolt doesn't it?"

"Yes." Leviathan frowned slightly regarding her.

"His nose blaze kinda looks like a bolt of lightning against a black sky and well I don't know the word for lightning bolt so thunderbolt will have to do."

"It's Fulmen." Leviathan told her, she glanced at him then at the horse as it snorted and shook its head, she smiled and patted its neck.

"He likes Fulminous."

Leviathan's eyes narrowed, he could see the power around her and the horse. Was she communicating with it? He had to get her back to Antyn and inside. He stopped his horse and turned it around.

"Time to head back." He instructed as she looked at him with a frown.

"Oh, that's a shame I was just starting to really enjoy this time together. I like it when it's just us."

Leviathan smiled and gave Tyg a smouldering look. "Do you want to lie in a field with me, Tygarya?" His voice was thick with innuendo and he waggled his eyebrows at her.

Tyg rolled her eyes. "Argh, would you stop!"

Leviathan's eyes went dark. "Tyg..." He muttered dropping into that low dominant tone. Tyg's eyes went wide as she realised what she had just done. Then she grinned like the devil as she dug her heels into her horse and took off in a gallop.

"No punishment if you can't catch me!" She called out as she disappeared down the road.

Leviathan grinned wickedly to himself and galloped off after her. As he gave his horse more stamina and strength using his magic he caught up to her horse and called out to her as he trailed along behind her. "But it's double if I do catch you..." He laughed at Tyg's horrified expression, then she set her jaw, and focused her eyes on the road. "First to the gate." She said and crouched low behind her horses head, standing up in the stirrups and let the reins go, putting her arms around the horse's neck. Her horse surged forward.

"Bloody hell." Leviathan exclaimed and grit his teeth at her recklessness. He couldn't give the horse another shot of his power, it was lathered and stressing already, its heart would explode. He was going to have to concede this one to Tyg, and he hated losing, but lucky for her, her carefree joyous behaviour had rubbed off on him.

As Tyg raced her horse through the gate she pulled it up and walked it down the path, letting its muscles cool down as it breathed harshly. She patted its neck. "Thank you." She muttered to it as she saw Leviathan coming up behind her. She grinned and stood up on the horse's back, balancing as it walked slowly back to the corral. Leviathan sat up as he reached her and walked his horse along the path behind hers, looking up at her in admiration of her balance.

"Tygarya, what the hell are you doing?"

"Celebrating." Tyg grinned.

"Look out for the trees..." Leviathan said sharply as a low hanging branch was coming up behind Tyg's back. She glanced backwards and as she reached it she jumped up onto the branch, sitting down on it then swung backwards, hanging from the branch by her knees, swinging upside down as Leviathan stopped his horse directly below her and looked up. Tyg was grinning at him. He grabbed her hair that was falling in front of his face as many lengths of it had come loose and buried his nose into it inhaling deeply. "Tyg, what are you doing now?"

"Having some fun." Tyg said.

"Hmm..." Leviathan grunted as he moved his horse sideways. He watched as Tyg let her knees go and flipped round to land lightly on the ground on her feet. He slid from his saddle and grabbed her round the waist and pulled her into him, pressing her against his chest as he kissed her, lifting her off her feet.

"I should spank you for that performance." He whispered in a husky tone.

"Why exactly?"

"You have an audience." He said causing Tyg to look over her shoulder. She saw the Lord and the Master and the two soldiers all staring at her from the start of the path. They had obviously all come looking when her horse had returned without her on it.

Tyg hung her head. "Sorry." She always felt like she kept messing up.

Leviathan lifted her chin with two fingers and looked into her eyes. "Tyg...baby..." He didn't want to see her get sad. His jaw clenched tight. 'Gods, why does she affect me so much?' He thought.

"Cheer up, I'm not mad...come on...let's go collect your horse." He grabbed the reins of his horse and put his arm around her shoulders and walked up the path to the waiting men.

"My liege, is everything okay?" Lord Gravelle asked.

"Fine, Gravelle, Tygarya was just playing around." Leviathan said. "We'll take him and his name is Fulminous..." Master Haldon took Leviathan's horse and walked off with it.

Tyg paused. "Wait, what?" Tyg looked at Leviathan in shock.

Leviathan smiled down at her. "You're going to need a horse to travel back to the capital. He's yours Tyg, that's the surprise."

"Mine!" Tyg squealed in delight and jumped into Leviathan's arms, wrapping her arms around his neck and her legs around his waist as she crashed her lips against his. He caught her a bit stunned by her reaction and staggered backwards as he held her easily with one arm around her waist and grabbed her by the hair at the back of her head and kissed her back slashing his tongue into her mouth as she caged his head with her elbows and kissed him back just as passionately. He growled deep in his throat and pulled his head back as he remembered they weren't alone.

"Fuck, Tyg...settle baby." He muttered. Tyg grinned and dropped her legs lowering herself back to the ground.

"Thank you so much, Lev...I love him."

"Then go see him and say goodbye, Master Haldon will drop him to the Estate tomorrow, we need to be getting back." Leviathan said grinning. Tyg sprinted off around the corner heading to where Master Haldon had the horses once again penned. He had removed both their saddles and was brushing Fulminous down. Tyg jumped the fence as Haldon stepped back surprised and wrapped her arms around the horse's neck. It stood calmly and lowered its head to her shoulder and quivered. Leviathan frowned again when he saw the exchange as he came around the corner with Lord Gravelle.

"Looks like you made her day, my Liege." Lord Gravelle said pleased.

"It does look that way doesn't it?" Leviathan said smugly.

As the carriage pulled up outside the Estate Antyn was there waiting for them. As Tyg stepped out he could see how happy she was.

"So you found one you liked then?" Antyn said casually.

Tyg grinned at him. "Fulminous."

"What?" Antyn looked stunned.

Leviathan came up beside Tyg and put his arm around her shoulders. "That's what she has called him."

"But that's..."

"Yes, apparently she read it in a book." Leviathan dropped his arm from around her shoulders. "Go inside ahead Tygarya, you need to bathe before dinner." He kissed her forehead and gently pinched her chin before patting her on the rump to send her on her way.

"Okay, thank you again, Lev....really." She beamed a beautiful smile at him, her eyes sparkling like the ocean with the sun glinting off the waves.

Leviathan chuckled and covered her eyes with one large hand. "Stop Tygarya, for fuck's sake...you have thanked me enough on the ride back here, my lips are numb."

Tyg grinned cheekily as she sauntered off, flicking her hair back and swaying her hips. "Tygarya..." Leviathan growled in warning.

They heard Tyg giggle impishly before she quickly changed her gait and hurried off.

Antyn folded his arms as he watched her walk away. "A leash might not be your worst idea, you know?"

"Hmm." Leviathan snorted in amusement enjoying the memory of her straddling his lap and kissing him ceaselessly all the way back, before becoming serious. "She communicated with the horse, Antyn."

Antyn dropped his arms. "What the hell, are you sure?"

Leviathan scowled at him but said nothing. Antyn raked a hand through his hair. "It could be that her power isn't far off fully awakening...we guessed around twenty. We need to keep very aware."

"One of us with her at all times?" Antyn asked.

"I think that's best."

"She's becoming quite the little temptress..." Antyn looked back to where Tyg had gone.

Leviathan turned to look at his brother his eyes darkening dangerously. Antyn smirked. "Just be careful when you do finally take her, Leviathan, that she doesn't end up taking you too..." Antyn walked off.

Leviathan' jaw clenched as he balled his hands into fists. He really wasn't sure he could give that assurance and that bothered him greatly.

12

As they headed out of the city Antyn pulled his horse in alongside Tyg's. He noticed the side-eye Leviathan gave him and smiled to himself.

"How are you liking the horse, Tyg?"

"He's wonderful." She answered with a wide genuine smile and patted Fulminous's neck sending ripples of a shiver through it.

"And you named him Fulminous?"

"Yeah, it suits him, don't you think?" She gave Antyn a breezy smile. She was in a good mood, setting out on this adventure of a life time, finally leaving the city behind.

"Lev said it was like you were actually speaking directly to the horse?" Antyn commented rather pointedly, he glanced at Leviathan with a little grin as Leviathan turned in his saddle to scowl back at him.

"Not talk to him, exactly...that would be silly. I just have this affinity with animals, I would rather their company I guess, and animals seem to know that. I guess I understand their body language and communications more."

"Than humans you mean." Antyn asked amused, a little more relaxed by her explanation.

Tyg's top lip curled up on one side. "Yes, Antyn, I much prefer animals to people...happy now?"

"What about to Sorcerer's?" He asked with a rogue smile.

"Enough, Antyn." Leviathan growled from just in front of them.

Tyg smiled a little at Antyn's insinuation and looked over at Leviathan under her lashes. He was a majestic sight sitting tall and straight-backed in the saddle on his mighty war horse, his hair drifting in the breeze that blew down from the mountains covered in winter snow.

His eyes, on instinct of being watched, slid to Tyg over his shoulder and she looked away quickly only to return her gaze to him to find him staring back at her with an amused smoulder.

She heard Antyn chuckle at their exchange. "It seems a given I think..."

Tyg grimaced at Antyn's witnessing the little flirtation. Yes, she enjoyed this new experience of feeling butterflies every time their eyes met and Leviathan had been almost sweet most of the time since patching their strange relationship finally on board ship and things had progressed back smoothly to affection after he gave her the horse, but there was still that nagging feeling that she wasn't here by choice and his dominant possessive nature over her was in all honesty frightening to her. Saying she was his and belonged to him and that was destiny as the prophets foretold, she wondered sometimes if he was a little crazy. Knowing he was powerful and ultimately stronger than her had her on the back foot with how to handle him. To know he had a magical power that could enter her mind and give her unfathomable pain was something that made her blood run cold, but it instantly heated when she looked at him.

Did he actually like her? Or was he incapable of affection and only knew possession and control. It confused her and made her doubt her own feelings, was she slowly being coerced and manipulated into this attraction using mind control and positive and negative reinforcement? Or was this merely the way of things when you liked someone, and she did like him...when he wasn't being a domineering jerk.

She had fallen into a moody silence as she reflected and startled when Leviathan came alongside her horse and took her hand, kissing it sweetly then holding it on his thigh as their horses walked along the long flat road side by side.

"Ignore him, Tygarya...and don't over analyse anything that is happening between us. What will be will be, enjoy the moments we share."

Could he read her mind? She gave him a small frown. "But behave and obey."

His return look was unreadable as he met her challenging gaze, but then a small wry smile crept over his lips. "Yes, my dearest. Let your mind be free of thoughts and just do what I wish."

Tyg dropped her gaze to the pommel of her saddle. "I suppose in a way I've been doing that most of my life...obeying orders blindly."

"Exactly..." Leviathan scoffed. "What most people think of as a free life is in fact quite controlled by external forces that their minds just accept...laws, finances, contracts and the need to fulfil so many obligations like family and work."

"I get what you mean....but this thing between us is vastly different, don't you think?"

Leviathan squeezed her hand and looked forward with a strange expression. "You are completely free to think and feel however you want to, Tygarya, but my stance that this is fate will not change."

"So I must belong to you?" Tyg yanked her hand back. This was exactly the sort of thing she was just thinking about, he came over all sweet but underneath it there was the control and possession. Was it just his way or should she actually try to run before it was too late? Could she even run, would he stop her if she just ran from him right now?

Leviathan clucked his tongue. "Tygarya..."

He didn't get to say anything more as she turned her horse and broke the line, digging her heels into her horse and galloping off across the grasslands to the left of the road.

"Well, fuck...I didn't see that happening?" Antyn exclaimed. "I thought you had her?"

Leviathan growled deep in his throat, his eyes flashing golden green as he pivoted his horse around and galloped off after her, his great war horse Titus more than capable of catching up with a little boost from Leviathan's power.

Antyn put a hand up to stop the column of soldiers accompanying them. "Let's stop for a rest and wait for the lover's tiff to sort itself out."

"At once, sir!" The Captain of the platoon of twenty soldiers yelled back before trotting his horse off down the line to direct his soldiers.

Antyn sighed and chewed his lip in thought as he watched the two horses gallop off, getting smaller as they reached some distance away before he saw the back one catch up, an arm reach out and the other person get dragged from their horse and dumped on the ground.

He winced at the hard impact. "Hate to be you right now, Tyg."

Tyg tumbled from her horse as it broke its gallop and cantered to a stop close by. Leviathan pulled his horse up short and sprang from the saddle stalking over to where Tyg was just getting her wind back, coming up on her hands and knees and towered over her.

"What the fuck was that?!" He demanded.

Tyg turned, planting her bottom on the ground and leaned back on one hand to look up with a craned neck at the dark foreboding figure yelling at her as she tried to get her breath back.

She grimaced and shrugged. "I don't really know..." She panted. "I just wanted to see if I took off whether I could just go."

Leviathan glared down at her with a stunned look for a moment before lifting his head and looking away, raking a hand through his hair. He licked his lips and snorted in an exasperated and incredulous laugh. "Are you fucking serious? You took off to see if I would give chase?"

Tyg shrugged and sat up, wiping her hands free of dirt.

"Of course I would, you fool!" Leviathan yelled, sounding a little confused.

"Yeah, but for what reason?" She asked, looking up at him again, squinting as the light was behind him.

He seemed to take pause and glare at her in silence again before huffing and walking away a few steps. He looked up at the world around him. "Why me?" He asked perplexed.

Tyg watched him as he put his hands on his hips and his head dropped with a heavy sigh. As she went to stand up his right hand whipped out behind him in her direction and she felt herself unable to move as a tight tension came into her head.

"You don't move!" He ordered in a very pissed off tone. "You will just listen."

He slowly turned around and his expression was deadly. "You don't get to test me, Tygarya! I have made this very clear to you since the day we first met. My resolve has not changed, nor is it ever likely to."

He stalked slowly forward in such a menacing way that Tyg felt her heart start to thump erratically. "Are you really as stubborn as a mule when it comes to trusting someone or are you just stupid and don't listen clearly? I'll say this again for you so listen up this time and take note! You are the one I have searched for, you are special and you are important to me in ways I can't inform you of yet. You are nothing like what I expected to find, something easy to manipulate and to control, yet your fiery wild nature is exactly what I find so goddamned attractive about you."

He reached her and stood over her outstretched legs, crouching down. He took her jaw in one large hand and lifted it making her look him in the eye as his fingers dug into her cheek.

"You are not here by choice because I need you, that is true. But don't, for one minute, ever question the affection I am building for you. This was never my intention and I have never felt such a strong attraction for anyone."

Tyg blinked in shock at his words as his grip weakened. His hand lifted to caress her cheek as his eyes that held hers softened slightly.

"I am cruel by nature, a product of a cruel upbringing. I am possessive and demanding by the pure need to have things my way, you already know these things, don't test my affection for you to not hurt you. You know I will. I do not want to but by my own creation, and yours, I will do whatever I need to, to keep you by my side. Why do you think you are of such a special creation as to be able to endure what I can give out? I do not want to hurt you, Tyg. That is why I tell you to simply behave and do what I say." His eyes closed for a moment and he sighed bitterly.

Tyg held her breath.

As his eyes opened he let her go and stood up, looking down at her. "Just stay and be mine." He held his hand out to her.

Tyg stared at it.

Did she have any choice, he just basically said she didn't but he was making it seem like she did. She was so confused.

Her hand raised on its own accord and slipped into his. He grabbed it firmly and pulled her to her feet, pulling her into his chest and wrapping his arms around her in a strong embrace.

She felt his lips kiss her head and she tilted her head back to look up at him. He pulled his arms back and his hands came to either side of her head, holding her securely as he looked down at her with a pleased smile.

"I'm going to fuck up. I'm going to need space sometimes. I can't be meek and submissive like some dainty princess." Tyg said calmly in a monotone as she held his gaze.

His smile was sardonic. "I know, I don't want you to be...but allow me to guide you, listen to my warnings, and heed my expressions. Allow yourself to trust that I know better in this world."

"You want me to curb my very nature to accommodate yours." Tyg accused with a frown.

"Yes, I make no qualms of that. I am the stronger beast, Tygarya. That is the will of the world and of nature itself."

Tyg smiled and laughed bitterly. "Then I suppose that's that then..."

Leviathan frowned, his thumbs stroking her cheeks as his eyes searched hers.

"...because I like you, Leviathan, and I do feel a deep connection to you like this destiny, fate thing just might be real." She smiled passively at him.

Leviathan grinned before crushing her lips with his and invading her mouth with his tongue, lashing hers with a passion ignited by triumph.

He left her breathless and clinging to him when he finally relented, taking her hand and leading her to her horse.

"I'm glad we had this chat, Tygarya...but no more doubt, okay?"

She mounted her horse and looked down at him as he held the reins. "Okay...but will you ever tell me what it is that makes me so special?"

"I will, when the time is right. Until then let's just focus on making us better." He led her horse over to his and mounted up, nudging his horse into a trot and heading back. Not giving her the reins he led her horse back like he would a captive.

Tyg was silent and contemplative as he led her horse back to the waiting company and he let her be, knowing she was probably feeling quite confused and unsettled by his frank words but they had worked their purpose and got her back under control.

She was fairly easy to manipulate with words backed by force and he figured that was how Palin had controlled and trained her from a young age. He really had to take his hat off to Palin, he had known what he was doing in breaking and training a being as dangerous as this one.

13

Tyg was still quiet and sullen as they continued their journey, Leviathan choosing to give her, her space for now as long as it didn't go on for too long.

As they stopped for a rest Antyn sought Leviathan out, finding him alone, staring off in the direction of the mountain range far away, quietly contemplative. His own words had hit home within himself regarding his own affection for the girl and he was having to deal with it begrudgingly. He heard someone approaching and turned his head.

"What happened out there, Lev?" Antyn asked.

The look on his face was benign. "Not much, she was testing my resolve, I set her straight."

"I thought you had her under control?"

"So did I...it seems our little silver haired sociopath is still very wild at heart and not convinced that obeying me is her only option."

"You put her right on that, I hope?"

Leviathan clucked his tongue. "Of course, however I feel there may be room still for her to try to possibly escape me again."

Antyn ran a hand over his hair. "You need to shut that down."

"Don't panic, brother. She knows I am not of a nature to try and curb my own personality traits to prevent hurting her."

"How is that a good thing?" Antyn huffed.

"She's basically the same as me so she understands, if she doesn't fall into line she will be punished. If she does what I say she will be able to stay relatively free to be herself."

Antyn sighed, rubbing his eyes, confused.

"It's the law of nature, Antyn. The weaker submits to the will of the Alpha, she may not understand human idiosyncrasies but she understands that."

"She agreed to stay on that premise?" Antyn scoffed, finding it hard to believe.

"Yes." Leviathan chuckled. "She is a simple creature to understand deep down."

"Fuck...like her affinity to animals, you know what this shows, don't you?" Antyn said with a concerned tone.

Leviathan seemed quite relaxed as he smiled into the wind. "Yes, it confirms the other side of her parentage, as we had surmised by the prophet's descriptions."

Antyn looked astounded. "This is..."

"Yes, brother..." Leviathan stepped past him, clapping him on the shoulder. "This is a great time to be alive!" He walked off back to the road where his horse was.

Antyn turned around. "Lev..."

Leviathan paused, turning to look back.

"Be cautious. We can't have her run, not until we have full control of this continent, otherwise she may..."

"I know, don't fret, Antyn. "I'll play nice with her, make her fall in love with me." Leviathan smiled. "I do actually like the girl and am quite attracted to her wild vivacious nature...I intend to keep her close and let her know it."

He walked off leaving Antyn there sucking on his teeth. "That's what I'm afraid of."

119

That night at camp Tyg was standing in front of a large camp fire watching the flames dance while she enjoyed the heat. Her hands wrapped around a hot cup of mulled wine to chase away the chill of the last of winter's nights. Her fur lined cloak was drawn tight around her body and her hood was up against the wind chill.

There was snow on the ground in patches here and there now they were more inland, the weather was getting steadily colder with the deepening of winter the more inland they went as they skirted the foothills of the start of the mighty Alps that stretched off to the south.

She gasped in a breath, stiffening as she felt two arms come around her and squeeze her waist as a large warm chest pressed to her back. She breathed in the scent of the man, enjoying the warmth his body gave her against the wind.

"Are you cold?" Warm breath blew on her cheek as Leviathan's face appeared over her shoulder and he stared into the flames of the fire.

"Yes, it's getting colder the further we travel."

"Enjoy my warmth then, a perk of being a sorcerer..." He hooked his chin around her hood and got his face inside so he could press his lips to her neck sending his power through that skin to skin contact and warming her body temperature.

She couldn't help but moan out a little breath of pleasure at the sensation as she closed her eyes and tilted her head to give him better access.

"You know, Tyg...there are better ways to warm you up?" He breathed against her with a small sexy chuckle.

Tyg gave a husky chuckle back. "I'm sure there are..."

Leviathan straightened up, pushing her hips with his hands and making her turn around in his arms to face him. She gasped and startled as her cup sloshed and Leviathan grabbed it from her, lifting it away to avoid the wine splashing on them before tossing it away and pulling her tight to his body.

"That was close." He rumbled with an amused sparkle in his eyes as they caught the firelight.

"You have extraordinary reflexes..." Tyg said looking up at him impressed and wary. "Is that part of being a sorcerer?"

Leviathan ran his hands over her head and down to her shoulders, sweeping her hood off so he could see her face properly and shrugged. "A little, but I am just as skilled and practised in fighting and hunting to have naturally fast reflexes."

Tyg gave him a little judgemental yet teasing once over. "For someone so big."

He smirked roguishly. "You have no idea yet how big I am."

Tyg instantly blushed and dropped her head. "Stop it."

He chuckled and put a hand to the back of her head, pulling it forward so her forehead pressed to his chest. "Sorry, I couldn't resist that one." He grinned as he looked into the flames.

She huffed, but her arms tucked into his coat and came around his hips, her fingers gripping his belt. "How old are you? You sound like a horny teenager when you say things like that."

"Know a lot about horny teenage boys?" His growl was mocking and teasing as he started absently wrapping her long braid around his hand.

"Of course not, but I'm sure it's not what an old Emperor should be saying..."

"Hey..." He thrummed deeply, yanking on her braid and lifting her head up to lock eyes with her. "Enough of the old, cheeky!"

"Aren't you though?" She grinned at his indignant tone. He didn't look a day over thirty but she had read in fairy tales that people with magic could live for hundreds of years.

He squinted at her, enjoying this frivolous nonsense. "For someone deemed immortal, no. I'm still very much a spring chicken, don't worry..." He pulled her head back further making her mouth open and covered it with his, lashing his tongue into her mouth as his other hand came to the side of her face.

She kissed him back, moaning into his mouth and pulling on his belt so his hips bumped into her. He groaned deeply, dropping his mouth from hers and to her neck, just behind her ear.

"Don't do that, baby."

"Why?" She breathed out, panting.

"You'll get yourself in serious trouble."

"You said you would wait for me to be ready." She answered coolly.

He lifted his head to look her in the face, searching it for her sincerity. "So you're just teasing me?"

Tyg bit her lip at the dark intensity in his eyes. "No, but...I don't know if I can yet."

"Well, I know how far you have let me go thus far...so will you let me go that far now?" His hand ran up her side and cupped her breast, squeezing it in a testing manner. "You want me to lick this, like the other day?"

"Oh, gods..." Tyg breathed out, knowing she was blushing as he chuckled fully aware they were surrounded by soldiers. He dropped his hands and grabbed her wrist, spinning on his heels and walking to her tent, dragging her along.

"I think a quick little kissing session before I make you go to sleep, little tease."

As he pulled her into the lavish tent and sat her down upon her camp cot he knelt in front of her and took her face in his hands looking into her eyes that were clouded and unsure.

"Tell me where your head is at, baby?" He asked gently probing.

Tyg gazed into his beautiful azure eyes and let out a little sigh. He dropped his hands to her thighs, grabbing hold of her hands and holding them as he waited for her to answer him.

She looked down at their hands saying nothing.

"You're confused by your feelings, that's quite normal."

Tyg looked up, chewing her lip for a moment then shrugged. "I guess...I just don't know enough about myself, you, any of this...it's a lot to take in."

"I understand that, Tygarya, but I need you to understand I want intimacy and pleasure with you, I want good times, good conversation, fun and everything that comes with spending time close to you. I don't want to hurt you..."

"I know that, I want those things too."

"Then relax, for fuck's sake...let yourself enjoy where this goes."

Tyg shook her head. "I can't...not tonight."

Leviathan scowled and stood up. "You tried to run away today, we had words...but don't pout about it. If you have questions I'll answer them."

"No, I think you made yourself perfectly clear." Tyg couldn't hide the sarcasm in her tone.

"So you're going to continue to fight destiny?" Leviathan growled out, raking a hand through his hair in frustration.

"No..." She admitted, making him look at her with that vulture gaze. "I guess I'm just scared of going too fast and getting hurt...not physically, I don't care about that, but..." She stopped and Leviathan could see the tears standing in her eyes unshed as she took a stuttering breath in.

"I'm not going anywhere." He said in a smooth deep voice. He knew she meant heart-broken like she was over her first love. Antyn had told him how she had cried by the man's grave before leaving Arial.

She looked up at him with a small grateful smile that he understood.

Leviathan lifted his arm. "Come here, baby...you are far more sweet natured than you give yourself credit for." He cooed gently.

Tyg stood up and came to him, hugging around his waist and burying her head. He folded his arm around her and with his other hand lifted her chin. As she looked up at him she lifted on her toes and kissed him chastely but softly with her full lips.

"I'm really attracted to you too." She breathed. "But this is all so new and scary...and I don't like myself being scared of anything but..."

He pressed his lips to hers, cutting her off, and found her mouth already open for his tongue. He explored inside enjoying the musky flavour of the mulled wine still on her tongue mixed with the sweetness that was her.

As he pulled back he spoke low. "Stop overthinking every damn little thing, Tygarya...I keep telling you, all you have to do is put your trust in me and follow what I say, what I do...you'll be fine."

His hand clenched into her hair at the back of her head and he kissed her again, more forcefully, tipping her head back and covering her entire mouth as his tongue lashed around hers leaving her completely breathless and dazed.

He grinned as he wiped her bottom lip, satisfied he had managed to quell her fears. "Have a good rest, Tygarya, we have a long way to travel. I shall see you in the morning."

He stepped out of her tent and shrugged his shoulders against the cold briefly before making his way to the tent next door.

As he entered Antyn looked up from where he was lounging on a cushion in front of a small coal brazier.

"Everything back on track?"

Leviathan smirked. "Of course, she's quite besotted."

Antyn frowned. "And you look quite smitten."

Leviathan snorted in amusement. "Do I? I suppose I am..."

"Lev?"

"Relax, Antyn...what happens between myself and Tygarya is only what is destined to...besides we have a long month in front of us and I doubt she's going to allow me to take her virginity before we reach home."

14

I t had been a mesmerising and spectacular month of travelling through the broad expanse of Tylandria for Tyg, everything was new and amazing, although fairly similar to the land of Arial. The farmlands, the towns they past through. There was one major city that was built around a large agricultural station for buying and selling livestock at auction set up at a crossroads of the main arterial highways. Leviathan had been amazing, patient yet frisky with her during the travel and she was really feeling like by the time she reached his home she would definitely be ready to give up her virginity to him. However, Tyg was getting pretty weary after the long slow days on horseback travelling a meagre twenty five to thirty miles a day and was glad when they were finally nearly at their destination looking forward to not riding a horse for a very long time.

They entered the town of Delton which was only one more day's ride from Estafeld, Capital of Tylandria, the eastern most city and home to the Adramelech Castle, Leviathan's home. Tyg could sense something in the air. The townspeople were overjoyed to see the Emperor in their town and cheered and surrounded them as they entered. Tyg noticed their company turned and went out to the side of the town where there was a large meadow. Leviathan instructed the soldiers to erect their tents in the meadow to one side of the huge bonfire that had been erected.

"What's all this?" Tyg asked.

Antyn looked at her surprised. "You don't celebrate Beltain in Arial?"

"Beltain? No...what's that?"

Leviathan frowned. "Nothing...don't worry about it."

Tyg looked at him then back at Antyn. "Tell me what it is."

Antyn looked at Leviathan. "Whatever...tell her if she wants to know so badly?"

Antyn turned to Tyg smiling. "I love Beltain, it is a fire festival that celebrates the turn of the vernal equinox and the coming of spring. They burned the fields back of the old withered crops and now begin sowing out the new, the animals are having their early babies and everything is fertile. It's like a celebration ritual for bountiful crops but young people use it as a fertility ritual to find a partner. It can be quite the spectacle." Antyn had a whimsical look on his face.

Tyg looked away. "I see, I didn't realise spring was nearly here..." It was then she noticed a few yellow flowers poking up through the tundra and old snow.

"We spent three weeks on board ship, and now a month journeying to here...plus our winter is about a month off from Arial's...so yes spring is nearly upon us and we will start preparing and food will be plentiful ready for our campaign in the summer." Antyn rubbed his hands together. "This is perfect timing..."

Leviathan snorted. "Antyn only likes it because it means he gets to sleep with lots of young women who throw themselves at him during the fire dance."

"The fire dance?" Tyg asked intrigued.

"A provocative dance the girls do round the bonfire to attract their chosen mate...or usually anyone who's willing to take them into the darkness and fuck them on a cool spring night." Antyn explained.

"Antyn!" Leviathan growled.

"What? Don't tell me you're worried about Tyg's sensibilities, she swears worse than a fish monger."

"Antyn, shut up!" Leviathan muttered.

Tyg smiled to herself and she looked away as Antyn grumbled to himself annoyed. "Fine, but I – for one – am going to enjoy tonight and the festivities of tomorrow night."

"You're going to stay tomorrow night?" Leviathan asked.

"Yes, I've already seen a particular young lady that I really want to get to know."

Leviathan rubbed his forehead. "Fuck's sake."

"Fuck for fuck's sake." Antyn said laughing as he slid off his horse and wandered off.

Leviathan glowered at Antyn's back as he walked away. Tyg giggled making Leviathan turned his vulture gaze on her. "What's so funny?"

"This festival...it seems to affect people in strange ways."

"Indeed it does." Leviathan muttered.

"I want to stay and see it." She levelled a challenging look at him. Things had been going well with her behaving since their little chat and they had been like a couple in full courtship mode the whole way here, she deserved a reward.

"Must we?" Leviathan rubbed his forehead again. Why couldn't he ever refuse her of anything?

"Please, Lev, I'm new here...I've been good..." Tyg asked sweetly.

"The castle is only a day away...I want to get you home."

"Please." Tyg whined at him, grinning broadly, her large luminous eyes sparkling beautifully.

Leviathan sighed. "Don't make me regret this."

"Oh, you won't." Tyg said strangely causing Leviathan to frown, suddenly suspecting she was up to something.

Leviathan turned away and called a soldier over. "Go to the barracks on the east side of town immediately and tell Major Keinly to send some extra men over to guard our encampment and to escort us into the capital in two days."

"Yes, my Liege."

Later Tyg found Antyn lying in the grass watching the town girls flitting round the unlit bonfire, giggling and skipping.

"What are they doing?" Tyg asked as Antyn looked up at her with a raised eyebrow.

"Practising."

"Practising dancing?" Tyg asked.

"Hmm." Antyn sat up. "What do you want, Tyg?"

She sat down, her eyes still on the girls. "Tell me more about this fire festival." She looked nervous and had a faint blush on her cheeks.

Antyn's eyes went wide. "Wait...you're not thinking..."

"Maybe..." Tyg glanced at him but quickly looked away back to the girls, her lip caught in her teeth.

"Fuck, Tyg...I don't know if Lev will go for it...he hates festivals and of them all this one is..."

"Just tell me, please."

"Well, okay." Antyn was suddenly feeling flustered at the thought of Tyg partaking in Beltain. "But you know you're going to have to follow through with it...don't play games with him."

"I know..." Tyg gave him a shy smile.

"Shit...okay..." Antyn grimaced and looked away. He wasn't sure how he felt about Tyg finally giving herself to his brother, he felt a little pang of jealousy.

Tyg walked over to where the young girls were laughing and dancing. There were several young soldiers and men from the town standing around watching them in small groups and they all turned to stare as Tyg walked over. The girls all paled and curtsied. They had seen her arrive with the Emperor and had heard the stories of her, recognising her easily with that long silver blond hair and large luminous blue eyes.

Tyg frowned. "Please don't do that, I need your help."

"Help?" One young girl asked as she looked up. Tyg smiled at her.

"Yes...I'm not from here and I want to learn about this Beltain festival...can you help me?"

The other girls giggled as they stood up and circled her.

"You want to know for the Emperor?" One girl asked boldly causing the other girls to jab her and shush her.

Tyg laughed musically, making them look at her wide eyed. "Actually, yes."

One young lady stepped forward. She had lovely golden hair and slate blue eyes. Tyg gave her an appreciative smile, she loved seeing blond haired, blue eyed people and they were common place in this land, it reassured her that she was home. Still, no one seemed to have the silver hair she had. This young woman though was the one Antyn had been eyeing from afar. "Your laugh is very musical, do you sing my Lady?"

"Yes, I do." Tyg smiled at her.

"I could teach you the Fire song, perhaps the Emperor would like to see you sing at our festivities tomorrow night, rather than dance..." The girl suggested coyly. She seemed to know that the Emperor would perhaps not wish to see his betrothed dancing for everyone to see.

"Sounds perfect..." Tyg was surprised at the quick uptake of the girl, understanding things perfectly. "What's your name?"

"Eleanor, my Lady, daughter of the Mayor of Delton."

"Come with me, Eleanor." Tyg turned and walked off back to the tents. Eleanor turned to her friends and danced on the spot in excitement for a minute as the others fawned over her being asked to join the girl they called a Princess, then she turned and ran to catch up to Tyg.

Tyg was sitting in the main imperial tent with Eleanor, talking quietly together discussing the fire song. Tyg was hesitant to actually practise singing it, not wanting Leviathan to find out, so she was learning the words and just softly humming the tune when Leviathan strode in with Antyn behind him abruptly throwing the canvas back.

He stopped in his tracks and levelled his vulture gaze at the blond girl sitting with Tyg. Eleanor quailed under that gaze as she hurriedly got to her feet and sank low in a deep curtsey keeping her eyes to the floor.

"What is this, Tygarya?" Leviathan asked coolly. His possessiveness and jealousy, it seemed, encompast females too, or perhaps he was appalled at having a peasant in his tent Tyg wasn't sure. Although she was the Mayor's daughter, that should account for something?

Antyn stepped round Leviathan and smiled. "Well, hello there...and who might you be?" Eleanor got all flustered as she quickly looked up and again lowered her gaze, blushing prettily.

"This is Eleanor...daughter of Delton's Mayor." Tyg said as she rolled her eyes at Antyn's antics as he turned on the charm.

"Eleanor..." Antyn practically purred as he sat down in a chair, leaning back and crossing his legs staring at Eleanor with that same vulture gaze Leviathan always had for Tyg.

"That doesn't answer my question, Tygarya. What are you up to?" Leviathan growled.

Tyg rolled her eyes again and got up walking over to Leviathan she put her arms around him. Eleanor's eyes were wide with awe to be in the same room as the Emperor as she trembled, standing politely silent, her hands clasped in front of her.

"You keep saying I should try and interact with people more...well..."

Leviathan looked down on her with an amused scowl. He had made no attempt to put his arms around her. "Tygarya..." He said wearily.

"What?" She frowned at him in confusion about what could possibly be annoying him.

"I don't care what you say, Tygarya...this is not like you. You are up to something." Leviathan said, he looked up and saw Antyn had leaned out of his chair and was reaching up touching Eleanor's cheek as he crooned something to her while she was still frozen in fear in a perpetual curtsey. Leviathan's jaw clenched. Tyg looked over and smiled to herself. "Antyn!" Leviathan growled.

Antyn dropped his hand and sat back in his chair. "Just getting to know the locals, Lev...just like Tyg is..."

"Knock it off, Antyn."

Antyn stood up and Tyg saw his eyes were glowing. Tyg bit her lip and looked at Leviathan. She stepped away from him as he folded his arms. The look on his face was pure menace. Tyg made her way over to Eleanor and grabbed her hand and pulled her to the exit.

"I think you should go now...I'll catch up with you again tomorrow...thank you for today."

"Oh...okay, yes...thank you, my lady." Eleanor curtsied in front of Leviathan again. "Imperial Majesty."

Tyg saw her out and stood at the tent flap looking at the brothers. Leviathan had walked forward and stood in front of

Antyn, looking down on him as if daring him to do something. Antyn's eyes were still glowing as he scowled at Leviathan.

"What's the problem, Lev?" Antyn asked coldly.

"You're the problem, brother...sleeping with all these village strumpets...feeding them your power, it's disgusting."

"It's fun...besides you do it to Tyg...you hypocrite."

Leviathan grabbed Antyn by the throat. "Shut up, Antyn."

"Lev." Tyg said quietly as she came up behind him.

"Go away, Tygarya!" Leviathan growled. "I'll deal with you for all that eye rolling later!"

Antyn had grabbed Leviathan's wrist and they were staring at each other intensely. Tyg felt like the air between them was electrified, they had been getting moodier every day leading up to this point and had thought maybe Antyn was a little jealous of her and Leviathan getting along so well after their chat when leaving Asbel.

"This is my fault, Lev, I brought Eleanor in here...I knew Antyn liked her."

Leviathan flicked his gaze to her briefly, then back to Antyn. "Still doesn't mean he can speak back to me."

"No, you're right, of course. And Antyn also needs to know that you haven't done that 'thing' to me since the ship."

It was Antyn's turn to look briefly at her. He grimaced and the glow went out of his eyes. Leviathan dropped his hand. "I'm sorry. Lev." Antyn said rubbing his neck. He turned and walked out of the tent. Leviathan took a deep breath and lifted his arm.

"Come here, Tygarya." Tyg smiled and walked into him. He wrapped his arm around her and grabbed her chin, lifting her face as he kissed her. He lifted her off her feet and walked to the divan and pushed her down on it as he kissed her passionately. "You are simply amazing." Leviathan said to her then as he leaned over her. He picked up a lock of hair and twined it through his fingers.

"Why did you do that?"

"Do what?" Tyg asked as she played with a ring on the finger of his other hand.

"You know what, Tygarya...you took the blame and you lied."

Tyg shrugged. "I didn't want to see you fight, it looked like it would have been quite scary."

Leviathan clenched his jaw and regarded her a moment. "You know I do blame you."

"What? Why?" Tyg's eyes went wide.

"You are wearing off on my brother, he would never have stood up to me like that before you came along."

"You can't really blame me for that."

"Yes I can, and I will." Leviathan smirked amused. "I should spank you."

Tyg sat up. "You're the second person to talk about spanking me since we got here in your damned Empire!" Tyg said coolly. She regretted it instantly and bit her lip as Leviathan's expression went deadly.

He grabbed her chin harshly making her wince. "Who the fuck said anything about touching you let alone spanking you!"

"Lev, calm down please, you're taking it out of context..."

"Then fucking explain it to me, Tygarya, and quickly."

Tyg sighed. "After the incident at your Estate in Asbel City, Antyn was angry with me too and just said...'If I was allowed to even remotely touch you I would fucking have you publically spanked, at the very least." Tyg tried to imitate Antyn's voice.

Leviathan relaxed a little and smirked, letting go of her chin. "Don't do that to me, Tygarya, I thought someone had threatened you."

"If someone threatened me I would kill them." She answered with a deadpan expression "What did he mean, if he was allowed to even remotely touch me?"

Leviathan looked at her strangely. "You haven't figured that much out?"

"No..."

Leviathan chuckled to himself and rubbed his eyes with one hand. "You really have no idea?"

"No." Tyg said getting annoyed, he sounded like he was saying she was stupid.

"It's the law, Tygarya...no one is allowed to touch you, my consort."

"No one...?"

"Not without consent."

"Consent from who?" Tyg narrowed her eyes.

"From me, of course." Leviathan grinned highly amused now.

"What if I touch them...?" Leviathan's face went dark instantly, answering that question. "I mean like I just took Eleanor's hand before..." Tyg quickly explained.

"Oh, that's okay, she's a girl...you don't like girls, do you?"

Tyg startled and shook her head. "So that's why you got grumpy when I helped that guy stand up back in Asbel City..."

"The Lord Chamberlain...yes."

"Well how am I supposed to know these things if no one bothers to take the time to tell me?"

Leviathan scowled. "That was supposed to be Antyn's job, I'm sure it's been mentioned...perhaps I should have him spanked."

Tyg stifled a giggle. "Oh, that would be a sight."

"Tygarya, for fuck's sake." Leviathan scowled deeper. "Don't even imagine it...otherwise I will punish you."

Tyg smiled at him. "You're going to talk to Antyn about this, aren't you?"

"Yes."

"Because..." She looked into his eyes with interest.

"Because he mentioned you and spanking in the same fucking sentence." Leviathan grumbled.

"Not because he failed to tell me the law?"

Leviathan shrugged. "And that too..." He said nonchalantly as he picked up a lock of her hair and held it to his nose.

Tyg thought it best to drop the conversation while Leviathan was back in a semi good mood and seemed to have forgotten about her eye rolling. "Leviathan..."

He smirked. "Yes, Tygarya." His voice was back to being a smooth baritone.

"Is there any chance of a bath tonight? We've been on the road for weeks, my hair can't smell very good anymore."

Leviathan chuckled as he looked at her with a dark expression. "Fuck, Tygarya...first the image of spanking you, now the image of you bathing..." Tyg's eyes widened as Leviathan stared intently at her. Tyg bit her lip. Leviathan grabbed her chin and reached up with his thumb and pulled it out of her mouth. "That's a nasty habit you're getting into...but I'm sure I can arrange a bath for you, my dear..."

"Thank you." Tyg said beguiling as she suddenly grabbed his hand and put it under her shirt and onto her breast and grabbed a handful of his shirt and pulled him down over her, lifting her head to meet his as she kissed him. He growled as he kissed her back caressing her breast. Tyg was always surprised with how gentle he actually was though, yet the thought of being spanked made a small part of her want to do something bad.

He lifted his head and looked at her with a strange smile. "It seems this Beltain festival is having an effect on you too."

Tyg gave him a very alluring look. "Perhaps it is..."

Leviathan frowned and sat up. "I'll go see about that bath...then we can see what I can do to you for rolling your eyes at me before...perhaps I should make spanking your punishment..."

Tyg's eyes widened with shock as he left giving her no recourse to that statement. "Damn it!" She breathed out. She felt a nervous flutter in her stomach and squeezed her thighs together. Was he seriously going to spank her? No surely he jests just to tease her? Like she would ever let that actually happen...

15

"Ah...Lev...I really think you should come outside and see this." Antyn burst into his tent the next evening just as it was getting dark and the festival was starting. As far as Leviathan was concerned he had left Tyg with Antyn to watch the bonfire. He didn't want anything to do with it or the festival. He hated festivals.

"What is it, Antyn? I've seen plenty of bonfires with dancing girls in my lifetime..."

Antyn grinned. "Not ones that included Tyg in them..."

"What the fuck!" Leviathan went straight to jealous rage as he stood up and practically shoved Antyn out of the way and stormed from the tent.

As he approached the festivities the townspeople bowed and moved out of his way. He saw there was a chair set up for him and the bonfire had been lit, but no Tyg. He grimaced and turned to Antyn who had run up behind him with a huge smirk on his face.

"Neat trick, brother...but where is Tygarya?"

"No trick, Lev..." Antyn grinned widely. "Look...here she comes now."

Leviathan turned and stared. He actually felt like his knees were going to buckle underneath him and he quickly made his way to the seat.

"Fucking hell!" He muttered as he just stared at Tyg as she walked out of the darkness and into the light of the fire and torches, like some mythical goddess with her nymphs dancing around her throwing petals.

Tyg was dressed in a flowing white gown that trailed off her shoulders and dragged after her along the ground, her feet bare. Her waist was cinched with a thick band of gold and the bodice was like the togas that they wore in Gua del Mar, leaving her arms bare and showing ample cleavage. On her shoulders the material was clasped by bands of gold. Her hair was down and on her head was a coronet of early spring flowers.

As Tyg started to sing the Fire song the girls all started dancing around the bonfire. Tyg looked through her eye lashes at Leviathan and danced her way closer to him as her voice soared and travelled magically on the still air. Everyone around the bonfire was silent, the only sounds were the musicians and Tyg's pure voice reverberating on the air like magic.

Antyn sat down next to Leviathan with a smug smirk. "You keep saying she is amazing...you are not wrong."

"Antyn..." Leviathan's voice was hoarse and thick.

"Yes, brother?" Antyn was surprised at the confused tone in Leviathan's voice.

"Why is she doing this?" Leviathan asked, not taking his eyes off of her.

Antyn looked at him, he saw Leviathan's knuckles were white as he gripped the arms of the chair. He was seething with possessive anger. Antyn smiled to himself.

"Leviathan...this is all for you. Don't get mad, this isn't some stunt of hers...she has been planning this, for you, since yesterday...with Eleanor's help."

"Planning what exactly?" Leviathan growled.

"Really, Lev? It's obviously been far too long for you..." Antyn said amused.

"Antyn!" Leviathan's voice was palpable menace.

Antyn patted Leviathan on the shoulder. "She plans to take you to bed tonight, old chap...so don't disappoint her..."

Antyn didn't get to finish his sentence as Leviathan stood up after he heard the word bed and strode off. Antyn watched fascinated, as did the whole town, as Leviathan walked straight up to Tyg and stood in front of her like a dark impenetrable wall. Tyg seemed a little surprised, but her eyes glowed as Leviathan took her hands and held them to his chest as she finished the song. As soon as the last note left her throat, Leviathan wrapped her in his arms and kissed her, dipping her back as he held her, just like back in Arial. Tyg wrapped her arms around his neck and kissed him back. He swept her feet out and picked her up, to great cheers from the townsfolk, as he simply walked off with her back to his tent. Antyn watched, his eyes sparkling then turned to watch Eleanor.

Inside the tent Leviathan laid her down gently on the bed, their lips still locked together. He sat up and took the coronet of flowers off her head. Tyg sat up and pushed Leviathan back on the bed, she hitched her dress up and straddled him, putting her hands on his chest. He was looking at her intently as he rested on his elbows. Tyg leaned forward and kissed him again. He sat up and put his arms around her, holding her steady as he pulled his head away. She regarded him as she sat over his lap as he regarded her intently with an eyebrow raised in question. She grabbed both his hands and brought them round and put them inside her dress onto both her breasts. Leviathan's eyes went dark as he felt her warm flesh under his hands instead of lace, her breasts were bare. Tyg reached up and slipped the dress off her shoulders. It fell to her waist leaving her chest fully exposed. Leviathan looked at her appreciatively as he played his thumbs over her nipples. He put one hand round onto the small of her back and held her in place as he leaned down and kissed one nipple. He heard Tyg gasp and flicked his eyes up to see her looking down at him, her eyes wide and innocent, but they were glowing with a strange light. Leviathan grinned against her and opened his mouth, sucking her nipple into his mouth and playing with it with his tongue. Tyg gasped again and placed her hands on his shoulders to steady herself. He raised his head and brought his hand from her other breast to her cheek.

"Tyg...are you sure about this?"

Tyg looked into his eyes and bit her lip, she nodded shyly.

"I need to hear it, Tyg." Leviathan said as he stroked his thumb down her cheek and across her bottom lip, pulling it from under her teeth.

"Yes...I'm sure, Lev." Tyg breathed as his eyes burned into hers. "I believe destiny brought us here on this day, please..."

Leviathan thrummed a deep rumble in his throat and his eyes glowed at that word. He rolled over, putting her on her back as he moved on top of her, pushing her knees apart. He ground himself against her as he kissed her breasts, then sat back and removed his vest and shirt and leaned back over and kissed her again as his hand travelled up her inner thigh. He watched her eyes as he stroked a finger down over her cleft testing her resolve, feeling the silky lace material dampen. Her eyes were wide, her face flushed and she moaned. He noticed her eyes cloud over and darken as her pupils dilated before she closed them in pleasure with another moan. He was surprised at her readiness but didn't want to rush this momentous occasion. He sat up again and pulled her up, startling her. He pulled her off the bed, gently to stand in front of him as he undid the gold belt and the dress fell to the floor. He took a moment to let his eyes feast on her naked flesh standing before him, just a flimsy pair of lace panties between him and heaven. He met her eyes as he pulled her to him, kissing her stomach and trailing his fingers down her spine. He brought his hands round to her hips where he hooked her panties with his fingers and slowly pulled them down. She dutifully stepped out of them and he lifted them to his face, making her eyes go even wider, as he breathed in deeply, smirking.

"Oh, Tygarya...you are a sight right now...how I've dreamed of this..."

He tossed the panties and grabbed her waist pulling her up so she again straddled him, she grabbed his face in both hands and kissed him deeply. He lifted his fingers back up to between her legs and pushed a finger slowly inside her. She moaned against his mouth as he groaned in response, he could feel her trembling.

"Oh, Tyg...so tight, but so wet, you are ready for me."

He kept up his gentle probing, turning and laying her down on the bed as he kissed her, then moved back down kissing her neck and her breasts. She moaned and arched her back as he pushed his thumb against her clit then pushed another finger into her. After a few minutes of slow deliberate probing Tyg was breathing hard and fast. Grinning Leviathan took the moment to sit up on the side of the bed and remove his boots as she watched him, slightly annoyed that he had stopped. She went to sit up but he pushed her back down using his power. "Stay still." He ordered her in a thick growl as he stood up and removed his pants. "The sight of you naked sprawled over my bed waiting for me is a sight I don't think I will ever tire of." He pulled his pants down revealing his cock.

Tyg mewled a strange sound at seeing his erection in front of her, looking more than a little scared. He smiled down at her.

"I'll be gentle, Tyg, trust me, only once I've made you properly ready for me will you get this..."

He leaned over her kissing her deeply as he knelt between her legs, pushing them apart more, bending her knees up as he again pushed his fingers inside her. He groaned at her wetness as she mewled again and arched her back against his probing willing him to push further inside her, lost to the pleasures he was making

142

her feel. He continued probing her swirling his fingers round, stretching her, preparing her. Tyg suddenly bucked against him with a loud breathy moan and bore down on his fingers, he felt her tighten around his fingers again.

"Bloody hell..." Leviathan muttered as he lifted his head with a smirk. "Oh, baby, come for me." He pressed his thumb against her clit, rubbing it.

Tyg's eyes flew open and met Leviathan's as she reached the pinnacle and her body went rigid for a moment before she cried out in ecstasy as her body shuddered, she threw her head back and closed her eyes, her mouth wide open in a rapturous moan as she grasped out at the pillows for something to grip on to. Leviathan gently kept probing with his fingers and raised up and kissed her passionately as her body trembled with the last of her climax.

"Tyg, that was beautiful to watch, baby." He gazed into her eyes as she smiled shyly and blushed, as she panted. "I'm glad you weren't shy and didn't hold back anything from me."

He felt her silken cleft was slick for him now. He positioned himself against her wet opening, removing his fingers and grabbed her chin making her look at him. She felt the head of his erection push up against her and her eyes widened in surprise again. "Oh, my..." She moaned as she looked into Leviathan's eyes. He paused, locking his gaze with hers.

"I'm going to have to hear it again, Tyg, tell me you're sure because there is no going back now. After this you are completely mine."

"I'm sure, Lev...please, I'm sure." Tyg wrapped her arms around his back and threw her head back and cried out in a mixture of pain and need as he thrust into her. He stopped inside her, feeling her tightness and looked at her until she recovered then slowly withdrew and thrust again. She cried out again, this time more of a moan.

"Okay, baby?" He whispered in her ear as he kissed it.

"Yes, I'm...oh fuck..." She couldn't talk, it was too much.

Leviathan grinned and thrust into her again and again as they both gave in to the pleasure. He pressed his forehead on hers as she clung to him, dragging her nails into his back as she wrapped her legs around his waist and took him wholly into her.

"Oh, Tyg, baby, you feel so fucking good." Leviathan groaned huskily into her neck.

Tyg moaned and threw her head back again unable to speak through the pleasure she was feeling. Leviathan grit his teeth.

"Bloody hell!" He breathed as she bucked against him suddenly bringing her hips up to meet his thrusts. He held her hips firmly to keep her still as she grabbed him by the hair and pulled his face to hers. She kissed him fervently and threw her head back again and cried out in climatic pleasure as she shuddered and spasmed around him.

"Fuck!" He growled at her aggression as he came hard and fast behind her, he shuddered and moaned at the core pleasure of his release.

He slowed then pulled out and lowered himself to lay beside her on his side and pulled her into him as they both got their breath back.

He trailed his fingers across her smooth perfect skin, watching her intently. She was biting her lip again. "Stop doing that." He muttered as he reached up and pulled her lip out from her teeth. "Don't get all shy and demure now, baby...you just gave yourself wholly with me...there is no wall between us anymore...nothing holds us apart...you are completely mine now."

Tyg looked up at him and met his eyes. She raised her head and kissed him. He kissed her back and played with her hair, brushing it over her breasts and around her nipples. She lay her head back down and blinked slowly. Leviathan grinned wickedly.

"Don't you dare go to sleep on me, Tygarya...I haven't finished with you yet, I'm just giving you a rest before the main event."

"What?" She managed to look startled.

Leviathan laughed as he kissed a nipple and sucked it into his mouth, then kissed up to her neck as he circled a finger around her clit. She moaned as her body bucked in response to his touch. He chuckled against her neck, as she arched her back for more.

"So responsive, baby...I like it..."

"Oh, fuck...Lev..."

"Get on your knees..."

16

When Tyg woke in the morning it was in the arms of Leviathan, holding her firmly against him as he slept. She looked up at his face, her head on his bicep. She had only ever woken up in the arms of one other man and she couldn't believe how more right this felt. She remembered Stills words about her being meant for something more once again and it brought tears to her eyes.

Leviathan's eyes flicked open, almost like he sensed her anguish. "Good morning." He said with a smile, then noticed the tears in her eyes. He leaned up on his elbow, dragging his arm from under her. "Are you okay? Did I hurt you?" His eyes were dark and his jaw clenched. There had been no blood when he had cleaned her up, but with the high activity and flexibility Tyg did every day that came as no surprise, he believed she had been a virgin and was pleased.

Tyg shook her head. "No...nothing like that." She looked at him with large luminous eyes that made him feel weak. He smiled at her in understanding.

"I know, I feel it too...this just feels right." He smiled endearingly at her.

Tyg nodded her head slightly as Leviathan ran his hand up the side of her neck and round to the back of her head and pulled her to him, kissing her. As Tyg ran her hands up his chest and then round to his back she kissed him back eagerly. He growled deep in his throat and rolled up on top of her, running a hand up the inside of her thigh. He pushed her legs apart and slid down her body, kissing her stomach, and then moved down further. He flicked his eyes up to her face briefly with a smirk.

"I saved the best for last for you, baby." He breathed against her soft downy light coloured pubic hair. He lowered his mouth to her clit, licking his tongue up and round it then sucking it into his mouth. Tyg gasped and moaned arching her back in pure pleasure at the new things his tongue was doing to her.

As Leviathan lay down next to Tyg, spent from the night's and now early morning's activities, he pulled her body into his and held her close as they both got their breath back. Tyg looked at him with a grin.

"If I had known what this was like I wouldn't have waited so long."

Leviathan growled a deep rumble in his throat. "Tygarya, do not say that you would have done this with other men sooner, for fuck's sake!"

Tyg's eyes widened. "No...I didn't mean that...only I wouldn't have waited so long with you...but I was so nervous about it."

Leviathan smiled. "The timing was perfect...you are perfect. You have just made Beltain my favourite festival." He kissed her nose, then sat up. "Now, get up!" He whacked her on the rump as he stood up and stepped over to his clothes, making her give a cute little squeal.

"What? Why do we have to get up...it's only early...come back." Tyg muttered as she stretched out on her stomach and lay her head on her arms, watching his naked back, with the amazingly hot dragon head tattoo, walk away. His back muscles flexed sexily as he raked his hands through his long hair.

Leviathan looked back at her naked, stretched out on the bed, for a moment tempted for another round then shook his head. "No, get up. I want to get you home as quickly as possible...now more than ever."

Tyg sat up smiling sweetly. "That's nice."

Leviathan glanced at her amused. "No, it's not." He picked up the dress, looked at it then threw it in his chest of belongings. He looked back at her as he dressed. "I'll get your things brought over...and get a bath drawn. You must be tender..."

Tyg pulled the covers up over herself and lay back down. "Okay, that's nice too." She said smirking, he must have forgotten about her healing ability, but she liked the dull ache while it lasted.

Leviathan walked up and stood over her, he had only put his pants on. The sight of him shirtless with his hair down around his face was quite a sight, but Tyg saw the dangerous glint in his eyes and held her breath as he leaned down and grabbed her chin.

"It isn't nice, Tygarya. You are mine, completely now. I want to take my possession home where it will be safe." He smiled on one side of his mouth as he dropped her chin and walked out, grabbing a shirt and his boots.

Tyg's eyes blazed ice blue fire as she watched him leave. "You're not fooling anyone!" She called after him. She heard his laughter and couldn't help but smile herself. Not realising in that moment the truth of his words.

Leviathan was back in only a few moments carrying her large chest of belongings all by himself when it usually took two soldiers. Tyg opened her eyes and watched him from under her lashes. She had laid back down and very nearly dozed off in her languid bliss. She absolutely felt like she had made the right decision, everything felt perfect and complete, maybe there was something in this destiny thing after all.

He put the chest down and walked over, sitting on the edge of the bed. "Are you hungry?"

Tyg grimaced as her stomach suddenly gnawed at her. She hadn't felt hungry until he mentioned it. "Starving."

He grinned at her. "Get up...don't you dare fall back to sleep, Tygarya." He said in that low commanding tone. "I can't organise a bath but have some hot water coming so you can at least wash, you can bathe in the castle baths once we get there."

Tyg looked at him and sat up. "Yes, my Liege." She said smirking.

Leviathan was looking at her breasts. He reached out and grabbed her hair, flicking it back over her shoulders so it didn't obscure his view of them. His eyes slowly raised to Tyg's and the dark smouldering look in them made her stop breathing. He grabbed her and kissed her fiercely forcing his tongue into her mouth as he held her by a fistful of hair at the back of her head. He stopped and breathed heavily, pressing his forehead against hers.

"What the hell are you doing to me? Now I've had a taste I can't seem to get enough of you." He whispered. Tyg frowned and was just about to question what he meant when...

"Hello?" A voice called out on the other side of the tent flap. Leviathan growled and let Tyg go.

"Get dressed." He said as he stood up. They both recognised the voice of Antyn. Tyg quickly got up and grabbed some clothes out of her chest. Leviathan stood watching her a moment.

"The dress, Tygarya...we reach the Capital today." He ordered low and gravely.

Tyg looked at him with a scowl, then threw her pants back into the chest and pulled the black dress from the chest. He turned to the entry.

"What?" He asked as he looked out. "What the fuck is all this, Antyn?"

"Breakfast."

"Why?"

"I just figured you could both do with breakfast in bed...but typical of you, you're already up."

"I want to get home."

"No doubt you do...especially now, huh?" Antyn's tone was noticeably facetious.

"Shut up, Antyn."

"Just let me in..." He huffed.

"No." Leviathan response was firm.

"Oh, come on...unless Tyg's not actually up yet..." Antyn tried to look around Leviathan's shoulder.

"Antyn...I'm fucking warning you..." Antyn saw the possessive glint in his brother's eyes and flinched, he had seen that look before.

"It's okay, Lev..." Tyg's voice called out. He pulled his head back into the tent and looked at her. She was sitting on the edge of the bed brushing her hair, looking regal. She smiled at him. "Let him in, I'm starving."

Leviathan frowned but stepped back and allowed Antyn to come in. He was carrying a tray of freshly baked sweet breads and sliced fruits. Another man following him had a pot of tea and cups on his tray.

"Starving...of course you are!" Antyn said smugly as he walked in.

Tyg's eyes blazed. "That's enough out of you!" She said in a menacing voice, brandishing the hairbrush at him.

Antyn baulked and looked at her with a frightful look as Leviathan snorted and folded his arms.

"I'm sorry, Tyg." Antyn said. "That was inappropriate."

"Maybe I should just let her deal with you, brother." Leviathan said amused.

Antyn glanced at him with a grimace. "Sorry, Lev." He downcast his eyes. "I really just thought it was an occasion to celebrate...it's not every day my brother – the Emperor – gets himself a legitimate bona fide consort in his bed."

Tyg's eyes flashed as she went to stand up. Leviathan reached out a hand and pushed her back with his power, then flicked his wrist and sent Antyn flying back, doubled over, like he had been sledge hammered in the gut. The man with the tea tray put it down and fled in terror.

Leviathan stalked over to Antyn as he scrambled backwards. "Lev...?"

Leviathan bent down and picked Antyn up by the throat, lifting him off his feet, walked him to the tent flap and threw him outside. "Go home, Antyn...now!"

Leviathan turned and walked back into the middle of the tent, his jaw clenched and his eyes blazing golden green. Tyg got up and put her arms around his waist and rested her head silently on his chest. He looked down on her surprised. No one would ever dare approach him when he was angry before...before her...but she was fearless and knew she could calm him down.

He wrapped his arms around her as his eyes softly glowed azure blue, and rested his head on hers. "Thank you, Tygarya."

She looked up at him smiling. "Are you okay?" She looked at his deep blue eyes.

"Yes, Tygarya, I am...Antyn just needed reminding of his place." He smiled at her and hooked her chin with a finger. "You really do constantly amaze me...but never more than last night."

"Good, I'm so glad it all worked like I wanted." Tyg said shyly then looked up and grinned. "So, can we eat? I really am starving."

Leviathan chuckled and let her go. "By all means, Tygarya my dear."

Antyn flew to his horse, saddling it in a fury, muttering to himself.

He knew this would happen, that damn girl had managed to get a choke hold on his brother by sleeping with him. This was dangerous, he needed Leviathan to stay objective to their goals – his goals!

They both knew the prophecies were vague at best on how Tyg was to be of use to Leviathan, they both knew that to usurp the power within her may result in her actual death.

He couldn't risk Leviathan putting the girl's life before their plan.

"I'll go home, brother, but only to do more research and hopefully be able to convince you to not let this girl melt that black heart of yours!"

17

This was it...home sat before her. She looked at the massive city with its huge castle that sat perched up on a craggy hill, the city sprawled at its feet round two thirds. A massive cliff face taking up the other third making the castle a formidable and amazing sight to see.

Leviathan, sitting upon his huge black stallion next to her, was quietly contemplative as he looked across from atop the hill they were on and stared at his home. He glanced at Tyg and saw wonder in her eyes, he smirked. "Impressed yet?"

He saw Tyg's face scowl and her lip twerked in a smirk. Oh, she wasn't going to give him the satisfaction of admitting she was impressed yet. She turned to him and shrugged. "Seen one castle you've seen them all." She looked at the city below. "Must be a burden with all these people to look after."

Leviathan snorted a chuckle. "Bloody hell." He shook his head. "Well in any case, are you ready for this?"

"I will never be ready for this..." Tyg muttered and Leviathan saw the sheer terror in her eyes. She had been warned that their entrance into the city would be met with large crowds as their approach had been announced by more than one herald.

"No one will touch you, my dear, don't worry...there won't be a mob or anything, that's why the extra soldiers."

Tyg looked at him and smiled. "Of course..." She said gratefully and also remembered the no touching law.

"Come on, let's go home..." Leviathan said and raised his fist to indicate to the soldiers around them that they were moving out.

It took another hour to reach the city streets. They were lined with people, right from the lower city, right up through the city proper and to the outer courtyard of the castle that led up to the massive entrance doors. There were soldiers lining the path all the way as they wound up through the city. Tyg had been forced by Leviathan to ride side saddle because of the large split that went up the side of her dress, he was not happy to have her riding a horse normally and exposing one long naked thigh to all and sundry. Just the look of her knee high boots with the large tread like army boots made people look at her strangely. Leviathan had argued with her about that too, but she was not wearing court shoes, in fact she had thrown them at Leviathan's head when he had tried to hand her some. So she had compromised on the side saddle as long as she got to keep the boots. She was now looking very regal with her hood half up just concealing her hair with her long fur lined cloak draped round her shoulders and down over Fulminous's rump. She had to admit she probably did look like a princess, which made her very uncomfortable. Fulminous seemed to know what was going on and started prancing his front legs as he bowed his head, his mane shaking and shimmering in the light.

"Show off." Tyg muttered.

As they reached the main courtyard leading to the castle steps they stopped and Leviathan dismounted. Tyg went to get off her horse.

"Stay there." Leviathan ordered her as he came round and took the reins from her and started walking her horse towards the castle steps. The inside courtyard was lined with wealthy looking people, aristocrats curious to see the rumoured girl. Tyg noticed no one else from their escort came with them. Tyg grit her teeth and snarled at Leviathan.

"This is so fucking embarrassing, what are you doing?" She mumbled as she folded her arms and scowled at the passing faces.

"Tygarya, unfold your arms this instant and act like what you promised me." Leviathan growled harshly without even turning around.

"Do you have eyes in the back of your head?" Tyg asked as she dropped her arms. She heard Leviathan chuckle.

"I can feel your angst from here, Tygarya. I figured you were pouting."

"Pouting? I'll give you fucking pouting, wait till later on tonight, mister."

Leviathan stopped the horse and walked back to her. Tyg bit her lip, surely he wouldn't do anything about her smart mouth right out here...would he?

He settled his vulture gaze on her with a smirk. "Don't think I won't rip you off that horse and ravage you in front of this crowd, Tygarya...it would probably earn me even more respect if I did." Leviathan laughed at the startled look on her face. "Just behave." He said to her with a last smouldering look then went back to leading the horse the last few paces to the steps. A servant ran up and took the reins as Leviathan came back again and help her off the horse. As he held her waist he deliberately lowered her down tight against his body. He inhaled her scent as he did so. Tyg stared at him when she was finally on the ground. "Pervert." She muttered, but her cheeks were blazing.

Leviathan chuckled. "I'm so glad you managed to wash your hair this morning for today...you smell absolutely divine, my dear." He took a lock of her hair that was down, she had the front twined up in two small braids holding the front back. The rest was down and as he lowered her hood he brought the lock to his nose inhaling deeply. Tyg frowned and looked around him.

"Ah, Lev...there are official looking people staring at us..."

"Let them...they're just jealous." He said as he continued to smell her, leaning down into her neck and nuzzling it.

"Lev..." Tyg said more insistently as she shivered against him. He felt it and growled in his throat like a hungry beast. Now he had tasted her, he just wanted more.

"What?" He muttered in challenge as he kissed her neck. She melted slightly against him at the touch of his lips. He ran his hand round to her back and pulled her hard up against him as he dropped the lock of hair and trailed his hand up onto the back of her neck and brought his face up to hers. "It's alright, Tygarya...they will stand there all day until I'm ready...and finished with you."

"Oh..." Tyg said but it was swallowed as his mouth covered hers and he passionately kissed her, laying his mark for everyone to witness that this strange silver haired beauty belonged to him. The passion of last night was still fresh in both of their minds and Tyg was soon kissing him back eagerly. Leviathan heard a coughing sound and lifted his head with an annoyed cluck of his tongue. But then the crowd of aristocrats that lined the castle courtyard erupted in cheering. Leviathan grinned at Tyg who had started to blush with a furious look of embarrassment on her face.

"I think the crowd liked that...see what I mean." He teased.

"They are all fucking perverts." Tyg muttered. "Can we get out of here now..."

"So eager, Tygarya..." Leviathan smirked.

"Don't make me regret last night..."

"Never, quite the contrary, I intend to relive every minute of it tonight."

Tyg bit her lip, causing Leviathan to scowl and using his thumb he removed her lip from her teeth. "Alright, Tygarya, let's get you home...come on..."

He grabbed her hand and stepped up the steps to the waiting officials who upon seeing Tyg's face, eyes and hair properly all went pale themselves as they all bowed their heads low and greeted their Imperial Majesty home. Leviathan ignored them and swept straight past them and inside, dragging Tyg by the hand behind him. They all followed him in and once inside the large foyer Leviathan turned Tyg to them all.

"Tygarya...This is my Lord Chamberlain of Estafeld, R'hyan. He is responsible for everything that goes on in this castle and city." R'hyan bowed his head.

"Such a pleasure to finally meet you, Lady Essyndyl. I have heard so much about you and it pleases my heart to finally see such a beautiful woman upon the Emperor's arm."

"Ah, thank you." Tyg said awkwardly.

"And this..." Leviathan continued. "Is the Lord Steward, Marcius, he is responsible for overseeing the day to day running of the people inside the castle...making sure everyone is doing their duties...he is also the one to which you will go if you require anything."

"Okay..." Tyg was already feeling overwhelmed and by the looks of it she had several more people to meet.

"Marcius will take over the rest." Leviathan said as he stepped away from Tyg and walked off with R'hyan to a secluded spot and started talking together in low tones. Tyg grit her teeth in annoyance.

Lord Steward Marcius smiled at Tyg's expression. "It is expected that his Imperial Majesty take a moment with the Lord Chamberlain after being away for so long, my Lady." He explained when he saw her expression. "I doubt he will have much more time to spend with you today. He will be in meetings with his ministers most of the week I dare to say..."

Tyg glared at Marcius and her eyes changed to ice blue, he opened his eyes in terror and stepped back. "Oh my...I'm sorry my Lady I did not realise that you were a ......"

"Marcius!" Leviathan growled as he came back over.

"A what?" Tyg asked frowning.

Leviathan smirked. "He thinks you're a warlock...or I should say a witch...because your eyes change colour and glow."

"What the fuck?" Tyg said, which made all the servants standing around her go pale in fright.

"And swearing isn't lady like..." Leviathan added with a chuckle. "Have fun, Tygarya, but behave." Leviathan bopped her on the nose then walked off again with R'hyan leaving Tyg fuming at him.

"So you're not a witch then, my Lady?"

"No...I'm Elvian apparently." Tyg was thinking about Corvyn, so that's what he was. She grinned happy to finally know. She looked up and stared confused at the Steward's terrified face.

"What have I done now?"

"Y-you're an Elvian?" He stammered.

Tyg grinned. "Yes...and a highly trained one, so don't piss me off!"

"Tygarya!" She heard Leviathan growl out from in his corner with R'hyan. So he was still keeping an eye on her. She smiled to herself feeling a little better about things.

"Please continue...Marcius, was it?"

"Ah, yes, my Lady, please forgive my surprise."

"Yes, I'm not supposed to exist...blah, blah...can we move this along..." Tyg rolled her eyes she was getting bored and antsy.

"Very well, my Lady...please let me introduce your ladies-in-waiting..."

"I'm sorry, my what?" Tyg asked not sure she had possibly heard right.

"Your ladies-in-waiting...they are here to attend your every requirement, and supply you with the necessary womanly company that you require when you are not required to attend his Imperial Majesty, of course."

"Wait just one second, Marcius..." Tyg scowled and her eyes started to glow faintly as she looked over at the three young women that were stuck in a perpetual curtsey in front of her with their heads down. "Are you telling me I have to have these women around me all the time?"

"Well, no...you don't have to all the time but...a woman needs female company and they are to aid you in dressing and bathing and other such requirements."

"No." Tyg said simply.

"What?" Marcius asked a bit stunned.

"No, Marcius. What do you not understand about that?"

"But your person must be attended when dressing and bathing."

"I most certainly do not...Leviathan!" Tyg yelled out.

Leviathan lifted his head with a large grin, like he had heard the whole conversation and was just waiting for her to call for his help. Tyg scowled further, her top lip lifting in a formidable snarl.

"Oh I see, like that is it...leave the poor uneducated girl to flounder about on her own under all these required protocols...very amusing for you, is it?" Tyg sneered at him as he wandered over.

Everyone flinched back at the way Tyg addressed the Emperor but they were all astounded when he just chuckled in response. Which only made Tyg's wrath worse.

"Perhaps, my Liege would like to wait until I kill a few of these fucking servants until he decides it's not funny anymore!" Her eyes flicked to a guard and the sword at his hip.

"Alright Tygarya, that's enough." Leviathan said in a low tone of warning, the grin dropping from his face.

"Right, well tell him that I don't want or need any fucking women hanging around me, certainly not to help me dress or fucking bathe. I've lived my entire life on my own or surrounded by hardened criminals, I don't need them."

"Tygarya! Calm down." Leviathan said as he finally reached her and grabbed hold of her shoulders. His eyes started glowing as he took in the power that had started building up around her. He pulled her into his chest and held her as the staff all stared horrified. She stood stiff in his arms. "Tyg...come on now...it's just introductions for fuck's sake, can you really not even handle that much human interaction...what about when you organised those balls back in Arial. I thought you could do this with some decorum, you made a promise to me." Leviathan talked calmly but with authority as Tyg slowly relaxed into him and finally put her arms around his waist, laying her head on his chest with a huff.

"I'm sorry..." She mumbled. "I was usually the one in control of those situations...here...I'm not, I feel cornered."

He grabbed hold of her shoulders again and pulled her out from him to look her in the eye. "No, I am in control here...I learnt my lesson back in Asbel City, so trust me, Tyg. You are meant to be here, this is your home so you can treat it as such." Leviathan pressed his forehead to hers. "Are we good?"

"Please get rid of the women..." Tyg breathed.

Leviathan smiled down at her and turned, tucking Tyg under his arm.

"Okay...no ladies-in-waiting attending you, but they will still be held here in court since they have a contractual obligation to attend. Did you get that Marcius?"

"Yes, my Liege." Marcius bowed his head and sent the three women who were cowering nearby away to their rooms.

"Okay...for now, Marcius, let's just keep this simple, introduce the maid that will be entering Tygarya's rooms and then let's just show Tygarya to her rooms shall we?"

"Certainly, my Liege..." Marcius snapped his fingers at a young maid who scurried up with large terrified eyes and curtsied in front of the Emperor. "This is Peony."

"Nice to meet you, my Lady..."

"Right." Leviathan let Tyg go. "Marcius is going to show you to your rooms now...can you behave?"

Tyg scowled at him. "Yes."

"Good...I have so much work to do...I'll be back when I can." He grabbed her head and kissed her fondly on the forehead and walked back to where R'hyan was watching with a bewildered look on his face, he muttered something at Leviathan that caused him to chuckle earning another shocked look from his chamberlain and they walked off out a door.

Tyg looked at Marcius, who was also staring at her with bewilderment.

"What?" Tyg said confused with all the funny looks.

"His Majesty is different around you..." Marcius said quietly as he indicated for her to go with him. Tyg noticed that all their luggage was starting to be brought into the foyer from the horses as she walked off with Marcius.

"What do you mean different?" Tyg asked curious.

"You are still alive, after talking that way to him."

"Still alive? Shit you mean he kills people for swearing at him?"

"Yes." Marcuis answered honestly and matter-of-factly.

"And he gives me shit about killing people..." Tyg muttered, then caught Marcius's stumbled step as he again looked at her shocked. Tyg grinned. "I did say I was an Elvian...so yes I have killed people."

"My Lady...I'm not quite sure what you want me to say to that."

Tyg laughed. "Nothing, Marcius, just relax..."

"Very well, my Lady."

18

When they got to Tyg's rooms she was speechless. Rooms wasn't really how she would describe it...more like a mini palace within the castle. She had expected a room with a bed, what she got was opulence and finery with a large four poster bed and a chaise lounge, a small roll top desk, a fireplace with beautiful upholstered chairs. A lounge room and a bedroom fitted with its own privy room. Tyg walked around the rooms amazed, touching all the different expensive fabrics. Marcius smiled to himself, finally a normal reaction from this strange girl.

"Is everything to your liking, my Lady?"

"I guess..." Tyg answered a little overwhelmed. "Wait, why?"

"If you wish to change anything or add anything please just let me know."

"Oh, ok...thank you...and sorry about before...I'm not used to all this...I haven't come from all this like what you would expect I guess of an Emperor's..." She hesitated on saying the word.

"Consort, my Lady?" Marcius finished her sentence with a smile. Tyg scowled but said nothing. "His Majesty did send a detailed letter outlining certain things, so I understand some of what you're saying, my Lady."

"Good, so can we stop with the 'my Ladies' because technically I'm not one?"

Marcius laughed. "His Imperial Majesty said you would say that, and no...we cannot, it is protocol."

Tyg grit her teeth. "Damn him."

"I must ask you to refrain from cursing him, please." Marcius said grimacing.

"Why?"

"Because I would be duty bound to report it."

Tyg laughed that musical laugh causing Marcius to stare at her wide eyed. "Report away, Marcius." She flailed her hand in the air as she turned her back on him then flopped down on the bed and sighed. He bowed his head from the view with propriety as he ignored her last comment.

"I will leave you to rest and unpack as it seems your belongings have arrived." He stepped out of the bedroom and waved the servants carrying her chests in, they bowed to her and left. Marcius closed the door.

Tyg got up and went immediately to the balcony doors and threw them open. She looked out and down and in her head was already working out how to get in and out of the room undetected. There was no way Leviathan was going to keep her trapped inside this stuffy castle like he tried to do in Asbel. Tyg leaned on the balustrade and looked out over her view of the city and the surrounding countryside. It was certainly an impressive looking place. It was going to be difficult getting in and out, she was glad she didn't have the massive cliff face below her but it was still a fair way down. She mapped the interlocking roof lines of the different parts of the castle and adjoining buildings to the massive walls then down to the rooftops of the town that almost abutted the walls in places nearer the front of the castle walls where the ground was more a gentle slope down the massive hill upon which the castle sat. It wasn't impossible, not for someone like her. She went back inside happy she could finally get changed and out of the constrictive black dress.

Marcius knocked politely on her door and entered only when she said he could, a couple of hours later. Tyg had already had Peony the maid bring her some late lunch and unpack her clothes into the drawers provided and she was sitting in front of the fire sipping a lovely glass of white wine. Marcius smiled pleasantly at her to see her looking more or less relaxed now within her rooms, although he baulked at what she was wearing. He refrained from saying anything about it as it looked like she was well accustomed to wearing these types of clothes that made her look more like a ruffian than a princess.

"Settling in, my Lady?"

"I suppose so...where does Leviathan sleep?"

"Ah...not too far away, my lady...but it is improper to ask." Marcius said to her.

Tyg rolled her eyes, here we go with proper and improper again, that made her think of Corvyn. She really hoped he had received his leave, she missed him. "How far exactly?" Tyg asked him looking up at him with her eyes glowing. "And don't speak to me about what's proper, because I don't give a damn about proper."

"My Lady, his rooms are just down the halls in the next tower. In fact his rooms are the tower." Tyg got up and looked out the window that faced the large pentagon shaped interior quad that was the epicentre of the castle. She looked up and saw four towers with evenly spaced building between making up the inner palace of the castle along with the tower she was in.

"Which one?"

"The one closest to you on the right."

Tyg looked over at it and smiled. It was the furthermost tower from the city, the one poised over the precipice of the cliff. She could see a window and a balcony from where she was.

"So, what can I do for you, Marcius?"

"There is still a couple of hours of daylight left, my Lady...was there anything you would like to do...a tour of the castle perhaps?"

"Can you show me the mineral baths that Leviathan has told me so much about?"

"The baths?" Marcius said surprised. "Of course..." He smiled, so she was just a girl after all.

"Thank you..." Tyg got up as Marcius held the door open for her and he escorted her down into the depths of the castle.

Tyg noticed the walls became bedrock and Marcius led her to a large wooden door that had a lantern on either side of it.

"The baths." He said as he opened the door.

Tyg walked in and stared in shocked fascination. The whole vast room was lined with marble slabs and in the middle was a large pool of water that you could tell was hot by the steam that hung over it. The water had a sulphuric mineral smell to it which told Tyg it was the natural hot spring that Leviathan said was under the castle. The water had a slight green look to it but still seemed extremely inviting to her.

As she looked around she noticed benches to sit on to remove your clothing, barrels of fresh water to rinse yourself off, that were hooked up to piping so it rained down on you, a stack of robes to wear after and also a stack of white fluffy blankets. Tyg walked over and picked one up.

"What are these?"

"They are towels to dry yourself...you don't have towels where you are from?"

"Not like this, how are they so fluffy?" She asked as she nuzzled her face into one.

Marcius shrugged amused. "I don't know, ask the people who make them."

Tyg flashed a grin at him at hearing the slight sarcasm in his voice, she was wearing him down already. "Can I get some of these sent back to Arial?"

"I suppose so, talk to his Majesty."

"Hmm." Tyg walked back to the water, noticing the ornate lanterns that lined the walls. She guessed there must be natural fissures in the rock on the ceiling that enabled the steam, smoke and fumes to escape...and heat the castle, she remembered Leviathan saying.

She knelt down and dipped her hand in the water.

"I'm afraid there are no separate men's or ladies bathing, as this is predominately a male dominated domain and the servants do not come down here. So if you ever want to bathe, let me know so I can post a guard at the door."

"Okay..." Tyg murmured as she stared at the water.

"Or you can just bathe now." Tyg turned startled at the deep commanding voice. Leviathan was standing in the doorway looking amused.

The Steward bowed low. "My Liege."

"Lord Marcius..." Leviathan acknowledged him as he walked in. Tyg stood up and smiled at Leviathan.

"I'm very impressed." She said as he lifted his arm beckoning for her. She walked in under his arm and he placed a finger under her chin lifting her face up.

"Well finally." He answered amused. "So?"

"So what?"

"Do you wish to bathe now?"

Tyg grinned. "Very much so."

Marcius bowed again. "I will return to my duties then, my Liege."

"Certainly, Marcius." Leviathan dismissed him without even looking at him.

As the Steward closed the door Tyg looked up at Leviathan from under her lashes. "Are you going to join me?"

Leviathan smirked. "I was searching for you everywhere...the maid told me where you had gone."

Tyg started unbuttoning Leviathan's shirt as his smirk got wider. "You didn't answer my question."

"No, I didn't...did I?" Leviathan chuckled as Tyg opened his shirt and pulled it off his shoulders, then started running her hands down his exquisite chest. She kissed him on the pectorals and glanced back up through her lashes as her hands went to his belt.

He placed his hands over hers stopping her, then stepped away and sat down on a bench looking at her still amused, but his eyes had darkened. "Your turn." He said as he watched her. "I see you've ditched the dress already..."

Tyg smiled at him and undid her corset belt, dropping it on the floor then untucked her shirt and pulled it off over her head. She looked at Leviathan with an eyebrow raised. He smirked back.

"And the rest..." He said waggling his fingers at her.

"What about you?" Tyg asked as she unlaced her bustier.

"I'm the Emperor...you do as you're told."

Tyg scowled at him. "So your fantasy finally comes true..."

"My fantasy?" Leviathan said with an eyebrow raised, but his eyes darkened even further.

"You know...every time I mentioned bathing..."

"Oh..." Leviathan chuckled in a way that made Tyg shudder and something deep within her clenched. "Yes...so is that a promise is it?" Leviathan said in a low husky voice as he watched Tyg undress.

Tyg threw her bustier at him. He laughed as he caught it.

"Promise?" Tyg asked.

"That my entire bath fantasy is going to come true right now?"

Tyg inhaled sharply as she looked at him wide eyed Leviathan laughed and then started taking his boots off. "Yeah it is..." He smouldered at her as Tyg smiled and did the same urgently.

Tyg had said goodbye and good night to Leviathan regretfully after that, he had made his apologies but she understood he was busy and probably would be all night. Not to bother, he had taken some time to come and see her, make love to her and tell her, that was all she could ask of such an important man.

19

The next morning Tyg went and stood out on the balcony to watch the sunrise. She leaned on the thick stone balustrade and looked out at the staggering view. She could see a part of the city, farmland and in the distance to the other side a great forest and mountains. The perfect all round view. She would enjoy morning coffees out here when the weather wasn't so brisk.

Tyg heard someone enter her room and turned to see Peony nervously enter and look up at her. Tyg smiled and walked back inside as Peony went about her early morning chores then delivered Tyg a simple breakfast of fruit, bread, cheese and tea.

Tyg gave the breakfast a cursory nibble, as she sat down, noticing Peony standing nearby looking pensive.

"Do you need something from me?" Tyg asked.

Peony nodded, she was so fearful of this woman, she gave off the same dangerous unfathomable vibes as the emperor, one wrong move and you're dead. Tyg regarded her as if reading her thoughts.

"You don't have to fear me." Tyg muttered as leaned back in her chair and regarded the young maid, estimating her age as about fourteen.

"I was just wondering if there was anything I could do for you, my Lady?"

"Do...?" Tyg thought about it. "Yes, actually there is." Tyg stood up and walked to the door. "Show me the libraries."

"The libraries?"

Tyg's eyes flashed. "Is there something wrong with that?"

"No, my Lady, nothing at all...at once." Peony swallowed hard in panic and dived out the open door to lead the way.

"Oh good, for a minute there I thought you were going to say I wasn't allowed in the libraries."

"Oh, no...nothing like that my Lady, it's just the other ladies that stay here never ask to see the libraries."

Tyg rolled her eyes. "Why am I not surprised, why are they even here?"

"Well, they have always been here..."

Tyg stopped walking. "What do you mean always?" She settled an icy stare on the girl. Did Marcuis not say this castle was male dominated?

"Ah, well not the same ladies of course, they change all the time, but well, before you came along..." Peony hesitated at the hard look on Tyg's face.

Tyg grit her teeth. "Before I came along ladies were here because?"

"Well for the Emperor..." Peony muttered looking at the ground.

"I see..." Tyg said looking up the hall in thought. "And are any of those particular women still in the castle?"

"Ah...one...I think." Peony hardly whispered it.

"Take me to see her." Tyg said flatly, her eyes blazing.

"Ah...yes, my Lady."

They arrived at some rooms that were, Tyg noticed, on the opposite side of Leviathan's tower to her rooms. They were all here...the other three, her ladies in waiting, from the other day as well. They were all sitting in a large room doing embroidery and chatting over tea.

Tyg leaned on the doorframe and smirked at them. They all stopped what they were doing and looked up at her with large terrified eyes, taking in her all black leather male attire. All but one, the one Tyg hadn't met yet.

She was elegant, and surprisingly petite. With long chestnut coloured hair and large brown eyes. She was wearing a simple pale green gown that showed off her attributes nicely. She was nothing like Tyg had expected.

Tyg looked at the other ladies. "Get out." She growled as she stepped into the room and stalked towards the one woman with murderous intent. The other ladies scattered and fled as the one stood up with a hand on her chest, her eyes wide and fearful.

"What's your name?" Tyg asked as she heard the door shut behind her.

"Melody." The one answered meekly.

Tyg blinked, not even her name was what she had expected. Tyg walked over to where there was a tray with wine on it. She poured herself one and came over and sat down at the table, putting her feet up on the table and leaning back causing Melody to baulk slightly at the lack of 'ladyness' this scruffian exhibited.

"Sit down." Tyg growled. Melody sank back into her seat. "Tell me why you are here?" Tyg asked her then as she took a casual sip of her wine.

"Why I'm here?" Melody stammered, confused by the question.

"Are you hard of hearing?" Tyg growled again.

"No, my Lady...I'm here because, well...I mean to say...I'm here so that..." Melody's eyes fell on the dragon's head ring on Tyg's finger and her expression went flat.

"Look, I understand you have probably fucked the Emperor before me, I don't really care about that...what I want to know is why you are still here now?"

Melody's face flushed at Tyg's language and she looked down at her hands, but said nothing.

"I see...you think you can compete with me, Melody?" Tyg's voice sounded like blades cutting through flesh.

Her eyes came up and there was a moment of a challenge, Tyg saw them flash. "Not compete per se...but I believe I am in a position to continue to be a worthy concubine to the Emperor."

"You're a witch?" Tyg dropped her feet off the table and had her hand around Melody's neck so fast she didn't even get time to blink. Tyg pulled her to her feet. She was only five foot four so Tyg lifted her off her feet to look in her eyes. Melody gripped Tyg's wrist in a panic, gurgling and struggling to breathe. Unable to speak any incantation while being choked.

"This is the only time I will say this so listen very carefully. Leave this place, today!" Tyg dropped her and turned away. Melody fell back into her chair and grabbed her throat coughing and gasping. She looked up as Tyg walked from the room and closed the door with real fear in her eyes. She was used to people being afraid of her being a witch, why wasn't this uncouth girl afraid of her, but attacked her completely unafraid? Her aura was incredible, was that why the Emperor had chosen her?

Tyg scoffed, did she really think I would share? Did Leviathan think he was going to be able to continue this behaviour and sleep with other women while sleeping with her? Absolutely not! If he wasn't going to give himself completely to her then she wasn't going to allow him to have the audacity to call her his property like he did.

She stopped.

No, she wouldn't go storming in to confront him on this, she would let him come to her and explain. No doubt little Miss Melody will kick up quite a fuss.

20

Tyg was nestled into a large leather chair in a nice tiny little nook in the libraries reading a fascinating book on trolls when she heard a commotion out in the main library room.

"Where the fuck is she?" Tyg heard Leviathan's voice and flinched. It was angrier than she expected it to be, which annoyed her even more.

Seconds later he found her.

Tyg looked up from her book as he stood in front of her, her eyes a cool ice. "Leviathan, is there a problem?" Her tone was slurred with obvious sarcasm as she smiled prettily.

Leviathan chuckled menacingly and raked a hand through his hair looking like the apex predator he was.

"You bet there is." The level of menace in his voice caused Tyg to put her book down, she placed her hands on the arms of the chair and crossed her legs in a challenging display of calmness.

"Really?" Her voice matched his. "Do you want to explain to me why exactly there is a problem?"

Tyg smirked when she saw that Leviathan actually hesitated. He seemed to re-evaluate her and straightened up to his full height and folded his arms. That vulture gaze fell on her then, but it was dark and smouldering.

"Oh, I get it...marking your territory were you?" Leviathan said in that low tone.

Tyg tipped her head sideways and regarded him with a smile. "Merely cleaning house."

Leviathan raised an eyebrow. "Can I ask why you didn't come to me?"

"And ask your permission to chuck your ex-fuck toy out of your castle, I don't think so? This is now my home, is that not what you said?"

Leviathan growled and his gaze darkened. Tyg stopped breathing, shit was that too far?

Leviathan advanced on her and placed his hands over hers on the chair, locking her wrists down as he lowered his face to an inch in front of hers and gave a menacing chuckle.

"Yes, Tygarya, I have fucked her...once, about four years ago...she is here in this castle not because she is, as you like to say, a fuck toy...but rather because she has nowhere else to go, since her family estate burned down a year ago, killing her parents."

Tyg held his gaze. "Doesn't explain why she is here, in this castle...you could have put her anywhere, Leviathan...literally fucking anywhere but here, and don't you dare fucking say you felt sorry for her because I know that emotion does not exist inside of you. You are lying to me. She all but threw it back in my face that she is a concubine of yours! She leaves, or I do Leviathan, like you I don't share!"

Leviathan pulled his hands away like he had been burnt and stood up, his eyes looking a little wild as he paced away raking a hand through his hair and turning his back to her. Tyg grimaced to have his lies confirmed to her, she had hoped he wasn't.

"Listen, Tyg..."

She stood up and walked past him to the door on silent feet and left without another word.

"...you've managed to misunderstand something..." He turned and noticed with a jolt that she was gone. "Wait!" Leviathan yelled out as he ran through the library not finding her. "Fuck." He growled out, wiping a hand down his face. "This girl, I swear!"

Tyg bolted back to her rooms, she actually felt...well she didn't know what she felt...this felt similar to when Stills died...okay not that bad...but it hurt in the same place...did Leviathan just break her heart?

Thomas's words came back to haunt her. 'I fear he will end up hurting you.' Is this what he meant, she had thought physically because he did that all the time. She didn't like this feeling, not one bit, it made her feel vulnerable, it made her feel...human. It was not something she expected at all and it left her angry, sad and powerless all at the same time. This type of hurt was why she had been so nervous about giving herself to him.

She was okay with Leviathan being with other women before her, but not while he 'owned' her would she allow him to bed other women as well! That was a mockery and a humiliation of her status of importance to him in the eyes of others.

As she entered her rooms Tyg looked over and saw Peony was changing out the water decanter with fresh water. Peony froze when she saw Tyg's face, shocked to see such an expression upon such a fearless person. Tyg realised then that tears were falling down her cheeks, she dashed them away and went into her bedroom.

"Peony..." Tyg called out. "Get me a large bottle of Volka...now!" Tyg slammed her bedroom door shut and fell on her bed grabbing her boots and pulling them off, hurling them across the room one by one. She should have just killed that bitch as soon as she dared say she was worthy of being a concubine.

Tyg had to give it to her; Peony was fast. Tyg was extremely happy to have her hands wrapped around the neck of the large decanter of the fiery clear liquid. She chugged it back like it was water and had nearly cleared half the bottle when she heard Peony squeak as someone thumped on the outer door to her rooms.

"What took him so long?" Tyg muttered as she turned to the open door of her bedroom to see Leviathan standing there already. "What took you so long? Did you have to go console Melody first? Was the poor girl upset?" She snarled and slurred. "Or have you come to see when I'm leaving? I got to say, that was quick work, huh...not two days of being together..." She muttered incoherently.

Leviathan frowned. "You're drunk? How did you get drunk so quickly?"

"Nup, not nearly as drunk as I intend to get." Tyg held up the bottle in salutation and drank heavily from it again.

Leviathan's eyes went wide as he watched her gulping back the alcohol. "Oh, that's how." He muttered. "Right, enough of this." He stepped forward and grabbed the bottle from Tyg's grasp pulling it away from her lips. He put it down on the side table by the reading chair. "Bloody hell, I really didn't picture you for the neurotic jealous type. You're more like me than I thought."

Tyg stepped back and her eyes went black. "You really thought I would be okay with you having other women while sleeping with me!?"

Leviathan's jaw clenched tight. "Tygarya...don't you fucking dare. Listen..."

"I just gave up my fucking virginity to you, you bastard, and you really thought I wouldn't be annoyed to find out that your favourite scrap of meat was still living in the castle, waiting in the wings for me to screw up enough that you got sick of me? Flaunting the fact that she, a witch, was so much more worthy of the Emperor than me a lowly criminal!"

Leviathan raked a hand through his hair and he hissed through his teeth. "Fuck Tyg, is that what you think?" He was speechless she saw herself in that light.

"Why was she still here, Leviathan? She said she was to be a concubine."

He sighed and sat down in the chair by the fire. "Tyg, she was here when we left for Arial, we found you not expecting to find you, remember, I keep saying it. I had no idea of the whirlwind that we were going to find ourselves in, I still don't even know how to explain it myself, and to arrive back here...there is so much to sort out...war plans...bloody paperwork...I forgot about her being here because she means absolutely nothing to me."

"Then why lie to me."

"I haven't." Leviathan's growl was gritty and dangerous.

Tyg stared at him expressionless, her eyes still black.

He took a deep breath and met her gaze calmly. "Tygarya..." He growled again, his tone getting deeper and more menacing. "Calm the fuck down...if you want the full story, here it is...I didn't lie when I said it was four years ago...you didn't give me time to explain...you took off so fast, and I was shocked by your vehement reaction. I took so long getting to your room because I had to talk to R'hyan and Melody and get her removed from the castle. She is R'hyan's niece, that is the only reason she is still here, here is where he lives too...I guess he hoped after one drunken night of sleeping with her I would possibly go back there, but honestly I'm seriously not interested and never actually was, and I have told her that before now. I do not know why she said that about being a concubine."

"You were drunk?" Tyg's eyes settled back to an icy blue and she sat down heavily on the bed.

Leviathan turned to regard her. "Yes."

"The Emperor, got so drunk he didn't know what he was doing when he slept with his Lord Chamberlain's niece?" Tyg was still not going to let this go...she hadn't really cared if he had slept with women before her...hell it was obvious he had, but to have one under her nose...not happening.

Leviathan rubbed his eyes with the fingers of one hand as he tipped his head back onto the back of the chair. "Does it really matter, Tyg, seriously? Whatever she said to you wasn't true, I have no intention of having concubines...I sleep with one woman at a time, always have."

Tyg stared at him silently again. No if it was in the past it didn't matter, she had just said so to herself and to Melody.

"No." Tyg muttered. Leviathan lifted his head and glanced over at her. She was sitting with her head down, then as he watched she collapsed back with a loud huff, throwing her arms out, over the bed. He noticed she was barefoot and wondered briefly how a shackle would look around her ankle.

Leviathan smiled to himself and picked up the Volka bottle and took a swig of it, flinching at the strength of it. "Was that so hard to admit?" He wiped his mouth on the back of his sleeve.

"Don't push it." Tyg growled. "If it wasn't for the fact that she challenged me on it, I had already told her I didn't care about the past."

"She challenged you on it?" Leviathan got up and walked over. He stood in front of her, his knees lined up with hers as he looked down at her prone form sprawled on the bed.

"Yeah, I asked her if she thought she could compete with me, and her fucking witchy eyes flashed at me."

"So you grabbed her round the throat..." Leviathan scratched his jaw. "Not the story I got from her."

"Ha! I bet...must have been a good night for her to cling on to hope for four years calling herself a concubine." Tyg said as she lifted up on her elbows looking at Leviathan with a silly grin, then the grin slipped from her face and she bit her lip as she looked over his fine form towering above her.

He appraised her sultry little lip bite and chuckled. "You're drunk, Tygarya, sleep it off."

179

"Why...I'm not sleepy...in fact I'm quite charged up now..."

Leviathan's eyes darkened and he leaned over her. He placed a hand on her stomach and ran it up over her hot skin pulling her shirt up and exposing her stomach. He planted a kiss on it not dropping his gaze from hers. Tyg's breath hitched at the heat she felt at that soft touch. He lifted his head slightly with a cocky tilt and smiled at her. "You need release, baby?" His tone had dropped to a sultry purr.

Tyg's eyes widened and she bit her lip once more, goose bumps travelled her skin making her shiver. "Bloody hell, Leviathan, when you talk like that..."

Leviathan's eyes darkened further. "I don't hear a no..." He reached down and started undoing her belt and pants, then hooked his hands under her buttocks lifting them off the bed, so he could pull her pants down and off. Then he sank to his knees and spread her legs apart, hooking them over his shoulders and planting a kiss to her pussy as Tyg collapsed back on the bed with a moan of pure pleasure.

Leviathan had Tyg wrapped in his arms as they lay on the bed, her back firmly against his chest as he nuzzled her hair.

"You are going to wear me out Tyg if I have to start doing that every time you get yourself worked up over something silly."

"It is a good way to relax." Tyg chuckled. "But why am I the only one naked?"

"If you are not careful I'll tie you to this bed and tease you up and never let you relax and leave you here naked until I see fit to return." Leviathan growled in her ear.

Tyg shuddered and Leviathan felt it. He chuckled. "Oh baby, please let me."

"Ah, no...I don't think so." Tyg shivered against him.

Leviathan moved her hair and kissed her neck, licking up to her ear.

"I suppose I should thank you..." Tyg said as she turned and grinned up at him.

Leviathan groaned. "Do I want to know where this is heading?"

Tyg laughed. "Don't be like that, I'm not that bad am I? I wanted to thank you for not putting me in the same rooms as all those other women in the castle."

It was Leviathan's turn to laugh and he chuckled against her throat. "I'm not a stupid man, that would have been very reckless." He sucked on her neck then kissed her mouth. "Besides, I chose this room because I can see it from my bedroom balcony." He looked at her. Plus this room is isolated and containable...

Tyg smiled. "Yes I know, I already figured that out, but tell me why I don't get to stay in your rooms? Marcius wouldn't even tell me where they were?"

"Really?" Leviathan seemed surprised. "I'll speak to him about that, if you want to be in my rooms you are most welcome, baby, in fact I was rather hoping you to be spending your nights with me when I am not busy. These rooms are just a space of your own that I thought you would appreciate."

Tyg smiled. "Baby in the bedroom..." Tyg muttered to herself.

Leviathan grinned against her as he continued to kiss her neck. "Problem?"

"No."

"I didn't think so." Leviathan sat up giving her rump a playful smack. "Now if you can promise to finally behave, I need to go back to my work. Is this little problem resolved?"

"Yes...alright. I might nap..." She stretched languidly and grabbed a pillow nesting it under her chin.

"Best you do, because I'm looking forward to tonight, Tygarya." He grinned as his eyes shone with his power.

21

"Why is this pompous ass telling me I can't go into the city?"

"Tygarya...nice to see you too." Leviathan said with an exasperated sigh, frowning as he looked up from his desk and put his elbow on the desk resting his head on his hand, to see Tyg storm into his office followed by the quaking steward not an hour later.

Leviathan's Lord Chamberlain, R'hyan shook his head. "And he is correct, you can't just go wandering off into the city without proper protocols, Lady Tygarya. You have to go escorted, you are basically the Emperor's consort now...you may have had freedom to come and go as you liked in your previous life but not here." He said it stiffly still reeling from the morning's encounter regarding his niece and first day of the onslaught that was the Elvian princess raised as an assassin.

"Consort!" Tyg scoffed making Leviathan raise an eyebrow at her.

"Well, that is the polite term...even though we aren't married." Leviathan said amused. "What would you like to be known as?" Tyg looked at him, her eyes blazing. "Tygarya, calm down. You can go, just let the Lord Chamberlain organise it." Leviathan said in that low tone. "I'm hardly going to let you just wander off by yourself regardless, so get that idea out of your head right now or I'll assign you with a permanent guard."

"Fine." Tyg huffed after a stare down with Leviathan for a few seconds, much to the relief of everyone in the room, and sat down in a leather chair.

"What do you want in the city anyway?" Leviathan asked her leaning back in his chair and waving the Steward and the Chamberlain away. They both bowed and left, closing the door.

"I wanted to find a leather worker..."

"What for exactly? We have one that works for the army exclusively...I could send for him?"

"Oh really?" Tyg looked up at him. "Well, that's okay then...but I still want to go..."

Leviathan smiled. "I understand...you're curious about the city." "Yes!"

"Tell you what...tomorrow is Farmers market, they have a fair and music and entertainment...I'll take you."

"Really? That would be nice." Tyg smiled beguilingly at him.

"No, it isn't...I have a request of you though." Leviathan smirked.

"What's that?" Tyg asked suspiciously.

"That you look like what people expect when they see you."

"The Emperor's consort." Tyg muttered sarcastically causing Leviathan to frown.

"Tygarya, must you..." He said weary.

"It's bad enough you call me 'yours' like I'm property...but for everyone else to think the same thing...it's degrading."

Leviathan chuckled. "Actually, Tygarya, it's for your safety...knowing what you are to me makes everyone think twice about doing anything to you."

Tyg stared at him, he didn't get it. She was hardly some princess from a faraway land, she could look after herself better than most. She sighed and gave up. "Fine, whatever I have to do to get to see the city..." Tyg frowned. "...you mean wear a dress right?"

Leviathan chuckled. "Right."

"Okay...I can do that."

"Good, now come here." Leviathan held his hand out to Tyg and she stood up and walked over to him. He grabbed her arm and pulled her down onto his lap in the chair, sliding his hand round the back of her neck and kissed her.

"Leviathan..."

He smirked. "Yes, Tygarya."

"Can I ask you a question without you getting all cranky and possessive like you do?"

Leviathan raised an eyebrow at her as he leaned away putting his elbow on the chair arm and leaned his cheek on his knuckles. He lifted his other hand from her neck and grabbed a lock of her hair as he meet her eyes and inhaled its scent. That seemed to be his go to as his permission to continue.

"Where is Antyn?"

Leviathan looked at her surprised a moment then his eyes darkened. "Why do you care?"

"Don't be like that, he's your brother...I just haven't seen him since you sent him home from that town after Beltain and he's my teacher..."

"He is at his house."

"Wait, what? He has a house?"

"Yes, Tygarya..." Leviathan sounded bored as he twirled her hair around his fingers. "He does, at the university."

"Oh..." Tyg said surprised with a smile. "Surrounded by books..."

Leviathan raised his head and smiled. "Would you like to go to see the University?"

"Yes, please." Tyg beamed a truly beautiful smile at him.

"I'll send Antyn a message...an olive branch...okay?"

Tyg kissed his lips. "That's nice."

Leviathan smirked and grabbed a fistful of hair and pulled her face back to his. "No, it really isn't." He kissed her deeply as his other hand undid the buttons on her shirt and slipped in to grasp her breast.

It was a short time later that a knock sounded on the door and the guard stuck his head in.

"Lord Chamberlain, my Liege." The guard announced with wide eyes as he stared at the scene in front of him before hastily down casting his eyes. Leviathan had his booted feet up on the desk and was leaning back in the massive leather chair reading.

Leviathan wasn't even looking at him. "Yes, let him in."

As Lord R'hyan entered he halted. "Ah, my Liege, I can come back..."

"Don't bother yourself R'hyan, just get used to it." Leviathan said amused as he looked up from the papers he was reading with a smirk. He stroked the top of Tyg's head as she lay curled up on his lap and chest. "You will come to value these calm times." Leviathan chuckled to himself and placed the papers on the desk. R'hyan noticed the soft glow in the Emperor's eyes and swallowed hard. "So what can I do for you?"

"General Barrock is wanting to do an inspection of the new troops in training with you as soon as possible."

Leviathan sighed. "Right, well how about dawn tomorrow?" He casually lay an arm over Tyg's body, resting his hand on her thigh. R'hyan swallowed and averted his eyes. Dressed as she was in all black leather she looked like a pet black cat getting petted by its master.

"Very well, my Liege, I shall let him know...also we need to revisit our conversation from earlier regarding Lady Tygarya's trip into the city tomorrow."

"Do we?"

"Yes, my Liege, I was just trying to organise the guard."

Leviathan smirked. "Don't go crazy R'hyan, she can look after herself, plus I'll be there. Enough to hold back the crowd, a couple of additional warlocks from my Royal Guard and a couple of Elite tagging along should be fine. Let's not cause too much of a fuss, this isn't a formal visit and I don't want it announced. I want it to be seen for what it is, I'm taking my beautiful young lover out to spoil her a little." He looked wistful as he stroked his hand over Tyg's hair.

"Very well, my Liege." R'hyan answered with a stiff bow. "It will help the public to see you in a different, more congenial light with a beautiful woman on your arm."

"Oh, there's something else you can do too." Leviathan said as he picked up a lock of Tyg's hair and started twirling it through his fingers.

"My Liege?"

"Send someone to Antyn's and tell him I'll be round to see him with Tygarya tomorrow so he had better clean up his act."

"My Liege...so you have seen the report?"

"Yes, R'hyan...next time just put it on the top, don't try and hide it in amongst other papers. I will deal with my brothers drunken bouts of stupidity as needed."

"My Liege." R'hyan bowed again and went to leave. "Oh and Master Migel is here waiting for you, my Liege."

"Good, send him in."

Leviathan grabbed Tyg's shoulder and gently shook her. "Tygarya, time to get up." His eyes glowed and she stirred and sat up. Leviathan put his feet on the floor, keeping an arm around her waist.

A man walked into the room and bowed low. "My Liege." His head remained bowed and his eyes on the floor as Tyg turned around in Leviathan's lap and regarded the man curiously.

He was middle aged, with a massive burly chest and some of the biggest forearms Tyg had ever seen.

"Master Migel here, is our resident Leather Master Craftsmen." Migel finally straightened up, not knowing where to look with the beautiful silver haired maiden sitting on the Emperor's lap.

"Oh...okay...that was fast, thank you."

Leviathan smiled at her as she stood up and walked around the desk, holding her hand out to Migel. "Pleased to meet you. I'm Tygarya..." Tyg said cheerfully.

"And I you, miss." Migel looked a little confused as to why this young girl was introducing herself to him. "Master Migel." He looked at her hand nervously, Tyg frowned and dropped it remembering the no touching law.

"So you work with leather, make the army uniforms?"

"Mostly, miss, I have workers and apprentices."

"But you're the best?"

"It would be boastful of me to say so..." Migel said with a wry smile.

Leviathan was sitting, leaning back in his chair one leg bent up with the ankle over the knee of his other leg, he had an amused lopsided grin on his face. "He is the best, Tygarya, that's why he works for me."

"I thank you for your kind words, my Liege." Master Migel said bowing his head.

Tyg looked at Leviathan with a frown. "Something wrong, dearest?" Leviathan asked as he scratched his jaw with his thumb.

"This is all a little too formal, with all the belly scraping that goes on how the hell do you actually ever get anything done around here?"

Leviathan laughed as Migel gulped in fright. "Oh, my dearest, you certainly are not one to mince words are you..." Leviathan turned to Migel. "You have my permission to be frank, open and honest, master, just relax...would you like a drink?"

Tyg saw Migel visibly relax as his shoulders hunched slightly. "Yes, my Liege, that would be wonderful."

"Good...Tygarya...pour this man a drink." Leviathan indicated over to the far side where the drinks cabinet was. Tyg grinned and went and poured three drinks. She handed Leviathan his one first, with a slight bow of her head. She fluttered her eyelashes at him. His eyes were deeply amused and darkened slightly. "Thank you, baby."

Tyg stiffened and bit her lip but recovered and went back and retrieved the other two drinks. She handed one to Migel and indicated for him to sit in the chair in front of Leviathan's massive ornate desk. Tyg sat in the other one.

Migel took a shaky sip and regarded the two powerful individuals before him. He had already had a quick run down from the gossip mill about the girl, the soldiers that accompanied them on the trip from Asbel had plenty to say regarding her explosive nature and the many fights her and the Emperor had had describing them as torrid love spats that could destroy the world. He was very wary as he glanced from one to the other furtively.

Leviathan raised his glass to his lips and regarded Tyg over the rim. "Everyone is waiting for you...you are the one who wanted him here."

Tyg flashed an annoyed glance at Leviathan. "Yes, I know that...let the man have a drink first...he clearly needs to relax."

Migel just about choked on his drink as he heard the way the girl spoke to the Emperor. He suddenly really didn't want to be here. He looked up at her. "Please, miss...tell me how I can be of assistance to you?"

"Okay...see these pants I'm wearing...I need more made, and I need a couple of tops to go with them, like I see some of the army wearing...a jerkin type and also I need a harness designed and made that can carry two swords...across each other...on my back."

Migel's eyes just about popped out of his head and he glanced at Leviathan who had sat up. His eyes gone dangerously dark.

"Tygarya...why the hell would you be needing all that?"

Tyg looked at Leviathan. "I'm trying out a new look..."

"No, you're fucking not. You're not an assassin anymore, Tygarya, you don't need to dress like one or carry weapons." Leviathan could picture the look in his head now and although he liked what he imagined he did not like the thought of anyone else seeing it nor the thought of her walking around ready to kill at a moments notice.

"Leviathan." Tyg said through gritted teeth. "I will wear what I want to and that includes my weapons...I want them back."

"No, you won't. You belong to me so wear what I want." Leviathan's tone dropped and Tyg's eyes narrowed. Migel quivered in his seat.

"I do my part for you, Leviathan...I wear a fucking dress when you ask it of me, I wear leather any other time now, what's the problem? The weapons? I am not giving them up, you wear them."

Leviathan's eyes narrowed too. Having her wearing her small arsenal could cause problems, but it might be better for her if she actually did. "Those sketch books that maid did of dresses...did you bring them with you?"

Tyg frowned confused. "Yes...but..."

"Go and get them."

"Now?" Tyg didn't get where this was going at all.

"Yes, Tygarya...now...we will wait." Leviathan sank back into his seat with his drink in hand looking smug.

Tyg stood up looking at Leviathan with a perplexed look and left the room. Leviathan called the guard to get R'hyan in there immediately.

R'hyan's office was adjacent Leviathan's so he was there in no time. He bowed and looked curiously at Master Migel. "My Liege?"

"R'hyan, go find me the best dressmaker, seamstress - whatever they're called - that this city has...and bring her to this office...now!"

R'hyan flinched and bowed. "At once, my Liege."

As he left Leviathan leaned back in his chair with a mischievous glint in his eye. "She thinks she's so smart..." He muttered with a glance at Master Migel and winked at him. Migel chuckled nervously into his glass and gulped back the whiskey not knowing what the hell was going on. This was a side of the Emperor never seen by outsiders.

Moments later Tyg returned and nervously handed Leviathan two small notebooks. As she returned to her seat Leviathan started flipping through them. As she watched him she saw his eyes get darker and darker, he flicked his eyes up to her several times as both she and Master Migel sat in confused silence. Tyg stopped breathing at the hungry look in those eyes.

"Tygarya..." Leviathan said in a deep raspy voice that made her shiver. "Some of these are..." Leviathan paused as he closed his eyes and shuddered. Tyg's eyes went wide as the implications of what was about to happen suddenly dawned on her.

"Leviathan..." Tyg went to hastily say.

"Quiet." He muttered with a warning look. Tyg chewed on her bottom lip, suddenly very nervous, while she waited. He grinned at her with that vulture gaze penetrating her.

The guard knocked on the door and opened it sticking his head through. "Lord Chamberlain R'hyan has returned with the woman, my Liege."

Tyg frowned and looked at the door. "Let them in." Leviathan said cheerfully as he stood up.

R'hyan walked in with a tall elegant looking woman with grey hair tied back in a bun. She wore a simple dark grey dress with a white pinafore over the top. The pockets of which looked full of interesting items like tape, scissors, pencils and – Tyg noticed – a measuring tape.

Tyg groaned and sank down into her chair, gripping her temples with the fingers of one hand so that her face was hidden. She heard Leviathan chuckle as he walked up and took the lady's hand as R'hyan introduced her.

"This is Mistress Hermione Daughtry, said to be the leading seamstress in the entire city, my...ah...niece recommends her highly." He glanced awkwardly at Tyg.

Leviathan kissed the lady's hand and pulled her by it over to his desk as Tyg groaned again.

"Mistress Daughtry, what a lovely pleasure it is to meet you. I had just one simple question that I needed you to answer for me." Leviathan said as he picked up one of the notebooks and opened it to a certain page. "Can you make this?"

Mistress Daughtry's eyes went wide and she grabbed the book. "Oh my! I've never seen...oh my goodness..." Her eyes came up and looked at Leviathan. "Your majesty, this dress is quite different from the fashion of today...who...?" He smiled and pointed to Tyg. Her eyes went even wider. "Oh my." She said again as Tyg grumbled under her breath and folded her arms giving them both a surly look.

"So? Can you make it or not?" Leviathan asked with a growl. "Her measurements are conveniently on the front page..."

"Yes...yes...I believe so, your Majesty." She bowed her head low as Leviathan took the notebook back and turned to another page and handed it back.

"And this one?"

Mistress Daughtry was speechless but nodded. Leviathan took the notebook back and put it on the desk grabbing the other one and opening that. "And this one?"

"Oh for fuck's sake, Leviathan, what is your deal?" Tyg muttered annoyed, her eyes blazing.

Mistress Daughtry quailed at Tyg's language in front of the Emperor but meekly nodded her head to his question.

"Good, thank you Mistress Daughtry, you will be hearing from my Lord Chamberlain in the next day or so no doubt." Leviathan dismissed her and R'hyan with a wave of his hand. R'hyan took the lady's elbow and steered her shaking body from the room. Leviathan sat down in his chair looking very pleased with himself as he straightened the two notebooks in his hands then put them securely in a drawer.

"Here's the deal, Tygarya..." His tone was serious as he leaned his forearms on the desk, his hands clasped together. Tyg sat up gritting her teeth, as Migel looked fearful once again. "You may have your leather outfits and your sword harness and whatever else your beautiful angelic heart desires, my dear." The silvery way Leviathan said it made even Migel shiver. "But..."

Tyg rolled her eyes. "Here it comes."

Leviathan's eyes went dark. "Oh, you didn't just roll your eyes at me, did you, Tygarya?" He growled with pure venom suddenly, cutting off his own sentence. "How delectable." The words rolled off his tongue in a thrum of contentment.

Tyg looked at him with wide eyes, that voice she knew only too well, the one that said playtime was over. "I'm sorry...I didn't realise..." Miguel glanced sideways at the girl to suddenly hear real fear creep into her voice.

"Too late..." Leviathan grinned mercilessly at her.

"Okay..." Tyg looked down at her lap sulkily, biting her lip making Leviathan growl deep in his throat at the sudden submission. "Continue what you were going to entrap me with."

Leviathan smiled at that. "Entrap you with...yes indeed." Tyg's eyes came back up to his, glowing ice blue once again in defiance. Migel was watching with terrified fascination...how the hell were these two supposedly lovers?

"I have decided Tygarya, like I just said, to let you have your outfits...but you will let me have mine...so for every outfit you have master Migel and his workers make for you...or anyone make for you..." Tyg frowned, damn, she had thought that was a loophole. "I will have Mistress Daughtry make one of these dresses for you also."

"Bastard." Tyg muttered, but her top lip twitched. Leviathan saw it and smiled.

"I'm glad we could come to an arrangement. Now I think it's about time you let master Migel run back to his workshop."

"Hmm." Tyg snorted and glanced at Migel. "We didn't even get an answer out of him whether he could or would do it?"

"Oh yes, my Lady, I can do anything you need." Grateful to be leaving.

"Great." Tyg said in a monotone, all the pleasure of it being taken away now.

"If you would like to come by sometime we can discuss it in detail and I can design what you want."

"Thank you, Migel." Tyg said with a soft smile.

Migel stood up and put the glass down self-consciously on the edge of Leviathan's desk. He bowed low to Leviathan. "My Liege."

"Master Migel, it's been a pleasure." Leviathan grinned. Migel froze for a second, he had never seen the Emperor smile before. Perhaps this twisted game was love...

Tyg looked at Leviathan as Migel left and found him watching her intently with that vulture gaze. "Was that altogether necessary?" She asked with a flinty tone.

"Yes."

"Do you need to make everything between us this game of control?"

"It's not a game, Tygarya...I have control, the sooner you realise that the better. This request should have been brought to me so we could discuss it."

"Argh!" Tyg rolled her eyes and stood up.

"Tygarya...seriously!" Leviathan growled in a husky voice.

"Gods, Leviathan, you say I mood swing but you mood swing faster than a hormonal pregnant woman with twins!" Tyg spat out. Leviathan laughed and threw himself back in his chair. "Oh and just so you know, you may think you have won by getting those dresses made, but you need to ask yourself one question, Mr Control Freak?"

"Oh, what's that?" Leviathan asked highly amused.

"Does your possessive control freak self really want other people seeing me in some of those dresses?" She smirked. "I'm going to the libraries!" She muttered as she went to the door.

Leviathan snorted. "I might just make you wear them in the bedroom, just so I can rip them off you and ravage that amazing body of yours."

Tyg halted as she inhaled sharply and stared at him. She didn't know how to respond to that blatant sexual comment, she was far too inexperienced and he seemed to enjoy shocking her with his vast repertoire. "Sadist." She muttered.

Leviathan grinned at her his eyes dark and glittering. "I think you figured that out a little too late to save yourself...pleasure doing business with you, my dear and remember you also owe me for two eye rolls later tonight, which I will enjoy taking out on your flesh." Leviathan said as Tyg swung the door shut.

"Damn you!" Tyg muttered on the outside of the door and stormed off down the hall with the guards watching her amused.

22

Tyg was summoned by a servant to dinner later that evening when she failed to show before the first course was due to be served.

She was still feeling a little put out by Leviathan's manipulation that afternoon and it was clear on her face as she entered the dining room. Leviathan's eyes narrowed slightly at the pouty expression, seeing that she wouldn't look him in the eye. Instead her eyes wandered around the room, the walls were a dark sensual red with black wood framing. The only thing in the room was the large dining table and great paintings on the walls, the biggest paintings Tyg had ever seen. They were strangely erotic with naked women lounging on day beds with fruit and wine being fed to them by burly sinister looking men leaning over them with leery looks. There were three paintings on three walls, the fourth wall was windowed and heavily draped with matching velvet curtains, now drawn closed.

"Get that look off your face before I bend you over this table and spank you, Tygarya." Leviathan's deep voice made her gaze slide to him as she sat down in the chair held out by the butler. The butler baulked with his gaze to the floor.

Tyg looked up at him and gave him a small smile. "What sort of room is this?" She muttered in question to try and deviate the conversation.

Leviathan chuckled. "You like it?"

"Not particularly...why do you have such paintings in a room where a person is supposed to have the appetite to eat?"

Leviathan rubbed his jaw, his smirk amused and relaxed. "They were a favourite of my father, same with the room colour...I don't know, I quite like them."

Tyg looked away and back to the painting on the wall in front of her. "Really? I would have thought it would be Antyn that liked them."

"Quite right." Leviathan laughed, lifting his wine glass after the butler had poured his drink. "Actually they were painted by a very famous painter from Gua Del Mar. They are very expensive."

"Still better in a sex dungeon than in a dining room..." Tyg watched the butler pour her drink and he glanced up at her with a twinge of his lips at that comment. She smirked back at him and raised her glass to her lips enjoying the deep rich burgundy. "I do like the colour of the walls though..." She held her glass up comparing the colour in the glass to the walls.

"Hmm..." Leviathan snorted, amused. "I think the colour would look good on you, perhaps I shall get Miss Daughtry to find a fabric of that colour for one of those dresses."

Tyg flicked him a sour look. She already had a dress of this colour thanks to Lord Kor.

He grinned at the reaction then the smile slid from his face. "How do you know about sex dungeons?"

Tyg baulked a little at the slight change in his tone. She put her glass down and gave him a straight forward look. "I know about such things but I'm lucky to have never seen the inside of one."

Leviathan leaned on his forearms, giving her an interested and intense look. "Do tell..."

Tyg watched as the butler came back in, announcing the soup course as two young women came in carrying their first course and placed them down, bowed and left.

She lifted her spoon and dipped it into the creamy soup, tasting it.

"Tygarya..." Leviathan prompted.

"You seriously want to hear stories about my time as an assassin?"

"I have been wanting to know more about that side of you for a while now." He said with genuine interest, leaning back in his seat and taking his wine glass with him.

Tyg stared at her soup for a long moment before speaking. "Palin took me to another city called Annul because he found out there was a Lord there that was going to become the Lord Mayor and that couldn't be allowed to happen. He liked young girls, ones with something special about them, exotic." Tyg lifted her gaze to Leviathan to find him looking raptured in her story but grim. "I'm talking young girls...Palin hated that sort of thing and took it personal."

"He never tried to touch you?"

"No, never!" Tyg looked insulted and Leviathan's mouth twisted.

"I guess he knew what you were so..."

"What's that supposed to mean?"

"You could have killed him at any time, Tygarya, he wasn't that good of a swordsman, not compared to you."

Tyg looked a little startled then dropped her gaze back to her soup and started running her spoon through it lethargically.

"You knew you could take him, why didn't you?"

"Why would I? He was my boss, I had made an oath to stay loyal to him. He had never done me wrong, saved me from a life in a brothel or a slave."

"Hmm..." Leviathan snorted derisively knowing that would never have happened and sat forward taking up his spoon, dipping it in his soup and putting it in his mouth a couple of times before looking back at her. He could just imagine what would have happened if anyone had tried to get Tyg into a brothel, it would have been a blood bath, maybe Palin knew that too. "So, you were sent in as bait to this man?"

"Yeah...it was the only way to get close to him so I could kill him." Tyg looked away like something was bothering her.

Leviathan frowned at the strange look on her face. "It all went smoothly, no problems?" His voice had taken on a harsh edge and Tyg looked back at him with a sardonic smile.

"He never touched me, if that's your concern."

"Of course it's my concern. You belong to me, I don't like the thought of any man touching you before me."

Tyg stared at him for a moment then started giggling under her breath, covering her mouth with her hand. "You're too much."

His eyes darkened instantly. "Why?"

"You've had other women, yet you're so perversely happy that I was a virgin."

His frown was dark and dangerous as he glared at her. "Tygarya..." He growled but then fell silent as the butler returned to check if they were ready for the next course.

Leviathan dropped back in his seat and waved his hand. "Take it away..." He sounded annoyed and Tyg gave him a little frown. Neither of them had taken more than a few spoonsful of the soup.

She remained silent and let the maid come back and take her bowl, replacing it with a plate with a thick slab of steak with steaming vegetables.

Tyg grinned at the succulent looking steak, something she couldn't afford to eat back home very often. She picked up her knife and fork with great enthusiasm.

"You like steak?" Leviathan asked, his tone mellowing out as he decided to drop their last conversation.

"Hmm..." She thrummed as she sliced off a chunk and stuck it in her mouth. Her face lit up with joy as she chewed and she gurgled a moan in her throat as her eyes rolled back in her head.

"That good?" Leviathan commented with a husky chuckle. "I might get jealous of the steak if you groan like that..."

Tyg looked up from under her lashes with a smoky look as she slowly took the steak off her fork and grinned as she chewed.

Leviathan's eyes went dark and broody instantly as he put his cutlery down and reached out a hand to grab her chin. "Do that again and this dinner will be over, I haven't forgotten that a punishment is due to you."

Tyg pulled her head back with a jolt. "You were serious?"

He smirked to see the worry in her eyes as he calmly picked up his cutlery and resumed eating. "Deadly, you will learn. I will teach you."

"Teach me what exactly?" Tyg asked with trepidation creeping into her stomach.

Leviathan chewed his steak in silence for a long moment watching Tyg's mind ticking over with growing disquiet as she stared at him waiting for an answer.

He smirked cockily as he licked his lips. "You'll have to wait and see."

Tyg grabbed her wine and took a large swig of it, looking into the glass and swirling the contents around as she frowned. "You're not going to do that head thing, are you?"

Leviathan gave her a heavy look. "No, far from it..."

"So you're not actually planning to hurt me?" She seemed relieved.

Leviathan's chuckle was dark making her stomach stir again. "Oh, Tygarya...it wouldn't be a punishment without a little bit of pain, now would it?"

Her eyes narrowed in a challenge. "And you think I'm just going to go along with this punishment?"

He placed his cutlery down again, piercing her with that vulture gaze. "You will."

Tyg scoffed and deliberately rolled her eyes to the ceiling. "I highly doubt that!"

Leviathan was up and out of his chair in the blink of an eye grabbing Tyg by the wrist and yanking her from her seat making it fall back as he lifted her up onto his shoulder and stalked to the door.

Tyg struggled against his biting grip around her thighs, banging her fists into his back. "Put me down!"

"I warned you." His voice dripped with deadly intent and he smacked her backside hard. "Now stay still!"

Tyg yelped at the force of the smack and tried to get some leverage, until he smacked her again even harder.

"I told you to stay still unless you want to feel the bite of my power!" His growl reverberated through her making her pause.

She heard voices mutter "majesties' and she looked up as Leviathan kept walking to see both R'hyan and Marcuis standing in the hall looking shocked.

"I'll be retiring to my rooms for the remainder of the night, no disturbances!" Leviathan bit out as he walked away. Tyg saw both men quail and bow their heads flicking strange sympathetic glances up at her as she strained to lift her head to look back at them.

Shit, this did seem quite serious...

23

"Tygarya time to get up."

Leviathan walked out of the privy room and pulled the blankets off of Tyg who had snuggled back down and gone back to sleep after Leviathan had already told her once to get up. She loved Leviathan's bed and his room, when he had forcefully carried her here in front of the Chamberlain and Steward and taken her roughly in this very bed the night before she had seen their faces and knew women had never been taken to his rooms before, even the servants around his private tower were all male. It was a deeply masculine room, dark and brooding, just like him, but the bed...the bed was huge. It had to be the biggest bed Tyg had ever seen and the most comfortable, with a lovely semi soft mattress that you sunk into just the right amount with wonderful fluffy duvets that Tyg loved to snuggle up under her chin. She had never known such luxury and she definitely intended to spend a lot more time in this bed, Leviathan or not and regardless of the fact that he had done terrible things to her body as punishment for her indiscretions that day. No, terrible wasn't the right word...Tyg blushed to think back, she had no idea how to put last night into words, but the worst thing about it was she hadn't entirely hated it.

It was barely dawn and Leviathan had already been up for an hour, being woken by his manservant as requested, early so he could go and meet with General Barrock on the parade grounds and inspect the troops during training. These men were soon to be sent to Enyana to bolster the troops already there as Leviathan started his next campaign through to Kolastan, planning for a summer campaign once the heavy spring rains had dried up. Hence the trip to Arial to procure more steel grade iron to make more weapons that weren't prone to cracking or snapping in half.

"Why do I have to get up? They're your troops so go and inspect them." Tyg said in a surly voice as she sat up and grabbed the blankets pulling them back over her.

"Don't you dare lie back down, Tygarya...I'm warning you!" Leviathan growled. Tyg heard someone out in the lounge room of Leviathan's quarters. "That's breakfast...get up or I swear I will smack that firm little ass of yours until you can't sit down this time!"

"Alright...alright." Tyg grumbled and shifted over to the edge of the bed and put her feet on the floor. Knowing full well it didn't matter what he did to her she would heal quickly from it. She looked at her wrists, she could almost still feel the burn of the ropes he had used to suppress her, but no sign of them remained now. She remembered Leviathan had been very happy about that.

She only had the clothes she was wearing the night before in here so she picked them up off the floor and redressed in them. Lucky for her it wasn't a dress.

As Tyg moved through into the vast lounge room she saw Leviathan's manservant bow towards her. She smiled at him and walked up to Leviathan. He was sitting at a small table under a window, it was just big enough to sit two people, one at each end, and was the perfect place to enjoy an intimate breakfast. The view out the window was breath taking. It was the last tower of the castle and the northern most window, so the views were unobstructed as this tower was built straight up out of the bedrock which plummeted down a craggy rock face for a hundred feet, the most impenetrable side of the whole castle.

As Tyg sat down and grabbed a piece of buttered toast she gazed out the window at the lightening sky as the sun slowly rose.

"So why exactly do I have to come with you?"

Leviathan levelled a cool gaze at her over a cup of steamy coffee. "Because I order it of you, is that not answer enough for you? Even after last night's lesson?"

Tyg glanced at him and caught the look. "Fine..." Tyg looked back out the window, blushing a little.

"Oh, and wear your sword." Leviathan muttered casually, his eyes not leaving her face.

Tyg turned back to him, her eyes wide. "What? Really? You mean you're going to let me be armed in your presence? Am I going to train?"

"No, not train...not today, my dearest...but Ra'chek will take some persuading to allow you to enter his training grounds."

Tyg grinned. "A demonstration then?"

Leviathan smirked. "If you like."

Tyg stood up. "I better go get it then..."

"Hurry back." Leviathan watched her sprint from the room, his eyes dark and contemplative. Today was going to be a big day even bigger than last night had been for her, his control was starting to take effect and she was so far accepting it with flying colours.

As Leviathan stepped out onto the training grounds, Ra'chek had several soldiers lined up in tidy inspection lines. Tyg followed along behind Leviathan, wearing her black assassin's clothing and her daggers and sword. She felt the most comfortable she had in a while, finally being allowed to bear arms again in Leviathan's presence, she had even braided up her hair, something she also had not been able to do very often since the event with the mercenary.

As Leviathan stepped up to Ra'chek and the other officer that was standing beside him Tyg noticed both of them stare at her with unbridled distain.

"Wow, feel the vibes." Tyg muttered as she folded her arms and looked around the training ground. It was a large quad of bare hard packed earth. On the outside of the main castle buildings on the eastern side of the castle, it was on a tier of land specifically designed for its purpose. The surrounding buildings were the quarters of the soldiers housed at the castle and Leviathan had told Tyg earlier that the castle housed up to one thousand troops at any one time, called a Regiment, that was usually under the control of a Colonel and his under officers, however General Barrock was in attendance to oversee training of an extra 1500 troops that were there at the moment due to the impending invasion of Kolastan. It was from these fresh troops that Ra'chek, the Master Trainer, had summoned for inspection by the Emperor himself. Tyg looked over the troops and estimated that there were perhaps one hundred of them standing before them, the best ones, she surmised. When they approached the edge of the grounds Tyg saw the practise areas were terraced down the hillside and on every ground stood soldiers at attention.

"Shush." Leviathan breathed at Tyg's sarcastic comment as he looked out over the soldiers below.

Tyg sighed and looked back at Commander Ra'chek and General Barrock as they both bowed their heads to Leviathan as he approached them and focused on the soldiers in front of him.

"My Liege." They both said, keeping their heads bowed. Tyg noticed the soldiers didn't move, but kept standing to attention, their focus unwavering even in the presence of their monarch.

"At ease." Leviathan said to the two officers. They both straightened and Ra'chek's jaw clenched as he regarded Tyg.

"My Liege, women are not allowed here."

Leviathan settled his vulture gaze upon Ra'chek. "By whose authority?" He asked in a cold dangerous tone. Ra'chek's eyes went wide as he realised his mistake and bowed his head again.

"My apologies, my Liege."

"Hmm." Leviathan snorted as he walked past Ra'chek and started looking over the lines of troops standing in front of him. General Barrock grimaced and shot Ra'chek a warning look. Ra'chek frowned and straightened once Leviathan had walked past him. Tyg smirked at him as his gaze flicked to her causing Ra'chek to clench his jaw and give her a look full of pure distaste as he took in the weapons she wore and the attire she was dressed in. General Barrock stood with one hand on the pommel of his sword giving her much the same look as she followed dutifully along behind Leviathan looking around with curiosity. To them she looked like nothing more than a pet dutifully following its master.

Leviathan turned and regarded Ra'chek and Barrock a moment then grabbed Tyg's hand and pulled her forward.

"This, Commanders...is Lady Tygarya Essyndyl, my betrothed...she is also half Elvian, the last of her kind."

Tyg grimaced as Leviathan pulled her forward, she hated being put in the spot light. At the mention of her being Elvian Tyg saw the looks on both commanders' faces turn dark and dangerous and Barrock tightened the grip on his sword. Tyg felt the whole troop of soldiers stiffen at the word.

"My Liege?" General Barrock exclaimed. "What is the meaning of this?"

Leviathan regarded Barrock intently. "Exactly what do you mean, General?"

"Elvians are to be killed on sight, my Liege, you know this?"

"I know nothing of the sort, General..." Leviathan stepped in front of Tyg as she gasped at hearing what Barrock said. "The war is long over and that law was put in force in my father's day...I no longer condone or validate it, besides they are all gone..."

Barrock's eyes widened and he bowed his head. "My Liege..."

Leviathan smirked and turned to Ra'chek. "Do we have a problem?"

Ra'chek bowed his head, gritting his teeth. "No, my Liege."

"Good, then let it be known that if anyone takes offense to Lady Tygarya being here, they take offense personally to me...understood?" Leviathan's eyes were glowing intensely. Both commanders swallowed hard, everyone knew the penalty of offending the Emperor was death.

"Yes, my Liege." They both stammered.

"Very well, let's see a demonstration from these newly trained soldiers then shall we?"

"Certainly, my Liege." Ra'chek said as he stepped up to the soldiers and started barking orders. Leviathan grabbed Tyg's hand and stepped back to allow Ra'chek to lead a demonstration. General Barrock stood beside Leviathan, one hand still resting on his sword the other tucked behind his back.

They watched for several minutes as Ra'chek led the soldiers through drills, making them do press ups and other such exercises then take their swords out and go through the motions of certain sword strokes and steps. Leviathan watched silent as a statue his vulture gaze never wavering.

"General..." Leviathan suddenly spoke, causing Barrock to straighten to attention and clip his heels together. "Go and get Ra'chek to break this up into groups and get them to do some proper sparring, this display is telling me nothing more than these men can learn a few dance steps."

"At once, my Liege." Barrock inclined his head and strode over to where Ra'chek was standing.

"I can tell you what it tells me." Tyg muttered bored.

Leviathan glanced at her with an eyebrow raised. "Go ahead?"

Tyg looked at him with a slight smirk. "That none of these boys are ready for killing."

"Hmm." Leviathan snorted with amusement. He said nothing else as he watched Ra'chek and Barrock split the soldiers into groups of ten and form circles around the grounds, then started sparring one on one in the centre of each circle, using wooden practise swords.

"Come..." Leviathan said to Tyg, taking her hand as he slowly walked around the grounds watching at each circle of combatants momentarily before walking to the next one and so on. Tyg noticed that Ra'chek and Barrock watched Leviathan carefully.

Tyg looked at the soldiers fighting each other and after seeing several examples couldn't help but lift her hand to stifle a yawn. Leviathan turned to her amused.

"Is this boring you?"

"Sorry..." Tyg smiled apologetically.

"Tell me your thoughts?" Leviathan dropped her hand and folded his arms, staring at her with interest.

"Oh...you really don't want my thoughts on this...trust me...it's your army." Tyg said evasively looking away and scratching at her head.

"Tygarya." Leviathan growled.

Tyg sighed and looked over to where Ra'chek was watching them, then turned and looked over to see General Barrock watching them interested also. "Look, I don't want to piss anyone off here..."

"You're starting to piss me off, Tygarya...I asked you for your thoughts."

"Fine..." Tyg almost rolled her eyes, but stopped herself with a nervous cough. Leviathan smirked at her, his eyes darkening a fraction. "It's all too static, don't you think?"

"Explain." Leviathan said intently.

"Well, look around you...everyone in every circle seems to be doing exactly the same steps...they aren't fighting, they are just going through the motions that they go through every single day...that's a fast way to get killed. No one actually fights like that."

Leviathan frowned and glanced around himself for several minutes then turned back to her. "What would you suggest?"

Tyg grinned. "They need a real fight...they need passion...they need to feel their lives are at stake...remove the wooden swords."

Leviathan's eyes widened slightly and a slow grin spread over his face. "Ra'chek!" He yelled out over the din. Tyg watched as Ra'chek came striding over and bowed his head to his Emperor.

"My Liege, is there a problem?"

"No problem, I just want the wooden swords put away and for the soldiers to fight with real steel."

"Ah...my Liege..."

"Now, Ra'chek." Leviathan growled. As Barrock strode over and stood beside Tyg, glancing down sideways at her in quiet thought. Tyg glanced up at him and smiled, showing teeth. He frowned deeply and looked away. Tyg realised suddenly that the men on this continent grew a lot taller than back home, here she didn't stand out for her height, only as a tall woman, as most soldiers seemed to start around her height and as she was soon to learn warlocks were always impressively tall.

"My Liege, this will result in injury and possibly some deaths." Barrock said firmly.

Leviathan glared at him. "What do you think will happen on the battlefield General? If these soldiers go out there fighting like these bored spectres with no idea of the passion the man coming at them has to stay alive they will all perish...they need to know what it is like to scramble against a foe just to stay alive!" Ra'chek had returned after giving the order to distribute steel swords, Leviathan turned to him. "You have been too soft on them during my absence, Ra'chek." Leviathan sounded angry and his eyes were glowing. Several soldiers that were nearby and could hear him were quaking in their boots.

"Something else..." Tyg muttered as she stepped next to Leviathan.

"Hmm?" He glanced at her.

"Have any of them fought against anything other than swords?"

Leviathan looked at Ra'chek, who was staring at Tyg with a lethal glare. He glanced at Leviathan and blinked.

"Of course!" Ra'chek said indignantly. "All of them are trained to fight with and against axes, daggers, maces, hand to hand combat... really, My Liege..." Ra'chek glanced at Tyg with meaning in his eyes that said Leviathan shouldn't be listening to her.

Leviathan's jaw clenched. "You think I shouldn't listen to an Elvian about how to fight?"

Ra'chek paled and glanced at Tyg again, she folded her arms and smirked at him, her eyes blazing into pale ice blue fire. Barrock grabbed the hilt of his sword.

"Have they learned the skills enough to be able to change fighting styles in a blink of an eye to adapt quickly to whatever comes at them?" Tyg asked confidently turning and facing Ra'chek.

"That comes with experience." Ra'chek growled.

Tyg's eyes blazed. "So you would send these young boys into battle knowing that....what...twenty...fifty percent will probably die in the first onslaught?" Tyg's voice was filled with disgust.

"Tygarya." Leviathan warned and reached out and grabbed her shoulder, pulling her closer to him to keep a tight rein on her. Taking the inert power from her that was building up.

Barrock sneered. "You obviously have never been in battle yourself, young lady." He empathised the lady. "Otherwise you would know that is just how war works, no one likes it, it is just what it is. These soldiers are expendable."

"It doesn't have to be..." Tyg growled.

"What do you mean?" Barrock growled back at her confused.

Leviathan grinned, he was very happy with this progress and he finally stepped into the discussion.

"Tygarya..." He said deathly quiet causing everyone to turn to him. Tyg looked up at him and saw his eyes looking down at her intently. "Show them."

Tyg grinned and turned to him in excitement. "Are you serious?"

"Yes."

"Really, my Liege...I must protest." Ra'chek stammered.

"Go right ahead, Ra'chek and I'll have your head on a pike at the gates!" Leviathan growled, levelling a cold deadly glare at him.

24

Tyg bounced on the balls of her feet. "I need a staff." She said matter-of-factly. Barrock grabbed the shoulder of a young man standing behind him and hauled him out of the circle he was in.

"Go and retrieve a staff...now!" He ordered the young soldier and he took off at a dead run.

Leviathan placed a hand on Tyg's shoulder again pressing her to the ground. "Settle down, baby." He muttered. "You're too excitable."

Tyg flashed him a beautiful smile and rolled her shoulders. "Do you realise how long it's been..."

"Since what?" Leviathan looked at her amused.

"Since I've been in a real fight..." Tyg was practically bursting with vivacious energy all of a sudden.

"So your pet Elvian is bloodied up then I see." General Barrock sneered, folding his arms.

Leviathan looked at him with a baleful glare. "You are lucky to be one of the few men I would take such a comment from, Barrock." Leviathan said in a deathly calm voice.

Barrock scoffed. "I just hope you know what you're doing, my Liege." He looked once again at Tyg and saw her holding her elbow with the hand of the opposite arm as she stretched out her shoulder, then changed to the other side.

The soldier returned with the staff and held it out to General Barrock with a bowed head.

Barrock looked at it with distain and indicated for the soldier to hand it to Tyg. The soldier baulked and swallowed hard as he held it out to the beautiful young girl standing in front of him giving him a most dazzlingly beautiful smile as she took the staff from his hands.

"Thank you." Tyg said cheerfully, then suddenly spun the staff around above her head, then around her back briefly and bringing it to in front of her face then bringing it to rest under her arm. Both commanders stepped back in awe at the short display. Leviathan squinted his eyes and smirked as he rubbed a thumb down his jaw. "This will do." Tyg said as she looked around.

Leviathan chuckled. "Right then....an opponent..." Leviathan looked at Ra'chek questioningly.

"I'll need four opponents." Tyg said calmly.

"What the hell?" Ra'chek blurted out enraged. "You precocious brat!"

"Ra'chek!" Leviathan warned in a deadly voice. "Why four, Tygarya?"

"This is about different fighting styles, isn't it? Let each man come at me and use a different weapon, and I'll show them how to adapt quickly and efficiently to each attack. As I deal to one, then bring in the next one."

Leviathan grinned wickedly, his eyebrows raised. "Okay."

"Are you serious!?" Ra'chek said infuriated. "She's basically saying she can beat my soldiers..."

"That's exactly what she is saying, Ra'chek." Barrock said to him annoyed. "So choose your best four men and let's get this over with."

Leviathan watched Barrock intently. "Indeed, General." Barrock raised his eyes to meet Leviathan's and didn't look away. They stared at each other for a long moment before Barrock conceded and down cast his eyes. Leviathan grinned, he was enjoying himself immensely.

Ra'chek muttered to himself as he stormed off looking for his four best soldiers, returning shortly with them in tow. Tyg looked them over, they were all young, lean well-muscled. Ra'chek called a halt to training and the other soldiers gathered around to watch the demonstration.

When the four soldiers were told what they had to do they all looked at Tyg with wonder and fear in their eyes, none of them wanted to fight a girl. Tyg grinned.

"Can I have a moment to warm up, since these boys have already had time to do that?"

"Of course, Tygarya." Leviathan said amused as he stood with Ra'chek on one side and Barrock on the other, as a large circle had been opened up. Tyg walked into the middle of the circle, holding the staff and stood still, closing her eyes for a moment to calm herself then proceeded to go through a series of moves, throwing the stick around, twirling it, twirling herself and jumping into the air, twisting and turning, smacking the staff down on the ground with astounding force that sent shock waves through the ground under nearby watchers feet. Tyg stopped after a couple of minutes to awed silence. She looked at Leviathan and walked up to him. She bowed her head to him as he watched her with amusement.

"I'm ready, my Liege." She looked back up with eyes that sparkled with life and Leviathan's darkened with lust. Tyg, breathing heavy from her exertion, grinned a lopsided smile and winked then turned away walking back to the centre of the circle. Leviathan chuckled and dropped his arms, placing his hands in his pockets confidently. He was well pleased to see that Tyg was more than willing to do his bidding without question when the time came.

Ra'chek shouted a name and a young boy no older than she was walked into the circle with a sword in his hands, he grinned widely as he approached Tyg, appraising her body up and down. Tyg grinned back, her gaze settling on his. Her eyes slowly started to turn ice blue again and blaze. The boy hesitated and turned to Ra'chek.

"Hey, no one said anything about her being a witch!" He yelled worried.

"I'm not a witch..." Tyg said deathly calm behind him.

He turned back and looked at her strangely. "What are you then?"

Tyg chuckled, the sound making every ones blood run cold. "Oh, I'm something much worse."

General Barrock hissed through his teeth. "Bloody hell." As he tightened his grip on his sword.

"Calm yourself, General, she has no power." Leviathan warned him as Tyg leaped straight at the young soldier with no warning.

"Can you control that?" Barrock asked with a tinge of fear in his voice.

"Of course I can." Leviathan scoffed.

Tyg had launched at the soldier, staff in hand and had lunged out with a jab to his face as he stepped back and whacked the staff away with a swipe of his sword. Tyg leapt into the air, placing the butt of the staff on the ground and vaulting up from it. She came down behind the soldier, back to back, turning and whacking his right arm hard then spun on her heels and whacked his left arm in the same way then spun to face him and crouching down on one leg as the other leg was extending out to the side she swept the staff out aimed at the soldier's legs. He quickly jumped and staggered backwards narrowly avoiding getting his ankle smashed. Tyg stood up and circled the staff round and rested it in the pit of her arm. She stalked around him grinning widely, as the soldier rubbed his arms from where she had bruised them. The soldier came at her, slashing and thrusting his sword. Tyg avoided all the front on swings by just dodging her upper body back and forth. She laughed and he lunged full on at her and she dodged and turned as he flew past her. She reached out with the butt of the staff on the ground and deftly tripped the soldier up. He staggered and fell and Tyg jumped on him, placing the staff around his neck as she held it from behind and pulled him up off his feet, strangling him with the staff. He flailed around clawing at the staff at his throat. Tyg growled at him.

"Use your dagger, you fool!" She placed a foot on his back and pushed him away sending him staggering forward. "You don't think quickly enough. If I had wanted you dead, I would have stuck my dagger into your kidneys just then." The soldier baulked hearing her.

Leviathan scratched his chin and glanced left and right. Both General Barrock and Ra'chek were standing with their arms folded. Ra'chek looked flushed and slightly embarrassed.

Tyg spun the staff again and the soldier went on the defensive lifting his sword and fending the staff off several times as Tyg dodged and weaved right and left, the soldier was having trouble keeping up on where she was when suddenly he was forced to his knees as Tyg's staff connected heavily with his left shoulder with an audible crack. He grunted in pain and looked up at her as she once again jumped up over him and came down behind him, placing the staff against his throat, this time the soldier had the foresight to raise his sword between Tyg's staff and his own body, blocking her from being able to strangle him again. Tyg laughed.

"Good! Now what?" Tyg asked as she kicked the soldier's knee out from under him as he tried to stand. As he was forced back to his knees, Tyg grabbed the dagger off her belt with her left hand and held it to his throat, dropping the staff, sweeping the soldiers sword down with it. She grabbed a handful of his hair pulling his head back and leaned into his ear. "I think you're dead, boy." She growled at him and then stood up shoving him face down into the dirt. She turned and looked at Leviathan with a grin.

"Next." Leviathan muttered under his breath as his eyes locked on Tyg's. Tyg bowed her head at him and turned to retrieve her staff, sheathing her dagger.

Ra'chek grumbled and called another name.

Tyg stood watching as the next young soldier came into the ring holding a short sword and a small axe. Tyg smiled in delight and stalked around the circle. He raged at her like a bull, his sword arm low and his axe hand high. Tyg appraised him, standing still till the last possible minute, standing side on to his approach, her head down, her eyes focused on him. It was hard for her to evaluate how to fight and not kill them...she was trying to keep control. As he reached her Tyg raised the staff to meet his momentum, the butt crashing into his chest as he ran full into it. He roared as he staggered back, like he just hit a wall. He lashed out and caught the staff with his sword, cutting it in two. The crowd of soldiers watching yelled in triumph. Tyg jumped away laughing, the two broken pieces of the staff now in both her hands, she changed her fighting style to two stick fighting and instantly sent a barrage of strokes against the soldier, turning and twisting and jumping at him forcing him back as he was forced to defend with axe and sword at close quarters. Tyg dropped one stick and punched the soldier in the face, breaking his nose. He stumbled back as Tyg stood still. He wiped at his face as the blood streamed down.

"You fucking bitch!" The soldier said.

Tyg laughed. "You can't fight close quarters and hold onto your weapons like that, moron." Tyg knelt down and drove the other stick into the earth, then stood up and held her arms up low inviting him forward. She was looking at him from a position where her head was down, making her look evil as she grinned at him. "Come on." She yelled at him. She held no weapon and he still held on to his axe and sword.

"She's insane." Barrock breathed as Leviathan frowned.

"Of course she is, she's Elvian." Ra'chek said as he spat on the ground. "They hold no fear of death."

The soldier grinned and came at Tyg slow and deliberate, swinging his axe round. Tyg laughed again.

"Confident all of a sudden..." She said to him as she paced a few steps to the left, keeping him in her sight over her shoulder. As he reached her the soldier slashed at her with his axe, widely at her head. Tyg dodged it, grabbed the wrist of his sword hand and stepped in close, pressing her back to his chest, lifting his arm up over her shoulder, tilting forward and sending him flying through the air and crashing down onto his back, she wrenched his sword from his grasp and held it to the side of his throat as she stood above his head.

"Dead." She muttered smiling then drove his sword into the ground right by his ear, turned and walked away. She walked up to Leviathan.

"Problem?" He asked her as she came to stand in front of him.

"I'm finding it harder to not hurt them...sorry." Tyg downcast her eyes. General Barrock frowned deeply and glanced at Leviathan. He didn't like the look he saw.

"Don't worry about hurting them, Tygarya....what were you saying about fighting to survive...this is what they should be trained to handle...if they get hurt or killed, it's their own faults."

"No..." Ra'chek said. "It would be my fault."

Leviathan glanced at him. "Indeed." The deathly venom was clear in Leviathan's voice.

"I am barely keeping it in check though...." Tyg muttered. Barrock's eyes went wide and he stepped forward.

"Wait...what is she talking about?"

Leviathan rubbed his thumb down his jaw. "Her Elvian blood."

"What the fuck!" Ra'chek exclaimed. "You mean she could berserk?"

"We cannot let her continue, my Liege." Barrock added.

"Rubbish...next." Leviathan said his stare intense as his eyes were glowing softly.

Tyg looked at him and met his eyes. He stared intently at her. "Kill them, Tyg."

"My Liege!" Both Commanders yelled then both went quiet as they saw Tyg grin a hideous animalistic grin and showed her teeth in a snarl. Her eyes slowly went black as she gave in to the battle lust.

"Send both of them in at once, Ra'chek!" Leviathan ordered. "Tell them no holds barred, try and kill her."

Tyg stepped away, drawing her sword and her dagger, walking backward away from Leviathan, with a cocky saunter, she chuckled and raised her dagger in his direction as he folded his arms across his chest and met her gaze. She smiled at him and brought the dagger up to her forehead in a salute then turned to face the two soldiers that stepped into the circle. They were both holding a sword each, but one had a small hand held crossbow. Tyg licked her lips when she saw it. It held a one bolt shot, already loaded.

"Like that is it?" Tyg said in a deadly voice. "Bring it, hot shot." Tyg stood side on to him as he raised the cross bow and fired the shot. Tyg dodged her head, and heard the five inch bolt whistle past her ear as she felt it slice past her cheek. She lifted the back of her hand to her cheek and looked at it as it came away bloody, she licked the back of her hand and ran her tongue along her teeth. The soldiers both looked at each other and swallowed hard. Tyg chuckled again, a maniacal sound.

Leviathan had stiffened when the bolt was loosed but visibly relaxed with a deep breath when Tyg dodged it. He chuckled too when she licked her blood off her hand.

"Fucking hell." Barrock breathed. "Who trained your pet Elvian, my Liege, you certainly didn't have time too?"

"She was already a trained assassin when I found her." Leviathan said with a chuckle.

Barrock stared at Leviathan unbelieving for a moment. "Gods save us all."

Tyg suddenly sprang into action and sprinted over to where she had left the broken stick in the ground, she jumped up, stepping onto it and used it to launch herself into the air, twisting high up in the air, she brought her sword round aimed at one soldier as she deftly threw the dagger at the other soldier in the opposite direction. As she came down her momentum forced the soldier meeting her sword to stagger back, as the steel on steel rang out. Tyg twisted immediately away and rolled on her shoulder coming up several feet away, she glanced over at the second soldier to see him staggering back with her dagger protruding from his chest. She grinned mercilessly, he was the one that had shot the crossbow at her. She turned her attention back to the other one as he advanced on her. He flicked his sword around, and Tyg raised an eyebrow.

"Don't tell me someone finally with some talent?"

He grinned at her and sent a flurry of sword thrusts and jabs at her, causing her to fight defensively finally. She dodged and weaved and returned his strokes evenly for a couple of minutes. As their swords clashed together Tyg found herself face to face with the young soldier as they pushed against each other, Tyg felt the bite of a dagger in her side and she glared at the boy as he grinned and head butted her in the face making her nose bleed. Tyg staggered back a couple of steps. The crowd of soldiers cheered the young soldier as they saw the dagger in his hand dripping bright red blood.

Leviathan stiffened and narrowed his eyes. "Tygarya." He growled.

Tyg never even heard him as she raised her hand to her mouth as she tasted blood. She was lost to the call of death. She fixed the soldier with a death stare and circled round with him. She glanced to her left and saw the sword of the other soldier lying on the dirt, he had managed to crawl away to be tended. Tyg picked it up and the grin on her face made everyone's blood go cold. The blood was all over her teeth and dripping down her chin.

She turned to face the soldier and started spinning the two swords around with expert ease. The young soldier's eyes went wide. She spat blood out onto the ground and advanced on him. She just kept coming, for every swipe and thrust he tried she just swept them aside and attacked, calmly deadly, with absolutely no emotion. The perfect killing machine. Never over exerting herself, simple movements, she actually looked like she was giving a demonstration. She didn't even flinch when the soldier cut her arm, or when he cut her leg. All she did was return cut for cut and gave him two more for each one, then started a barrage of slices and cuts mercilessly like she had with Raven, until he was finally staggering from loss of blood, his dagger had fallen from his grasp as he lost the feeling in his left arm. He staggered and fell to his knees as Tyg stood over him and grinned like a demon from hell.

"Enough!" Ra'chek yelled.

Leviathan turned and looked at him.

"There is no use to my best man losing his life this day!" Ra'chek pleaded with Leviathan. "Call off your monster!"

"My monster? That's my future wife you're talking about." Leviathan chuckled then sent a stream of power into Tyg's head.

Tyg dropped like a stone in the middle of the circle of soldiers, letting go of the swords and clutching the sides of her head as she suddenly let out a blood curdling scream of pain. All the soldiers stepped back several steps in shock as Leviathan walked slowly forward and stood over Tyg as she was curled into a ball. He let the pain do its job until he determined Tyg would be out. He then stopped his power and bent down and gently picked the incoherent form of Tyg up from the ground and carried her off the training grounds without a single word to anyone.

Barrock balled his hands into fists, he was shaking in rage. "Fucking hell! What the fuck was that!"

Ra'chek was staring at where Leviathan had disappeared with horrified shock. "At least he can control her." He muttered darkly and turned to face the soldiers screaming orders to get the young soldier to the infirmary and to get cleaned up and back to barracks.

As Leviathan made his way back to his rooms, Tyg's eyes started to focus again. He looked down and smiled to see they were as blue as the sky. They were, however, very angry looking.

"What the fuck did you do that for!?" Tyg yelled at him as she squirmed in his arms.

"Keep still." Leviathan ordered.

"Like fuck, Leviathan...put me down!"

"No."

He adjusted his grip on her as she struggled and threw her over his shoulder as he walked. Tyg struggled against him until he whacked her bottom hard with the flat of his hand.

"Behave!"

The looks from the people they past made Tyg blush with embarrassment until he finally reached his tower and walked in, through the main rooms, up the winding staircase and into the bedroom suite of rooms where he threw her down on the bed and ripped her sword belt off her and her boots, her leather jerkin then grabbed her by the shirt and pulled her up to his mouth, kissing her forcefully. Ripping her shirt open and exposing her breasts as he grabbed one in his hand as he held himself over her with the other. Tyg felt the heat of him press against her as he lowered himself down over the top of her slowly with a commanding presence.

"Lev..." Tyg breathed between his tongue lashing into her mouth.

He lifted his head slightly and trailed kisses down her neck as she grabbed handfuls of his shirt and let out a moan. He looked at her and smiled, then pulled her lace bustier down and sucked a nipple into his mouth. His mouth felt so hot against her, and she arched her back and let out another moan. This felt different, more urgent, more lustful...she grabbed Leviathan's shoulders and pushed against him, rolling him over and straddling him.

Leviathan looked up at her and grinned, flicking her braid over her shoulder as she smiled down at him. She took the remnants of her shirt off and wiped her face of the blood then kissed him fervently. He held her head as she kissed him, then as she raised her head he smirked.

"Battle lust." He muttered.

Tyg growled and ripped open his shirt and started kissing his chest. He placed his arms under his head as Tyg reached for his belt and undid it, pulling his pants down and exposing his erection. Tyg glanced up at him and he smirked again as Tyg lowered her head and sucked his hard cock into her mouth. He closed his eyes and hissed through his teeth.

"Easy there tiger..." He said after only a brief second and reached out one hand and grabbed her braid and pulled back on it. Tyg lifted her head and looked at him. He sat up and pulled her mouth back to his. He flipped her onto her back then and sat up. He removed his boots and pants then undid her pants and pulled everything off.

"You're the one needing release right now, baby." He muttered in a deep sexual tone making Tyg shiver in delight as he bent his head, while grabbing her thighs, pushing them apart. He licked up her cleft as Tyg cried out in a needy mewl.

25

Leviathan was holding her in his arms, her head on his chest and one of her arms laid over his chest, as she lay with her eyes closed in contentment.

"You understand why I did what I did?" He asked her as he kissed her hair.

Tyg looked up at him with a dark scowl. "Maybe...doesn't mean I have to like it."

"How else could I have stopped you from killing that boy?"

"You told me too!" Tyg sat up indignantly.

"Yes...but Ra'chek preferred you not to."

Tyg snorted. "And he is?"

Leviathan chuckled. "You really have no respect for authority, do you? Would you have preferred I jumped in with my sword?"

Tyg glanced at him horrified. "Ah, no."

Leviathan raised an eyebrow. "You no longer want to cross swords with me?"

"No, not after seeing you in action."

Leviathan chuckled. "You think I'm a better swordsman than you?"

"You are..." Tyg said grudgingly.

"You're right...I am." Leviathan said smugly as he sat up and swung his legs off the bed and stood up. "Do you wish to bathe before we go to the market?"

Tyg looked up at him in surprise. "Oh, I forgot about that?" She looked out the window to see the sun wasn't even at its apex yet.

Leviathan levelled an amused look at her. "Hmm, I'm sure you would love to lounge around in my bed all day, Tygarya, but I cannot."

"Alright, I'll go and quickly bathe..."

"Good girl, then come to my study once you are dressed."

As Tyg was making her way back to Leviathan's study she stopped at a cross intersection when she saw General Barrock standing there, his attention fixed firmly on her, one eyebrow raised as he appraised her in the sleek dark blue and silver dress she was wearing for the market.

"You look different." He muttered darkly.

Tyg scowled at him realising he wouldn't have seen her in a dress since he was not present at their arrival. "What do you want, Barrock?"

General Barrock smiled, it wasn't pleasant. "I just wanted to let you know a few home truths."

"Oh...like what?"

"The Emperor is lying to you...it is still law to kill Elvians, although we had thought they were all dead...extinct." He stared at her intently. "He created his own Hunters and has always tracked down and slaughtered Elvians and half breeds...ever since the Jaegers were banished to their castle."

Tyg frowned and looked at the floor, making Barrock more confident.

"...so you should think hard about why you are here and still very much alive, little lady..."

Tyg raised her head and fixed Barrock with a dark glare that made him clench his fist around his sword hilt. "Even if that is true,

I am here to change his mind about Elvian's and show him just how useful we can be." Tyg was just saying something, anything to try and smack that smug look off Barrock's face, without violence. She was actually in turmoil right now about whether what he said was actually true. Leviathan still wouldn't say why she was here.

Barrock grinned. "Keep telling yourself that...you're useful alright, like a trained dog will bite on command..."

Tyg clenched her fists and was just about to lash out at the general when they both froze at a familiar voice at the end of the corridor.

"Why are you walking the halls with my General, Tygarya?" It was drawled and sounded like velvet. "Was the affections of a Captain not enough for you?" The dark dangerous tone made Tyg swallow hard, and the implications of him mentioning a 'captain' was not lost on her. The look of fear on her face was not lost on Barrock either as he frowned at her. So she clearly feared Leviathan too, Barrock thought as they both stood still as the rapping sound of Leviathan's boots coming closer filled the halls.

"What the hell?" Tyg said as she stepped away from beside General Barrock with a disgusted look.

General Barrock glared at her. "The feeling is mutual, don't worry." He muttered equally as disgusted.

Leviathan smirked, coming to a stop before them both. "I came looking for you...you were taking too long."

"What? Geeze, Leviathan, you told me to go bathe."

"And come straight to my office, not stand around in the halls chin wagging with other men."

"My Liege...I waylaid Lady Tygarya...I apologise." General Barrock bowed his head.

"For what, General?" His voice hardened. Tyg wondered if he would actually tell the truth and earn Leviathan's wrath.

"Merely to tell her that Ra'chek has confirmed a time slot for her to have the training yard three days a week."

Tyg looked at Barrock surprised, Leviathan caught the look.

"Funny that she is only just hearing that information now, General." Leviathan stepped up to Barrock and placed an index finger on the General's chest. "I do hope you didn't take it upon yourself to try and threaten my consort in any way while I was not around?"

The look Leviathan was giving Barrock was frightening and Barrock wouldn't meet his gaze. "No, my Liege." He answered quietly.

Leviathan turned to Tyg. "Tygarya...what was the general talking to you about? And, don't lie to me..." The threat was very real in his voice.

Tyg's eyes were wide and she licked her lips as her mouth went dry. She owed this man nothing. "Ah...he was telling me something about Elvians that he thought I should know."

General Barrock stared hard at Tyg as Leviathan growled. "What exactly did General Barrock feel you just had to know?" Leviathan's voice was calm and deadly.

"Ah...just that you created Hunters specifically to track down and kill Elvian half breeds, he wondered why suddenly you had a change of heart when it came to me."

General Barrock suddenly dropped to his knees with a gasp of pain. "My Liege..." He pleaded as Leviathan glared at him, his eyes blazing with light. Tyg could see Barrock was shaking with pain. So it wasn't just her Leviathan could do this to...no wonder everyone feared him.

"You've over stepped your authority, General." Leviathan's voice sounded like a file rasping over metal in its vileness.

Barrock sank down and pressed his forehead to the floor, genuflecting before Leviathan's feet. Tyg looked away, nervously chewing on her bottom lip, at Barrock's humiliated submission.

"Forgive me, my Liege." Barrock grunted out through the pain he was enduring at Leviathan's power clamped inside his head like a vice.

"You are asking something I have never done before, General, what makes you so special?"

Tyg frowned at those words and glanced at Barrock still down on the floor. He was human so Tyg knew he couldn't take this for much longer.

Other people had gathered at the end of the hall and Tyg wondered if Leviathan would feel obligated to kill the General because of them watching just to maintain his fearsome reputation.

Tyg stood up straight and faced them. "Get lost! Go!" Her eyes blazed in icy fury as the terrified servants fled.

Leviathan turned an amused gaze at her. "You want me to *not* kill him?"

Tyg shrugged. "You do what you want...I just got rid of any pressure to do one thing over another due to witnesses."

Leviathan raised an eyebrow at her in surprise. "You think I would be swayed to kill General Barrock because some petty servants were watching?"

"You rule by fear, don't you? Not by showing any leniency."

Leviathan's jaw clenched and he grabbed Tyg by the wrist and stalked off down the hall leaving the general gasping for breath as Leviathan stopped his power flow. Barrock raised his head and stared at the retreating figures, one dragging the other behind them unceremoniously then stood up and dusted himself off, staggering as he wiped the blood from his nose with the back of his hand.

He frowned deeply thinking about the exchange he had heard. Tyg had just saved his life by putting Leviathan's anger on to herself.

General Barrock wasn't sure how he felt about that. He cursed bitterly and staggered off in the opposite direction.

Leviathan reached his office and practically threw Tyg into the room. The door slammed shut on its own. He took a deep breath in and stared at her with that vulture gaze.

Tyg stared back unafraid to meet his gaze. "What!"

"Why do you constantly undermine my authority?"

"I don't...I didn't..." Tyg looked confused.

"The mere fact you stand in a hallway and argue with me says you do!"

"We weren't arguing...were we?" Tyg frowned. "Gods, Leviathan, you are too confusing!"

"I'm too confusing?" He took another deep breath and rubbed his thumb on his forehead, closing his eyes for a moment while he collected himself. "What did Barrock actually say to you?"

"Just that I should know that you used to hunt Elvians and half breeds and slaughter them...is it true?"

Leviathan looked away and walked over to the cabinet behind his desk where the whisky decanter was and poured himself a drink.

"You want one?" He offered, holding the decanter up.

"Sure..." Tyg said, still waiting for an answer. He poured her a glass and held it out to her, making her walk to him to get it. As she took the glass he took her chin in his other hand and made her look up at him.

"It's true, Tyg...I'm sorry...my father went to war against the Elvian race to free the human race from their slavery years ago and so I guess I was raised to hate them...until I met you."

"So this hunting of them still goes on?" Her eyes were wide.

"You're the last of your kind as far as we know, Tygarya." He said softly.

"You wiped them out!?" Tyg stepped back from Leviathan's hold and drained her glass, placing it on the desk, her hand unsteady.

"No, what numbers were left were exiled from this continent and sailed east into the unknown. There may be a few half breeds still in hiding here and there....mainly in other countries I would say, that's the only way to explain your existence."

"Leviathan...I..." Tyg didn't know what to say. She turned and silently left the room as he watched, not making any effort to stop her, his face grim. She made her way silently along the halls to her rooms where she locked the door and fell on her bed. Genocide of an entire race of people, her race of people, well half of her. A war mongering race that kept people as slaves from what she had read, a people whose strength and agility was second to none, an unbeatable race. That was until Leviathan's father had come along and changed history by creating the Jaeger.

Leviathan's eyes blazed with a rage so deep he smashed the glass in his hand as he clenched his fist. "Damn you and your big mouth, Barrock....you may have just ruined everything!" He muttered darkly, then called out in a massive roar. "R'hyan!"

He stood with his palms pressed to the desk, watching the blood from his cut hand spread across it slowly as R'hyan scrambled into the room.

"My Liege?" He noticed the blood. "Are you hurt?"

"Don't worry about that, cancel the outing and go get my brother here, now!"

26

As soon as Antyn walked into Leviathan's office he knew something was terribly wrong. He sat down in the chair opposite Leviathan and raised an eyebrow.

"What happened?"

Leviathan was sitting with a hand over his face, the elbow resting on the arm of his chair, looking extremely moody. He glanced sideways at Antyn and had watched him from under his hand as he sat down. When asked the question Leviathan dropped his hand and leaned over the desk, putting his forearms on it, and hunching his shoulders.

"Tygarya knows about what happened to the Elvians."

"Oh?" Antyn's eyebrows raised in surprise. "Did she read it somewhere?"

Leviathan's mouth twisted cruelly. "No, General Barrock took an instant dislike to her this morning and decided to tell her."

Antyn's eyes narrowed and he leaned his elbow on the chair arm and tapped his chin with his forefinger in thought. "What exactly did he say?"

"He told her straight, I created the Hunters and systematically slaughtered them all after my father decimated them and made them go into hiding."

"Shit! Is the general still alive?"

Leviathan scowled darkly and looked away. "Yes..."

Antyn looked at Leviathan's expression and guessed. "Tyg stopped you, didn't she?"

"Somehow...yes." Leviathan sat back into his chair with a huff. "We need to fix this, and fast. I do not need her to withdraw from me like on board ship."

"Hmm." Antyn went back to tapping his chin and thinking. "Weren't you suppose to come to visit me today?"

"I was supposed to take her to the market and then to the university...she wanted to know where you had disappeared to, when I told her you lived at the university she wanted to go there."

"To see me?" Antyn grinned.

Leviathan looked at Antyn with a frightening glare. "I'm already in the mood to kill someone, Antyn, don't push it." He growled in a low venomous tone.

Antyn baulked. "Sorry, Lev." He straightened in his chair. "I think you should continue with the day as planned..."

"Really?" Leviathan seemed surprised. "Tygarya has locked herself in her room."

"Exactly...she loves drama and can hold a grudge...and we don't want a repeat performance of on board ship, like you say?" Antyn explained. "I believe the best way to deal with this is to drag Tyg out of her reverie and force her to act normal...she'll come back around a lot quicker."

"I don't know...I don't need her going psycho in the middle of the streets."

"We also don't have time to squander with her moping about feeling sorry for herself...we have an invasion to plan."

Leviathan frowned. "I haven't seen you at any invasion meetings, little brother."

"Ah...well...I've been doing my own planning...don't worry."

"So what do we do?"

"Leave it to me." Antyn said as he stood up. "Just be ready to leave..."

Antyn knocked on Tyg's door.

"Tyg...it's me...open up."

The door was unlocked and opened as Tyg stared at Antyn with a shocked expression. "Antyn, you're here? Why are you here?"

Antyn smiled. "Can I come in?"

Tyg stepped back from the doorway allowing Antyn to enter and then closed the door.

"You're not supposed to do that." Antyn instructed.

"Do what?" Tyg asked confused.

"Close the door when a man is in your quarters."

"Oh! Really?" Tyg frowned and looked at the door.

"No, but leave it now...come sit...tell me what happened."

Tyg hesitated. "He sent for you, didn't he?" She asked darkly.

"Do you want a repeat of what happened on board ship?"

"No." Tyg answered sullenly, looking at the ground with a dark remorse.

"Well, neither does he...therefore..." He pointed to himself and grinned.

"What can you change? You certainly can't change history." Tyg said as she sat down.

"No...but history is just that, Tyg...leave it there."

"But he slaughtered Elvians to the point of extinction after his father destroyed them, he just had to go that far."

"What do you care? You weren't even aware you were part Elvian, you are also part something else...what if they are all dead as well?"

"Are they?" Tyg's tone dropped. "You should know." She gave him a scathing, untrusting look.

Antyn raised an eyebrow. "Actually Tyg, I don't know...you could be half human, you could be half troll...I don't know, it's all pure speculation."

"Half troll?" Her eyes went a little wide.

He chuckled at her shock. "Figure of speech, you get what I'm saying though..."

Tyg frowned deeply as she mulled things over. "If Leviathan had people hunting half breeds down and killing them, why was he searching for me?"

"We told you that." Antyn frowned as he answered carefully.

"Did you?" Tyg asked suspiciously.

"I said we never expected to find you there...you were a complete surprise to us, to be honest we didn't know who or what we were actually searching for anyway, until our eyes landed on you, then we just knew."

"So why didn't Leviathan just kill me when he saw me?"

Antyn smiled. "In that pale blue dress? Never crossed his mind."

Tyg thought back. "Is that why he followed me into Karon's office that night?"

"He wanted to know how it was that you existed, yes...and from there you did nothing but confuse and intrigue him..."

Tyg's frown eased a little.

"Tyg..." Antyn called in a quiet tone. "Let's go to the market...and then I'll show you the university...let this go."

Tyg looked up at him, her eyes unfathomable.

"You're still dressed to go out and look absolutely beautiful...you do still want to see the city? It would be a shame to let such beauty go hidden and wasted in here. Plus this is a rare opportunity for you to see the city you now live in, you know he's not going to let you out often."

"Yes, of course I want to see the city, but...now...I know why everyone looks at me like they do." She looked away again, her expression almost sad. "I feel even more on show..."

Antyn's eyes widened a bit as he realised her doubt. "No one can hurt you."

Tyg glanced back with a look of distain. "I know that."

Antyn chuckled. "There's the girl I know...please come..."

"With Leviathan?" She asked coldly.

"He was your original date, be a bit rude to ditch him now." Antyn swaggered with a roguish smile.

"Hmm, and I suppose you participated in the killing too?"

Antyn smiled triumphantly. "Never, I'm a cleric, not a warrior."

"Oh..." Tyg twisted her mouth as she gave him an ambiguous look. Antyn smiled in return.

"What, you don't believe me?"

"You carry a sword..."

Antyn shrugged. "And I can use it too...doesn't mean I have to."

"Okay, fair enough..." Tyg shrugged and looked away.

"So...are we going or not?" Antyn stood up, waiting, holding his hand out to her.

Tyg looked at it with a slight sneer then stood up on her own. "Okay...once again I'll be the one to make all the concessions!"

Antyn looked at her sharply. "You're the one that makes the problems..."

Tyg scowled at him darkly. "Do you want me to do this?"

Antyn sighed and rubbed his eyes with the finger and thumb of one hand, exasperated. "Why are you so difficult?"

Tyg frowned and stalked to the door grabbing her cloak off the hook and holding it scrunched up in one fist. "I'm not purposely being difficult, Antyn...when are you and him going to realise that I really am trying here! I'm a nothing, a no body...thrown into this imperial life where suddenly everyone knows who and what I am and judge, hate and fear me for it! I'm used to a life of obscurity not this shit show!"

She stormed off down the hall leaving Antyn staring with startled surprise in her wake. He grimaced as he realised that she was quite right, before following her out.

27

T yg was surprised to see the market was very similar to back in Arial, except a lot larger, it spilled out of the large market square with its ornate stone monument to their Emperor in the middle and down the side streets. Hawkers and vendors lining the narrow streets on one side as people bustled past on the other, leaving a very narrow channel for people to actually stop if they were interested in any wares being sold. It resulted in a chaotic and raucous atmosphere. There were street performers on every corner blending music and laughter to the general cacophony of sound.

Everything came to a standstill when the Emperor's carriage arrived, his soldiers clearing a path along the main boulevard to the square as they came. As the black and gold carriage stopped and the footman opened the door people stared in curious wonderment. They could plainly see the Imperial Guards, Warlocks and Elite as well as the black and gold dragon's head livery of the Emperor but no one believed the Emperor himself could possibly be inside and was actually visiting the market.

So when he stepped out and straightened up to his impressive giant height of nearly seven foot the whole market square full of people hushed and fell to their knees, heads bowed in reverence and fear.

"Enough!" Leviathan roared out over the crowd. "Carry on about your business. I am here merely to escort my lovely princess and show her the wonderful sights, crafts and wears available in my city's famous market. Make me proud!"

The crowd erupted in cheers, applause and congratulations as they scrambled to their collective feet and waited with bated breath to get a look at the woman that the Emperor had called his. Many lifting up on tip toes and craning their necks over the rest of the crowd as the soldiers formed a tight fence keeping them all at bay.

As Leviathan turned back to the carriage and held his hand out, he saw Tyg's bitter expression and he couldn't help but try and suppress a little smirk making his top lip twitch.

"Tygarya, behave." He said to her under his breath.

Tyg scowled as she put her hand in his and allowed him to help her from the carriage.

"How can you stand this every day?" She muttered as a hushed awe fell over the crowd at the sight of her emerging from the carriage.

"I've never known anything else." Leviathan stated matter-of-factly.

Antyn stepped out after Tyg, straightening his coat and looking around, he heard the comment and remembered Tyg's fractious words earlier. "Well, just remember, Tyg is far from used to this sort of pandering attention so go easy on her, brother."

Tyg looked at him with surprise and he smiled at her. "I listen...you only need to speak more often..."

"What's this?" Leviathan asked, seeing that something was being conveyed beyond the actual words spoken. He levelled his vulture like glare upon Antyn with an eyebrow raised.

"Nothing, Lev...just something Tyg said to me earlier when I was convincing her to still come down here."

Leviathan frowned at the two of them. Tyg looked at him and gave him an ambiguous look. "I'm sure Antyn will tell you all about it later...can we go and look at the stalls now?"

"Hmm..." Leviathan snorted, giving Antyn another sideways glance before allowing Tyg to pull on his hand and lead him away.

Antyn smiled to himself and followed along smiling at the townsfolk as they all stared after the Imperial couple.

Tyg, Leviathan noticed, seemed to be in the market for something specific as he became aware of the fact that she kept bee-lining for any stall that was selling ornately decorated, jewelled, hand crafted daggers.

As she was studying one particular one, testing its weight and shocking the vendor as he paled watching her spin the blade around on her hand Leviathan couldn't help but be curious as to what she was up to now.

"Planning on a little night time excursion or just adding to the arsenal?" He enquired smoothly.

Tyg looked up at him with a grin. "Adding to the arsenal...I lost a couple of daggers along the way..."

Leviathan looked away, containing his mirth. "If you are talking about the ones you used against me, my man and that assassin...I figure you're in for quite an expense looking at these..."

Tyg turned and gave him a haughty little frown. "You should be paying...since you're the one who never gave any of them back."

She lifted the knife up, waggling it as she spoke.

Leviathan grabbed her wrist and yanked it down to her side with lightning speed, startling her and making her flinch back. "Do not raise that in my direction, Tygarya." He growled under his breath.

"What?" Tyg gasped at him as his eyes flashed. She noticed the guards had all stiffened and reached for their swords. "I wasn't...I..."

"Regardless, if you were merely gesticulating as you spoke...be more aware!" Leviathan growled, he let her wrist go and stepped away as Tyg hurriedly put the dagger back on the stall's display.

"I'm sorry...I didn't realise..." She murmured, looking at the ground as Leviathan waved his hand to the guards for them to relax.

She saw Leviathan's hand come back and go under her chin, lifting it up to look at him as he gave her that formidable stare.

"Tygarya...nothing that can be deemed as a dangerous weapon may be pointed in my direction for any reason...that's a law...on penalty of death."

"More rules..." Tyg groaned and pouted at him.

"More rules." Leviathan did smile this time as he brushed her pouting lips with his thumb. "Let us not forget what you did on board ship before arriving here..."

"Hey, Lev..." Antyn called out. "I'm going to go check out a certain herbalist I know...I'll be back soon..."

"Very well..." Leviathan huffed as Antyn made a swift disappearing act into the crowd and was gone.

"Let me guess...a woman?" Tyg surmised.

Leviathan gave her an impressed look. "You seem to have grasped my brother's personality quite well in only three months..."

"I know people like him." Tyg replied off hand.

Leviathan's eyes narrowed as he stepped closer to Tyg and lowered his head to her ear. "You mean you know men like him? What men exactly do you know that like to flirt and bed women haphazardly?" The tone in Leviathan's voice was dangerous.

Tyg's expression faltered and she bit her lip before turning into him and placing a hand on his chest and looking up at him with a wary look.

"Lev...you do remember where I come from, don't you...? It's literally only been...what...three months like you say?"

He growled in his throat as he cupped her cheek with one hand. His menacing aura was picked up by the crowd surrounding them and a hushed apprehension went through it as the couple looked at each other.

"Just because I remember does not mean I have to like it."

Tyg twisted her mouth. "I didn't particularly like it either..."

Leviathan brushed her soft skin with his thumb and stared at her lips for a long moment fighting the want to possessively take them right in front of everyone to declare just who this woman belonged to.

His jaw clenched tight as he dropped his hand and looked away with a bleak expression on his face. What this woman, no...young girl, did to him was becoming more obvious.

He felt the crowd relax as a murmur started up.

"So are you going to purchase a dagger or should we move on to something else perhaps..." He said coolly, putting his hands behind his back and stepping away.

Tyg took the hint, she had felt the uneasy tension around them. She glanced at the two warlocks that were standing just behind her and saw their eyes were flinty. Her gaze travelled beyond them to the guards and then to the strange elusive men in the green robes that shifted quietly through the crowd unnoticed by most.

"I would really like to find a baker...I feel peckish for something savoury but sweet..." She looked away as if searching through the crowd.

Leviathan shook his head, amused again as his mood changed easily back by Tyg's willingness to yield. "Savoury but sweet? Is there such a thing?"

"Of course there is..." Tyg grinned as she turned back to him and he couldn't help but be astonished by the way the light was hitting her side profile, sparkling off the silver tones in her hair.

He grabbed her around the neck and pulled her roughly up to his mouth, making her lift up on tip toes and braced her hands against his chest in surprise as she let out a little squeak of alarm into his mouth as hers was invaded by his dominating tongue.

The crowd hummed with whispers and gasps.

As Leviathan pulled back he looked down at Tyg's upturned face as her eyes fluttered open. "You are beautiful, Tygarya..." His eyes hardened like he was making his mind up about something as they roamed her face. Tyg held her breath in apprehension at what this mercurial dangerous man could possibly be thinking. "I wish to buy you something..."

Tyg stared up at him speechless for a moment as he smiled down at her, no longer caring about the façade of protocol any longer.

Leviathan turned away to talk to his retinue following behind. "You..." He pointed to one man who flinched in fright. "...go and find Tyg something from a baker, she wants savoury but sweet." The man baulked, but bowed low and scurried off as Leviathan turned to the next one. "You...find a reputable jeweller...I wish to pick out something for Tygarya to wear."

Tyg swallowed. "To wear?" She asked as the other retainer also left in a hurry to do the Emperor's bidding.

Leviathan was regarding her with dazzling interest as his fingers trailed around to her collar bone and lightly traced it, making Tyg blush and feel hot under his sensual touch in such a public place with so many people watching. She could hear the murmurs of the crowd as they all excitedly watched.

"A necklace..." Leviathan announced.

"You don't need to do that." Tyg said feeling a little embarrassed at Leviathan's sudden want to buy her jewellery, what had gotten into him all of a sudden? This was not normal behaviour.

"I want to...I'm feeling strangely spontaneous." Leviathan said with a one sided smirk. "Besides, ladies of high standing always wear lots of jewellery, yet you only wear my ring." He said as he dropped his hand to her hand and lifted it up, stroking his thumb over the large dragon's head. Tyg twisted her mouth at the fact she wore it all the time because she couldn't get it off.

She looked at him with bewilderment. "Are you sure it's not heat stroke?"

Leviathan's lips pressed together and his gaze pierced her with an amused glare as the day wasn't even particularly warm.

The retainer returned, puffing and pointing. "A jeweller, my Liege...this way..."

As Tyg was pulled along by a determined Leviathan she looked at all the stalls they were passing and at the people staring. Leviathan's city seemed to be thriving. Tyg squinted as she saw something small flit through the crowd of on lookers. She smiled to herself, there they were...

The child pick pockets...

The scourge of every city...

And they were probably making the most of this pressed in crowd...

It made Tyg feel more at ease knowing Leviathan's capital city wasn't perfect.

As she looked up from where she had seen the child move through the crowd she noticed a small stall selling trinkets and dainty little bracelets.

"Stop! Leviathan!" She tugged back on her hand, trying to rein him back in his long purposeful strides.

He halted and looked at her with a raised eyebrow. "Problem?"

Tyg noticed all the guard around them looking around nervous and alert.

"No problem...I just want one of those...not a fancy necklace..." Tyg pointed over to the small stall and the crowd seemed to open up, making an avenue revealing the stall at the end as the old lady behind it startled and got all flustered at the sudden attention before she scampered around to the front of her stall and fell to her knees, bowing her head to the ground.

Leviathan frowned as his eyes flicked over the little wooden stall. "Those are cheap...I meant for you to have something better."

Tyg's expression darkened. "I have no need for expensive gems or gold...but I have always wanted one of these..." She spoke as she walked forward in a rush, slipping her hand from his, before Leviathan could pull her away.

She looked at the assortment of little silver chains with their dainty charms and pointed at a particular one that had two tiny silver balls attached to a fine silver chain. Tyg lifted it as the old lady nervously stood up and came over, casting furtive glances around at all the guards, not knowing if she was allowed to stand up or not, when no one spoke to her she made her way back to the other side of her stall, bowing her head at Tyg. Tyg heard the little jingle of the silver balls indicating they had something inside them that made them ring and jingle like bells.

Leviathan loomed up over Tyg's shoulder, glowering down at her and the thing in her hand. "What do you want that for?"

Tyg looked up at him with a strange whimsical sparkle in her eyes that made Leviathan's instantly darken in response.

"I will wear it around my ankle and dance barefoot and..."

"Enough!" Leviathan growled, snatching the anklet from her, aware of the amount of ears listening in. He opened his fist and stared at the item for a dark moment.

Tyg smiled to herself as Leviathan grabbed her hand, flicking his other at his servant to pay for the anklet and walked back to the carriage, putting the dainty anklet in his breast pocket on the inside of his coat.

Market day visit was now over it seemed.

She had seen all she needed to see...she had come specifically to find any trace of an underground network...seeing the pick pockets confirmed it.

She was relieved to finally get out of the milling crowd full of stares and whispers as they reached the carriage and got in. She saw the other servant was back and he came up to the open door of the carriage holding a little bag full of sugared dough balls out to her, his head bowed low. She smiled and took them with a small thank you.

Leviathan looked over her shoulder, his hand coming over and his fingers dipping into the bag to draw one of them out. He held it up, inspecting it with a raised eyebrow.

"Just try it." Tyg laughed at him as she took one out and bit into it. She looked up at him smiling as she chewed. Leviathan stared at the sugar on her lips as she licked it off.

Leviathan grabbed her around the back of the neck and pressed the dough ball to her lips as Tyg looked at him startled. He pulled it away and grinned devilishly as he saw her lips covered with the fine sugar. He leaned in and licked it off. Lifting away from her slightly as he grinned again, wickedly.

"That's not the way you're supposed to eat them." Tyg said to him with a little sarcasm.

"It is the way I eat them, and it's delicious." Leviathan held the dough ball up to her mouth. "Eat." He purposely mushed it into her lips as she opened her mouth, making sure a lot of the sugar was left on her lips before he melted his lips back to hers and kissed every little morsel off.

Tyg suddenly pulled her head away. "Wait..." She yelped out as she remembered something.

Leviathan's hand clenched into her hair not letting her pull away. "What now?" He asked harshly.

"We were supposed to go to Antyn's manor house at the university..."

Leviathan glared at her. "You dare mention my brother's name right now?" His voice deepened to an angry growl.

Tyg stared up into his fierce glare. "But...the books..."

"Tomorrow! Right now I want what you promised me."

"Promised you?" Tyg's brows knit together in confusion.

Leviathan reached into his pocket and pulled the little silver anklet out, holding it up in front of Tyg.

"You dancing for me, wearing nothing but this."

Tyg's eyes widened. "When did I promise such a thing?" She breathed as her cheeks blushed.

Leviathan leaned in closer, his breath hot on her face as his fierce glare locked on to her.

"You either do what you said you would, or I will punish you instead, either way you will not be seeing any books today."

Tyg blinked at him and swallowed, tasting the sugar still in her mouth. "Okay..." She barely managed to speak the word before Leviathan crashed his mouth back to hers.

28

The following day Tyg woke up to find herself sprawled across Leviathan's bed completely naked and alone. She sat up and groaned as she wiped a tired hand over her face. He had been rough with her yesterday again, annoyed at her for not being focused on his affections and instead mentioning his brother's name. Such small things could set him off in a tirade of jealous dominant behaviours that Tyg found herself afraid of. On top of his voracious appetite he was unpredictable and she knew he had the capacity for extreme cruelty and violence.

So did she...

But not when it came to someone she liked...nor did she ever think to mix such things with sex.

Which begged the question, did Leviathan actually like her? Or was he purely just attracted to her body...a body that could endure such cruelty and pain easily and heal perfectly. She shuddered to think what she would do if he ever went that far...

She looked at her wrists and rubbed them. Although there were no marks remaining from last night it was still imprinted on her mind that he had tied her wrists so she couldn't fight him off. It confused her and left her feeling out of sorts.

She didn't know how to take this increasing level of discipline in the bedroom, especially given the fact that her body seemed to ache for more of it. She didn't know if this was normal or not, she had no one to ask, and being so young compared to Leviathan, obviously inexperienced and naïve, although she actually had no idea how old he was. She had asked of course but never got an answer, only that age didn't matter to someone who was going to live forever...he looked thirty at most but something told her he was older than that, perhaps not by much but certainly old enough to be considered a wise and learned Emperor.

She sighed and stood up, dropping a thick burgundy robe around herself with the intention to head to the baths through the maze of back halls to wash away the remnants of last night.

It was still chilly now as winter was having a last ditch effort with a sleety rain storm lashing the windows and as she walked through to the living area of Leviathan's private quarters she saw the fire was blazing in the hearth. She made her way over to it and picked up another log, throwing it in and standing before the fire enjoying the warmth.

The door swung open and Tyg turned to see Leviathan standing in the large open frame. His vulture like glare with those burning azure blue eyes settled on her and seemed to soften slightly.

"Tygarya...you're awake."

"No thanks to you..."

Leviathan's jaw clenched at her flippant comment. "What's your problem?"

"Yesterday..." Tyg hesitated and she knew she was probably blushing as she looked away from his intense stare, fully aware that he was now stalking towards her. "...it was..."

He lifted her chin. "Look at me." He ordered in a clear deep tone.

Tyg shifted her eyes back to his.

"You enjoyed every part of yesterday, why do you have a problem now?" He scrutinized her face, his eyes narrowing.

Tyg didn't really know what to say, she had never been with anyone but Leviathan...and only been with him like that for a week, she had no idea if this sort of thing was normal between a man and a woman, but she was pretty sure the tying up and endless teasing of her body was not.

He stroked down her hair, picking up a long lock and twining it through his fingers, bringing it to his nose as he held her chin and looked at her complex expression.

"Tygarya...do not over analyse it. You do what I want...and in turn I give you pleasure as a reward for your good behaviour...or punishment for bad. Simple."

Tyg stared at him, her eyes paling and starting to glow.

"Tyg..." He breathed softly. "You are mine and in everything you will give me control."

He dropped his hands and walked off to a chair and sat down, stretching his legs out towards the fire as Tyg stood still and watched him, her eyes still glowing brightly. He looked at his pants and wiped a hand over his thigh like he was wiping dust from them.

"If you don't calm down, I will put you back in the same position I had you in last night." He relaxed back and lifted a hand, an apple lifted from the fruit bowl over on the little breakfast table and flew into his hand. He took a big juicy bite and then lifted those piercing eyes back to her.

He smiled through his chewing, a little juice dropping onto his chin, as he saw her eyes had calmed back to a pretty sky blue, but she still looked at him with a slight challenge in her eyes.

He lowered the apple and rested his arm on the chair. "Come here."

Tyg bit the inside of her mouth but slowly walked towards him, coming to stand in front of him as he drew his legs up, planting his feet on the floor, and widened his knees so she could stand between them. He looked up at her.

"How long are you going to keep this up, Tygarya?"

"Keep what up?" Her voice was chilly.

He lifted the apple and took another bite, looking amused now as he chewed rather noisily. "This pretence that you hate the thought of being mine, or under my control. I know you relish it."

Tyg looked away, her mouth twisting as she bit the inside of her mouth to refrain from saying what was going through her head. He was an egotistical bastard!

"That's right." She stated, earning a raised eyebrow from Leviathan as he took another bite of his apple. "You won me fair and square killing Palin, even I can't argue with that."

Tyg saw a strange flash of green and gold enter Leviathan's eyes as he grabbed her by the arm and yanked her down with an angry growl, wrapping his hand around her throat as she crashed down to her knees in front of him.

"You think that is what makes you mine?" He squeezed her throat and leaned over her, his face coming close to hers as she gasped for breath. "You have been mine since the day you were born, Tygarya! And you will be mine up until the day you die only by my hand! You were created for Me!"

He threw her back in disgust.

She fell onto her back and coughed, turning to her side and holding her throat as she gasped in a few deep breaths. She looked back over her shoulder at him expecting to feel the sharp pain of him entering her head.

He was watching her, his eyes glowing. "Say it!" He ordered.

Tyg baulked and looked away, putting her hands down to enable herself to move away from him.

Suddenly she couldn't move as she felt Leviathan's power settle over her.

"Tygarya..." His voice was menacing and made her shiver. The realisation of actually having no freedom of choice where

Leviathan was concerned settled over her as thickly as his power did.

Tyg huffed in defeat. "I'm yours...happy." She felt a twinge of pain in her heart. "Is that all I am to you? A possession?" She breathed out.

She felt him come over the top of her and he flipped her on to her back, crouching over her. He flicked her hair back from her face and ran his fingers down her cheekbone and over her lips, his touch was gentle and loving, confusing her even more.

"How many times do I have to say this, Tygarya...you are extremely important to me."

"But you won't say why."

Leviathan's jaw ticked as he sighed and stood up, looking down at her as she felt him release her from his power's formidable grip. "I came to check on you, make sure you were okay after yesterday's play...clearly you are not. I should have realised, you are young and therefore confused about your own feelings towards that sort of thing...and how much your body will now crave it."

She sat up onto her elbows and looked up at him with a caustic glare.

"Follow me." He ordered stepping away from her and towards the door. He waited on the threshold, looking back at her with a challenging raised brow.

Tyg got to her feet, adjusting the robe around herself and walked towards him. "Where are we going?"

His brows lowered in annoyance to her question then he turned and walked off down the hall.

Tyg rolled her eyes and followed.

As they reached the bottom levels of the castle Tyg knew they were heading to the baths. She smiled to herself as he walked in and turned to her, pulling her into his body and embracing her gently.

"Tyg...trust me in the knowledge that I know what your body can take."

Tyg flushed as he ran his hands under her robe, over her shoulders and lifted it away from her body so it fell from her and pooled at her feet. He ran his hands down her arms and turned her around, kissing her on the shoulder as his hands kneaded into her back muscles. She groaned at how good it felt.

"You are an incredible gift that has been given to me, I will not do anything to jeopardise that." Leviathan was talking to her in a deep soothing tone as he worked his hands over the muscles in her back, shoulders and neck. He felt her body giving to him, arching back into his touch, like always, it was so responsive. "I know what you need, Tyg...we are very similar creatures...except I give and you will take. Perfectly suited for each other."

He kissed her shoulder again and then tapped her bottom. "Get into the water."

Tyg walked over to the edge and stepped down into the warm water, turning around and watching Leviathan undress.

29

Tyg was shocked as she walked onto the university grounds and looked around at the large stone buildings, sprawling lawns and paved walkways. There were several scholars walking past going to and fro, some were openly discussing topics as they went by, others were alone, heads down and scurrying like timid mice.

General Barrock huffed, sticking his chest out and waving his hand nonchalantly. "Well...that's the library over there...but Lord Antyn was supposed to be here waiting for you."

"To take me off your hands?" Tyg sneered.

"Exactly." Barrock rebuked. "Baby sitting psychopaths isn't part of my job description."

"Funny, I would have thought anything the Emperor ordered you to do would be part of your job description." Tyg lifted her top lip and snorted a derisive laugh.

"And so here I am..." Barrock muttered, conceding the point. "But you are no better off it seems...a slave to his wants just like us all."

Tyg glared at him in shock at those poignant words.

"Tyg!" Antyn's voice called out and they both turned to see Antyn striding across the lawns. She was always quite surprised by Antyn's handsome features, he tended to get over shadowed by Leviathan's striking looks, but he was definitely a very good looking man in his own right, it was no wonder he was such a ladies man...it wasn't just his position as Prince of the realm.

"Tyg..." Antyn puffed out as he reached her. He waved his fingers at General Barrock. "You can go now, General."

General Barrock puffed his chest out, bowed his head, turned and left.

"This way, Tyg..." Antyn started back across the lawns. Tyg stared at the building over to the left that Barrock had said was the library.

Antyn stopped when he realised Tyg wasn't following him. "Tyg?"

"Isn't that the library?" She pointed to it.

"Yes...but I'm taking you to my house first...come on." He turned away again and Tyg followed him this time. She noticed that a couple of royal guard followed along behind them at the respectful distance.

Behind the massive learning halls of the university was a tree-lined avenue of white stone terrace housing. They looked uniform, neat and well kempt with shiny black doors and Tyg could see there were brass name plates on them. She walked closer to one and jumped up the three steps to the door to look at it.

Professor Mandrake.

Tyg jumped back down and did a few long quick strides to catch up with Antyn. He looked at her sideways with a small smile. "You could have just asked..."

Tyg grinned. "Not my style."

Antyn laughed in a relaxed manner, enjoying the day now the rain had stopped and the sun had broken through chasing the clouds away..

"So all the professors live here?"

"Most, some choose not to...depends on if they have a family I think..."

"Oh...and which one is yours?"

Antyn gave her a proud ambiguous look. "I have the manor at the end of the road." He pointed and Tyg could see a good sized white stone manor in the same style as the terrace houses standing proudly at the end, it had a small black wrought iron fence across the front with a little grass square either side of a white gravel path to the front door. In each of the squares of grass was a tree, symmetrically matching. They were showing their early spring foliage of striking red leaves, the way the boughs bent and wavered in the gentle breeze made them look like a maiden's red head of hair.

Antyn swept the gate open and ushered Tyg through and up to the door.

As he opened it Tyg could see he was eager for her to like it. She smiled and walked in to a small area with a coat rack and the stairs to upstairs in front of her. "This way..." Antyn stepped past her after closing the door and walked off down the hall next to the staircase. Tyg thought the house looked very familiar to the one she used to stay in with Barion and May. She felt a little pang of what she could only guess to be home sickness.

She wondered if she should write a letter to Dane...or perhaps to Luke to see how they were doing. Did any of them wonder about her?

Antyn led her through to the kitchen and beyond that was a glass conservatory that opened out onto a little garden that stretched back to a large brick wall perimeter that Tyg guessed was the outer wall of the university grounds. There was a large oak tree in the back yard and its limbs shaded the area well.

Antyn turned and opened his arms out wide and smiled. "What do you think?"

Tyg smiled. "I like it, it reminds me of home."

"Home?" Antyn frowned. "Don't let Leviathan catch you saying that."

Tyg gave him a deadpanned look before looking away and looking up at the back of the house. "It's quite large for one guy...how many bedrooms?"

"Ah...it's actually not that large...and three."

"Hmm..." Tyg wondered if perhaps she could stay here...close to the books she wanted to read. She wanted to read them all, her thirst for knowledge was unfathomable since having access to them. "So where's your library room, every manor house has one..."

Antyn laughed. "You think so...come on...I must show you something you may find interesting."

He took her back into the house and through the downstairs, showing her the kitchen that she had already seen, the dining room, the front reception lounge and then to a small room no bigger than a servants single room. He unlocked it with a flick of his fingers and when he opened the door Tyg was struck by the musty scent of old books. As she walked in she gaped at the bookshelves that lined the walls filled with books and scrolls, some spilling out onto a small table that was in the room. The room was cold and Tyg noticed it had no fireplace.

"It's cold in here."

"Yes, I keep that temperature because some of these books need to be kept from perishing..." He pointed up and Tyg looked up at the ceiling to see a large green magical array spinning slowly over head. Antyn walked over to one bookcase that had several scrolls piled up on its shelves. "Some of these scrolls are extremely old and very delicate..." Tyg blinked, she sometimes forgot Antyn was a sorcerer too.

"What are they?"

Antyn gave her a strange look, almost like he was thinking about whether to answer her or not. "They are scrolls of prophecy..."

"Prophecy?" Tyg startled and stared at the scrolls, her fingers itched to pick one up and look at it. Antyn seemed to read her mind. "No touching."

"Why do you have all these here? I would have thought Leviathan would keep them at the castle if you guys believed in such things?"

Antyn smiled as he looked at the scrolls then back to Tyg. "Believing in such things is what led us to you in a way, Tyg and this is what I do...I study the scrolls."

"Oh..." Tyg drifted to the books and looked along the spines reading their titles.

Some were huge and heavy volumes impressively bound with embossed leather covers with gold leaf and silver inlay. Tyg wanted to touch them and looked at Antyn to see him watching her carefully.

"I wouldn't...those are books on magic, called Grimoires." He smiled amused. "Some have wards of protection over them from prying eyes."

Tyg frowned and twisted her mouth. "Yeah, but you can obviously pick them up?"

"Yes, I can."

"So you're not going to let me?" Tyg pouted and scowled at him.

Antyn chuckled and shook his head. "I'm afraid not, Tyg...those books are not for you...here..." He walked across to the other side of the hall into another room full of books, a study with a desk and bookcases lining the walls. "All these are free for you to read if you so wish."

Tyg walked over and looked at the spines, pulling one out and running her hand over the cover. It was green and gold embossed and the title was 'The Great Discovery Works of Leopold Durant...an indexed encyclopaedia of plants.'

Tyg opened it up and saw that the pages were filled with drawings depicting leafs and flowers with detailed side notes. "This is original?" She gaped in wonder at it as she drifted her fingers over a delicate water colour painting of a strange looking pink flower.

"Of course, all the books in here are originals...that's why they are here, this is my private collection." Antyn said with a flourish. "Some are hundreds of years old."

"Of course..." Tyg rolled her eyes as she flipped the pages of the book, fascinated. "I wish I could draw like that..."

"We all have our talents, Tyg..." Antyn chuckled, then coughed at the sharp look she gave him as she snapped the book shut and put it back on the shelf. "Oh, and you can read these books here, but you can't take them out."

"Out of this room or out of your house?"

"Out of this room." Antyn smiled at her as Tyg looked over to where a large arm chair sat in the corner with a blanket draped over it.

"Okay..." Tyg nodded solemnly as she picked up another one.

"These ones on this shelf you are free to take out into the conservatory...I like to read out there." Antyn pointed to a couple of shelves of books that looked more like ordinary story books and Tyg stepped over to pick one up and look through it.

"Okay, thank you..."

Antyn frowned as he looked at Tyg, she seemed unusually quiet...moody even.

"So, what happened to you guys yesterday? Leviathan left a message to say he was cancelling your visit and you guys just left, but now you show up today looking pensive to say the least?"

Tyg looked up from the book she was perusing, her eyes cold. "You know him." She muttered.

"Indeed I do...and I can see that whatever happened is weighing on your mind...you can talk to me." Antyn tried to sound as empathetic as possible.

Tyg closed the book and placed it back on the shelf with care. "It's probably not a subject I can talk to anyone about, that's the problem."

Antyn frowned at that a little confused. "No one, not even me?"

"Especially you." Tyg scoffed in a mumble.

"Why is that?" Antyn folded his arms and looked insulted.

Tyg sighed, rolling her eyes at him. "It's not a slight against you, Antyn...it's just...um...very personal..." Tyg looked away and Antyn saw her discomfort and her neck redden.

"Oh...one of those problems...well, perhaps you shouldn't shun female companionship quite so quickly..."

Tyg glared back at him then walked to the door, opening it and walking out.

Antyn scratched his cheek wondering what on earth was going on...but one thing he was sure of, Leviathan was getting too close to this girl and her with him.

He followed her out to find her waiting for him in the hallway. He looked at her with an eyebrow raised in question.

"Can we go to the university library now?"

"Don't you want some tea first?"

Tyg sighed. "Do I have to?"

"No, you don't have to...but I really think you should try to talk to me about what's bothering you."

"Why?"

"Because there is no one else for you to confide in, especially given that your topic is the Emperor and not for just anyone's ears..."

Tyg stared at him and folded her arms. "It's embarrassing."

260

Antyn's eyes held hers. "Gloss over it and get to the actual issue...I know you've only been with Lev, and I also know how intense he is...so I can only imagine how intense the last week must have been for you since you surrendered yourself up to him."

Tyg's glare turned into a dark glower. "See that, right there...surrendered myself up to him...that's the same attitude he has."

"Ah...I see...so it's the whole 'she's mine' thing..." Antyn shrugged. "Unfortunately that's just Lev..."

"He said I've been his from the day I was born."

Antyn's eyes widened at that. "Really...he said that?"

"He did...care to explain?"

"Ah...if he didn't then I'm not..."

"Then this conversation is over!" Tyg growled out through gritted teeth.

Antyn sighed dramatically causing Tyg to look at him sharply. "At the end of the day, Tyg, I don't believe Leviathan will do anything to lead you to ruin. Just be a good girl and do as you're told and some day you will be married to the most powerful sorcerer on this earth."

Tyg swallowed hard and looked away, still feeling conflicted.

Antyn watched her then looked away with a small regretful smile, sorry that he had to lie.

30

"Tygarya, why have I been given a report of you talking to druids in deep discussions while at the university?"

Tyg turned to regard Leviathan as he walked into the antechamber of his rooms. She was sitting curled up in a chair by the fire reading. Another week had flown by with Tyg visiting the university three times in the week and had formed a little following of professors hovering over her to answer her questions in the hopes she gives them a good word to either the Prince or the Emperor.

"How come druids all seem to be old men, but warlocks and sorcerers stay young for years?"

"Druids don't have the same abilities to slow the aging process...they are botanists and alchemists and healers...they only have very basic magic, but great understanding in their chosen field of study." Leviathan folded his arms. "Now answer my question."

"My hair." Tyg said simply.

"What?"

"That's why I'm talking to druids...my hair." Tyg said amused as she continued to read, turning a page deliberately.

The book went flying out of her hands and across the room, hitting the wall and falling to the floor. Tyg looked up at Leviathan who was standing staring at her with that vulture like glare.

"Well that was unnecessary..." Tyg remarked with an eyebrow raised.

"Tygarya...I'll give you one more chance at this." Leviathan's tone was low.

Tyg sighed, narrowly avoiding the compulsion to roll her eyes. "You know how I have been using coconut oil to keep my hair nice?"

"Yes." Leviathan smirked. He loved her hair and now imported coconuts from the Paradise Isles near Arial especially for her.

"Well, I've been reading these books about different plants and what they're good for and it got me wondering..."

"Wait, you've been reading books on botany?" Leviathan reached out his hand and the book on the floor came flying back into his hand. He flicked through it. "I thought you were reading fairy tales." The book she was currently reading was about metallurgy.

Tyg snorted. "I read a lot of things..."

"Hmm...perhaps I should take more interest in what you're reading." Leviathan put the book down on the table. "Continue..."

"Really? I thought I was done explaining..."

"Nothing is done until..."

"Until you say it is....yeah, alright..." Tyg rolled her eyes as Leviathan smirked, his eyes darkening at the movement. "I went and spoke to the druids about coming up with a formula for my hair that would include certain plant extracts that would help keep my hair even nicer."

"Even nicer..." Leviathan muttered as he stepped over and grabbed a lock of her hair and twined it through his fingers.

"So do you approve, my Liege?" Tyg asked.

"I approve..." He pulled on the hair in his hand a little harder, making Tyg frown slightly. "...and await the results with baited breath."

He leaned over the chair, putting his hands on the arms and locked eyes with her. Tyg stared at him, her eyes wide and watchful, his tone had dropped.

"Sorry?" Tyg asked breathlessly.

Leviathan smiled, realising she had no idea she had just rolled her eyes at him, leaned in and kissed her on the lips. "You're lucky you are you...although I hardly know why I even think that way..."

He said with a curious lilt as he stood up and took his coat off, dropping it over the back of a chair.

"You know, I might even be able to market it when it's finished..." Tyg said trying to change the subject back to her hair product, she wasn't sure where this conversation was heading but it made her nervous.

Leviathan stopped and turned. "Tygarya, how many times do I have to say it, you don't have to earn money."

"I know, but I like to...it's nice to have my own money...and this isn't earnt from killing people."

Leviathan rubbed his eyes with one hand as he collapsed into the opposite chair to hers. "Fine...I suppose I should be glad you're not suggesting you want to continue killing people for money."

Tyg sat up. "Fine? Are you serious, I can do it?"

Leviathan looked at her with a lop-sided smirk as he rested his cheek on his fingers, his elbow on the chair arm. "Yes, Tygarya...earn your money...as long as it's legitimate and you pay your taxes, your workers, those druids and do everything within the law."

"Taxes? To you?" Tyg frowned.

"Yes." Leviathan smirked, clearly amused by the look on her face, seeing her mind ticking over.

"Perhaps I can negotiate those taxes...I hear they're quite high." Her eyes twinkled as she regarded Leviathan with as much business acumen as she could gather.

Leviathan's smirk got wider. "They're high because we are at war...expanding our territories."

"But surely being the Emperor's consort gives me some sort of discount?"

"Oh..." Leviathan chuckled. "So you're happy to be known as my consort now...but why should I?"

"Because you want to make me happy?" Tyg gave him a beautiful smile, getting up and slowly stepping towards him.

"Do I?" He said with suspicious amusement. His eyes intent and darkening with every slow step she made in his direction.

Tyg knelt before him, causing him to arch an eyebrow at her. "Do you?" She breathed as she put her hands on his thighs and looked up at him as she slid her hands up higher. He breathed a little amused chuckle but his eyes got darker as his pupils dilated.

"Of course I do, Tygarya."

"Well..." She smiled in triumph. "I'm willing to make you happy in exchange..." Tyg reached for his belt and started undoing it.

Leviathan growled and leaned forward, pushing her away. She fell back looking startled. "Enough, Tygarya. You are not a whore, don't act like one, even with me!"

Tyg looked stunned and a little hurt at his words. "I was only playing around with you...I wasn't serious..."

"Perhaps, but don't do that! Don't ever try to manipulate me."

Tyg moved back onto her knees and looked up at Leviathan contritely as he stared at her, his eyes glowing.

"Now you can stand up, and get in there." His tone had dropped and was hard as he flicked his head indicating the bedroom.

Tyg baulked, startled at the sudden order, she had come to learn what that tone meant for her. "What?" She stood up, worried.

Leviathan smirked, standing up and grabbed the back of her head tugging on her hair, leaning closer into her and lowering his voice to a husky whisper. "You can go into the bedroom now and wait for me."

Tyg's whole body suddenly went cold and she shuddered. "But..."

Leviathan spun her with a quick flick of his fingers and pushed her with a gust of wind at her back towards the bedroom door. "Last chance to go willingly, Tygarya, are you not even aware that you rolled your eyes at me before...and now I'm just in the mood to collect."

Tyg's stomach dropped and she looked back over her shoulder with a little look of fear. Leviathan chuckled as she turned back and quickly made her way to the door.

"You see your place? Made for me...I am literally the only man in the entire world that could get that reaction from Tygarya Essyndyl...am I right? I control you, not the other way around."

Tyg grit her teeth as she opened the door and stepped inside the bedroom. He was right, but only because he was stronger, faster and more powerful than anyone, including her. So did that actually make her just a possession?

She had been blinded to Palin's real intentions concerning her, was she being slowly blinded by this powerful Emperor as well?

She turned back towards him as he came into the bedroom behind her and kicked the door shut.

"Leviathan?"

She was swamped by him as he grabbed her up in a strong embrace his mouth consuming hers, silencing her. Devouring her every breath and making her mind go blank.

31

As the weather started to heat up so did the castle activity, preparing for the onset of summer and the start of the army's next campaign into Kolastan. Supplies were brought in and stockpiled before being shipped out and the whole castle seemed to bustle with people coming and going where it was usually graveyard quiet and reserved within the halls. People scattered out of the way as the Emperor walked sedately through the halls, his long strides purposeful as he went in search of the one person he found himself actually missing, not being able to spend much time with her as he organised for the coming summer campaign.

"Tygarya?" Leviathan's voice called out to her as he opened the door to her rooms. She looked up at him from behind the desk she had acquired. Leviathan frowned at the scene in front of him and walked over, looking at the papers in front of her. "What's all this?"

Tyg looked up and smiled at him, leaning back in her high backed leather chair. "Purchase forms for my hair product."

"You're kidding? It's already being sold?" Leviathan picked up a paper and read it.

"Of course, it's been a whole month." Tyg replied with a little huff, did he really have no idea of the passing of the weeks he was so busy?

He saw the name on it was Lady Marion DePont. He shook his head, laughing. "Well, it seems you're a business woman now." He perched on the corner of the desk, bending one leg up slightly and grabbing the ankle with his hand as he rested it against the thigh of his other leg. "I like the look of you behind that desk...very sexy."

Tyg grinned at him. "You want to sit on my knee?"

Leviathan laughed. "No, but I do have concerns this may take up too much of your time."

"What else do I do?" Tyg pondered in confusion of his statement. "I only train three times a week for two hours a day..."

"Spend time with me." Leviathan growled.

Tyg startled, her eyes going wide. "I only work when you work..." Tyg said a little bitter at his controlling attitude.

"Hmm...is that why I haven't noticed this before?" Leviathan said with a strange look in his eyes.

"Leviathan...you said I could do this." Tyg scowled. If his possessive narcissistic attitude took over she knew he would try and strip everything from her, and she couldn't let that happen, she had bigger plans of expansion. "I spend all my spare time beside you...I always come when you ask it of me."

Leviathan was watching her with that vulture gaze. "Quite." He stood up. "And I require it of you now, come with me Tygarya, I have a surprise for you."

Tyg was shocked. "A surprise?" He held his hand out to her with a smile.

Tyg took it and stood up. He pulled her into his arms and ran a hand over her hair, picking up a lock of it and holding it to his nose, inhaling the scent.

"Your hair is so soft now, Tyg..." He breathed, dropping her full name. "I definitely approve of how you are spending your free time, relax."

Tyg reached up on her toes and kissed him on the cheek. "Thank you."

He tightened the grip on her hand pulling her behind him as he led her from her room. "Come on...this surprise I think you will really like."

Leviathan led her to his rooms and when he opened the door to the living area of his vast private apartments she noticed one of Leviathan's man servants was standing by the fireplace, in front of him was a small wooden crate on the floor. Leviathan let go of her hand and folded his arms with a whimsical look on his face as his servant stepped away, bowing his head.

Tyg approached the box suspiciously, glancing at Leviathan several times as she walked up to it.

"Just open it, Tygarya!" Leviathan ordered in impatient frustration.

Tyg crouched down and flipped the lid off it with a quick movement. The view that hit Tyg's eyes made her gasp and fall onto her knees. She peered into the box with a smile of childlike wonderment and absolute adoration. The eyes that stared back at her were wide and full of wonder.

"Leviathan..." Tyg breathed as she reached into the box and wrapped her hands delicately around the small bundle of creamy coloured fur.

The kitten instantly started purring.

Tyg held it up in front of her face, its striking blue eyes a match to her own, its grey coloured face and paws making it look adorable. Tyg kissed its little nose and it rebelled against her affection by reaching out a paw and placed it on her mouth.

"I don't think it likes kisses." Leviathan said amused.

"Rubbish...I just didn't ask for permission." Tyg muttered causing Leviathan to frown. Tyg put the kitten down on the floor and watched it crawl up her knees onto her lap and start playing with the cord of the lacing of her new leather bodice she had received from Master Miguel a few days prior.

"He's the most adorable thing I've ever seen, Lev...thank you."

Leviathan stepped over and knelt behind her, putting his arms around her shoulders and kissed her hair. "Good."

She leaned back into him as she stroked the kitten's soft fluffy fur. "Why?"

"Why not?" Leviathan retorted ambiguously. "I don't need a reason to buy my betrothed a gift."

"Lev..." Tyg breathed as she turned in his arms to look at his face. "He is more than a gift." Tyg said seriously.

The kitten jumped off Tyg's lap and pounced at the crate lid and started chewing it. Tyg turned fully around onto her knees facing Leviathan and cupped his face with her hands. His eyes instantly started glowing with a dark luminosity at the serious look in her eyes.

"Leviathan...I think I love you."

Leviathan scowled, but his eyes were bright as he brushed her hands away and scoffed. "Nonsense, don't get carried away, Tygarya, it's only a cat."

"He is not 'only a cat' how dare you!?"

Leviathan chuckled and stroked her cheek. "I worry you are lonely when I'm not with you...I know you have no interest in making friends with anyone in the castle so I thought an animal companion might be more suitable and you have been more than the perfect consort these last few weeks."

Tyg grinned. "That's so nice of you."

"No, it's not nice, Tygarya." Leviathan grumbled as he ran his hand up the side of her neck and grabbed a handful of her hair and pulled her face to his. He kissed her passionately, swirling his tongue into her mouth. Tyg kissed him back, pushing him down onto the floor and lying on top of him. Leviathan pulled her head back by her hair and regarded her as she looked down at him grinning.

"So we are doing this...here?" Leviathan asked smugly as he ran his other hand down her back and over her buttocks. He squeezed it and pushed her down, grinding her against himself. Tyg bit her lip to feel his hard erection.

"We can do it anywhere you like..." Tyg breathed and deliberately rolled her eyes.

Leviathan's smirk slid off his face and his eyes darkened dangerously. He grabbed her by the shoulders and rolled over, pinning her underneath him.

"You did that on purpose." Leviathan growled.

Tyg blinked slowly at him. "Perhaps my punishments are not severe enough." She had become quite used to and enjoyed his play now. Leviathan growled as he stood grabbing her by the wrist and hauling her up to her feet, then throwing her over his shoulder. He walked off to the bedroom grinning from ear to ear as Tyg calmly submitted to him.

Antyn was with Leviathan in his office going over their campaign plans when Tyg walked in the next morning, the kitten on her shoulder.

Antyn's eyes widened then went to Leviathan. "You did it then?"

Leviathan shrugged. "Obviously."

Tyg grinned. "You knew about this?" She asked Antyn.

"Yeah, he mentioned it..." Antyn said darkly.

"Mentioned what exactly?" Tyg pressed.

"Tygarya." Leviathan growled. "Stop it, or I'll take the little beast back."

Tyg's eyes widened in fright. "You can't!"

"Then stop looking for a reason." Leviathan scolded as he turned back to his work. "I told you already."

Tyg scowled and folded her arms then one side of her mouth tweaked up in a smirk. Leviathan wasn't looking at her but Antyn was and he raised an eyebrow at the expression on her face as their eyes met.

"Did Leviathan tell you that I told him I'm in love with him?"

Antyn's eyes went amazingly wide and his mouth dropped open as Leviathan growled deep in his throat and stood up, throwing the pen he had in his hand down on the desk. His eyes started to glow as he turned to look at Tyg.

"Get out, Antyn...now!" Leviathan roared as he stalked towards Tyg.

Antyn gave Tyg a look that conveyed a 'why did you say that?' look and fled the room.

Tyg looked at Leviathan with fright as the kitten, sensing the change of vibe in the room, jumped off Tyg's shoulder and ran under the chair nearby.

Leviathan had her by the throat. "Don't ever say such things to anyone...especially my brother!"

"Lev...I..." Tyg stammered, confused.

"I told you it was nonsense!" Leviathan growled.

Tyg didn't understand why he was so angry, did he not want her to love him? Wasn't that what a consort was supposed to do and be? Did he hate that word that much that he couldn't even hear it from her?

"I don't understand...Lev...please..." Tyg beseeched him as he squeezed her throat.

Leviathan let her go and stood over her while she coughed. He rubbed his eyes with the fingers of one hand. "Just don't, Tygarya."

"But why?" Tyg demanded, glaring up at him.

"Because that's a bloody order, that's why!" He barked back just as fierce.

Tyg straightened up, her eyes flashing. "So that's all the explanation I get?"

Leviathan's jaw clenched tight as he levelled that cold vulture gaze on her. "Yes."

"Fine!" Tyg said as she rolled her eyes.

Leviathan's eyes went dark and deadly and he grabbed her by the back of one arm and pulled her into him, grabbing her chin. "Those bloody eyes of yours, Tygarya!"

Tyg stared at him, her eyes blazing ice blue. "I don't know I'm doing it until it's done!"

"I know...it shows your condescending manner, that's what pisses me off!"

"I'm sorry..." Tyg suddenly back tracked as she felt Leviathan's power enter her mind.

"You will be..." Leviathan grabbed the back of her neck and leaned down and kissed her hard, bruising her lips and forcing his tongue into her mouth.

His other hand he put on the small of her back and turned them both around in a semi-circle then pushed her backwards until she hit the desk. He spun her round to face the desk and pushed down on her neck making her bend over it.

"Lev..." Tyg protested in a heavy grunt as the force made the air leave her lungs.

He smacked her ass cheek hard as she clamped down on her lip to stifle a yelp. It stung through the tight leather of her pants.

"Five this time I think...now count!"

Once done he lifted her up and spun her round. He pushed her back so she was lying on the desk as he kissed her controllingly, his tongue invading every part of her mouth. His hands ripped at the laces of her leather bodice then pulled her undershirt up over her head as he lowered his mouth to her breast and nipped at her nipples through the lace of her bustier.

"Lev..." Tyg breathed as she struggled against him, but was stilled by his power still in her mind as he straightened and grabbed her belt buckle.

"I know what you're going to say, Tygarya...but don't worry, no one can get through that door."

He grinned as he pulled her boots off, then her pants and pushing her knees open. He took a moment to appreciate her lying naked over his desk completely under his control. "A quick refresher lesson on who is in control here." He growled, before he lowered his mouth to her wet core making her moan and close her eyes, arching her back up in pleasure.

When Antyn returned a couple of hours later he found Tyg asleep on Leviathan curled up like a cat, like back in Asbel City. Antyn frowned as Leviathan smiled at him.

"You're still doing that?" Antyn asked with distaste.

"Of course...I like it." Leviathan said arrogantly.

"I told you...she's not a pet, Lev."

"I know that, brother." Leviathan growled annoyed.

Antyn looked around and saw the kitten was asleep on one of the chairs. "Did you put the kitten to sleep too?"

"No, Antyn." Leviathan breathed with an annoyed sigh. "The kitten played with the things on my desk for ten minutes then jumped over there and fell asleep...it's what baby animals do."

"Hmm...so why do you really do this to her?"

"It calms her...keeps her out of trouble."

"That you know of..." Antyn scoffed, folding his arms.

"What do you mean by that?" Leviathan raised his eyebrows at Antyn with a dark expression.

"Don't forget how sneaky she is...that's all. She could be up to something you just don't know about it."

"You don't trust her?" Leviathan said amused as he stroked her hair.

"Seems to me that her brain needs to be constantly stimulated."

"It is, with her new business...it's keeping her busy enough."

"You hope, I know you are syphoning off her power while she sleeps on you."

"If you know that, why bother asking...you're just wasting my time...and yours. Besides it stops her headaches...makes her a nicer person."

Antyn sat down in the other chair in front of Leviathan's desk. Leviathan watched him with an eyebrow raised.

"She really said she was in love with you?"

"Only because of that thing..." Leviathan pointed to the kitten who had raised its head when Antyn sat down, and was now licking its paw.

"Oh, I see...I didn't think she would be the type to throw it out there like that over a gift, but then...I didn't peg you for the romantic gift giving type either..."

"Fuck up, Antyn! It wasn't a romantic gift...it was a companion for her...she likes cats not people."

Antyn smirked and looked away.

"What's so funny?" Leviathan asked through gritted teeth.

Antyn gave him an ambiguously amused look. "I like pussy too."

Leviathan rolled his eyes and huffed. "Grow the fuck up! Did you come back for any specific reason or just to annoy me?"

"Only to say I got the report finally on the iron ore we got from Arial."

Leviathan smiled. "And?"

"It's good quality stuff...so with our good quality coke we should get some very nice high grade steel out of it."

"Excellent, when does production start?"

"The new blast furnace is due for completion in two days."

Leviathan's eyes clouded. "It was supposed to be finished last week."

Antyn scowled and scratched his chin. "The accident on site delayed things a bit."

"I thought you said the accident was minor?"

"It was...kind of...not really major..." Antyn said evasively.

"Antyn..." Leviathan growled his tone dropping menacingly.

"It's all under control, Lev, don't get all angry...I can probably get a trial load put through tomorrow for you...how's that?"

"Better...I want a full report before we leave for Enyana next week. I don't want to get there and find out we have no weaponry or armour."

Antyn's mouth twisted like he knew this already. "And have you decided what you're going to do with Tyg?"

Leviathan looked up, his eyes narrowed and scary. "You just said she can't be left to her own devices, she'll be coming with us."

Antyn didn't look surprised and nodded. "Okay, I figured as much, it's for the best...I really don't think we should be leaving her alone, she's a wild card...if she had been the spoilt princess we both assumed to find keeping her locked up in the palace would have been easy, but this girl...she's a smart cookie and getting smarter with all these books she consumes."

"Hmm..." Leviathan agreed. "I don't particularly want to come back from conquering other countries to find my own palace burnt to the ground and the key to my ruling the world vanished."

Antyn was silent for a moment, taking in Leviathan's words. Did he still perceive Tyg as a tool only, somehow he doubted it...Leviathan was changing.

"Alright then...oh, one more thing before I go."

"Hmm..."

"You might want to curb your need to consume her power, Lev...you need to consider the possibility that doing that may hinder the awakening of her full power."

"Is that so...I'll take it under advisement. Although the time for her awakening being needed is not upon us yet..." Leviathan said with a sneer.

Antyn shrugged and stood up. "Okay, well just letting you know...oh and Tyg has asked me if she can come over to the university at some point to look at more botany books."

"Yeah, that's no surprise...its fine with me, just make sure she lets me know." Leviathan looked down at Tyg and grabbed a lock of her hair, twining it through his fingers and watching it like he was mesmerized.

Antyn saw the strange look in Lev's eyes and clenched his jaw. "Lev...be careful with her."

Leviathan raised his eyes to Antyn but he had already retreated out the door. "Damn it!" Leviathan scowled.

He looked back down at the sleeping girl and grimaced. He knew he was getting too close, but she really was perfect for him in every way. Prophecy confirmed it, and no matter how much Antyn said to keep his feelings in check it didn't matter in the end, because it was all preordained exactly what was meant to happen.

End of Part One

PART II

Consort, Possession or Useful Pet?

Antyn's
Prophecy Collection

The Phoenix will rise
at the time of its choosing
Betrayal, Survival
Life's last breath
will spark an awakening
of the darkness
and light
that dwells within
– Prophetic Poet 1661

32

Tyg stood beside Leviathan's shoulder watching the last of the supplies get loaded into the wagons ready for transporting to Enyana and beyond to Kolastan.

"Right, let's get a move on before we waste too much of this day!" Leviathan ordered, stepping away and walking to the front of the line.

As he walked Tyg followed, the eyes of the rows of soldiers watching them furtively as they stood to attention. Tyg knew they were all a little frazzled at her coming along. Leviathan had argued with General Barrock about it. Tyg felt a little off, she knew there was something unspoken about her and it unnerved her. Leviathan wasn't just bringing her along for enjoyment of her company, even she knew that much, and it made her feel like Leviathan did not trust her out of his sight. He was always like that, keeping a track of her daily, almost like he expected her to try and escape, but she didn't feel like she was being kept as a prisoner.

As they mounted up on their horses Tyg saw Antyn running over, waving a piece of paper in his hand. He grinned as he stepped up to Leviathan's horse and handed the paper up to him.

"This just arrived by raven...good news."

Leviathan opened the rolled up letter and read it silently as Antyn leaped up onto his horse and waited for a response.

"So they know we are coming..." He said solemnly. Tyg listened attentively.

"With the approach of summer, they obviously guessed we would return and come for them, this could be a diversionary tactic to stall for more time." Antyn smirked gleefully.

Leviathan tossed the letter down to General Barrock who stood holding his horses head by the bridle. He took it and read it with a grim expression.

"Treaty?" He scowled and huffed out a breath. "What could they possibly have to negotiate with?"

Leviathan smirked as he took up his horse's reins and General Barrock stood aside, tucking the letter into his jacket. He went to his own horse and swung up onto its back, lifting his hand to signal to the troops behind to ready to march.

Tyg heard the bellows of the different officers down the line give the order and looked back over her shoulder at the procession.

"Impressed?" Leviathan asked her with amusement in his voice.

Tyg glanced back at him before looking away to the front. "I suppose...it is a grand sight...all those black uniforms and flying pennants."

Leviathan chuckled and looked forward spurring his horse into a walk. "Move out!"

Again the General conveyed the order with a hand signal and the orders bellowed out behind them as they started off.

As they moved through towns and villages they picked up more and more supply wagons and soldiers that were stationed to make sure the harvests were all made and bundled up, stored correctly for winter without being plundered and now ready for delivery to the battle front.

After another two weeks of travel the line of soldiers and wagons stretched back as far as the eye could see and Tyg looked back over her shoulder as they reached the peak of a hill to see the procession stretching back for miles as they crossed the border into Enyana. She caught Leviathan glance at her and she smiled at him.

"Impressive." She breathed with amusement.

Leviathan laughed, pointing in the opposite direction. "That's impressive..."

Tyg turned in her saddle and looked out at the view of the land dropping away to the sea, the sun sparkling off the waves and the golden sand beaches. It was a long way off but still looked as picturesque as Leviathan promised. Davios, Enyana's capital city clear in the distance was where the soldiers often took leave from their duties and training.

"So do we get to stay here for a few days' rest, it looks amazing?"

"Another time, we will make camp there tonight, then follow the shore line up, don't worry Tygarya, you will get to see plenty of the beach from here until we have to move inland again towards where the main camp is.

It took them another fifteen days to reach the campaign headquarters for the upcoming battle travelling only an average of ten to fifteen miles a day with such a large army in tow now. It was stationed twenty miles back from the border with Kolastan and inside a rich Lord's estate. The last few days had been interesting for Tyg, seeing the ravages of battle here and there dotted about. Some villages burnt to the ground, rubble where once stood a sizeable town yet the beauty of the land and sea seemed to hold a serene dream like quality to it.

The people would come out and stare at the procession with blank expressions, some with fear, as Leviathan's soldiers that had remained from the battle as peace keepers with Enyana lined the street, standing to attention as their Emperor went past. Tyg walked her horse up closer to Leviathan's as they started up the hill leading to the Lord's estate. He slid his vulture like stare across to her with an eyebrow raised.

"People don't seem happy to see you back..."

Leviathan's top lip twitched up a little on one side. "It usually takes a while for a conquered country to find its footing again under new ruler ship...I don't need them to like me...but this particular part of the country is not spared for the time being as we are close to the border here with Kolastan, so the people here are probably a little more on edge to do with that than anything..."

Tyg pursed her lips and looked back to the front as they approached the large manor house at the top of the hill that looked down upon the devastated town and its large steel mill where the iron ore from Arial had been delivered.

"Was this a hard war?" Tyg asked a little more subdued.

Leviathan turned his head to appraise her of her question. "It was hard fought...Enyana has many mineral deposits and the temperature is not as severe as most of Tylandria, therefore their crops are more lush...they always knew that trade with them would one day give way to a takeover and they fought bravely, they were trained and had good defences...but lucky for me not many warlocks of any real power." Leviathan's voice was sombre as he spoke and Tyg was surprised, thinking he would relish war.

"The capital took the heaviest casualties...the King amongst them, which was not my plan, but he refused to surrender...even after the years of positive trade between our countries." Leviathan grumbled.

"I thought you wanted to take over, so wouldn't you need to kill the reigning monarch?"

Leviathan brought his horse to a halt, looking back down the hill at where the procession of supplies had stopped, not needing to go up to where the Emperor planned to stay. "No, my plan is not to kill the current Kings, I want them to continue to rule, but under my guidance."

Tyg looked surprised.

Leviathan smiled strangely at her. "That is what an Emperor really is, an overseer, if you like."

"So what do you get out of it?" Tyg asked a little confused.

"Tribute, a percentage of crops each year and above all ultimate control over the masses."

Tyg pressed her mouth together seeing the dominant light spark up in Leviathan's eyes.

Their attention was taken by a couple of military officers coming down the stairs of the mansion and walking up in front of the horses, saluting sharply then waiting for them to dismount.

General Barrock dismounted and saluted in front of an officer that wore the identical uniform to him, but instead of four stars on his uniform he had five in a circle and gold tassels on his shoulders, before shaking hands with him less formally. Tyg guessed this General was the most important one.

"It's good to see you, General Barrock!" The other General greeted him warmly.

Leviathan stepped off his horse and walked to hers, taking Fulminous's head as Tyg dismounted. She was under a light cloak with a large hood, but it billowed in the wind as she dismounted and fell to her shoulders revealing her rare hair colour. The General of the Army stared at her with disbelief but seeing Barrock discreetly shake his head, said nothing.

Antyn leapt from his horse and approached with his usual gleeful smile and shook hands with the General of the Army and his accompanying officers.

"General Oltar, how have you been?" Leviathan finally turned to focus his full attention on the General.

"We had a hard winter keeping rooves over everyone's heads who had been displaced, mainly in Davios. Glad to see the back of it, but the soldiers are still able to be fed daily rations, so we're not complaining and the people are appreciative of our help. We headed up to here from the Capital over a fortnight ago and so we are well dug in now in preparation."

"Excellent..." Leviathan slid his gaze to the next officer standing beside the General as the General turned slightly to introduce the next ranking General beside him that wore the identical uniform and four stars as Barrock.

"You'll remember Chief of Staff, General Kloine..."

Leviathan waited for the man to salute him before stepping to the next one.

"And Lieutenant General Bayton..."

Leviathan nodded at them both. "Gentlemen..." He said before lifting his gaze to see where Tyg had got to. He saw her a little way off with Antyn.

"Major General DePerin and Brigadier General R'Hurin are with the main army down closer to the border, we scheduled a visit to the main encampment tomorrow, if that suits you, my Liege? That's where you will be able to make contact with those of your royal guard that accompanied the ore."

"Yes, that's fine." Leviathan said with a frown, still watching Tygarya and Antyn as they seemed to be wandering off around the edge of the hill looking at something.

"What's over there?"

General Oltar looked away and saw the Prince walking to the edge of the hill where a low stone wall perimeter kept the ground even. "Ah...on a clear day such as this you can just make out the encampment of the main forces, my Liege..."

"Hmm..." Leviathan walked off in the direction of Tyg and Antyn leaving the Generals all looking after him, before General Oltar looked at Barrock.

"What's the go there?"

Barrock sneered with contempt. "The Emperor has found himself an Elvian pet, he likes to keep her close on a short leash and under strict control...lucky for us, believe me, she's fully trained to kill."

"An Elvian?" The officers all muttered their disapproval.

"Trust me, the least amount of time you spend in her presence the better." Barrock insisted.

Leviathan stepped up behind Tyg as she stood looking out over the view, in the distance hundreds of small white specks of canvas tents could be seen scattered over the meadows as a haze of smoke from many campfires drifted over the top. Leviathan placed his hands upon Tyg's shoulders, looking over her head.

"Another impressive sight?" He asked with a tinge of teasing.

"Yes...how many soldiers do you have?" Tyg asked.

"One hundred thousand all together." Leviathan replied proudly, turning her to face him. "Now come back to the house." He glanced over at Antyn. "Both of you. That was rude to walk away."

"I only followed Tyg..." Antyn shrugged before walking back towards the waiting Generals. "Thought I had better as you were busy..."

Tyg frowned. "I don't need to be watched all the time...and by the looks on the faces of those Generals, I wasn't about to be welcomed..." Tyg folded her arms, her eyes focusing on the shiny silver buttons on the front of Leviathan's coat.

"It doesn't matter if you are welcomed or not...I expect you to stay by my side, I didn't think recognition was that important to you?"

"It's not, that's why I walked off..." Tyg said stubbornly. "I would much rather look at the view."

"Good, so if I tell them all to ignore you, that will be a good thing."

Tyg finally lifted her chin and looked up at Leviathan's face, meeting his eyes with a cold pout. "Just what do they see me as?"

Leviathan's brows furrowed as his piercing gaze locked with hers. "Doesn't matter. My opinion is the only one that matters and right now I'm getting pissy." His tone dropped and Tyg huffed, looking down again.

"Lead the way, my Liege..." She muttered.

Leviathan smirked, taking Tyg's wrist and stalked back to the main entrance of the mansion. The Generals all looked miffed as Leviathan came back with Tyg in tow. "Right, someone show me to my rooms, I wish to settle my consort in there, then we shall have a meeting...I want to see the results of the steel refinery."

"Can I not go with you?" Tyg asked pensively.

He gave her a look over his shoulder, turning to look at her fully. "Can you behave?"

He saw Tyg's expression tighten as her eyes changed colour. "What do you think I'm going to do exactly? What possible trouble can I get into surrounded by your entire army?"

Leviathan frowned and glanced away for a moment, taking in the faces of his officers as they stared grimly at the girl hidden under the black cloak. He saw Antyn standing close by looking mildly amused by the request.

"Alright, Tyg...stay by my side."

33

Entering the large manor they all made their way to the living area that opened up at the back of the house to a sprawling lawn and gardens that drifted off down the hillside. The room had been rearranged to accommodate the impromptu war room and the dining table from the adjacent room had been brought out and placed in the middle of the floor with a large map of the area laid upon it.

Leviathan walked in and up to the table, placing his hands upon the map and staring at it.

Tyg pressed in beside him and looked down at the map with a curious frown. "So what are we looking at?"

Leviathan smirked and traced a finger over the map. "We are here, that line is the main trade route between the countries that leads up into the main divide."

"It's hard to tell what's what looking at a flat map..." Tyg commented.

"The lines show how steep the terrain is, the closer together the steeper it is...see here, parts of Enyana are nice and flat and in the summer time hot and dry but in the winter it's cold and gets a lot of snow in parts near the mountains..."

Tyg listened intently as Leviathan strayed his finger over the map explaining.

"Kolastan is basically the end of this whole mountain range, cliffs, crags and impossible passes...the capital lies in an elevated valley that is practically impossible to reach in the winter so we have to wait until the thaw is complete before we can even make an assault upon this divide which of course has been heavily fortified in anticipation of our arrival. We need to get through that before I have any chance of getting to their capital." His finger slid up the map and tapped.

"And beyond Kolastan?" Tyg asked her eyes drifting to the edge of the map where the other side of Kolastan seemed to once again drop away to being quite flat.

"Gua del Mar...practically a desert. Small population, only one big city, they're more a nomadic people..."

"And are you going to conquer them too?"

Leviathan gave a small rueful smile. "Of course. I hope to do so this campaign."

It was later in the day when Antyn arrived back from the steel mill. Leviathan looked up from the map he was studying with a small grin on his face to see a folded blanket under Antyn's arm. Leviathan had been most happy with the high grade of the steel coming out of the large furnaces that had been built here, he had sought out the best blacksmiths, ones that were masters of their craft and held reputations for making many ceremonial and family heirloom swords for the wealthy, knowing the technique of folding steel to increase its strength yet still maintaining a thin sharp edge.

"Is that it?" He asked as he stood up.

Antyn smiled and handed out the blanket. Tyg looked up and could see something was clearly wrapped in the blanket. "As ordered..."

"Have you looked?"

"Of course, I didn't want to bring them all the way here if I knew you weren't going to like what you see..."

Leviathan smiled appreciatively and took the blanket, placing it on the table on top of the map and started unwrapping it. "Tygarya, come over here."

Tyg stood up, curious and came to his side as he flipped the blanket open to reveal two short bladed swords with black leather twined grips and simple silver cross guards, the pommels were silver, engraved with a gold plated dragons head. Leviathan picked one up and pulled it from its scabbard revealing a blade that shone like silver it was polished and sharpened to a very high quality. He turned it on several angles checking the edge and the workmanship before pivoting around and holding it out to Tyg.

"Tell me what you think?"

Tyg took the sword from him and felt the weight was good. "Is this what you've made for your army?"

"Not quite..." Leviathan said with a pleased tone. "These are for you."

Tyg lifted her gaze with a perplexed frown. "Me?"

"Your sword is of poor quality, and I know by talking to Master Migel back home that you were planning on getting another sword, yes?"

"I was...I have always planned to carry two..." Tyg murmured as she looked again at the sword. She had wondered why it was short compared to the normal regiment type sword, but now she realised...it was for her and Leviathan knew she was wanting to carry her swords on her back. She also preferred a thin bladed short sword. "I don't know what to say..." She breathed, her eyes lifting back to him.

He reached out and stroked her cheek. "I planned to wait until your birthday, but since we were coming over this way..."

"My birthday..." Tyg looked up with a small frown. "That's a long way away."

"That's why I couldn't wait. I didn't want to risk you getting another sword on your own...plus I brought the new harness Migel has made for you." Leviathan said, taking up the other sword and taking it out of its scabbard to check it over too. "You may need them, best to be properly prepared."

Tyg gave Leviathan a beautiful smile. "Thank you, my Liege. I will use them in your honour for protection of your realm."

Leviathan stared at her, shocked by her words, Antyn gaped at her before looking away with a frown. He placed the sword down and took the other one off her then pulled her into his body, kissing her deeply.

Antyn huffed. "Hello...still here..."

He got no response as the couple seemed to be getting even more serious with the kissing. He shook his head and walked out of the room leaving the love birds to it.

The response from Tyg had been perfect and cemented her loyalty to Leviathan, but why did that make his own heart tremor with apprehension?

34

Leviathan dropped the field glasses and sighed. He stood on the prow of a hill with his Generals behind him close to the border of Kolastan where the major trade route town sat impassable in the wide divide, fortified against them with several obvious barriers of stakes, pits and traps along the way. In the forefront was a small army massed on the flat and foothills where the border was clearly marked out with stakes.

"So it's war then?" Antyn asked.

"Hmm..." Leviathan snorted. "The longer I wait the longer I give them to build fortifications. There are already reports coming in of them increasing their soldier numbers at that town...their coming in from the south directly from the capital." He tapped the map being held by a couple of soldiers against the wind that blew. "This is where they look to be planning to try and cause a siege...I really don't want that hassle for too long."

Antyn shrugged. "I'm sure they started building those when you invaded Enyana. It is the most logical place to cross and the main road access from trade with Enyana. They would have stopped fortifying during the winter but as soon as the pass was open once again..."

"Probably, but the longer I wait the more they can build and the sturdier they become."

"Hmm...a siege is definitely time consuming considering we will probably get stuck with another siege once reaching the capital as well." General Oltar agreed bitterly. "It's about twenty miles back from this pass and no doubt fortified beyond even this...it's a narrow useless country without taking into consideration all the minerals, coal, gold and gems in those ranges."

Leviathan grinned, getting control of all those mines was the main reason Kolastan had to be taken this summer. There was one other reason this mountain range was so important, however.

Tyg noticed his eyes glow intently and his lip curled up on one side. "You know what happens in a siege situation, don't you Antyn?"

Antyn looked up and met Leviathan's gaze. "Yes, my Liege." Antyn's voice was cold and flat.

Tyg sat up. "What happens?"

Leviathan glanced at her like he had forgotten she was there. He smiled and stepped over to her putting an arm around her shoulders and pulling her into his side. "Let's just say, Tygarya, it's expensive both on money and resources to have soldiers of this number sitting around idle and I'm good at helping the other side negotiate a surrender."

"Oh..." Tyg's thoughts went to Corvyn wondering if he was on the front line somewhere just below them. "In that case I don't think you should wait."

"Is that so?" Leviathan gazed into Tyg's eyes with that intense vulture-like gaze returning.

"You're supposed to be taking territory, expanding your empire, aren't you? What's the point of ruling over rubble and ghosts because everything is destroyed? Force the siege and start negotiations."

"Rubble and ghosts?" Leviathan chuckled. "You do have a way with words, Tygarya."

"She's right, of course." Antyn added with a sigh. "Perhaps it is time to get over there and make your presence felt, your Generals obviously aren't good at negotiating peace treaties...we are massed only five miles from their border, the new weapons have already been distributed..."

"Hmm..." Leviathan groaned as he stroked his fingers through Tyg's hair. Tyg watched him intently as he thought about it. "It's still another week of travel through that terrain to reach the Kolastan Capital. They can take advantage of the terrain along the whole route decimating my army...not to mention those bloody sorcerers are out there somewhere...it's not ideal for us."

He turned to his Generals who were waiting patiently for his next orders. "Let's move the main army up to this line...half a mile from their border flags, it's time to make them start to sweat, meanwhile I want a small force to go set out and find another way around, if we can bypass this main divide and their fortifications to avoid a siege and trickle our forces unseen through some other pass we could effectively split their army in two and take the Capital while they are undermanned."

"Yes, my Liege!" General Oltar saluted with a vicious grin upon his face.

"As soon as the first ten thousand are in place start the attack, don't wait."

"Yes, my Liege!"

They rode into the area where the army was basing its main campaign strike into Kolastan two days later, Tyg looked around at all the tents and soldiers sitting around camp fires, sleeping on the ground or doing hard labour digging trenches and latrines.

There was still sporadic fighting going on just over the rise and flashes of coloured light from the warlocks, clashing of steel and screams of the injured and dying could be seen and heard.

"Why are you doing this again?" Tyg asked as her nose wrinkled up in disgust at the smell of thousands of unwashed soldiers. She was wearing a heavy black robe with a large hood drawn over her head to conceal her from the curious gazes of the soldiers as they past them by so was getting irritable as sweat ran down the back of her neck.

The soldiers all fell instantly to their knees and bowed their heads to the ground as they recognised their Emperor, but as word spread others came running to watch their Emperor approach and cheer for his arrival before hastily falling to their knees, rising again once he had past to continue to cheer.

Leviathan looked over at her and raised an eyebrow at the face she was pulling. "Because I wish to bring this entire continent in under control of one Empire, mine."

Tyg twisted her mouth with a little scorn. "You want to rule the world...that's right...so I'm guessing you're not really wanting to just slaughter everyone and move on to the next then and hurry this up..."

Leviathan smirked and looked back at the path through the encampment. "Correct, there wouldn't be much point to taking over a country if it ends up having no people in it to rule over....did you not make that same argument yourself?"

"So that's why this laborious way of doing it..." Tyg huffed.

"Laborious?" Antyn laughed from the other side of her.

"Well, I mean...you're both sorcerers so..." She gave them a wide eyed twisted expression.

"Ah...yes." Antyn nodded with an amused smile. "I get what you're trying to say..."

"There are certain protocols of warfare that dictate that if I was to use my power to take over through general genocide without any forewarning or attempts at peaceful negotiations I would be deemed a murderous tyrant and be called up for war crimes by the other nations and probably trialled for execution as a war mongering monster." Leviathan chuckled at the preposterous notion of it as Tyg looked at him with a dubious expression.

"Yeah, but you could still kill them all, right? I mean, no warlock can stand up to you?"

"Right, but like you just admitted, I'm not the only one with any magic and to use magic in a battle is as exhausting to the individual as actual fighting. I may be the most powerful but this isn't a one on one fight. If we have twenty warlocks and they have forty, who's going to win that?"

He gave Tyg a serious look. "Let's just say I would rather use my warlocks and exhaust them and leave my own power in reserve in case the enemy manage to get the upper hand. Besides, we aren't the only sorcerers, there is a cloister of them up in this very mountain range somewhere, about eight of them I think, at this stage I am not strong enough alone to take them out as a fortified group should they decide to come down and challenge me on behalf of humanity."

"Other sorcerers!" Tyg exclaimed. "I had no idea..."

"They fled when my father was killed by Tiagratis...he led them and they don't like me. They live in a secluded monastery shutting themselves off from the rest of the world but I don't doubt if I was to make too much noise that didn't sound like humans and warlocks fighting fairly they might investigate and try to take the opportunity to take me out."

Tyg didn't see fear or apprehension on Leviathan's face but there was something...did he not know where in the vast mountain range that stretched down the entire southern part of the continent they were?

"But I need people to be complicit to being ruled over by my Empire anyway and I wish to keep the sovereignty in tact within these countries I conquer so I require an amicable surrender by them, it would be a waste to have to decimate the infrastructures already in place and working, and deal with insurrection and rebels, besides my long term plan is where my power will shine." Leviathan looked off with a whimsical smirk.

"So no dramatic beheadings of Kings then..." Tyg drawled.

"Sorry to bore you, Tygarya."

"And so why do you feel the need to rule over these countries again?"

"Because humans should not be left to govern themselves, I have a plan to make everyone exist to do only what I want them to do." Leviathan said in a hard tone.

Tyg heard the narcissistic tyrant words and bit her lip from asking any more. He sounded a little crazy but she wasn't going to point that out.

It was pretty clear that Leviathan held his human subjects with little regard.

As they settled into a large fortified tower room where the first battle progress meeting was taking place Tyg listened with little interest as the Generals explained that progress was going well...there had been minimal losses and injury on both sides and the other side had easily fallen back and settled in behind those fortified walls within the pass for Leviathan's army to lay siege upon them, all as planned.

"Let the negotiations begin then...we know they never received winter supplies from Enyana this past winter thanks to us, their food stores will be already low. There is no way they can sustain a long siege." Leviathan stated. "Send a messenger of rank to deliver an offer of parley."

Tyg's head came up as the Generals saluted and left. "Are you all pirates now?" She grinned in good humour.

Leviathan swivelled around to regard her with that vulture glare as Antyn chuckled to himself and leaned back in his chair grabbing a fistful of nuts from the bowl on the table and fed them into his mouth.

"It's a general term, Tygarya..." Leviathan said in a droll tone. "You've been quite obnoxious all day...asking a lot of repeat questions."

"I'm bored. I thought I would come to the battle zone and get to fight."

Leviathan clucked his tongue. "Did you...as if. You're here purely to stay close to me, nothing else."

Tyg scowled at him.

"Just behave, Tygarya." Leviathan muttered wearily.

35

It had been two full days already of trying to meet with King Davalos. Every morning Leviathan would go out and meet in a white truce tent with Lord Frameur and get excuses for why King Davalos was not meeting with him today, then the rest of the day was spent wasting soldiers assaulting the massive first wall of the fortifications blocking the pass.

"Argh! That bloody Lord Frameur is starting to really piss me off!" Leviathan stormed into the drawing room, throwing off his gauntlets. It was the second day of trying to get King Davalos to the negotiation table. Leviathan had it on good authority that he had journeyed down from the capital but so far he had been keeping a very low profile.

"What's he done now?" Antyn asked, looking up from the table he sat at looking over paperwork.

"He has once again got into King Davalos's ear and now he is refusing to negotiate surrender at all. It's like he's waiting for something...and I'm getting sick of the excuses."

"That is becoming tiresome, that Lord Frameur is really goading for this war, isn't he?"

Tyg's head came up when she heard that. Corvyn was in that army that would be sent back to the battlefield to storm the fortifications that were by all accounts impenetrable, all the warlocks were called up to try and break the defences and wards.

"I can kill him if you want." Tyg offered cheerfully from the divan she was lying on reading.

Both Leviathan and Antyn turned to stare at her. Leviathan stepped over to her with a droll smile.

"Nice offer, but how exactly? Because it's not like I couldn't just do that too...if it wasn't for the fifty foot high walls guarded by archers and warlocks...that position is impenetrable and we can't seem to find a way around it either, reports are back saying the other two passes have been blocked by convenient rock falls. I cannot win this with a frontal assault and he knows it, but there's no way to get anyone on the other side of that damn wall either."

Tyg stared at him like he was stupid for a moment. "I'm a trained assassin remember...it's what I do. If you really think Davalos will negotiate with you and that Frameur's the obstacle to a peaceful treaty, I can remove him for you with very little fuss. I could even get inside that town and open the gates for you if it meant a quick end to this boring waiting around while men die assaulting that wall looking for a weakness."

Antyn stared at her, raking a hand through his hair, then turned away troubled. Leviathan sat down on the divan next to Tyg's hip with an avid expression.

"It's lovely for you to offer, my dear, but it's not really that simple."

"Of course it is...just get me some intel. Tell me what to expect at the wall and where to find him and I can do the rest. "

Leviathan looked at her like he was considering it. Antyn turned back and baulked when he saw Leviathan's expression.

"Lev...she can't."

"Why can't I?" Tyg sat up looking at Antyn as Leviathan put an arm around her shoulders.

"Because Lord Frameur is a warlock, that's why he's been here controlling this pass for years...you wouldn't be able to get past his protection wards..." Leviathan explained.

"Oh...that's a shame." Tyg said almost too casually.

"But you're right...something has to be done about Lord Frameur, he is becoming quite the obstacle, if I can't take this pass there's no hope." Leviathan looked at Tyg, lifting her chin with one hand and letting his eyes wander her face. "Although, there may be a way for you to get close to him...let his wards down..."

Antyn grimaced. "No, Lev...she can't...you can't allow it....she's betrothed to you now."

"What?" Tyg asked looking between the two of them.

"She's too innocent, too naïve...she could end up getting hurt...and could you handle that?"

"What are you talking about?" Tyg said annoyed, her eyes going to Leviathan's as he stroked her cheek with his thumb, still holding her chin.

"Flirt with him, get invited into his rooms...bait yourself."

Tyg's eyes went wide and she pulled her head back from Leviathan's grasp. "Oh!" She looked down, blushing. He remembered her story about the Lord in Annul.

Leviathan frowned. "No, Antyn's right...you can't." Leviathan stood up and walked back to the table. "We'll have to think of something else...and quickly because no doubt King Davalos has almost finished massing his troops to the south ready for an all-out assault to break the siege and we don't really want the hassle...perhaps I should send the warlocks in on an offensive."

Antyn watched Leviathan's body language, he saw the way Leviathan had rounded his shoulders and hung his head. Antyn grimaced gritting his teeth. It was clear manipulation. Antyn looked over at Tyg and saw her looking at Leviathan with a worried look on her face. Leviathan was taking full advantage of the fact that Tyg didn't want to have to send the army into a battle it couldn't easily win – or at least that Captain - her empathy was going to get the better of her under Leviathan's manipulation.

"Now wait a minute..." Tyg said surly. "What do you mean I can't?" She turned to Antyn. "And I'm not innocent and naïve, do you know the shit I've done?"

Antyn frowned and looked away as Leviathan turned back to face her. "That's not what we meant, Tygarya. You haven't had much to do with people, social interactions on an intimate level...have you ever actually flirted with anyone?"

"She flirts with you all the time." Antyn muttered condescendingly.

"Besides that, Tygarya is...shall we say...comfortable around me now...but before back in Arial she didn't, she was like a scared rabbit."

Tyg gave him a filthy look.

Antyn rubbed his forehead. "No, not in the normal definition of flirting...but your relationship is far from the normal definition of anything." Antyn said bitterly.

"Excuse me...I am right here..." Tyg said caustically. "And what do you mean 'far from normal'?"

Antyn looked at her. "Forget it."

"Yes, Tygarya, don't listen to Antyn's nonsense...but answer my question."

Tyg thought about it. "Flirted? No, I suppose I never really have flirted with anyone besides you...I've seen people flirting though..." Tyg remembered back to Thomas and Miss Belmont, her all giggling and hiding her face, batting her eyelashes. "...seems all a bit stupid. I've been courted before though...but again that was one sided..."

"What?" Leviathan's expression went flat as did his tone.

"Lord Kor? I told you about him...he courted me on agreement for two weeks, after that I told him to get lost."

"That bastard that put his hands on you at that banquet...yeah, I remember." His voice was stony quiet. "What about that other guy...the one just before me?" Leviathan asked his eyes going dark.

Tyg was surprised then she scowled, she didn't want to talk about Stills, it made her heart break even now. She shook her head. "No...I only knew him for a day and liked him, so I kissed him."

Leviathan and Antyn looked surprised at that. "You just walked up to him and kissed him?" Antyn blurted out, causing Leviathan's expression to darken even further.

Tyg was staring at her hands, deep in thought. "He was teaching me how to use a bow...he put his hand on my stomach to correct my posture and..." Tyg absently placed a hand on her stomach remembering the little flutters. "I remember he used to look at me with such a deep gaze, like you do..." Tyg glanced up at Leviathan and caught the look and looked away again "Like that...sort of. He said plainly he liked me and that he wished he could kiss me, so I just kissed him."

"After just a day." Leviathan growled.

Tyg looked back up her eyes going ice blue. "You kissed me after an hour! Remember?"

Leviathan smiled then. "Yes, I do...you little thief."

Tyg smiled in spite of herself and looked away again. "So anyway, no I've never flirted with anyone, but looking back...I guess plenty of people have tried to flirt with me, but you're right...I guess I was too naïve to see it."

"No, Tyg...that's not being naïve, that's being aloof...you're sociopathic, they didn't interest you so you were completely closed off to them not even aware of their feelings." Antyn explained.

Tyg scowled at him. "Whatever...I'm sure I could do it though."

"I still don't think it would be a good idea."

"I only have to get alone with him, yes? It's not like I actually have to let things go anywhere..."

Leviathan smiled, walking back to Tyg and sat down next to her again. She looked up at him as he brushed her hair back, flicking it over her shoulder. "Let's just give it some thought, shall we?"

"But how long have you got?" Tyg asked. "You said Davalos was massing his troops for another offensive behind that town's fortifications, which could be a slaughter for your front line...which you're trying to avoid, aren't you?" He had said he was going to put his warlocks to the front.

"Maybe another couple of days." Leviathan nodded.

Tyg smiled at him and blinked slowly, looking back up at him under her lashes. "Shall we sleep on it then?" She placed a hand on his chest, playing with a button on his shirt.

"Fucking hell." Antyn muttered and stood up. "That's it I'm out." He walked off muttering to himself.

"Well, Tygarya, you certainly know how to clear a room, but that's not the effect we're going for." Leviathan chuckled amused. Tyg screwed her face up at him.

"It's exactly the effect I was going for..." She grabbed a fistful of his shirt and pulled him towards her as she lay back down on the divan, pulling him over the top of her as he laughed.

"Tygarya, you do that to any other man and I will kill him." Leviathan said quietly as he lowered his mouth to hers hovering just above her lips as his gaze darkened. "...and then punish you accordingly." He kissed her possessively.

Later that evening Antyn found Leviathan in the kitchens of all places. He was sitting at the small table pulling a roasted chicken apart.

"Lev? What are you doing in here, I've been looking everywhere. You do know the servants will bring food to you?"

Leviathan laughed as he stuffed another chunk of chicken meat into his mouth then grabbed a glass of red wine next to him and gulped it back, smacking his lips. "I know...but I was starving, couldn't wait...blame Tyg."

"Blame Tyg?" Antyn said confused. Leviathan levelled a strange smug look at him. "Oh..." Antyn muttered. "Work up an appetite did you?" He said sullenly.

Leviathan just grinned at him. "What do you want?"

"To talk about her actually and what you're trying to get her to do..."

"What's that?"

"Lev, don't play dumb with me...I saw your manipulations, but really...is it wise to encourage this side of her?"

"Don't tell me what to do, little brother."

"I just don't think encouraging her blood thirsty need to kill is a good idea, she's hard enough to control at the best of times." Antyn shuddered. "And what's to say if you send her off on her own over the border that she doesn't defect or disappear into the mountains."

Leviathan threw a chicken bone onto the plate and rested his forearms on the table regarding Antyn seriously. "Not even, not when she's doing it solely for my pleasure, at my request? Don't you get it, Antyn? She would do anything for me right now...and isn't that exactly where we wanted her to get to? Things have been good, very good." He grinned with a strange dreamy look in his eyes. "She's been settled and behaving...I think she needs this test of her loyalty."

"Not at the price of you falling in love with her and besides you know damn well she offered to kill Lord Frameur because she doesn't want to see that warlock Captain possibly hurt on another

ANNETTA LINCOLN

open assault. She has no idea where in the army he is so probably thinks he's up there since you purposely mentioned it."

"Shut up Antyn, you swing that term around but you have no idea what it means...if you did you would be more cautious using it around me and I am fully aware of her emotional attachment to that bloody warlock! Why do you think I keep him out of her sight?" Leviathan growled and his eyes went dark.

"I call it as I see it...ever since you started sleeping with her you've changed...you're getting sentimental, Lev."

"Shut up. Antyn." Leviathan growled in warning, his eyes flashing.

"Admit it, you have feelings for this girl."

Leviathan shrugged and sat back in his chair, wiping his hands on a napkin and throwing it on top of the plate before answering. "It's hard not to...she's amazing...on every level, made perfectly for me and my needs."

"Seriously, Lev, you need to focus."

"No, what you have is jealousy, little brother. Now shut up and let me do what needs to be done."

"So, you're going to send her out there?"

"Yes, if she wants to go and prove her loyalty to me, why should I stop her?" He tilted his head at Antyn with a cocky smirk.

"So, no second thoughts about getting her to use herself as bait to get close enough to kill Lord Frameur?"

"No, I have every faith she will succeed with no problems, it's not like she hasn't done it before back in Arial. This is exactly what she's trained to do, go in on a mark and kill him."

"Except for the flirting...how do you feel about the fact he's going to put his hands on her...going to try and kiss her, grope her?"

"He'll be dead for it anyway." Leviathan growled.

"Can you stand the thought of her flirting back with him?"

306

"What's with all the questions, Antyn?" Leviathan asked annoyed. "She's got a job to do and she'll do it...because I want her to do it."

"That makes you no better than that Palin guy."

Leviathan sat forward leaning over intently. "She is mine, was always meant to be mine, he had no right to have her. Okay, so he did a real number on her turning her into this sociopathic killer...doesn't mean I can't now utilise that." Leviathan said calmly. "She is what she is, we all need to adapt to what's in front of us."

"Fine, but I worry you don't realise what you're going to feel at seeing her get close to him, whether you expect it or not."

"Don't worry about me, little brother." Leviathan got up and walked out of the room leaving Antyn staring at the chicken carcass on the table. He leaned back in his chair and rubbed his eyes with one hand, heaved a heavy sigh, then got up and walked out of the kitchen.

36

The next morning Leviathan sat up from the bed he shared with Tyg and raked his hands through his hair. "Get up." He said to her as she stretched and yawned.

"Why?"

"Because I have another attempt at getting a meeting with King Davalos and this time I want you to come with me."

"In a dress no doubt..." Tyg scowled as she dropped her head back on to the pillows.

"If you're up to doing what we discussed..."

Tyg looked at him as he turned and leaned over her putting his arm on the other side of her shoulders. He picked up a lock of hair and twirled it round his fingers as he looked down on her smiling. "If not, just come in your leathers."

"If you ask this of me, you must realise one thing." Tyg said as she sat up, looking Leviathan in the eye.

"What's that?" He asked with a small frown as he leaned back slightly.

"I will succeed...no matter what."

Leviathan's frown deepened and he looked her straight in the eye. "I'm getting the feeling that means something more than it should."

Tyg looked away thoughtful. "People call me a berserker."

"Yes, I've seen it in action." Leviathan said ruefully.

"But I'm not...I'm worse than that."

"Worse? You're not really making any sense, you're talking about when your eyes go black?"

"Yes. It's hard to explain...I go inside myself...I focus on the task at hand and I mean it...a cold hard focus...nothing will stop me from my target...nothing."

Leviathan looked at her surprised. "I think I understand, it's your Elvian nature."

"Do you really?" Tyg looked at him her eyes an intense ice blue. "I've had women and children in my way before, Lev, and I haven't even hesitated."

Leviathan looked at her silently but his jaw clenched tight.

"And I felt nothing...nothing!" Tyg wrenched her eyes away from his and pulled her legs up hugging her knees. "I scare myself..." Tyg let out a laugh like a sob. "The only thing that scares me, apart from you, is myself."

"You regret it now though...?"

Tyg shook her head. "No...that's just it...I don't, I would do it all again."

Leviathan rubbed his forehead and looked away. He stood up and wandered over to the windows looking out at the rows of vines of the estate they were staying at, a mile back from the frontline. He turned then walked back and sat down next to her again taking her hands in his he kissed them then put them into his lap.

"Tygarya, you have been used and abused. Trained to put your feelings aside and remain completely unemotional to get the job done. Don't blame yourself. Sometimes I wish you were like that all the time, maybe that's why your emotions can run unchecked at other times...like a dam exploding. And those headaches, perhaps they are an indication of it?"

Tyg was looking at their hands. Leviathan gently took one hand back and lifted her chin and looked into her eyes, he noticed they were that strange cornflower blue. "I ask you if you want to do this...you can say no."

Tyg shook her head. "I'll do it...I just want to make sure you understand that if things go awry the casualties could mount."

Leviathan shrugged. "So be it."

"What if it makes Davalos go head long into war rather than the desired effect of getting him to talk of surrender."

"We can tackle that bridge if we need to, but if you can get at least that lower gate open to allow our troops in past that first wall, I don't believe Davalos will have much choice but to negotiate surrender."

"Alright then, let me get dressed...in a dress." Tyg rolled her eyes as she went to get up. "Can we find one that's been left behind by a lady of this region?" As she stood Leviathan grabbed her arm and pulled her back into him, between his legs and pulled her down. He tangled his hand into her hair and held her firmly, as she looked fearful.

"You rolled your eyes, Tygarya..." Leviathan's growl was ominous.

"Oh shit, it's a habit, I can't help it...Lev..." Tyg tried to pull back but he held her firmly by the back of her head. He grabbed her right leg around the thigh and lifted it so it was on the bed beside his left hip, then pulling her head down to the right he reached around her and grabbed her other thigh lifting it up so she suddenly found herself spun around and lying face down over his lap, her head and thighs held firmly by him.

Tyg was on her elbows struggling to get up as she grit her teeth. "Leviathan, fuck!"

"You know the consequences, Tyg, but you're lucky I'm short on time...next time it will be worse for you, I promise you that." Leviathan growled as he whacked her left butt cheek hard then pushed her off his lap onto the floor. He stood up and stalked out of the room. "I'll find that dress."

37

As Tyg walked into the tent where the meeting was taking place, following behind Leviathan and Antyn, she saw Lord Frameur turn and immediately smile at her his eyes wide and curious. She downcast her eyes and looked away submissively. Antyn had cast a spell over her hair changing it to a fiery red based on the common colour of the royal family of Enyana and their extended family.

"Emperor Adramelech, who is this lovely young lady you have brought with you to this meeting?"

"No one of concern, Lord Frameur but if you must know she used to be the Duchess Targatha." Leviathan muttered. Tyg looked at him when he said 'used to be' with a dark scowl, before turning to smile demurely at Lord Frameur as he stepped over with concern, taking her hand and kissing it.

"What a pleasure to meet you, Miss Targatha." Lord Frameur said pleasantly. "But what doth one mean by 'used' to be?"

"She's a lucky default of the war." Leviathan said simply as he collapsed in a chair. Tyg scowled at him in an obvious manner showing her discontent.

"How is it that you have kept her so?" He asked perturbed as he started to notice little details like her torn dress and unbrushed hair.

"She was the niece of King Hyston...so a hostage, a spoil of war shall we say." Antyn said with a meaningful lilt to his voice.

"Ah..." Lord Frameur sounded unsettled as he looked into Tyg's eyes and stared a long moment. Tyg frowned ever so slightly at him and her eyes changed colour. Lord Frameur blinked and looked away. "Oh my..." He muttered to himself as Leviathan smiled at him taking the bait.

"Yes, so I thought to utilise her as my servant from now on...she can get us all drinks...learn to be humble." Leviathan flicked his head in the direction of a table with wine and water on it.

"Ah, yes...very good." Frameur looked uncomfortable as he glanced at Tyg's miserable face while she set about her task acting forlorn and under duress.

"So Frameur, what's the excuse today?" Leviathan muttered rubbing his forehead.

"Excuse? I assure you Emperor Adramelech, that they are not mere excuses..."

"So where is he?"

"Where's the king?" Tyg interjected sounding surly, rushing up to Lord Frameur and falling to her knees in front of him. Everyone looked at her startled. This wasn't part of the script. Tyg's face was the epitome of sadness as she looked up with large tear filled eyes. "They said they were meeting the King today..."

Lord Frameur looked at her wide eyed as she grabbed onto him. "Can I meet this King of yours or not? I need to beseech his help."

"Ah...I..." He looked frightfully over at Leviathan whose face had dropped into a stony countenance looking frightening. Antyn rolled his eyes and sucked on his teeth.

Leviathan shook his head amused glancing sideways at Antyn who slowly sank into the chair beside him to watch the show. Tyg placed a hand on Lord Frameur's chest. "I would do anything to meet the King of Kolastan, I have heard he is a great man and I need help to escape this situation..." Tyg was being overly dramatic but then perked up with a giddy smile. "Does your King hold balls and banquets?" Tyg looked at Lord Frameur doe-eyed, acting like an airhead.

"Ah, yes he does, from time to time...." Lord Frameur stammered having lost all self-control the minute Tyg put her hand on him.

"Good, please I need to go with you, you need to save me?" Tyg said in a girly voice Leviathan and Antyn had never heard before but her eyes were glowing softly. Leviathan snorted, causing Tyg to turn to him.

"See what I mean...these conditions are abhorrent! I used to hold balls all the time and now this brute refuses to allow me to do anything but serve him, he's wicked! Keeps me confined in his own rooms no less, can you believe that! It's absolutely scandalous that a young lady such as myself be extorted to being a mere servant girl at his complete beck and call!" Tyg swooned and fell heavily on her hip. "Oh the humiliation is too much to bare, I get bullied by people who used to serve me! My father is dead! No one will help me here. Please you must help me!"

"We are poised to go to war again with this man and his King, Duchess...and you are a spoil of war, do you think I would just hand you over to the other side?" Leviathan stated, sounding bored like he had to put up with this nonsense from her all the time, he was playing along, but Antyn stood up and grabbed her shoulder and started to drag her back.

"I do apologise for this servant's behaviour, Lord Frameur, she will be sent back and punished accordingly."

"No, please...no more whipping!" Tyg turned to Lord Frameur, breaking free of Antyn's grip and fell against him. "Tell him he can't do this to me! I'm related to royalty, I have rights in wartime...he can't treat me like this! Please, I beg of you don't go to war, I hate war! Surely things can be sorted over a lovely sit down dinner and polite conversation, don't you think Lord Frameur, you look like a far more reasonable and civilised man than these monstrous brutes. Perhaps you would consider saving me in these negotiations..." She stroked her hand down his finely embroidered waistcoat.

"Well...it's just..." Frameur stuttered flustered by her vivaciousness.

"You can't let me down now my Lord, I'll give myself to you...my father spoke of you many times, I just know that you won't leave me here with this monster..." Tyg deliberately let the dress fall off her shoulder revealing a nasty black bruise, she had used charcoal and blueberry juice.

"Oh, he did?" Lord Frameur said his mouth going dry and his eyes roaming her body in the dress and seeing the bruise he swallowed hard as he helped her to her feet once more.

Tyg had put a hand on her own cleavage as she said it making Lord Frameur look straight at her bosom. "Oh wait, how rude of me..." Tyg said stepping back and taking her hand off Lord Frameur's chest and looking to the ground in dismay. "I have nothing to offer you, no riches anymore, they've all been stolen by these wretched soldiers. Are you single, like not married yet? Perhaps I could sacrifice myself to a marriage to you..." She leaned closer and whispered in Lord Frameur's ear. "Help me, please...I'm being held against my will by these savages, he has taken my body by force!"

Lord Frameur descended into a coughing fit and had to get a glass of water.

"Oh my goodness, please let me help you, Lord Frameur." Tyg took the glass as he sat down and held it to his lips bending over just enough so he could stare at her bosom again which was right in his face. Tyg caught him staring and smiled devilishly at him batting her eyelids. "Lord Frameur are you considering me?" She giggled which made Leviathan's eye's go dark and his jaw clench, he frowned and stood up.

"Right this meeting is over...get over here!" Leviathan grabbed Tyg by the hair and turned her to the door. "Out, and stop looking for a way to leave. I own you now, you obey me!" Tyg quailed away from him like she expected to get hit, looking back at Lord Frameur from around Leviathan with a pitiful glance and walked out of the tent with Antyn dragging her by her wrist. Leviathan paused and looked back with a small smug grin at Frameur's fraught expression. "If you want the little minx perhaps we could include her in those negotiations I'm trying to have with your King? She is rather a handful I would rather be rid of." He snorted and left the tent, he knew the fact that Frameur was a warlock meant he would be able to sense something about Tyg, although he had suppressed her aura the man might still suspect she was a witch, so a worthy steal.

He found Antyn and Tyg waiting for him. He grabbed her hand and pulled her at a fast walk the twenty yards back to their front line, then quickly found an officers tent and pulled her in there with Antyn in tow.

"What the fuck, Tygarya!" Leviathan growled.

"What?" Tyg said calmly folding her arms, no hint of the airhead persona left.

Antyn smiled. "Don't worry about it Lev, it will have a result you would never have expected."

"What does that mean?"

Tyg looked at Antyn. "He doesn't get it...?"

Antyn shook his head. "Remember I told you I always wanted you in any negotiation I did?"

"Yes, back in Arial at Lord Doven's." She gave him a pleasant grin.

"I'm sorry I forgot that, we should have had you there at the very first meeting."

"Would someone care to explain?" Leviathan said wary.

"Tyg just got her way into Lord Frameur's town without so much as a question." Antyn explained his eyes sparkling.

Tyg shrugged. "Well we don't know that yet but I'm sure once he finds the note I wrote addressed to the King beseeching his aid, they won't be able to ignore my plea..."

"Note?" Leviathan growled.

"I placed a note in his pocket, that's why I had to get so close...it also gives him a chance to steal me away to his side and save me from you." She battered her eyelashes at him as she grinned. Leviathan scowled at her facetious attitude before letting out a huff.

"Ah, I see now...he's one of those that needs to save the damsel in distress...but Tyg don't ever do that again." Leviathan growled his eyes darkening.

"Do what?" Tyg asked blinking at him.

He scowled but Antyn interjected. "I really don't think she knows until the moment, Lev, if you had seen her with Lord Doven...she's actually a really great actress..."

"Hm." Leviathan snorted. "And with Corvyn and with ourselves if you remember, she plays very deviously I admit but I meant shoving her breasts in his face."

Tyg grimaced as Antyn looked away. "Oh that..." Antyn hissed in a little disapproving breath. "...yeah, don't do that..."

"I'm sorry, Leviathan." Tyg walked up to him and placed her hand on his chest. "But one thing has me curious..."

"What's that?" Leviathan regarded her amused.

"Is that the sort of girl you expected to find when you sailed to Arial?"

Antyn flinched as Leviathan scowled deeply at her. "Not quite..."

"Not quite?" Tyg raised an eyebrow at him.

"Yes, Tygarya, not quite...certainly not so needy for a husband to save her or quite so...tearful or giggly."

"Are you sure about that?" Tyg asked running her hands up Leviathan's chest. He growled at her and grabbed her by her hair pulling her back from him and holding her out at arm's length. As soon as Leviathan touched her hair the colour drained from it as his powerful aura broke the spell.

"Tygarya, don't do that." Leviathan muttered. Tyg smirked on one side of her mouth as Leviathan smiled back at seeing her silver hair return. "Bloody hell, Tyg, you are a force to be reckoned with." He pulled her back into him and kissed her forehead. "Come on, let's get going."

Antyn walked to the tent flap and opened it for Tyg. As she stepped out she noticed the soldiers were all watching the tent after seeing a strange red haired girl being hauled in there by the Emperor. They all stared as she walked out, now revealed as the silver haired girl that was the Emperor's betrothed, none of them could collate why she was playing such tricks and wearing such a dress. Tyg suddenly wished she was wearing a cloak. When Leviathan stepped out and straightened to full height looking around Tyg wrapped her arms around his waist and hid her face.

"What now?" Leviathan muttered looking down on her with an eyebrow raised. "Are you still acting, what's the problem?"

Antyn dropped the canvas. "I think Tyg just became shy."

"What?"

"It's this dress...I hate dresses at the best of times because they make me stand out and get noticed, but this one makes me look ravaged, I don't like the stares. Stop them."

Leviathan laughed and put his arms around her. "Tygarya, you would be noticed regardless of what you are wearing, why do you think I make you wear a cloak in this heat most of the time?" Leviathan pulled her back and took her hand. The expression on his face was magnanimous. "I wouldn't normally say this, but I'm in a fickle mood after that whole acting stunt before so....learn to own it, Tygarya."

He then walked slowly through the soldiers holding Tyg's hand heading back to their horses. Tyg looked around scowling at the soldiers as they stared at her, then she noticed Corvyn. He was standing with his thumbs in his belt staring at her with a dark scowl on his face. She smiled and waved at him. He shook his head with discontent and turned away barking orders at his soldiers and muttering, he waved his hand causing his soldiers to go flying backwards, stopping them from staring.

Tyg heard Leviathan chuckle. "Now that is how a soldier should react, that man is a true leader."

"So promote him again..." Tyg said casually, causing Leviathan to look at her darkly as they reached the horses and he grabbed the reins of her horse.

"I might just do that...he's an incredible warlock."

Tyg noticed Corvyn's men line up around them to escort them back to their outpost. Had he been close by all the time, watching her? She smiled a little to know that fact but felt a little out of sorts that he had obviously kept himself hidden from her sight. Was that an order from Leviathan or did he actually want to stay away from her? That hurt a little, she thought they had come to an understanding, a friendship back in Arial.

As she reached her horse she was grateful to see her cloak was still there and threw in around her shoulders.

She heard Leviathan snort in amusement but he said nothing and allowed her to ride back to their outpost unfettered.

38

"So how are you going to do this, Tyg?" Antyn asked as they held a meeting once they were back in the tower house.

"I told him to save me, that I would try and get to the cemetery at the edge of the vines a mile east of the tower house if he could arrange for some soldiers to sneak through the woods and get me at midnight tomorrow night."

"How's that going to work and seem at all feasible?" Leviathan snorted.

"There will be a distraction that will gather your scouts in and focus to the west."

"What distraction?"

Tyg shrugged. "I don't know...think of something, it's not actually real...just make sure your scouts let those soldiers through to rescue me..."

"Sounds dangerous and a little blasé..." Leviathan grumbled.

"It was on short notice..."

"You think I'm going to let you just go with him in the dead of night...alone?" Leviathan scratched his chin. "I don't like it..."

"It's all your plan. Okay, how about I have someone like a bodyguard with me that I could say has to go with me because he has been my faithful retainer since I was young? That he managed to hide during the takeover of the estate and has aided my escape plan?" Tyg beamed a smile like she was proud of herself for coming up with that on the spot.

Antyn huffed. "It could work, that way she is still chaperoned at least, being a Lady in war time does have its protocols...which she proudly just proved we aren't adhering to..."

Tyg made a face at him. "I couldn't tell you what I was planning, I needed your reactions to appear naturally shocked."

Leviathan gave her a dark suspicious look. "Have someone in mind for that role, do you?"

Tyg's smile turned benign. "I'll need someone who is at least proficient with magic, since Lord Frameur is a warlock, and someone we all trust enough with my life..."

Antyn's eyes went wide and he started chuckling like a mad man, Tyg scowled at him. "By the gods, Tyg strikes again!"

"Shut up, Antyn." Leviathan growled, standing up and stalking away, raking a hand through his hair. He turned back and levelled that vulture gaze on her. "You do realise you could actually be putting that Captain's life in more danger than if he stayed here in the army?"

Tyg shook her head with a sour expression. "No, I don't think so."

Leviathan advanced on her, leaning down over her chair and boxing her in with his hands on the arms. "Do you like him that much?" His voice was harsh and savage as his teeth gnashed.

"I am familiar with his skills and I trust him to do a good job. You trusted him enough to put him in charge of me when you left Arial City...and promote him." Tyg answered him, her eyes locking with his in a challenge.

"She is right about that." Antyn spoke up. "In Arial he was invaluable, especially when dealing with Tyg and her conspiratorial ways, I think he could keep her from going too over the top."

Leviathan was still staring hard at Tyg. "Do you need a handler?"

Tyg pursed her lips, her eyes solemn. "Yes, I do."

Leviathan straightened up, huffing out a breath. "Very well, go get him."

Tyg grinned and grabbed her cloak, moving out quickly before Leviathan changed his mind.

Antyn watched Leviathan's face as he crossed his arms and glared after her. "You sure you can do this?"

"Shut up, Antyn."

Corvyn was standing talking to a soldier and looking down at a clipboard when Tyg turned her horse and moved up towards him, pulling the hood of her cloak down to reveal herself. The soldiers standing in front of him all baulked and bowed their heads making Corvyn frown and turn around. His eyes went wide to see Tyg sitting on horseback behind him. She stilled her horse and gave him a small smile as he gave the clipboard back to the soldier and stepped closer. He had left them at the gates of the tower house to return his men to guarding around the outer perimeter set a hundred yards back from the tower house, what was she doing out?

"Captain Corvyn, I presume?" Tyg said with amusement as she jumped off her horse.

"Lady Tygarya! What are you doing here?" He demanded, sounding a little bewildered, it was the first time she had seen him and been aware of him being close by and had instantly sought him out?

"Talking to you, should I not be?" She grinned at him. "You seemed to have kept yourself obscured."

He looked very uncomfortable as his soldiers stared at him like he was either God or completely insane. "It's probably not in my best interest to be seen as acquainted, my Lady."

"I just wanted to come and say, hi. Why are you being so formal?" Tyg pouted with a scowl on her face, he saw her eyes lightening.

"Protocol in front of the soldiers, of course." He said through gritted teeth wondering why the gods had chosen him for this girl's attention again.

"Oh, right...I was hoping for a hug. Don't friends normally hug each other when they meet up after so long?" Tyg's grin turned into a smirk as Corvyn baulked then saw her smug smile and knew she was teasing him.

"Perhaps a simple thank you instead would suffice?" He smiled back, rubbing the back of his neck.

"For what?" Tyg asked with a curious tilt to her head.

"For the three day leave we were given when we reached Davios, the capital of Enyana." Corvyn said with a sardonic twist to his mouth.

"You got some leave? That's nice." Tyg smiled cynically.

"I know it was you're doing and I hoped to get the chance to meet you and thank you one day." Corvyn's smile was full and showed teeth in a boyish way in stark contrast to his usual hard soldier grimace.

"Nonsense, you know nothing...besides you've been sulking around behind my back for the last few days haven't you?" Tyg looked at him with appreciation of that handsome smile and saw him flush slightly.

"Hmm...I was ordered not to appear friendly with you." Corvyn looked away with a coy smirk. "On that note, what brings you over here, does the Emperor know you've escaped?"

He was clearly teasing her but Tyg scowled at the true premise of it. "Negotiations are stalling...so I'm having to do something drastic."

"With that Lord?" Corvyn's head turned to look in the general direction of the fortified town. "Was that what this morning was all about?"

"We need to get in and stop this siege."

"Yeah, I heard about the expedition to find another way around coming up nil." Corvyn looked back at her and folded his arms with a serious look on his face. "The negotiation meeting today, why were you there, exactly?"

"Helping..." Tyg said a little vaguely, looking around at the soldiers nearby.

She was surprised to see Corvyn's face darken in disapproval. "Helping? In that dress you were wearing, and the way you were acting? What the hell is the Emperor's plan? And why are you looking me up?"

Tyg smiled at him. "Do you have a problem with me doing that?"

Corvyn rubbed the back of his neck. "I should...but no." He smiled warmly his eyes glowing softly.

Tyg beamed at him making him scowl suspiciously. "Good, because Leviathan sent me over here to get you."

"What?" Corvyn baulked and took a defensive step backwards.

Tyg laughed musically causing more than one soldier to look her way. "You're the only one I know here and I guess the only one Lev trusts to mind me and protect me while we're separated, having experience I trust you as well. Now I know you're a warlock you make a lot more sense to me."

Corvyn laughed in spite of himself. "So the Emperor calls for me to babysit you again, great..."

Tyg shrugged. "I suggested you actually."

Corvyn grit his teeth as he stared at her a little wide-eyed and frantic. "You did? Shit..."

"It's okay, Leviathan agreed...that's why he sent me over here to get you."

"So, he just wants me or my whole company?"

"Ah...I think just you, but just come with me and find out."

"Alright then..." Corvyn turned around and yelled. "Get my horse!"

A couple of soldiers scrambled away as Tyg mounted up and sat waiting. It didn't take too long for them to return with Corvyn's horse, leading it through the muddy paths. He swung up into the saddle and turned its head to face the right direction.

Tyg gave him a little wistful look before turning away. "We're staying up at the house..."

"Yes, I know." Corvyn said rather flatly before they put their heels to horse and trotted off.

As they entered the yard, passing the soldiers at the gates with a salute, Corvyn looked forward grimly to see the Emperor waiting for him with General Oltar and Prince Antyn beside him. As they dismounted Corvyn heard the deep voice cut through the silence and grimaced to hear the impatient possession.

"Tygarya...what took so long?" Leviathan held his arm up and Tyg jumped off her horse and walked obediently in under it while Corvyn handed the guard the reins to his horse and told him to wait with it, he figured he wouldn't be long.

"I had to find him first, his troop was a long way away you know, doing training..."

"Hmm..." Leviathan looked up and meet Corvyn's eyes. Corvyn came to attention and saluted, down casting his gaze.

"My Liege, how can I be of assistance to you?"

"Did Tygarya not explain the situation?"

"Not fully, I thought it best to not give anyone the opportunity to listen in on your plans." Tyg grinned up at Leviathan, but Corvyn could see the challenge in her eyes.

Leviathan glanced down at her with his jaw clenched tight. "My plans...sure." He looked up back at Corvyn. "You better come in then, Captain." He turned, pulling Tyg around with him and walked inside.

Corvyn glanced at Antyn and General Oltar. They both indicated for him to go first. He swallowed hard and stepped up and inside the house following the Emperor as Antyn followed but he noticed General Oltar stayed behind on the step.

"You're a very popular young man, Captain." Antyn said casually. "Who would have thought you would have made such an impression upon us all back in Arial, eh? Let's hope you can live up to your reputation now..." He chuckled and Corvyn glanced at him with a nervous startled look.

"I'm not sure I get what you mean?"

"You're a very competent warlock, I hear?" Antyn said changing the subject with a sly grin.

"Fairly competent, yeah..." Corvyn muttered.

"Play your cards right with this task and you could see yourself with another promotion and your own regiment to lead."

Corvyn stopped walking and stared at Antyn as Antyn walked a few more steps before realising and turning back to grin at him. "Problem?"

"To offer that sort of incentive before even reaching the room for discussions, this must be a task I'm really not going to like?"

Antyn laughed and turned away, walking off with a wave of his hand to follow. "You may be right..."

Corvyn's jaw clenched hard, the muscles ticking as he looked forward to where Leviathan was graciously allowing Tyg to enter a room first. "Bloody woman, what have you gone and done to me now?"

39

Once seated in front of the Emperor, Corvyn felt a trickle of nervous sweat run down his spine. He combed a hand through his hair as Leviathan clicked his fingers for a servant to pour a glass of water for him.

"I thank you, my Liege." Corvyn said politely, taking the glass.

"The only problem with war in the summer months, is the heat inside the armour...isn't that so?" Leviathan commented, leaning back in his large chair and letting his gaze sweep up to Tyg who was still standing beside him. He placed a hand on the side of her thigh, stroking her. "We are planning on using Tyg's skills as an assassin to break the siege."

He looked back at Corvyn to see his face was dark and disapproving. "You are one of the few people that know of Tyg's skills and have seen them in action. You are also one of the very few people who have had previous experience in commanding Tyg to calm down and control her actions."

Corvyn felt the sweat at the back of his neck turn cold. He really didn't want this assignment, he didn't want the Emperor's gaze upon him, especially when it had anything to do with Tyg. What he understood better than most was the Emperor's possessive feelings for the girl and he certainly didn't want to be killed due to any misunderstanding of feelings he himself may have towards her.

He could feel the Emperor's eyes boring into him, judging him with that strange jealous and dominant glare.

ANNETTA LINCOLN

"That being said, you are also the only one that she trusts to accompany her on this mission." Corvyn could hear the grating possessiveness in the Emperor's voice and grimaced.

"What exactly is the mission, my Liege?"

"She is posing as the late Duke of Esbury's daughter, Targatha...and a prisoner of war beseeching aid from King Davalos to rescue her from her oppressor...me." Leviathan smirked. "The act you saw this morning was setting the scene of her being humiliated and made to be a servant, bullied and soiled."

Corvyn's jaw clenched. "Okay...that makes sense, so they obviously bought it?"

"We shall find that out in due course, Tyg is planning to make her escape from here and meet up with Lord Frameur's men tomorrow night...I want you to be her chaperone."

"Chaperone?" Corvyn baulked. "Won't I just be killed as soon as they get her to safety?"

"Of course not..." Tyg butted in. "As my knightly retainer, you have been by my side since I was a child..."

He scowled. "I'm not that much older than you..."

Leviathan huffed, amused as Tyg laughed. "No, but I've read these things are quite common to have squires be paired with young maidens as their champion and protector from a young age."

Corvyn's eyes narrowed. "So you're still reading fairy tales I take it?"

Leviathan snorted in amusement as Antyn laughed. "I forgot why it is I like you so much, Captain, you do speak your mind!"

Tyg pulled a face at him and folded her arms. "It doesn't matter...it might not even come up, as long as I introduce you as my protector and that you fled and hid on my order when the estate was overrun by Leviathan's army so you could come back and get me out...I'm sure they'll believe it. Especially if we let it be known that you also managed to secret some of my family's wealth."

Corvyn looked at her dubiously. "They won't just take your word, will we have papers?"

Antyn sat up with a serious frown. "Papers can be forged...we have something better..." He took out of a drawer a piece of cloth with a large brass brooch on it. "This is the brooch of office that the Duke bestowed upon his high officials and the cloth of the Royal house...it doesn't mean you didn't steal it, but I'm sure if you have this on your person Tyg can make it convincing..."

"Of course I can." Tyg beamed a smile at Corvyn as he looked up at her, her eyes twinkling like the sun reflected off a lake.

Leviathan reached out and put his arm around her waist, possessively. "Half the work on this being believable has already been done this morning...we are just waiting for a formal reply to see if they try to start negotiations and include Tygarya in them, or whether Frameur will still stall and keep this siege going with the premise of helping her escape."

"Is there any real reason for him to want to end the siege?" Corvyn asked, scratching at the stubble on his cheek.

"Not really, except they will be short of food...due to the fact they normally get supplies for the winter from Enyana and that wasn't able to happen this winter just past, their food stores must be getting rather low."

"So what's the hurry for us to get in?" Corvyn asked darkly, glancing at Tyg.

Leviathan could see his reluctance in using Tyg in this way. "Because I wish to take Kolastan and Gua del Mar this campaign...and without something drastic happening we aren't getting over that wall." He stated unemotionally.

Corvyn's jaw clenched and he nodded. "I see..."

"And..." Antyn added. "...as you know, Captain, this fortified trading town is only the first obstacle, we can't take a month to get through here only to sit for another month on the doorstep of the capital...waiting for everyone to run out of food."

"So what exactly are you intending to do once you get inside those walls?" Corvyn asked, looking at Tyg with a piercing gaze.

Tyg met his gaze and smiled. Remembering his hazel eyes and the many times she saw this very same hard accusing look in them.

"Open the gates, kill Lord Frameur and hunt out the rumour that King Davalos is there and that Lord Frameur is preventing him from talks...if that is correct, capture King Davalos in such a way that he must agree to Leviathan's terms of surrender."

Corvyn wiped a hand over his face. "Forgive me, my Liege, but are you sure this girl can do all that?"

"With your guidance, Captain." Leviathan's deep smooth voice answered with a slightly amused lilt.

Corvyn's eyes lifted to Leviathan and Leviathan's eyebrow raised in question of that clouded look. "If I may be free to say..." Leviathan lifted a hand in acquiescence. "I'm against this whole plan, but will of course obey orders and complete them with all due diligence, but I want it recorded that if for any reason this fails and, gods forbid, Tygarya is killed...no recourse will be set upon me as being held as a responsible scapegoat...this will all be held on your own shoulders, my Liege."

Antyn gaped at Corvyn, as did Tyg. He was certainly not shy to speak his mind. Leviathan lifted a finger to his chin and tapped it while staring at Corvyn with a benign smirk for a long silent moment. The air in the room felt tense but Corvyn maintained his gaze.

"As Emperor I will bear full responsibility for this mission no matter the outcome, Captain. That goes without saying."

"Leviathan, how can you...?" Tyg went to interrupt but Leviathan pinched her waist.

"Quiet." His gaze never left Corvyn's. "I am entrusting Tygarya to your care, Captain, take the responsibility and if she dies don't come back to face me."

Corvyn's jaw clenched and he dropped from his seat going down on one knee, bowing his head to his Emperor. "I will die on that hill with her, my Liege."

"Okay, can someone stop this martyrdom?" Tyg spat facetiously. "This is getting ridiculous and off track...we have planning to do."

Antyn agreed and stood up. "Yes, indeed...no one is going to die anywhere, so let's make sure of that and plan effectively, shall we?" He placed a hand on Corvyn's shoulder. "Get up, Captain...we appreciate your solemn vow and that was a part of why you were chosen for this task, but not why we are here..."

Leviathan's gaze was still upon Corvyn as Antyn dragged him up to his feet. Leviathan pulled Tyg down onto his lap deliberately and held her there. Tyg wasn't about to struggle, seeing that dark look on his face and she almost rolled her eyes as he buried his nose into the side of her neck, making it very clear who she belonged to.

Antyn sighed and rubbed his forehead as Corvyn went red in the face and looked away.

"Antyn, take the Captain and explain the plan to him more thoroughly..." Leviathan said with a distinct dismissive tone.

Antyn gave Corvyn an apologetic look. "This way..."

Corvyn glanced back to see Leviathan holding Tyg's head, his fingers threaded through her hair and his fist clamped shut around it as he kissed her. His eyes however lifted to stare back at Corvyn from around the side of Tyg's head, they were glowing a bright blue and looked smug.

Corvyn turned immediately away and stalked from the room with Antyn fast on his heels.

"Sorry about that..." Antyn felt the need to say something. That display of Leviathan's had been childish.

Corvyn grimaced. "No need to apologise, the Emperor is quite obviously making his point." Corvyn sighed out bitterly. "I really don't understand why though."

"Because she likes you." Antyn said nonchalantly as he led Corvyn into another room. "And that is quite a rare feat."

Corvyn snorted. "I wished she didn't..."

Antyn gave him a strange look. "Oh, come now, you don't mean that..."

Corvyn gave him a serious glare. "How am I supposed to answer that without earning my head on the chopping block?"

Antyn laughed. "I don't care about things like that, Captain...only results."

"Results..." Corvyn groaned. "Bringing Tygarya back alive."

"Exactly...I'm glad you're far from a stupid man, Captain."

40

The night was clear and warm as Tyg sat in the cemetery with Corvyn and waited for midnight to pass, hoping to be rewarded with a rescue. The sounds of alarm bells ringing and horns blowing permeated the night in the distance as a large fire raged far to the East side of camp, the distraction was well under way.

"You look different in normal clothes." Tyg murmured in the quiet. Corvyn had been given a pair of brown buck skin pants and linen shirt with a long travel coat and a plain sword buckled around his hip.

"It feels weird." He grumbled. He was digging a stick into the earth, impatiently.

"You look nice, more your age...I forget how young you are in that officer's uniform."

"Hmm..."

"Still having trouble with people not respecting you because of your age?"

He glanced at her, surprised she even remembered a conversation from their time in Arial City. "No, not since coming back into the army."

"You're still in the Royal Guard?"

"Supposedly, but of course we were still sent to the front line to get the iron ore here, then there was no point going back knowing the Emperor was going to be heading here anyway."

"Ah, I see..."

Corvyn frowned at her sigh. "Did you hope I would return to the castle? I've heard rumours..."

Tyg chuckled. "Yeah, let's just say my first few weeks here weren't great...I missed your levelness to chat to. I really needed you with me."

"Hmm..." Corvyn heard the snap of a twig and stood up immediately, his hand going to his sword as he peered off into the darkness.

"Relax, it's them, they have been watching us from a distance for a while now..." Tyg said cautiously. "Don't make any sudden moves and get shot by an archer with a shaky finger."

She stood up and cowered behind him, placing a hand upon his arm and peering around him like a timid lady would.

"Please, this is my knight protector, don't harm us." Tyg called out as the figures in the gloom started towards them.

Corvyn had the swatch of fabric pinned with the brooch and draped over one shoulder and when the soldiers from the other side came up to them Corvyn saw the leader's eyes go to it, his expression grim. He looked up at Corvyn's face scrutinising him suspiciously.

"It's a long way from the Duchy of Esbury."

"I know that." Corvyn stated coolly.

Tyg squeezed his arm and came up to stand next to him. "I assure you I'm telling the truth." She sounded just like a haughty high born lady would.

"I just wonder, miss, how your protector was able to make it all the way here yet was unable to protect you when it came to you being taken and molested by the Emperor of Tylandria? Is he perhaps a coward that fled and hid?" The soldiers sneer was obvious on his face and his men snickered.

Tyg stepped forward, getting into the soldier's face before Corvyn could punch him with the clenched fist Tyg saw at his side. "I'll have you know my protector followed my orders! He did exactly what I asked of him to get to this point, if he had tried to stay with me during the invasion he would have been slaughtered and I would still be locked in the bedroom of that beasty Emperor! If it wasn't for him my family's wealth wouldn't be buried and those fires that are now burning as a timely distraction would never have been lit!" She stepped closer to the soldier who was staring at her with a pale face full of concern. "And it's Lady Targatha Esbury to you! Show me some respect or are you as bad as the Tylandrian army in the way you treat ladies of substance?"

The soldiers had all baulked and dropped their heads. "I apologise, my Lady...please we need to get going before those fires are put out...follow me."

Tyg glanced back at Corvyn to see him looking at her with a surly expression, she grinned at him and quickly followed the soldiers in the darkness through the small thicket that sheltered the local Lord's family cemetery then across the meadow to a stream.

"We need to cross this, my Lady..." The lead soldier said, looking at her feet with apprehension.

Corvyn was quick to sweep Tyg up into his arms and scowl at the soldier. "Get going! If we're caught out in the open like this we're all dead men."

Tyg coyly put her arms around Corvyn's neck and looked up at him with a small grateful smile. "Thank you, Sir Coalgate." She purred his pseudonym.

He looked down at her smug grin and his jaw clenched tight with disapproval. "Don't." He reprimanded. The soldiers all heard and gave him a sideways glance of approval that he was clearly a no nonsense knight and did take his job seriously.

"You're no fun." Tyg whispered as Corvyn trudged his way through the water of the stream.

"My feet are now freezing and wet...I'm not in a good mood."

"Aww, that's too bad...I'm enjoying myself, you can take that to warm your heart." Tyg was enjoying herself immensely and wondered if this was exactly the reason why airhead ladies acted so pitiful, perhaps they weren't so airhead after all. Being in the strong arms of a gentlemanly knight was quite an experience.

"How about I drop you right here in the middle of the stream?" Corvyn growled through gritted teeth, fully aware that Tyg was stroking the back of his neck with her nails. "Cut it out! This is serious..."

He let go of her for a split second letting her drop before easily catching her again. It was enough to make Tyg gasp and cling to him tightly. He chuckled in amusement and walked the rest of the way out of the stream. "You need to eat more, my Lady...you weigh less than a feather."

He could hear her seething and as he reached dry ground he dropped her feet immediately, stepping away from her before she could do anything in retaliation.

As he stepped back, however, he felt Tyg's fist curl in and grab his shirt, preventing him from going anywhere. He was always astounded by her brute strength and as her face came up to his, his eyes were wide with apprehension at what she might do to him.

His eyes went even wider when Tyg planted her lips on his cheek and battered her eyelashes at him. "Thank you, my brave knight, I must be such a burden to you..."

"Ah, no...you're alright, my Lady..." He flustered, going bright red as the soldiers all watched with strange amusement. Tyg turned her back with a little smirk and walked off, following the soldiers.

Corvyn grit his teeth as his fists clenched. "Bloody woman!" He muttered sulkily before following.

As they entered through a small trap door in the massive fortified walls that spanned the narrowest part of the ravine leading up to the town Tyg noticed the thickness of the wooden gates and the fact that there were two separate fortified walls with soldiers lining the top to go through before reaching a long open space that would be lined with archers on either side from the top of the cliffs. Tyg could see by the signal fires that large boulders were sitting ready to be pushed down into the narrow pass should the enemy ever get that far. It was impressive and they had to enter another fortified gate into the town where all the soldiers were gathered before finally being taken up to the keep that was again strongly fortified.

"There's no way Leviathan is getting through all that without some serious magic being used." Corvyn muttered to her.

She gave him a small smile of agreement, her eyes not holding any amusement.

Lord Frameur came sweeping into the large foyer of the keep with a flamboyant pride, seeing Tyg, spreading his arms wide like he was going to embrace her. Corvyn stepped in front of her with a challenging glare making Lord Frameur falter and glare back, his grey eyes sparking. Corvyn had suppressed his magic and hoped Lord Frameur wouldn't detect it.

"Who do we have here then?" Frameur asked a little miffed to be blocked.

"Lord Frameur, this is Sir Coalgate, my protector..." Tyg nudged Corvyn out of the way and allowed Lord Frameur to come closer as she took his hands in hers beseechingly. "He helped with my escape by making the distraction and getting me out of the

Tower House unseen. I really do owe him my life. As do I owe you as well, I thank you."

Lord Frameur's gaze softened when he looked at Tyg and he took a hand back to stroke down her hair. "No need, my Lady, it is my duty to help a lady in distress. I hope you will find your accommodations here far more relaxing."

"Yes, I am feeling rather exhausted after all that walking..." She feigned staggering and Lord Frameur caught her in his arms. She wiped her forehead in a daze and groaned. "Oh, my...I feel all dizzy..."

"Please allow me to take you to your room, my Lady." Lord Frameur swept her off her feet and started making his way to the staircase as she promptly faked fainting.

"Wait!" Corvyn bellowed out.

Lord Frameur stopped and turned back to give Corvyn a hard look. "She is in safe hands, sir knight, I assure you...follow if you like, but I'm sure Lady Targatha needs rest, food and a hot bath after her ordeal in the hands of Emperor Adramelech."

Corvyn saw Tyg's furrowed brow and steady expression and bowed his head. "Of course, forgive my impertinence, my Lord."

"Think nothing of it, sir...I understand you have a job to protect Lady Targatha and I thank you for your actions in making sure she was able to escape and make it here, she's been very brave but I fear her fragile countenance has had enough for one day."

"Of course, my Lord." Corvyn answered trying to keep his tone even. Fragile countenance?

Lord Frameur took Tyg up the stairs two levels and settled her onto a bed in a corner room that had been prepared for her.

She groaned and blinked her eyes open, grasping out for Lord Frameur's hand as he turned to leave. "Thank you again, my Lord."

He patted her hand with a pleasant smile. "Rest well, my dear, I will come check on you in the morning."

"And my knight…"

"I will ensure he is cared for, my Lady…" Lord Frameur looked up and saw Corvyn standing in the room, his face dark and threatening. "Ah, if you can assure him that he can leave you, I assure you will be left alone to rest."

"I'm not leaving." Corvyn stated, his deep voice calm and resolute.

The maid that had been in the room finishing the preparations glanced up at him with apprehension and a strange glittery daze as she took in his handsome features. He folded his arms and glared at her.

"Sir Coalgate, please rest…" Tyg said in a weak voice, laying her head back on the pillow and meeting his gaze. "Lock my door if that will appease you."

He bowed his head. "Certainly, my Lady."

Lord Frameur seemed a bit put out by that but he walked from the room with the maid and Corvyn followed him out, shutting the door soundly and giving Lord Frameur a hard look, holding his hand out expectantly.

The maid handed him the key and he thanked her graciously before turning to Lord Frameur. "I thank you for saving my ward and taking her in, my Lord, she has been through a lot as you say and I fear she could have lifelong trauma. She said she is prepared to marry you if that is the compensation you require after your King has acknowledged her freedom and bestowed her the right of her rank back upon her. So I will tell you now in confidence that I managed to save some of her family wealth and buried it."

Lord Frameur seemed a little flustered and puffed his chest out with pride. "I will be good to her, sir knight." He seemed very pleased to hear about the money.

"That's all I can ask." Corvyn answered grimly.

"You could be quite an asset here, sir knight...by your obvious physique you know how to handle yourself."

Corvyn smiled. "Well, I'm not going anywhere until Lady Targatha releases me from my oath."

Lord Frameur's eyes narrowed slightly. "Quite...well, this way...Gertie here will show you to a suitable room."

Tyg was up and leaning out the window as soon as she heard the lock turn. She couldn't make out much in the darkness, but could hear the jingle of armour as guards patrolled the perimeter of the keep. She was tempted to just leap from the window down onto the ledge of a small roof line about twenty feet below, but due to not having her leathers on and only a pathetically thin dress, she decided it was best to wait and check it all out in the daylight.

Corvyn returned about an hour later accompanying the maid, Gertie, who was bringing up food. It was a watery stew and Tyg wondered if perhaps they were indeed running out of food. It had barley in it and a few carrots, the meat tasted like dried beef.

"Is the siege hard?" Tyg asked the maid in a conversational tone as she set out Tyg's meal for her and poured her a goblet of wine.

"Well, it's quite scary, I hear the Emperor of Tylandria is a savage and vicious man with a god complex."

Corvyn spluttered a bit at hearing his Emperor being rudely described.

"Oh, he is...absolutely terrible..." Tyg agreed dramatically. "I meant the living conditions, are they hard, how are the food stores?"

"Oh, we're okay for now...the siege has just begun, so..."

Corvyn frowned at that and gave Tyg a look to get rid of the maid.

"Do you think you could organise me a hot bath before you retire for the night? I must smell awful..." Tyg lifted her hair and smelt it, wrinkling her nose up in disgust.

"Of course, my Lady, Lord Frameur has procured some lovely fragrances and oils for you. I'll get right on to it...he also has some dresses..."

"Oh, wonderful, is he a good man?"

"Oh...ah...yes, he is fair..." Gertie seemed a bit hesitant and Tyg's skin crawled a little to see the woman's cheeks blush.

She quickly left and Corvyn closed the door, looking back at Tyg with a dark look. "I don't like that reaction, you're going to have to be careful..."

Tyg screwed her nose up. "What Lord doesn't grope the maids...?"

Corvyn's jaw clenched. "He better not try and grope you."

Tyg blinked and gave Corvyn a small smile of appreciation at the sentiment. "If he does, you're going to have to let him, Corvyn...I need to get into a room alone with him, sooner rather than later...don't they seem a little too comfortable under siege?"

"Hmm...the meal isn't much so they are obviously rationing, but yes, I get that same feeling, I would very much like to get a look at their food stores, but I guess that's not the priority."

"No, you just keep a low profile tomorrow, I need to get closer to Frameur...perhaps try and get yourself a tour of the gates and fortifications..."

Corvyn folded his arms. "They're suspicious of me, so that might be asking a bit much...and there isn't any evidence of King Davalos being here."

"I guess we'll find that out tomorrow..."

"Hmm..." Corvyn rested his head back on the door and watched Tyg eat for a moment. "You look weird with that hair colour, I can't get used to it."

"Lord Frameur seems to like it." Tyg said coyly, looking up with a teasing smile.

Corvyn coughed and looked away. "He hasn't seen you with your normal hair." He muttered half to himself.

Tyg looked up with amusement. "And if he had?"

Corvyn's gaze settled on watching the flame inside a lantern flicker. "He would know you are far too good for him."

Tyg sat up, startled by the harsh response. "I'm not truly marrying him, Corvyn..."

"I know that." He pouted darkly.

She studied him, curious at his sudden cool aura and was just about to ask him if that was how he felt about her himself when a small knock sounded on the door.

"My Lady, we have the bath..."

Corvyn stood up off the door and opened it letting a guard in carrying a small metal tub and put it down on the floor in front of the fire that roared in the far wall.

Gertie came in with a couple of other maids all carrying large urns full of hot water and began filling the tub.

The guard approached Corvyn. "You may accompany me down to the soldier's quarters for a game of Switch and a pint of beer, if you are interested?" He offered gruffly.

Corvyn gave the man a nod. "I thank you for your offer...if my Lady is finished with me I will retire for the night and give you the key to lock yourself in." He looked purposely over at Tyg still eating her stew. Tyg returned his look with a mild smile.

"Of course, thank you, Sir Coalgate for everything you've done this night."

He bowed formally and left the room with the guard. He could take a hint when it was shoved obtusely in his face like that. He was being told to back off away from Tyg.

Gertie and the other maids made two more trips with hot water before it was ready for Tyg and they all stood in a line waiting for her to undress so they could help her wash.

Tyg felt her skin crawl. "Thank you, I can do this unaided...just leave the implements and organise for the water to be emptied tomorrow morning. Once I have bathed I feel I will be too tired to have the clanging and banging of it disturb me tonight."

Gertie and the maids curtseyed, putting down the brushes and scrubs and left the room. Tyg got up and locked the door, stretching languidly and stripping off. She fully intended to enjoy this bath.

41

The next morning the maids returned and Gertie had a couple of dresses for Tyg to choose from to wear. She frowned in distaste at the highly boned and corseted dresses with their hooped skirts and petticoats, they were well out of fashion back in Tylandria. One was a light blue and one was a dusky rose pink.

She was really going to hate today...

"Lord Frameur has requested that perhaps you might like to accompany him for breakfast, my Lady?" Gertie said with a little giggle.

Did they see this as a romantic fairy tale? Great...

Tyg had to bite the inside of her mouth to stop herself from saying something inappropriate.

"That would be wonderful, Lord Frameur is a most gracious host."

The maids all giggled again and looked at each other as they went about their tasks.

"May I enquire as to where my knight is?"

"Right outside the door, my Lady...it's whispered that he slept there..." One maid said, giggling. "He is certainly admirable in his serious approach to your protection."

Tyg heard the little lilt of affection. It seemed as though Corvyn was developing his own interested parties. "Yes, he will make a great husband for some lucky woman one day..."

All the girls gushed and giggled amusing Tyg enough to stir the pot a little more. "He is a poor knight of no true title, so perhaps he may find interest in any one of you pretty maids?"

They all gaped at her, Gertie blushing and then all curtseyed graciously at her.

"Well, help me get this blue dress on..."

When Tyg opened the door and saw Corvyn standing outside, she scowled at the amusement on his face as he took in the dress she was wearing. He was practically covering his mouth and swallowing the laughter.

"Shut it." She muttered to him as she walked down the hall. He fell in step with her and chuckled.

"Oh, no...you're going to hear all about how great you look, very womanly, very adorable..." Corvyn laughed, teasingly.

Tyg gave him a sideways glare seeing his face didn't match his humour. She clucked her tongue. "You heard what I said to the maids, huh?"

"Oh yes, I could hear every word and every giggle." His voice dropped into a very annoyed cadence.

"So as your mistress would you like me to marry you off to one of the maids here?" Tyg asked in a purr of discontent.

"Just try it." Corvyn growled.

Tyg laughed but they both became serious as they entered the downstairs dining room to find Lord Frameur waiting for them. She noticed a couple of soldiers standing in the room and grimaced.

"Lady Targatha, what a truly beautiful sight, Sir Coalgate said either of those dresses would be perfect for you, he wasn't wrong."

Corvyn paused in his steps as Tyg turned to look at him. He saw her eyes go almost white they became so pale blue and blazed with an ire so scathing he could almost feel it on his skin. He looked away with a faint flush running from his ears and down his neck as he rubbed the back of his neck with discomfort at being caught out in his petty revenge.

"Is that right...?" Tyg hissed through gritted teeth. "I'll have to make sure to thank him later."

Corvyn gave a nervous chuckle. "Ah, no need, my Lady."

Was this for the way she took her amusement from him last night when he had to carry her over the stream? She had never before had someone deal with her in such a petty way. She started laughing, a full melodic laugh that made everyone in the room gape at her in astonishment.

Corvyn's lip started twitching and soon he was laughing too.

Lord Frameur frowned at the two of them laughing hysterically to the point that Tyg was actually wiping tears from her eyes. It took her a long moment to get a hold of herself and she was panting, holding her chest and looked flushed.

She coughed and straightened, whacking Corvyn in the arm. He stiffened immediately and the laughter died upon his lips.

"I do apologise, Lord Frameur...think of us like siblings, we like to tease each other and I'm afraid you have been central to one such prank." Tyg explained delicately.

"Oh?" Lord Frameur wasn't sure if he should be appeased or insulted.

"To be honest I would prefer a dress that wasn't quite so...ah...flouncy. I do prefer something a little more understated."

"Oh, I see...and here I thought you were really a girl who liked to play princess..." Frameur seemed quite relieved. "To be honest I was rather hoping the opposite of you."

Tyg smiled and walked closer to Frameur, extending her hand and placing it upon his arm. "Believe me, I am very sedate by nature." She purred in a low tone, blinking slowly.

Frameur's smile turned slightly sinister looking and Tyg knew he was more than just interested in her, he wanted her. This should be easy.

"Shall we have breakfast?"

"Indeed, afterwards I have somewhere to take you." Lord Frameur said, taking her arm and leading her to the table.

A mighty boom sounded through the keep, followed by another, then another. It caused the mortar to move and dust to rise as the whole keep shook with the rumbling vibrations.

Lord Frameur cursed. "Damn, they have started their assault of the main wall..." He sat down and looked over at Tyg. "Never fear, dear, we are quite safe in here, it's just the sounds echo up the ravine, it causes the rocks to vibrate."

"Oh, I see...that's quite reassuring..." Tyg chewed her lip wondering why Leviathan would start assaulting the first wall now.

"No doubt the Emperor has discovered you are gone...it would be an obvious conclusion to think you have escaped to our side. I expected some sort of retaliation attempt." Lord Frameur chuckled. "He seems quite angry..."

Tyg pouted, was it a farce? A distraction maybe? "I'm not sure why he would be so upset to lose a person he thought of as nothing more than a maid."

Frameur gave her a strange brooding look and Tyg thought for a second that her ploy had been seen through, her grip tightened on her butter knife. Frameur's eyes narrowed at her ever so slightly and he smirked. "You don't know, do you?"

"Know?" Tyg's stomach sank. "Know what?" She glanced at Corvyn who was standing in a corner. His eyes were fixed on Lord Frameur wondering what he was going to say next.

Frameur reached out a hand and lifted Tyg's chin, turning it side to side as he studied her. "Your aura is quite amazing, Lady Targatha. I can't quite see through it...it's almost like you have been suppressed."

Tyg gasped for real, shocked by his words.

"I can see you have no idea what I'm talking about...but you appear quite intriguing and special." His eyes were intense as he scrutinised her.

Corvyn bit his lip and looked away, trying to act concerned and surprised for the wrong reasons. He was surprised, very surprised that Lord Frameur could so obviously see the suppression magic Leviathan put over Tyg's power to conceal it from warlock eyes. He had noticed the very first time he had seen her arrive into Enyana with the Emperor, he remembered what it had been like to look upon her before that, that ethereal glow of magic aura that intensified to levels that would stop the tracks of every person that wielded magic if they saw it. This was bad, if Lord Frameur even suspected her of being something akin to even a witch, he may expose her as a spy.

Tyg looked down at her plate unsure of how to proceed, she had no idea what he was talking about. Aura, what aura? Was this why Lord Frameur was all for getting married, did he think she was a witch...she was Elvian, maybe that's what it was he was seeing? She wondered what he would think of her knowing that.

She looked up to see Frameur still watching her with a faint smile on his lips. "I've shocked you..." He said amused.

"Do you intend to marry me because you think maybe I'm a witch?" She frowned up at him.

"I do believe you offered yourself as payment for your freedom, but ultimately it is, Miss Targatha. I mean, you have no lands or title anymore...the best you can offer is a strong womb to produce me a magical heir to carry on my line." Lord Frameur grinned savagely, revealing his true nature for all to see. Tyg noticed he had dropped the 'Lady' title emphasizing his point.

Tyg gave a benign smile back. "I see, and you think this is what the Emperor is angry about?"

"Oh, I'm positive it is. Whatever you possess, he definitely wanted it and now I have it."

"I see..." Tyg took a moment to sip on the glass of water that had been poured for her, glancing back at Corvyn who looked like death ready to strike should all this turn bad. She gave him an almost imperceptible shake of her head and saw his jaw clench tight. She looked back up at Lord Frameur and reached out to touch his hand.

He caught her fingers and held them as he smiled triumphantly. She downcast her eyes then looked back up through her lashes at him demurely. "I'm thankful you helped me escape him." She said quietly. "And I'm very lucky that you are a handsome and well-mannered man."

Lord Frameur lifted her hand and kissed it. "We will make an excellent partnership, my dear..."

After breakfast Tyg returned to her rooms to find many dresses being sorted out of a large chest by Gertie. They were all of simple design but very expensive fabrics and Tyg had to silently thank Lord Frameur as she quickly changed into one that was far more comfortable, it was still a dark blue, with a simple A-line design and square neck that showed a little cleavage, it had a large silver corset belt that cinched the waist and Tyg braided her hair into a long plait and pulled it over her shoulder.

Corvyn knocked on the door and entered, his expression dark and brooding.

Tyg dismissed Gertie and sat upon the bed, looking at Corvyn with an accusatory scowl. "Is that why Leviathan keeps me with him, for real?"

Corvyn huffed and rubbed his jaw. "I do not know why the Emperor keeps you...I'm not privy to that information."

"But you know about this aura?"

He looked uncomfortable but nodded. "Anyone who has magic is aware of your aura. The Emperor suppresses it for your safety. Somehow Lord Frameur was able to see that something is being hidden from him...you need to be very careful with him now."

"So do Elvian's have magic or is it something else?"

Corvyn was surprised by the question for a second. "Ah, yes...of course they do...you do have amazing strength, fast healing, the ability to use weapons with deadly accuracy...magic takes many forms."

Tyg stood up and went to the window, looking out over the town rooves and the large foreboding mountains that seemed to loom in from every angle.

"Tygarya...you have no time to think about that."

She turned and settled a fiery ice gaze on him. "So that's all because of magic?"

He sighed. "Hmm...it shows in the fact that your eyes change colour with your moods, Tyg...did you really not know about this?"

Tyg's eyes seemed to swirl with an inky depth.

Corvyn stepped closer, his frown deepening into concern. "Tygarya...calm down, there is nothing you can do, the Emperor does what he wants to do with all of us, you know that...but I'm sure it's not just about producing an heir. Now, we need to go, Lord Frameur is waiting for you to take you somewhere...this could be to do with the King."

Tyg looked up, startled out of her reverie by that statement. "Right..."

42

They were escorted down to the lowest level of the keep and out to the stables. Tyg saw Lord Frameur waiting with a small two person carriage. He took her hand and helped her in then sat down beside her, closing the door as Corvyn jumped up on the back tailgate with a soldier and they headed out.

"So where are we going?" Tyg asked, curiously, looking out the window and seeing them circle around the keep and take a small winding road up into the mountains behind.

"We are going to meet with the King." Lord Frameur announced. The way he said it made the hairs on Tyg's arms raise. Something about this was not right.

"Why is the King not staying within the Keep?"

"Because no one knows he is even here..." The sinister grin on Frameur's face made Tyg shuffle uncomfortably in her seat and wish she had her weapons. She looked up at Frameur's side profile and studied him. He seemed very confident about his position, and thinking back to all those times that Leviathan would come back from meeting with him with the King a no show was sending alarm bells off in her brain.

She toyed with the large dragon's head ring on her finger, closing her fist and jabbing at the horns as they stuck out. This was her only weapon...this would do.

They travelled up a small pass to where a cabin was situated. As they stepped out of the carriage Corvyn was instantly by her side and she knew instinctively that something was dreadfully wrong.

They watched Lord Frameur walk closer to the cabin and the air itself seemed to vibe and ripple in front of him.

Was that a ward?

"Tyg..." Corvyn whispered to her. "We need to be really careful..." He touched her elbow and Tyg felt a tingling sensation. "I'm placing extra wards over you so you can pass through that...but Tyg, I think there is a sorcerer inside. The magic feels different."

"What?" Tyg exclaimed in a hiss.

"Don't worry, he won't be anywhere near as powerful as Emperor Adramelech, but he may see through your disguise."

"Shit! Are you saying the King is a sorcerer?"

Corvyn shrugged and dropped his hand quickly as Lord Frameur turned around. "Come, Miss Targatha...your man can stay there with the others, no one comes inside."

"Do I have to, I'm scared?" Tyg feigned fragility but Frameur seemed to scowl with annoyance.

"Yes, come here...you need to understand."

Tyg demurely walked forward, looking back at Corvyn briefly as Frameur took her hand and walked her inside the cabin.

It was gloomy inside and it took a moment for her vision to focus. There were two men in the room, one looked old and sickly, sitting in a chair with a blanket over his knees while the other wore a cream coloured robe, like a monk would wear. He was standing behind the King looking at Tyg like she was extremely suspicious. Her hackles went up instantly as her eyes swept the room for dangers and anything she could use as a weapon.

"My dear, this is King Davalos...and the man behind him is his carer, Timothy."

"Nice to meet you..." Tyg did a little nervous curtsey.

"Why have you brought her here?" Timothy spat, clearly not happy with the situation.

"I need his signature on a document." Frameur answered unfettered. He took out a folded paper and opened it up. "I'm going to need yours too, my dear."

Tyg stepped to the table as he bent over it, straightening the paper out as Timothy retrieved a pen and ink and placed it on the table then pushed the chair that King Davalos was in up to the table. He grabbed the King's hand, lifting the pen in the other, dipping it into the ink before placing it into the King's hand and manipulating him to sign the document.

"King Davalos, your signature...right here, please sign."

King Davalos mumbled incoherently, looking up momentarily with a confused look that seemed to scream for help.

"What's wrong with him?" Tyg asked quietly.

"He's a coward, that's what is wrong with him." Frameur spat in disgust. "He was going to just talk surrender, said he had a dream showing that Adramelech bastard ruling over the world like a god. Can you believe that? I had to do something..."

Timothy gave Frameur a strange look that conveyed his disturbance at him telling her this stuff, but Frameur was clearly the one in charge here. Was it possible for a warlock to be more powerful than a sorcerer? Plus this sorcerer looked old, couldn't he stop the aging process like Leviathan and Antyn, even warlocks could slow the aging process?

"I refuse to bow to that psychopath just as Timothy here refused to bow to him years ago when he took over from his father. The man is insane, have you not noticed?"

Tyg grit her teeth, Lord Frameur was unstable. "Yes, he is."

Frameur gave her a rewarding smile and pressed his hands to either side of her head. "You see, you get it...we cannot surrender to that man!"

"Okay, but what am I signing?"

"A declaration of abuse at the hands of Emperor Adramelech and his brother, the fact that they stripped you of your lands and title and humiliated you, a relation of the dead King Hyston and that you have sought protection and clemency from King Davalos, to which he is signing his approval."

"I see..." Tyg took up the pen and scribbled some fake signature.

"Excellent..." Frameur took her hands and turned her back to face him. "...as soon as Timothy here finds the other sorcerers hiding in these mountains we will be able to band together and fight against him and his brother. Then we can get married...I will give you a most fabulous wedding."

"You don't know where they are?"

"It has been winter..." Frameur said as a dubious sounding excuse. "...but soon Timothy will set off along the trails, he was aware of where two of them were...but with the coming of that bastard Adramelech they may have scarpered." Frameur raked a hand through his hair with frustration. "Everyone are cowards!"

Tyg pressed in closer to him. "I'm glad you are not, my Lord." She looked up at him with a beautiful smile. He paused and looked upon her with an appreciative smile in response.

"Ah, my lovely Targatha...how I wish we could be wed this very day. I cannot wait for you..." His eyes sparkled with a dark meaning and he licked his lips.

Tyg lifted to whisper in his ear. "Perhaps we don't have to wait, meet with me tonight somewhere secluded with no eyes upon us?"

He gave her a very heated look as she dropped back to her heels and blinked up at him. "What about that pesky knight of yours?"

"I can get rid of him."

It was clear to Tyg that Lord Frameur had kidnapped the King and was holding him only for the purpose of maintaining control. The capital thought the King was at the Keep, yet the people of the Keep didn't know he had arrived and was actually being held captive by Lord Frameur.

She made a fuss of still being quite tired after her escape and excused herself from Lord Frameur's presence as soon as they got back to the Keep.

As Corvyn closed the door, his face was a mask of concern. "What the hell was all that about?"

"The King was in there as well as another man which I think was the sorcerer you could feel...but, he was old and seemed weak himself...the King is being poisoned and held against his will. Lord Frameur is in control."

"Fuck..." Corvyn scratched his jaw as he started pacing. "It was speculated that might be the case, Frameur is a renowned warlock..."

"Is he more powerful than a sorcerer?"

Corvyn gave her a worldly look. "Not all sorcerers are as powerful as Leviathan or Antyn, they come from the strongest bloodline and Leviathan literally has the power of two other sorcerers within him."

"So Sorcerer magic can be weak?"

"It depends on the bloodline and the person, if the person is of a weak and fragile body it may mean the magic within them is weak also...do you know his name?"

"Timothy."

Corvyn huffed in thought. "I don't recognise that name but the Emperor might. He has the names of all the sorcerers that lived during Morphun's reign."

"Leviathan's father?"

"Hmm...okay, so we need a plan, we really have to get Lord Frameur out of the way now, it's crucial."

"I'm meeting him tonight for a secret rendezvous, so make yourself scarce. After that we'll sneak down to the gates deal with the soldiers there and open the gates for Leviathan. Can you get word to him to be ready?"

"Yeah...I have a way." Corvyn's frown seemed to darken like the way wasn't pleasant for him.

"What is it?" Tyg asked.

Corvyn looked up at her grimly. "Nothing, a simple spell is all..."

"You don't look like it's a simple spell?"

His mouth twisted bitterly. "It causes some pain, similar to when the Emperor is in your head, so it's only to be used to communicate with him if completely necessary."

Tyg's eyes dulled into a death stare. "Is that how you communicated with him back in Arial when he was in Landau?"

Corvyn's expression intensified. "Yes." He looked at Tyg's curious gaze for a moment before sighing. "When he first ever enters your head he leaves a seed of power there so he is there at all times...I have a way of accessing that seed and reversing the contact to communicate a short message."

"A seed is planted in my brain?" Tyg felt a little sick.

Corvyn grimaced. "In all of us, Tygarya. He must be looking at the person to cause that pain but he can make you dream..."

Tyg shuddered. "I had no idea..." Leviathan was worse than she realised.

That night Tyg made her way through the Keep in the dead of night to secretly meet Lord Frameur in a courtyard for a naughty rendezvous. She was a little apprehensive not knowing how to get through his defensive wards if he kept them up even when close and personal with her. She was completely unarmed and Corvyn had warned her that the slightest tingling of her skin could indicate that Frameur's wards were about to be unleashed upon her. She knew to strike he would have to conjure a spell and that for a warlock took time and his hands and speech. Incapacitating his hands would be important, but if she was holding him down, that meant her own hands were tied too.

"Lord Frameur?" She called out through the darkness of the small courtyard garden, peering into the darkness and listening for any sound.

"Call me William." He crooned as he came out of the shadows against the side of the building and took her hands up in his.

He turned her and pressed her back against the cold stone. "Oh, my Lord, you scared me."

"Sorry, I did not intend to..." He lifted her hands and pressed them to the wall either side of her head as she looked up at him and as his mouth melded to hers she grit her teeth, tensing up.

He lifted his head and gave her a disapproving look in the gloom, but she could easily see it as the lights from the kitchens above shined down just enough.

"What game are you playing, open your mouth." Frameur demanded. "This was your idea, don't back out now."

"Of course not, William..." Tyg purred his name and she saw his eyes dilate. "You're just taking me a little by surprise at your fervour."

"Forgive me, I am in need of your taste." He murmured into her ear, one hand dropping and groping at her breast. She cringed into herself as he licked her neck, along her jaw and back to her mouth.

Lucky for her he had released her left hand, no doubt thinking she was weakest in that arm, but it meant he had released the hand with the ring. She wiggled and squirmed at his groping touch and opened her mouth to him allowing his tongue to invade her mouth possessively. He groaned in pleasure at her and dropped his other hand to start pulling up her dress. He grabbed her thigh and lifted her leg, pressing his crotch hard against her making her gasp out a little. She really hadn't prepared herself for this level of touching and it made her skin crawl and tears to prick behind her eyes, she really didn't like to be touched.

Tyg curled her left hand around his shoulder, bringing it up towards his neck, brushing it lightly as a caress as her other arm circled his neck on the other side. She tightened her grip when she realised she was getting no hint of any wards surrounding him, fisted her left hand and shoved the horns of the dragon's head ring into his jugular, tearing at it to open a wound large enough for his blood to spurt out rapidly. He gasped, trying to back away but Tyg spun around and shoved him up against the wall, clamping her hands over his wrists and holding them down, her mouth over his as he struggled against her. Her eyes were fixed upon his, looming large, bewildered and frightened in her vision.

As he bled out she had to keep him silent by forcefully pressing her body against him and covering his mouth with hers for the entire two minutes until he weakened, while holding his hands pressed to his sides to disable him from using his magic. A great flaw in warlock magic Tyg decided, a definite weakness to exploit if she was to ever come up against a warlock again. As he slumped against the wall she let him go and he slid down the stone to the ground. She crouched down over him and lifted his head, checking he was dead. She was covered with his blood, which also stained down the wall behind him. It was a gory sight, but hopefully no one would discover it until morning when Leviathan's troops were already inside the town. She stood up and spat her saliva out clearing her mouth of the feel of Frameur's tongue. She straightened her dress as best she could still feeling out of sorts at his assault and took a moment to take a deep breath, breathing out in a cleansing long sigh and shutting her feelings of rage off, he was dead no need to get self-absorbed, she still had work to do. She scaled the wall surrounding the Keep and dropped down into the town and made her way through the darkness to the town gate.

43

She met up with Corvyn behind a cart full of hay for the soldier's horses close to the barracks where the soldiers were sleeping, but he could see the dress was stained dark with blood all down the front of it. He handed her a satchel containing a pair of leather pants, a padded jerkin and a couple of long bladed daggers he had managed to steal that would fit her. He was dressed in a soldier's uniform and hoped she would look like she was a soldier out of uniform, being lax. He figured it could work if she flipped a uniform cap over her hair, long enough to give anyone enough pause before reacting anyway. He knew a simple pause was all she needed.

"What the hell happened?" He whispered hoarsely at her appearance.

Tyg looked down at herself grimly. "I only had this ring...I had to rip open his jugular."

Corvyn paled slightly. "Shit...and then hold him down?"

"Exactly..."

His eyes narrowed. "So no problem with any wards?"

"Nope..." Tyg said shuffling in the bag and pulling the pants out to change into.

"And did he call out at all?"

Tyg glanced up at him as she stepped into the pants and pulled them up. "Nope."

He didn't care for her nonchalant way of answering. "How did you keep him quiet?"

Tyg jumped up and down to get the pants over her bottom before doing them up. She pulled the dress off over her head and dumped it on the ground and quickly pulling the jerkin over the satin chemise she was wearing. Corvyn's jaw clenched and he looked away, politely.

"Do you really want to know? It might upset you and you might just go and tell Leviathan in some justified loyalty to him."

Corvyn's scowl deepened and he grabbed her arm, pulling her closer, scrutinising her face. "Is this all a game to you?"

She looked at him startled. "Of course not, I take killing people very seriously, and I did warn Leviathan I would do whatever was necessary to get the job done."

He huffed and let her go, wiping a hand down his face. "What the fuck did you do?" He muttered.

"I got close to him, like I had to...let's just leave it at that." Tyg took hold of the daggers and twirled them in her hands. It felt good to have weapons again.

"Fine..." Corvyn huffed.

"Don't say anything to Leviathan."

Corvyn grumbled. "I won't, I promise."

With Corvyn by her side they sneaked out of town using the soldier's gate, making their way down to the two imposing walls built across the ravine. Boredom made the soldiers lazy and unsuspecting making their job easier as no one even looked at them with any interest as they walked through the gates and down the road.

There was only empty space of about thirty feet between each wall as soldiers patrolled along the tops of them, behind the second wall were a select number of buildings where over two hundred soldiers slept and spent much of their days doing nothing. There was then the long space of the road up to the town fortifications that were again minimally guarded at night. Corvyn had estimated that there were probably only two thousand troops in the town, they were relying fully upon their fortifications and protection wards while the remaining troops were camped up in a valley out on the other side of town on the other side of the great valley where most of Kolastan's farming was, stretching away to the Capital. Corvyn had heard mention there were five thousand soldiers there.

"It's time to split up..." Tyg said in a no nonsense tone. Corvyn's jaw clenched tight but he knew this was the reason she was here and nodded.

"Where do you want me?"

Tyg thought about it. "There are between a dozen and fifteen soldiers along the top of each wall over night at any one time, I intend to take care of the ones on the front wall...I can get past the ones on this closer wall...I need you to start a fire that will draw the men from their sleeping quarters over there and make as many of them as you can leave the gate area. We want them in disarray and confused chaos when Leviathan's men come through that lower gate."

"Got it." Corvyn nodded. "Good luck."

Tyg grinned and stepped away, melting into the shadows and was gone. Corvyn let his wards covering his identity drop and sparked a flame in his hand, standing up he lobbed a fireball into the sky, bringing it down upon the large food tent then sent another up and over the town wall into the barracks, aiming for the warlock dorm.

Tyg past a soldier who was sleeping with his back against a pole that was part of the structure of the platform above, she saw he had a cloak draped over his legs and without hesitation she took it, wrapping it around herself and pulling up the hood. It was pitch black and the soldiers patrolling the second platform all stood within the lights of a couple of lanterns, talking to each other and smoking. She frowned in disapproval at their lax attitudes to their jobs, they would soon learn their lesson she thought as she slipped by them easily in their blindness of the dark shadows thanks to the lanterns.

The soldiers on the first platform were more alert, they had no lanterns as they did not want their positions to be given away from the enemy they knew was out there just waiting to pick them off the wall with an arrow.

Tyg saw they were all standing a good ten yards apart, occasionally one would walk down to another and they would talk for a moment, take a quick break then return to looking out at the darkness and the lights of thousands of camp fires beyond. She quickly approached and broke the neck of the first soldier, propping him up in the alcove of the ramparts he was posted at before stepping back to the opposite edge and crouching down in the darkness.

She waited to see if anyone had noticed or heard anything before crawling along the platform to the next one aware this could take some time, and time wasn't on her side.

After taking out five of the soldiers the next one walked off towards his fellow and they started talking, taking a smoke break and leaning on the ramparts, looking out. They talked softly so their voices didn't carry to their enemies but Tyg heard snippets of them discussing the number of fires there were out there.

She snuck past them and dispatched another two guards before they finished their smokes and separated. She thought about going back to deal with them, but then paused, holding her breath as she watched the figure of the one who had left his post walk past it and head to approach the soldier on his other side, one she had already dispatched.

"Shit..." She breathed, standing up and looming up behind the soldier in front of her, shoving her dagger into his ribs and angling to his heart as she covered his mouth with her other hand. She let him drop to the ground as the nosey soldier reached his dead companion and raised the alarm. Eight, she had dispatched eight so far, that left the two in front of her as well as a possible five behind her.

As the soldier raised the alarm Tyg was running, her daggers held low. She saw the other soldier in front of her also start making his way over as the one who raised the alarm was crouching down over the dead body. She caught up to the soldier, grabbing him by the back of his belt and jolting him to a stop as her dagger plunged into the back of his neck. He jerked and went limp, dropping like a stone. She ran forward just as the soldier crouching down looked back. He stood up, fumbling in shock with his sword to release it from its scabbard before feeling both of Tyg's daggers enter his body. She lifted him up by those daggers in his chest and threw him over the ramparts.

He screamed out a quick death cry before it abruptly stopped as he hit the rocky ground beneath. Tyg spun around to face the remaining soldiers who had all drawn their swords and were approaching cautiously.

"Fuck..." Tyg spat out as she looked at her options. It was just then that the first fire from Corvyn blazed up over the second wall, causing many shouts and alarm bells to start up. The men in front of her knew no help was coming to their aid, they had to stop this assassin on their own.

They had levelled out into a line clearly showing Tyg there were actually only four of them and were advancing on her while one was making demands.

"Who the hell are you? Show yourself!"

Tyg chuckled as she vaulted up onto the top of the thick stone rampart then jumped off spinning in the air to come down behind the soldiers as they gaped at her in disbelief, stalling.

She managed to thrust a dagger into the chest of the soldier second in line while thrashing out with her other blade to slice deeply into the sword arm of the man closest to the rampart, severing the nerves and making him clutch his arm and stagger backwards.

She snatched up the sword, avoiding a swiping arc from the sword of the third soldier before throwing her dagger at his face and turning to brace and make contact with the fourth soldier's sword with her own. They backed off each other as the soldier took stock of the fact that two of them were dead and the third wasn't going to be able to fight. He grit his teeth and glared at his foe.

"Who the fuck are you?!"

Tyg reached up and lowered her hood, grinning as the soldiers face went white and his eyes opened large in shock. "A woman!"

It was enough for Tyg to have an opening and whacked the flat of her sword down upon the man's wrist, making him drop his sword and then turned it to plunge into his chest. She walked him backwards to the edge of the platform and kicked him off her blade and off the platform, falling with a thud in the darkness. She turned to see the last remaining soldier was standing up, leaning back against the stone and holding his good hand out in surrender. He dropped to his knees and pleaded for his life.

An explosion of fire went up inside the town walls, distracting the man as his eyes looked behind Tyg, reflecting back the fire in them. Tyg moved in the blink of that eye, looming into his vision as her sword plunged into his chest, coming out through his back and imbedding into the stone block behind him. Tyg stepped back, releasing the blade and looked him over as blood gushed out of his mouth followed by a froth as he coughed. Tyg didn't wait for him to die.

She dropped down off the platform to where a small hatch was situated in the huge gate. She pried it open and let out a small low whistle as alarm bells and fire whistles continued to go off up behind the main town gate. Five Tylandrian soldiers appeared out of the darkness at her call. They were dressed all in black with black cloths over their faces, they would be responsible for taking out the guards on the second platform making way for the rest of the soldiers to move swiftly in and open the second gate up properly.

"Go that way, up and to the left, there is a platform that will allow you to walk along the top over to the next gate and drop down onto that platform, there are only about twenty soldiers there, but below them is about two hundred." She instructed.

Tyg watched them move off as a group of another ten soldiers came in and started to lift the large portcullis gate to allow the waiting lines of troops in.

While the soldiers on top of the second wall were all looking inwards at the fire they were dispatched without any warning alarm being raised as the soldiers on the ground were still fighting the fire Corvyn had lit amongst their tents. The five Tylandrian soldiers quickly dropped down and started raising the second gate as the ten that opened the first came up over the top and dropped down behind them to protect their backs. A few soldiers on the ground came to question why the gate was being raised. A scuffle ensued but it was too late.

A steady silent stream of a couple of thousand of Leviathan's troops quickly snuck through and took over the fortifications with very little resistance as Corvyn managed to blast open the gate to the town using his magic making the way easy for the soldiers to gain quick control.

After the first gate had been raised Tyg made her way out of the wall and down the road in the opposite direction to the soldiers waiting to get in. She found Leviathan storming and pacing back and forth in the darkness beside his horse at the back of the line of soldiers now entering the ravine as sounds of fighting and shouting could be heard. She grinned at his agitated movements and called out softly to him, stepping into the light of a few small lanterns surrounding him. He turned to see her covered in blood...it caked her hair and covered her face and arms, the light coloured jerkin stained with it.

"Tygarya..." He breathed in relief and stepped straight into her space, embracing her strongly and holding her head against his chest. "You are a marvel..."

He let go of her head and lifted her chin, kissing her and taking her breath at the passionate forceful action.

"Lev...seriously..." Antyn's voice interrupted him and he lifted his head, looking down at Tyg with a sparkle in his eyes as he licked his lips. He tasted blood and wiped his chin which was now covered in the blood smeared from Tyg's face.

Tyg grinned up at him. "I'm a bit dirty..."

He chuckled. "I can see that, I don't care. I'm just glad you came back to me." He looked up over her head into the darkness of the road as the last of the soldiers were going through the lower gate. "Where is Captain Corvyn?"

"Still inside, those explosions were his doing, he's opening the main gate."

"Then let's go and meet him up there..."

It was a short and ferocious battle in the end, once the Kolastan soldiers saw their fortifications had been breached and thousands of Tylandrian soldiers were streaming in they threw down their weapons and surrendered. No one knew where Lord Frameur was, no orders came and so in the confusion the soldiers decided to save themselves.

Leviathan swept into the Keep and was notified of Frameur's body being found and brought in. He felt Antyn walk up beside him as he looked over the dead man's body.

"She took a strange path to kill him..." Leviathan muttered before turning and walking out.

Antyn pressed his mouth together firmly inspecting the wound at the man's throat before turning to General Oltar to spread the word that Lord Frameur is dead.

Leviathan returned to where he had left Tyg in an upstairs living area.

"Where is the King?" He asked, looking at the cowering servants kneeling under guard as his soldiers were still clearing the rooms.

"Not here, he is being kept in a cabin in the mountains about three miles away."

Leviathan frowned, folding his arms. "Tell me everything."

44

The next morning Leviathan travelled up to the cabin after hearing Tyg's report concerning King Davalos and the sorcerer named Timothy, he brought Tyg with him as well as Corvyn leaving Antyn back at the Keep to control the takeover. He used the same carriage that Frameur had used to not give any warning of anything being out of sorts. It was expected that Timothy would be wary as the noises of last night's attack would have travelled up the ravines to here. As it was still early morning and the battle had only ended just before dawn with the Kolastan troops surrendering Leviathan hoped he hadn't found out that Lord Frameur was dead and the town was now his.

They saw Timothy step out of the cabin looking worried as the carriage approached. Tyg stepped out first as Timothy would recognise her as not a threat. She smiled and waved giddily to ease his fears and it worked as he visibly seemed to relax.

His face went pale then green as the seven foot figure of Leviathan stepped out of the carriage and straightened up, at the same time he sent a fork of purple tendrils straight at the unsuspecting Timothy smashing through his defences and ensnaring him within a spell that froze him to the spot.

Leviathan walked slowly forward as Corvyn and Tyg held back. He walked straight up to Timothy and looked down on him like he was nothing more than a bug, chuckling sinisterly.

"Well, well...if it isn't Timothy Von Drenan, it's been a long time..." Leviathan sneered as the frozen form of Timothy looked up with terror in his eyes. "Still a spineless conniving little weed, I see."

Leviathan looked calmly around the small clearing in which the cabin sat, taking in the sparseness. "Looks like you've been living rough...tell me..." Leviathan's eyes sparked into a faint glow. "Was it your idea or that fool of a warlock's to try and stand in my way?"

He lifted his hand to face the cabin and started twirling and twisting his fingers like he was unravelling something. Tyg, looking on fascinated, guessing he was dismantling the wards and spells held over the cabin that she couldn't see.

It only took him a couple of minutes and Timothy was looking at him with fear and awe as Leviathan turned his attention to Corvyn. "You can enter now..."

Corvyn and Tyg made their way to the cabin. As Tyg past Leviathan he reached out and grabbed her arm, making her spin around and hit his chest. She looked up at him, questioningly, but he simply touched her hair, returning it back to silver and dropping the suppression over her aura.

As the colour drained from her hair, the colour also drained from Timothy's face. Leviathan grinned savagely and turned Tyg around to face the other sorcerer. Dropping his power hold on the man so he fell onto his knees. He looked up as he was encased in ice, trapping him in something more permanent as Leviathan fixed him with a baleful stare. "You should have followed me." He stated calmly smug.

"How? How does she exist?"

"Recognise this do you?" Leviathan asked with a smug chuckle, indicating Tyg. "She came straight to your threshold and you didn't even know...that's how weak you are, Timothy. A half Elvian of Royal blood, alive and well and she belongs to me!" Tyg frowned at his words and looked back at him disgruntled. "Do you know what's going to happen now?" Leviathan asked the man as he let go of Tyg's arm.

Timothy's eyes glowed brightly, they were a rare green colour and sparkled like emeralds. "You're going to kill me."

Tyg stepped back and folded her arms, glaring at Leviathan wondering what that little display had been about.

"Yes." He answered coolly.

Corvyn came back out of the cabin. "Quick, we need to get this man back to a healer!"

Leviathan looked up, grimly and stepped past the sorcerer and towards the cabin. "You better hope the King doesn't die, Timothy...or I'll make your death linger for days just for my enjoyment."

Tyg saw Timothy blanch and dry wrench in fear.

Once Leviathan stepped inside the cabin Tyg's gaze dropped to Timothy and he looked up at her with a curious gaze. "How?" He groaned out.

Tyg twisted her mouth wondering if she should even talk to him, he might try something, some spell of persuasion was possible. Sorcerers didn't need their hands to weave spells. She backed up a step. Corvyn walked over and stood behind the sorcerer.

"Don't worry Tyg, his Majesty has completely incapacitated him...just don't talk to him. That will definitely piss his Majesty off."

Tyg huffed and walked off to the cabin, leaving Corvyn to watch over their captive. She entered to see Leviathan leaning over

King Davalos with one hand on the King's forehead, his eyes closed and his expression disgruntled.

The King groaned and his eyes blinked open as Leviathan also opened his eyes and stepped back. "King Davalos?" He asked, glancing up at Tyg for a second noticing her there. "We need to get him back to Antyn...I can smash the curse spells put upon him but I'm afraid it may be too late to save him."

He turned with a cluck of his tongue and went back outside. Tyg looked at Davalos and saw him make a move to sit up, he rubbed his eyes and blinked, looking around the room like he was surprised to find himself there. He looked up at Tyg with confusion.

"You actually look better than the last time I saw you..." Tyg said as she moved to pour him a glass of water and held it out to him.

He lifted his hand, but it was shaky and weak. Tyg put the glass into his hand curling his hand around it and letting him lift it to his lips. He took the smallest of sips and descended into coughing. Tyg took the glass back before he dropped it and placed it on the table.

Corvyn came back in with two soldiers.

"Tyg...move aside."

She stepped back so one soldier could take the King's shoulders and the other his feet and they lifted him up and carried him out. Tyg followed and as she stepped out of the cabin she stopped in shock.

Leviathan had Timothy by his throat, lifting him up off his feet and held aloft by pure strength with one hand. Timothy was like a ragdoll and as Leviathan lifted his other hand which held a dagger, he merely whimpered as Leviathan eviscerated him, cutting him from groin to rib cage, his guts spilling out to the ground between them. Leviathan dropped the dagger and stuck his hand into Timothy's body, searching up to grip his heart. Timothy's body convulsed, blood gushing out of his mouth as his eyes rolled back in his head.

"You have been found guilty and now you must die." Leviathan intoned in a deep voice. "From one sorcerer to another to accept your power, your knowledge, your wisdom and your lifespan..."

Tyg watched in fascination as an ethereal glow started to shine around Leviathan and Timothy. She felt Corvyn press to her back. He whispered in her ear. "This is why the Emperor is so powerful and so dangerous."

"...I accept these charges of blood, power and life from Timothy Von Drenan, may his death give purpose to his life."

Leviathan opened his mouth as a black smoke rose up out of Timothy's and entered Leviathan's. Once it stopped Leviathan ripped his hand out of Timothy's body, his fist holding Timothy's heart and dropped the withered corpse of Timothy to the ground. The heart was encased in flames and became dust in Leviathan's hand which he upturned and the ashes fell upon the corpse and blew away in the breeze.

Leviathan turned to stare back straight at Tyg, his eyes blazing with power.

Tyg swallowed hard, frozen to the spot. She heard Corvyn's hard breathing behind her and his hand poke into her back. "Move." He said through gritted teeth.

Leviathan lifted his hand towards her. "Tygarya, don't be afraid."

She stepped down off the porch of the cabin and made her way to Leviathan, placing her hand in his. He gripped it hard and pulled her into his body. "I cannot leave a single sorcerer alive to oppose me, Tygarya, no matter how weak." He said as explanation.

"Right, I get it..." She muttered back, not sure why he thought she would care. He leaned back and looked at her face, studying her reaction. He smiled and stroked a hand down her cheek.

"Of course, you would..." He seemed pleased and took her hand, leading her back to the carriage.

Antyn looked over King Davalos, placing several healing spells upon him and declaring he should return to health in a couple of days, but that he will forever be weakened as the damage done to his body was severe. Special care would be needed to prevent him from catching colds and fevers in the future. Keeping him comfortable in the Keep they sent a message out to the capital to let them know their King is in ill health and would be returning in a few days with the intention of completing a full surrender to Emperor Adramelech, to whom he now owed his life.

45

O n the second day of the town having fallen under Emperor Leviathan's hold, all the soldiers that had surrendered were being held inside their barracks under heavy guard while lines of troops of the Tylandrian Army filed up through the pass, into town and out the other side setting up in the valley where the majority of the Kolastan troops had been camped. It was a grand sight to see and Tyg was walking the ramparts of the Keep with Antyn when they stopped to look over at the main town square to see Leviathan standing before six men who were all on their knees and under heavy guard. Tyg noticed their hands were shackled in iron mitts and saw Corvyn guarding them with others from Leviathan's warlock guard.

"What's going on down there?" Tyg asked, leaning out and watching with curiosity.

Antyn stopped and looked over with a grim expression. "That is your Emperor being a cautious ruler."

Tyg gave Antyn a sideways glance. "What does that mean?"

"Those men are all warlocks, its fine to have normal human soldiers just surrender and be absorbed into our army, if they buck against our ideals then it's easy to deal with them as examples for the rest, but for men with magic..." Antyn's expression clouded. "It's dangerous to just assume they will change sides easily and you're either with Lev or against him and he won't leave any person with magic on an opposing side."

Tyg's brows drew down in thought. "So he's going to have them killed?"

"Yes. They chose the wrong side and Lev will not allow any magic to exist that he does not control."

Tyg watched fascinated as the warlocks were systematically slaughtered, their chins lifted and a dagger sliced across their throats then pushed face down in the dirt to bleed out as a final humiliation before their bodies were burnt to ash. Leviathan stood watching the proceedings with a grim expression, his eyes lifted and he saw Tyg standing on the parapet.

The stench of burning flesh soon reached Tyg's nostrils and she covered her face, pulling back from the edge and pulling a disgusted face at Antyn. "Let's go..."

Antyn chuckled and they made their way down into the Keep and through to the other side of the massive building away from the smoke.

"Are you perturbed by those executions at all, Tyg?" Antyn asked, curious, as they sat down in a lounge room.

"No, I understand."

Antyn looked her over for a moment before picking up a book.

Leviathan strode in a minute later, seeing Tyg sitting in a chair and looking out the window. "Tygarya, why did you watch?"

Antyn looked up, startled at the gruffness of Leviathan's voice. "We were walking the ramparts, it was my fault we were there, I didn't realise..."

Leviathan's gaze slid slowly to Antyn. "Did I ask you?"

"Was I not allowed to know you were slaughtering your enemies?" Tyg said facetiously. "It goes without saying there will be those within Kolastan that must be executed to make the rest fall into line, should I be shocked?"

Leviathan's vulture gaze settled on her as she spoke and she saw the edge of his lips twitch slightly before he raked a hand through his hair and looked away nonchalantly. "Not at all, I'm glad you understand...I thought for a moment you would be wanting to campaign for their lives."

"Why?" Tyg frowned and Leviathan could see she was completely perplexed.

He chuckled. "Because I forgot who you were for a moment...you only fight for those you care about, right?"

Tyg's eyes narrowed slightly, was he itching for a fight? She turned in her chair to face him more directly. "You seem quite annoyed by something, what is it?"

Leviathan sucked on his teeth and folded his arms. Antyn put his book down in apprehension, how was it that Tyg was beginning to understand his brother better than himself?

"You're right, Tygarya, there is something that has been weighing on my mind for a while..."

"Something to do with me?" She asked in a quiet tone, starting to feel the weight of his glare.

"Hmm...it's to do with Lord Frameur's body..."

Tyg felt a sinking feeling in the pit of her stomach. "What about it?"

"The method you used, it would have taken him longer to die than those warlocks out front just did..." He dropped his hands and walked towards her, bending over her and placing his hands on the arms of the chair, bringing his face down in front of hers as she pressed back into the seat watching him, wary.

"And?" Tyg asked. "I had no dagger to slit his throat or pierce his heart, if I had gone with a weapon he would have known immediately...I had to use my strength and this..." She held up her hand and flashed the dragon's head ring in front of Leviathan's face. "What's the problem, he's dead."

She met Leviathan's gaze and held it as he seemed to search into her soul for something. After a full breathless minute he stood up with a grunt and turned away. "You did your job, fair enough..." He stepped away towards the door and Tyg let out a long slow breath of relief. He stopped at the doorway and turned back, his eyes intense.

"I know you explained to me that you would do anything to complete the job, so I won't push this, but next time..." He paused, his jaw clenching. "...no, there won't be a next time."

"Leviathan!" Tyg stood up, affronted by his attitude. "What's the problem, he's dead, like you wanted. You have the town like you wanted, you even have the King, a sorcerer's power and Kolastan's surrender without even a week of siege."

Leviathan's gaze flashed as he glared back at her. "Tell me how far he went before you had the opportunity to use that ring, which I gave you, to open up his jugular? Tell me how far you went to keep him from calling out to the guards? Tell me how you kept him quiet for two whole minutes while your hands were full holding his hands from spell casting."

Leviathan had rounded back and was standing in the middle of the room. Antyn wiped a hand over his face in exhaustion. "Lev, we spoke about this before you even sent her out...you said you could cope."

Tyg and Leviathan were face to face, staring at each other. Tyg grimaced and folded her arms. "That's unfair, Leviathan...I did what I had to, there were no feelings in what I did other than to kill him...for you!"

Leviathan straightened up, his face grim as he blinked once then turned away and walked from the room clearly choosing to leave in his ire rather than stay.

Antyn let out a breath, standing up as Tyg looked at him with a perplexed expression. "It's alright, I'll go talk to him..."

"He's being ridiculous, you agree right?"

"Yeah..." Antyn grumbled before leaving.

Tyg dropped back in her seat, chewing her lip. How the hell did he manage to work out what had happened? Had he somehow read her mind? She was sure Corvyn wouldn't have said anything, he had promised her.

Antyn found Leviathan in the drawing room, looking through Lord Frameur's accounting books for the Keep, he was going to have to find someone to take over until the King was back in the capital and could make these decisions once again.

"What was that?" Antyn asked as he strode in and closed the door.

Leviathan looked up with just his eyes, broody under his brows. "What was what?"

"That just before, you know what I'm talking about. Are you seriously acting like a jealous lover right now?"

Leviathan leaned back in his chair, rubbing his eyes. "It just irked me that she didn't seem to contemplate how to kill him before he touched her."

"He had wards up, Lev, you're being unreasonable...I told you, you wouldn't be able to handle this...you're a possessive psychopath."

Leviathan clucked his tongue in annoyance. "Shut your mouth, Antyn, before I shut it for you."

Antyn sighed and dropped into a chair. "She is yours, through and through, she just proved that...quit worrying. She just handed Kolastan to you on a silver plate."

Leviathan grunted. "I'm just glad it was Timothy Von Drenan behind this and not someone like Drexel...this could have all gone horribly wrong letting her go in alone."

Antyn grimaced. "So that's what has you in a terrible mood..." He wiped a hand over his face and stood up, going over to a side table where there was a crystal carafe of some amber coloured liquid. He unstoppered it and sniffed it before pouring some out into two glasses. He walked over to Leviathan and placed one down in front of him. "It is something we can both blame ourselves for, we should have known the likelihood of a sorcerer being involved in Kolastan was high, they are out there somewhere..."

Leviathan picked up the glass and swirled the amber liquid around, staring at it. "I now know the likely whereabouts of two of them."

"Really?" Antyn said surprised. "Well, if taking Kolastan wasn't worth celebrating that news certainly is."

"Hmm..." Leviathan gulped back the alcohol. "I can't act on it yet...I need to focus on getting Gua del Mar first...it's only a hunch that Timothy had...but it does seem, by his memories that he was kicked out of the order and then later it may have disbanded through disagreements."

"Is that so...that is good to know, at least if they are all independent of each other they can't all come at you at once. Think about sending some warlocks out to explore the area..."

"Hmm, that might be beneficial...but it can wait. Let's get King Davalos back to his capital so he can formally surrender in front of his people."

46

They journeyed out onto the vast valley where their troops were camped, Leviathan sat upon his mighty war horse, Titus and had a line of Royal Guard and warlocks with him surrounding a carriage that was being escorted by ten Kolastan soldiers. He approached the closed and guarded gates of Kairo, the capital of Kolastan, stopping a hundred feet away from the gates and allowing the Kolastan soldiers to take the carriage containing their King the rest of the way. Leviathan watched solemnly as the soldiers were met with a contingent of people from inside the city before gates were opened and the carriage rolled inside.

A man sitting upon a white horse and flying the red and gold pennon of Kolastan, with the lion on it, rode up to within reach of Leviathan's archers. He held his hand up to stay their arrows and kicked his horse forward to meet the man.

"I thank you, Emperor Adramelech for returning our King to us, you have shown yourself to be a gracious man in the circumstances. We ask for a couple of days in which to confer with King Davalos in regards to what has transpired with Lord Frameur amongst other things. Please be patient, we will allow his Majesty to abdicate to you in due course."

"I don't want him to abdicate to me, only swear fealty to me as your overlord, he can continue to rule here in my stead."

The man looked a little taken back. "I see, well we obviously have much to discuss with his Majesty, we ask for patience."

"I'll give you three days...how's that."

The man bowed his head. "Most gracious of you, your Imperial Majesty." The man turned his horse and galloped back to the city.

Leviathan turned and moved back to where his army was camped only a mile away to wait.

A courtier wearing the colours of parley came through the front line and was escorted without delay back to where the Emperor had set up his headquarters tent after the short and bloody campaign. Giving King Davalos time to enter his capital alone and make his preparations with dignity for his formal surrender. He now owed his life to the Emperor and Leviathan knew he would not go against him.

Leviathan was lounging in an ornate chair that was set up like a throne in the middle of the meeting tent, casually eating an apple, one leg hooked up over the arm. Antyn was standing over at a desk reading reports when a Colonel entered with the courtier and stood him before the Emperor. The courtier fell to his knees and prostrated himself.

"Get up." Leviathan growled as he looked at the Colonel. "What is it?"

"He has a message from King Davalos, my Liege."

"Does he...?" Leviathan sat up and held his hand out. The courtier stood up shaking and took a sealed letter from his doublet and handed it to the Colonel who handed it to Leviathan. "Go and await instruction."

Leviathan waved the Colonel and the courtier out as he handed the letter to Antyn. Antyn had walked up and stood next to the make shift throne when the courtier had been brought in. He took the letter and walked back to the desk, grabbing a letter opener and wedging the wax seal open he unfolded the letter and quickly scanned it. He smirked and put it on the desk, turning around to look at Leviathan's waiting face.

"So it's done." He said simply. "This letter cordially invites us in to receive the King's formal surrender."

"Well it's about fucking time." Leviathan scowled then chuckled, wiping his mouth. "You know, you're right, we should have used Tyg from the start, this all ended so easily, with even the added bonus of a sorcerer's power to add to my own...let's get going."

"Well, the fact that King Davalos was already under duress from Lord Frameur certainly helped the situation..." Antyn said, frowning at the term 'used' but carried on. "How long do you intend to stay?"

"Only a week, long enough to determine that the people around King Davalos aren't as power hungry as Lord Frameur was..."

"That's quick..."

"Yes, I'll leave General Kloine here with half our troops, make their presence felt, we can sort any problems out on our return. We have to move on if we wish to take Gua del Mar...since this campaign seems to be going so well all of a sudden..." Leviathan scoffed as he stood up. "And all thanks to my little Elvian princess, I wonder what she will make of Gua del Mar?"

Antyn baulked. "Shit, I forgot what they were like with women, you better keep her on a leash."

"Oh, I intend to do more or less just that, don't worry and I look forward to what's going to happen if she even tries to roll her fucking eyes at me over this." Leviathan muttered as he left.

"By the way, where is she?"

A small smirk crept over Leviathan's lips. "Asleep."

Antyn frowned. "By normal means or by you?"

"Me of course, she's getting bored so better she sleeps until we need her."

Antyn rubbed a hand over his face. "You can't do that, Lev..."

"I can, it's only while I'm busy...an hour here, an hour there, it's no different from back home in my office..."

Antyn sighed and shook his head. "You know if Tyg ever finds out you make her sleep using magic, she'll try to kill you, right?"

"She can try..." Leviathan snorted.

47

Tyg was bored as Leviathan took residence in the palace of King Davalos and sat in council with his advisor's and government officials laying down how things were going to work from now on.

It seemed taking over a kingdom was complicated and full of red tape, discussions, negotiations and endless meetings which kept Leviathan, Antyn and General Kloine busy.

As Leviathan placed Kolastan under Marshall Law, Tyg found herself unable to wander around and cloistered within the palace under watchful guard. With one sorcerer already shown to be involved in a plot against him and not knowing where within these colossal mountains the others were made him extra controlling of her freedom.

She found Corvyn in the front courtyard of the palace talking to another officer one morning as she walked out onto the promenade balcony where the King usually stood and waved to the crowds of people when he opened the gates of the palace walls for special celebrations.

"Captain!" Tyg called out, leaning out over the balcony's stone balustrade and waving enthusiastically.

The officer facing Corvyn was also facing her and he looked up with wide eyes as Corvyn grimaced and shrugged his shoulders against her calling him out.

She could see the officer's mouth move and he pointed, then flinched at something Corvyn said. Tyg's mouth twisted in a surly pout as it was obvious Corvyn was choosing to ignore her.

She looked back over her shoulder and saw a soldier standing just inside the doors watching her every move. She stepped up to him and he stared back at her through his helm.

"Send someone to go fetch Captain Corvyn, tell him he is being derelict of duty and if he does not adhere to the Emperor's strict orders he knows the punishment."

The soldier glared at her for a moment then turned and walked off through the room and to the door, opening it he spoke to another guard out there then closed the door and turned around to glare at her again.

Tyg smiled and sat down in a chair to wait. The servants within the palace were still working and one was standing to the side looking at her in her leather gear and weapons with a very nervous look on her pale little face. Tyg flicked her gaze to the woman, she looked middle aged and wore a dark grey maid's uniform with a white lace apron. "Could I get some tea?"

The woman curtseyed. "Of course, miss. Would you like black tea with honey?"

"Sure..." She hadn't eaten much for breakfast and felt the start of a dull headache brewing. "Do you have anything sweet to go with it?"

The maid gave her a pleasant smile. "Of course, Miss."

She left the room and Tyg grabbed up the book she had been reading, there were different books in this palace and she was devouring them.

It didn't take long before Corvyn burst into the room, huffing with annoyance. "Tygarya, what is the meaning of this?" He demanded gruffly, pulling his helm off and tucking it under his arm as he swished his long fringe back from his eyes. "How dare you embarrass me with some trot about not following the Emperor's orders!?"

Tyg gave him a benign smile. "But you aren't..."

Corvyn sighed and rubbed his forehead. "In what way?"

"No one relieved you of your duty towards me, Corvyn...I'm here without Leviathan or Antyn, therefore aren't you supposed to be the one keeping an eye on me, not him?" Tyg pointed to the guard whose eyes shone through his helm with laughter as he straightened up slightly.

Corvyn met the guard's eyes and the guard quickly looked at the floor. "Get out." Corvyn ordered and the guard saluted, quickly making his escape as Corvyn turned back to Tyg who was looking at him with an amused smirk on her face. "You have got to be kidding me, Tygarya?" He placed his helm down on a nearby low cabinet, pulling his gauntlets off and putting them down too.

"No, not at all..."

Corvyn appraised her with a hefty stare before licking his lips and looking away to the open balcony doors. "Are you bored?"

"Yes, I am actually, how did you know?"

"It seems you only decide to come looking for me when you are...am I some sort of toy for you to play with when your master is gone out for the day?"

Tyg gave Corvyn a startled look that slowly narrowed down to a very dangerous glint. "Are you calling me a puppy?"

Corvyn sighed bitterly and dropped into a chair, raking his hand through his hair. "What's wrong?"

Tyg blinked and settled her gaze back on him with a serious expression. "Do you believe in prophecy, fate...all that?"

Corvyn sat up, surprised by this sudden question. "Not really, although I know for a fact that some prophecies have indeed come true in the past."

"What ones?" Tyg asked, enthralled by the notion.

Corvyn thought about it. "It was preordained that Morphun Adramelech, the Emperor's late father would go to war against the Elvian race."

"Preordained? How?"

Corvyn's mouth twisted and he swept his hand across in front of himself. "It was written in the stars..."

"In what way was it written?"

"It was said that the mighty House of the Dragon Sorcerer would rise to contest the might of the Elvian race and change history...which he did."

Tyg dropped her gaze to her tea cup and chewed her lip. Corvyn regarded her pensive response and scratched his jaw, feeling the coarse stubble. "Tygarya...what's the issue?"

"I don't like the feeling that my life is not my own."

"Are you unhappy being with the Emperor?"

Tyg frowned in thought at the question, Corvyn watched her with a small frown of his own.

"No, I'm happy...but does that matter, even if I wanted to leave he wouldn't let me."

Corvyn scratched his jaw, feeling the coarseness of stubble. "Tygarya, I think you need to stop overthinking things, you admit you're happy so why worry about if you weren't..."

She pursed her lips and looked away out the doors as a stirring breeze blew in.

"Find something to keep you busy..." Corvyn stood up. "And not me."

"And not me, what?" Antyn's voice came from the opposite direction to the main door and both Tyg and Corvyn startled.

Tyg's mouth twisted in ire. "Why are you sneaking around using the servant entrances?"

Antyn walked over with a cold smile on his lips. "You just never know what you'll find..." His gaze slid to Corvyn and Corvyn's jaw clenched at what he was getting at.

"Lady Tygarya called for my presence. Apparently she was under the misunderstanding that I was still to be her warder when both you and the Emperor were busy."

Antyn snorted, looking at Tyg. "Really? Do you realise the danger you are putting this man in, Tyg?"

She looked up at him with a dark scowl.

"It may be that you like the Captain's company, Tyg, as from what I just heard he seems to have an understanding of your personality, perhaps that is a comfort to you...but I feel I must warn you to leave the Captain alone."

Corvyn's jaw was ticking under the strain of keeping his mouth shut. Tyg merely smiled up at Antyn, leaning back in her chair.

"As a warrior this man is impeccable, as an officer he is becoming a great leader...but as a warlock he is unmatched...this is really the only reason Lev is being so lenient and allowing you to have the gall to even recommend this man to be your handler during the infiltration of this country..."

Corvyn flushed, getting hot under the collar. Antyn looked over to him and met his irate gaze with a calm benign smile.

"Do you understand, Tyg?"

She pouted and folded her arms. "Fine..."

"Good, you can go now, Captain..."

Corvyn saluted, spun on his heels collected up his helm and gauntlets and stalked from the room. "That bloody woman is going to get me killed." He muttered as he stormed off down the halls. He baulked, freezing in his steps to immediately straighten up and salute as Leviathan appeared at the end of the hall.

Leviathan walked slowly towards him, his eyes narrowing upon him, taking in his state of uniform and pale expression.

He lifted his gaze to look ahead and past Corvyn by without a single word.

Corvyn let out a relieved breath and hurried off, slamming his helm down upon his head and cursing ever having met Tygarya.

Leviathan strode into the lounge room to find Tyg sitting with Antyn, she didn't look pleased and Antyn looked quite the opposite as he looked up and grinned.

"What's going on? I just saw Captain Corvyn in the halls, somewhere he should not be."

Antyn glanced at Tyg as she fidgeted in her seat. "Oh, nothing...Tyg was bored."

Leviathan stepped up to her chair and glowered down at her. "Bored? What has that to do with a Captain in my army?" His voice dropped to a dangerous tone.

"She was under the misunderstanding that she was still under his wardship, so called him out on it. I've put her right on it."

Leviathan's gaze slid to Antyn even as he leaned down and placed his hands on the chair arms of Tyg's seat. "Get out."

Antyn didn't hesitate to stand and make his way to the door. "I did explain, Lev...perhaps don't leave your biggest asset to her own devices from now on."

Tyg looked up at Leviathan's face as he turned back to her. Impulsively she grabbed his face with both hands and planted her lips on his. She felt him tense with surprise for a moment before one hand lifted to grab her by her braid and pull her back.

"Tygarya..." Leviathan growled.

"I'm sorry...Antyn's right, I was bored so I called the only other person that I know, please don't punish him, I used your name to get him here."

Leviathan smirked a little. "So you threatened him?"

Tyg shrugged. "Kind of...I told him he was being derelict in his duty of me, that no one had relieved him of the job of being my minder..."

Leviathan couldn't help but chuckle and stood up. "Why do you feel the need to seek him out?"

Tyg shrugged. "I get honest answers from him...as much as he growls at me and tells me off for calling him out, he also sets me straight of concerns I have that I cannot talk to you about."

Leviathan frowned down at her and lifted her chin to see her face. "Concerns regarding me?"

"Regarding me." Tyg answered. "Why I'm here, what it all means..."

"Philosophical of you both..." Leviathan muttered. "I do not like it, but I understand...I do not however condone it."

Tyg blinked as he glared down at her, his thumb slowly stroking her cheek. It glided across to her lips and he mushed them lightly, his eyes glowing softly.

"Do you think I should forgive you?" He asked deeply.

Tyg's eyes were unwavering as she locked eyes with him. "No, but forgive him."

"Very well, you know what you need to do then..." He said, stepping back and letting her go.

Tyg swallowed hard and stood up, walking to the door feeling his dark presence right behind her, following her all the way up to the bedroom they shared.

48

Leviathan looked up from the map on the table as a young corporal came in and saluted. Tyg was lounging back in a chair at that table tapping her fingers on the top as Antyn sat over in a corner at a small desk going through acquisition reports. They had moved twenty thousand of their troops down from Kairo's valley and through the pass to the hilly lands bordering Gua del Mar. It stretched away into gold where the sand met the grasslands. The heat here was already oppressive.

"My Liege." The corporal puffed. "A message has been received from Gua del Mar."

Leviathan straightened up and walked over to the soldier as he dug into his jacket and pulled out an envelope holding it out with a bow of his head.

Leviathan took it, waving his hand in dismissal to the soldier. He pivoted on his heels and quickly left.

Leviathan broke the seal and opened the letter, as he was reading it Commander General Oltar accompanied by General Barrock came in.

"My Liege." He saluted. "I heard a message came..."

"Hmm..." Leviathan held up the letter briefly then continued to read it, walking back to the table and then placed the letter down on it. "It seems King Bahadur already knows about our intentions to continue our offensive strike towards his border."

Antyn turned around with interest.

General Oltar nodded. "We've had reports of scouts watching our progress, is he proposing a parley or surrender?"

Leviathan's mouth twisted in an amused smirk. "Neither...he's invited me directly to the palace. It says that if I intend on continuing my advancement he proposes, rather than use any force to destroy innocent lives, he wants a contest as per their customs."

"A contest?" General Barrock asked a little disbelieving.

Antyn frowned. "The Sabres are well known to deal with situations by duel, plus he knows he is seriously out numbered."

"It is why they are so formidable..." General Barrock agreed. "They fight and train as much as any soldier but it's like a religion, full of honour and prestige to battle in a dispute. Much like the Elvians except, they are notoriously suspicious of magic users, preferring to have their nation free of magic."

Tyg's head came up, her eyes sparkling with sudden interest.

"That's exactly what he proposes, a duel." Leviathan stated.

Antyn looked at Leviathan with interest. "You and King Bahadur?" He scoffed.

Leviathan actually chuckled derisively. "Hardly, no...champion verses champion."

"Champion?"

"And it states it cannot be myself...or you...and no magic will be allowed. A contest fought merely with weapons and brute strength. To the death." Leviathan's tone was sardonic.

Tyg sat up straight, her chair scraping. Leviathan's gaze lifted over to her on the other side of the table. She smiled at him and blinked endearingly. He raised an eyebrow at her.

"No." He said simply.

The Generals' reactions were mixed, Barrock blanched and grit his teeth. "Your champion must be one extremely skilled in sword defence, my Liege. The Sabres don't have their reputations as some of the best swordsmen in the world for no reason and the King's champion will be the best amongst them to be assured, they hold contests all the time, it's their biggest pastime, proving their prowess."

"I haven't even accepted this proposal yet, General…" Leviathan gave him a hard look.

General Barrock bowed his head. "My apologies."

Leviathan slid his gaze back to Tyg, a finger raised up in warning to stay silent on the matter as she glared at him, her mouth firmly pressed closed but it was clear she wished to speak.

"It has its merits…" Antyn piped up.

"Yes, it certainly does…if I can guarantee the win." Leviathan's eyes were blazing with intensity as he still stared at Tyg. She had looked away and was leaning over the table, her chin in her hand pouting at being silenced. "If I lose, this agreement then makes things messy, as I'm forced to invade anyway and break the agreement."

"May I collate a list of suitable candidates for you to have a look at, my Liege? It may help to make a decision based on performance?" General Oltar asked.

Leviathan finally looked away from Tyg and up to the General. "Sure…"

General Oltar signalled to Barrock and they both saluted before leaving.

"Why can't it be me?" Tyg finally blurted out once the Generals were out of the room.

"Because I said no." Leviathan commented casually.

"It has merits too…" Antyn quipped with a little side smirk.

Leviathan scowled and turned around to look at his brother with an eyebrow arched in question. "You want Tygarya to be my champion?" He scoffed.

Antyn grinned. "They'll never see it coming...you know what they're like."

"I do...and they will never allow it."

"Why not?" Tyg asked, sitting up and looking at Antyn.

"Because women to them are..."

"Antyn!" Leviathan warned, his gaze frightening.

Tyg's gaze shifted to him, suspiciously. "What are women to them, incapable?"

"Something like that..." Leviathan said nonchalantly, waving his hand. "Shall we go and meet with the messenger?"

Antyn stood up with a stretch. "Guess we should...this is an attempt at peaceful negotiations."

Tyg stood up too but Leviathan glared at her and pointed at her seat. "No, sit down, you are staying here."

Tyg opened her mouth to object but Leviathan's eyes sparked dangerously as he lifted his finger up again. Tyg grit her teeth and slowly sank back into her seat, folding her arms. She was so bored.

Antyn chuckled and walked out of the room.

Leviathan gave her one last look of warning. "Behave and stay put, Tygarya."

Antyn was waiting for Leviathan as he closed the door. "She's going to find out sooner or later why keep it from her?"

"I don't need her getting riled up and going off on her own to do something stupid."

"I thought you had a handle on her?"

Leviathan shot Antyn a hard glare. "Don't push it. My handle on her is only that I am stronger than her, a better fighter and my power is firmly inside her head."

"So you're saying she doesn't follow you around like a puppy because she loves you but because she knows she has no choice?"

Leviathan's smirk was vile. "Exactly."

"King Bahadur and his men would be envious of you for that. Their women are all just property after all." Antyn chuckled.

Leviathan snorted. "I will explain only as much as I need to and only if we do in fact agree to King Bahadur's invitation." He mulled something over. "Let's get Captain Corvyn promoted and give him a spot back in my personal guard with a select number of proficient warlocks under him...."

Antyn glanced sideways at him with a small twist of his mouth. "Sure about that?"

"He doesn't need to be in Tygarya's line of sight, but if I need him to watch her I know he's there."

"You trust him that much to be your support to fall back on where Tyg is concerned?"

"His loyalty has never been in doubt, Antyn..." Leviathan tapped his head. "I know exactly where his loyalties lie, he may find Tyg attractive and beguiling, but I think underneath the normal he recognises something deeper about her nature, an understanding of what she has gone through and what her mental state may be like. She certainly frustrates him to no end."

Antyn huffed, nodding his head. "It is certainly a strange connection they have...but they do work well together as proven here."

"Yes, and one I would rather keep where I can monitor it."

Leviathan walked up to where the messenger was being kept, he was standing by his horse with two Sabres flanking him all holding the reins of their horses looking relaxed and unthreatened.

When they saw him approaching through the mass of soldiers surrounding them they all couldn't help but swallow hard to see the tall powerful figure of a man who knew he was more powerful than anyone standing in front of him, his aura oppressing everyone in his path.

They all looked up at his impressive height and the two Sabres' muttered back and forth to each other in their own language as the messenger stepped forward and bowed his head respectfully.

"Emperor Leviathan...thank you for your time to hear our King's request." The messenger said with a formal tone thick in his attempt at the common tongue.

Leviathan gave him a disarming smile. "Of course...it is a request that has not surprised me, knowing your customs as I do."

The messenger kept his eyes down and nodded. "That is good to hear, where are you sitting with a decision, Imperial Majesty?"

"I'm debating it." Leviathan gave a little smirk. "Please allow my attendants to lead you to a tent for refreshments, you've obviously ridden a long way." Leviathan looked up over their heads like he could see the distance. "Although I am surprised you didn't seem too worried about crossing the border into Kolastan and travelling so far into enemy territory to get to where our troops were."

He saw the two Sabres snort and puff their chests out. So they can both understand the language...

"We were riding under colours of truce..." The messenger looked a little nervously at Leviathan.

"Right..." Leviathan said with a small nod. "Just the three of you?"

The messenger licked his lips nervously and looked around at the Sabres who were both now frowning.

"Because, you wouldn't dare to come over the border with a force now, would you?" Leviathan glared down at the messenger making him quake in his boots.

"Your Imperial Majesty, I assure you..." He dropped to his knees. "It was only to ensure we reached your line...without being caught out in a surprise attack from marauding troops."

Leviathan glared at him. "How many?"

"Only a platoon of fifty. Once we saw your main line they stayed back and the three of us approached. I assure you, Emperor Adramelech, there are no other troops."

Leviathan huffed. "Very well..." He turned and started walking away. "I will make my decision by tomorrow. You will stay here until then and take my answer back with you."

As Leviathan walked back into the large command tent he saw Tyg was still sitting at the table with the map on it, there was a bottle of red wine open and a glass in her hand. He huffed, impressed, pleased she had once again behaved at least. His eyes narrowed though as he saw she was reading a large brown leather book with gold filigree upon the cover.

"Where did you get that?" He demanded as he approached her, he lifted his hand up and the book went flying out of Tyg's hands and into the air snapping shut, floating across the room and into his own hand. It was a book on the customs and ways of the people of Gua del Mar.

Tyg looked up indignantly with a sour pout. "Amongst your things..." She placed her glass down on the table.

"And who said you could read it?" He demanded.

"Who said I couldn't?" Tyg retorted, folding her arms. "There were clearly things being kept from me and as you know, I will always find out in my own way."

Leviathan sighed and placed the book on the table, tapping his fingers on it. "So how did reading that help you?" His eyes came up to meet hers with that vulture-like gaze.

"I can see why you don't want me anywhere near them." She answered sourly.

He chuffed in amusement. "Good, at least I don't need to have that conversation with you...now come and help me find a champion..."

Tyg glowered up at him. "If these Sabre are as good as suggested you need me."

Leviathan raked a hand through his hair. "I don't trust you to go anywhere near Gua del Mar...what you would see there would flip your psycho switch."

Tyg grinned. "My what?"

Leviathan frowned and grit his teeth, looking away. "It doesn't matter, you are not going."

"You said you would only accept this King's proposal if you could guarantee the win..."

"Oh, and you can guarantee you can win?"

"Well...let's just say..." She pointed to the book. "I don't believe the hype."

Leviathan laughed. "You and I are in agreement on something at least...now are you coming or staying here?"

Tyg stood up, grabbing her coat. "Coming...definitely coming...but I still think you should pick me..."

Leviathan watched her as she grabbed her coat and slipped it on. As she walked over he stepped in front of her and lifted her chin, making her look up at him with large eyes in question.

"You would be my choice, Tyg, only if I could be completely sure you wouldn't step out of line. Gua del Mar is a place steeped in tradition, that tradition treats its women poorly but that is the way of it...they are considered property, a commodity used to build alliances and show status and wealth, you stepping in there could cause me far more problems than you could solve."

"I promise I won't do anything to embarrass you...let me do this."

399

Leviathan searched her face for a long moment as she blinked up at him.

"I'll think about it."

49

Tyg's head was swivelling around as they walked through the army camp and Leviathan noticed with a sour expression.

"Tygarya, what are you looking for?"

"Captain Corvyn, I never really got to thank him after the whole sorcerer murder thing...I meant to the other day before Antyn interrupted our chat and then you told me I couldn't see him."

"Sorcerer murder thing?" Leviathan chuckled. "You think of me as a murderer?"

Tyg glanced up at him with a small pout and shrugged. "Well, you did kind of kill him out of vengeance, didn't you?"

"Hmm..." Leviathan snorted amused, looking away and pointing over to a large black tent. "Your Captain is over there working in his new position. He is no longer a Captain, you'll be pleased to hear, I made him a Colonel of the Tylandrian army responsible for ten thousand troops, but I also gave him twenty warlocks under his personal command as a Royal Guard Officer."

Tyg gaped a little. "Oh, I guess he's pretty busy then."

"He is....he has several officers now under his command as well, he is learning how to effectively distribute orders and manage effectively, rather than doing the boot work. Plus having to effectively time manage himself with doing two jobs." Leviathan smirked as he looked away.

Tyg frowned and looked away in the opposite direction. It was pretty clear Leviathan was picking on Corvyn giving him so much responsibility, probably hoping he would fail.

"I would like to go and congratulate him." Tyg stated.

"Why?"

"It was through the work he did with me that made you promote him again, I feel I should say a few words."

"Really?" Leviathan scoffed. "I'll think about it."

Tyg grit her teeth and gave him a hard glare. He glanced down at her and his eyebrow shot up. "What do you want to say so badly that it's screwing up your face and causing unsightly wrinkles?"

"I wish you would just tell me I'm on a leash and be done with it."

Leviathan stopped walking and turned to face Tyg, she stopped and folded her arms, looking at Leviathan's feet and fidgeting uncomfortably. "What part of anything I've ever said made you think you weren't on a leash? I choose to make it a theoretical one I can just as easily make it a literal one, as I have told you before."

Tyg looked up with a fierce blaze, but when she saw the hard challenging look in Leviathan's eyes she backed off with a huff, dropping her gaze again. She really was at his mercy and he knew it. As much as she felt drawn to him and was attracted to him she hated this part of him. He really was a possessive over-bearing jerk, was he really very different from the Sabre in Gua del Mar that kept women as trophies?

Leviathan stepped close and lifted her chin on the tips of his fingers making her look up at him. "You're a loose unit, Tygarya...you need control. You know that right?"

"Doesn't mean I have to like it." Tyg huffed out. "It makes me hate you."

Leviathan's expression went flat and his hand slowly curled around her throat. He dragged her closer and up onto her tiptoes to meet his glare. "Choose your words more carefully, Tygarya."

"People call me your pet behind my back, is that all I am?"

"Who?" His tone was commanding and he squeezed her throat, causing her to grab his wrist and gasp for breath a little.

"Does it matter who? Everyone." Tyg stated, not backing down.

Soldiers were starting to stop and gape at the two of them, a couple of warlocks that had been trailing along behind them as part of Leviathan's guard shuffled on their feet anxiously. They could see the building power field between the two as Leviathan's eyes started to glow. One of them decided to take off and find the Prince.

Antyn was just stepping out of the large black officers tent with Corvyn after giving him some sage advice and instruction in his new position, along with General Barrock when the warlock came running up.

"Prince Antyn, please come...his Imperial Majesty...he has..." He puffed out pointing back to where he had run from.

"Spit it out man!" Antyn grumbled but Corvyn and General Barrock looked up.

"Shit..." They both breathed out.

Antyn looked up as the warlock finished. "He has Lady Tygarya by the throat...the power is building..."

"What the hell!" Antyn complained and took off with Corvyn in tow. General Barrock stayed back, folding his arms and clucking his tongue with irritation.

"That girl causes more problems than she solves..."

As Antyn approached he took in the scene, Leviathan looked pissed and Tyg looked unremorseful as she struggled in his grasp, she was just in the throes of kicking at Leviathan's knees when she reached for her dagger. He instantly let her go and sent his power

403

slamming into her head. She dropped like a stone, gripping the sides of her head as she screamed in pain.

"Lev! What the hell is going on?"

Leviathan shot Antyn a warning look making him freeze in his tracks. Corvyn ran up however and dropped to his knees next to Tyg and cradled her in his lap, looking up at his Emperor beseechingly. "My Liege, please stop!"

Antyn looked at Corvyn stunned. He had heard about how he had done this back in Arial, but to see the man basically sacrifice himself for the girl was a sight truly astonishing. He understood why Leviathan kept the man around now, he had a conviction to protect like a rock.

Leviathan's jaw ticked as his gaze settled on Corvyn. "Tell me who has been talking about Tygarya behind my back and saying she is nothing but a pet?"

Antyn baulked as Corvyn shook his head. "I do not know, my Liege, please...she can't answer if you're doing this."

Leviathan flicked his wrist and Corvyn was lifted off Tyg and thrown back but they could all see that Leviathan had stopped torturing Tyg. She was curled into a ball and panting as Leviathan bent down and brushed her hair back from her face.

Antyn came up as Corvyn gained his feet, wiping his mouth of a trickle of blood from biting his tongue in the hard impact with the ground.

"Tygarya..." Leviathan's voice was demanding.

She lifted her head and glared at him, smacking his hand away and sat up, resting back on her heels. She lifted the back of her hand to her nose and wiped the blood away. "I told you...I hear them all whispering, every time I walk through this grand army of yours." She spat sarcastically.

Corvyn came up to stand beside Antyn and Antyn put his arm out to prevent him from going any further.

"You have a death wish…" Antyn muttered to him.

Leviathan sighed and stood up, glaring around the camp as all the soldiers crowding around diverted their eyes. "If anyone speaks badly or loosely of Tygarya again, they will die…" He raised a hand and a black mist lifted from his palm growing thicker and larger and spreading throughout the camp. Tyg watched in awe as the mist seemed to get into everyone's ears and then dissipate.

Antyn sucked on his teeth while he watched. Once it was over he muttered. "Was that really necessary?"

Leviathan glanced up at him with a death glare then offered his hand to Tyg to help her to stand. She looked at it with distain and stood up on her own. "What did you do?"

"Perhaps you should return to the tent." Leviathan said coolly.

"What did you do?" She asked again more firmly.

Leviathan scowled darkly at her. "I solved your problem, for now…and when the rest of the army is in front of me I shall do the same to them."

"You cursed them?" Tyg asked, her mind spinning at the power and control needed to do that to the entire army that was camped here.

"I will not have anyone saying things that are untrue, Tygarya." Leviathan levelled that vulture gaze at her as she looked up at him with horror. "You said it to spite me, therefore anything said about you is obviously reflecting back on my reputation."

Antyn clucked his tongue and looked away with a sigh. "Gods, Tyg…when are you going to realise…"

"Realise what?" Tyg glared over at Antyn, her gaze sweeping over Corvyn as well, who was standing with his arms folded and staring at her with a fatherly-like disapproval.

Leviathan grunted and turned away. "We have things to do…get a move on, either go back to the tent or follow and keep your mouth shut."

He stalked off towards where General Barrock was. He looked pale and shaken at being cursed, he knew he was the one who had spoken to Tyg back at the castle and had heard the gossip amongst the soldiers and done nothing about preventing it from reaching her ears. He bowed his head as Leviathan approached him.

"Get me your five best swordsmen, I want to pick a champion, we will hold a short tournament."

"At once, my Liege."

Leviathan looked back and saw Tyg standing with Antyn and Corvyn. Antyn had given her a handkerchief and she was wiping her nose.

"What do I need to realise, Antyn? My place? Because, yeah, I'm getting it pretty clear right now." Tyg said sourly as she wiped her nose.

Antyn gave a sideways glance at Corvyn before answering. "You are more important than any of these soldiers, Tyg, he will kill them all and not even blink. Keep these sorts of things to yourself."

Tyg blinked. "I wanted to know if he agreed with the sentiments of his army, I mean where did they get the idea I was just a pet if not from the man himself?"

"Tygarya!" They all heard Leviathan's voice and looked up to where he was. "Tent or with me..." He said meaningfully.

Tyg hissed through her clenched teeth. "Leash indeed." She stormed off, making her way over to Leviathan. He took her hand and held it as he walked away, following the direction that General Barrock took to set up a clearing for the tournament fights.

Corvyn turned to Antyn, causing Antyn to look him in the eye with a critical gaze. "Is she really that special to the Emperor?"

Antyn's expression went flat. "Yes, and you would do good to remember that she is his betrothed."

"Why does he..." Corvyn went to ask but the look on Antyn's face stopped the words.

"Be very careful, Colonel...that curse is now upon you too." Antyn walked off, following where Leviathan went.

Corvyn chewed his lip and looked away, aware of eyes upon him watching curiously. He turned and saw the two warlocks that were supposed to be with the Emperor. "What are you doing standing here and gawking at me for?" He growled before stalking off, muttering.

50

The afternoon was spent watching the five best swordsmen that were present amongst the soldiers compete for supremacy. Leviathan kept Tyg's hand the whole time, not letting it go even once, even though it was getting sweaty between them.

He huffed, annoyed. "Is this it?"

"Well half our army is still back in Kolastan and Enyana...we only brought through thirty thousand..." General Barrock said defensively.

"What about you, General?" Tyg asked facetiously.

General Barrock gave her a dark scowl and drew himself up, squaring his shoulders with pride. "In my heyday perhaps."

Leviathan huffed as Tyg smirked. "Leave the General alone, Tygarya, he has done his part and is well decorated, that's why he holds the position he does."

"Thank you, my Liege." Barrock bowed his head, looking at Tyg the entire time with a smug smirk.

Tyg sucked on her teeth and pointed off to one particular young soldier. "He seems to be the best of them..."

"Really?" Leviathan scoffed. "Shall I make Colonel Corvyn compete, see how good he is?"

Tyg glanced at him and saw the sparkle in his eyes, she folded her arms and looked away, clamping her mouth shut.

Leviathan chuckled and Antyn rolled his eyes and smiled to himself, his brother sure knew exactly how to manipulate Tyg to shut up.

Leviathan suddenly let go of Tyg's hand and stood up. "I get your point though, Tyg...we really need to test the best to make sure they really are good enough to be called a champion." He drew his own sword and walked out into the cleared area. "I will fight him and determine if he is worthy to be called my Champion."

Antyn sat forward as General Barrock visibly tensed. "Ah, Lev...are you sure about this?"

Leviathan swished his sword around in an arc, loosening his shoulder. He looked over at the young soldier who was gaping at him in disbelief. He pointed his sword at the man and grinned viciously. "I'll go easy on him...come, fight!" He ordered with a bellow.

The young soldier licked his lips and took up his sword, inching forward into the cleared area as soldiers surrounding the space started cheering the young soldier on.

"Come on..." Leviathan called jovially. "It's not every day you get to challenge your Emperor...I'll go easy on you and only defend, show me what talent you've got."

The young soldier seemed bolstered by those words of encouragement and by the cheering crowd and stalked forward.

Tyg was watching Leviathan as the young soldier attacked, parried and stepped away several times, looking for an opening. Leviathan was amazing...she had seen him in action against Palin but to see him now it was more like a demonstration of excellent swordsmanship. She chewed her lip as she watched with awe at the speed and grace he had for someone of his size.

It was definitely confirmed, he was the best swordsman Tyg had ever seen.

After half an hour of sparring with the young man Leviathan called a halt and shook the soldier's hand. "Most excellent, I will deliberate seriously on whether you shall fight in my stead when we enter Gua del Mar. Thank you for today, I enjoyed it."

Leviathan smiled as the soldier bowed deeply in respect before walking away and heading over to where Tyg and Antyn were seated with General Barrock grinning with pride in his man. "Go reward the young man with a hearty meal from the officer's mess and get him a woman."

"Yes, my Liege." General Barrock laughed and walked off to congratulate his soldier.

"Come, Tygarya, let's head back to the tent." He held his hand out and Tyg stood up, walked to him and took his hand. "You've forgiven our disagreement?" He asked, lifting her hand to his lips and kissing it as his gaze settled on her with amusement.

"I'm not going to dwell on it..." Tyg answered, causing Leviathan to laugh.

"Then neither shall I." He walked off pulling her into his side as Antyn slouched back in his seat with a sigh.

He looked up and over the soldiers still congratulating the young man for his prowess and saw Corvyn standing to one side, his thumbs in his belt as his eyes watched the Emperor walking off with Tyg under his arm. Antyn sucked his teeth as he scrutinised the young warlock, he was powerful, one of the most powerful warlocks of his age that they had in their army and they had been watching him and his progress way before Tyg was ever on the scene. But the way he had kept his vow of making sure Leviathan didn't go too far with using his power on Tyg, even though the expiry date on that command was well overdue and was valid only in Arial, was astonishing and disturbing. The look on his face was indescribable to Antyn as he watched the Emperor and Tyg together, Antyn couldn't decide if it was brotherly or that of a jealous lover.

Corvyn suddenly turned his head and locked eyes with Antyn.

Antyn calmly smirked at him and Corvyn blinked and looked away disturbed at being caught staring before turning and walking quickly away, muttering to himself.

Antyn chuckled and stood up, stretching languidly before making his way slowly back to the command tent. It was decided, he was definitely to be watched carefully.

Later that evening Antyn entered the Emperor's private tent to find him sitting at a table drinking wine with no shirt on. His expression was brooding and dark as he was reading quietly. Tyg was asleep on the bed and Antyn suspected it wasn't a natural sleep, she also wasn't wearing much and was under a large fur.

"What's eating away at you, Lev?" Antyn asked seeing his brother's dark brooding expression as he sat quietly studying the book on Gua del Mar customs. "She's not giving you any more trouble?"

He looked up and closed the book, rubbing at the space between his brows as he rested forward on his forearms on the table. "No..." He sighed. "She's calmed back down on that, just needed some attention..." Leviathan smirked and Antyn knew what sort of attention he meant.

"I see...she's more highly strung than I thought."

"It's more that she has a very low opinion of herself, thanks to her poor upbringing, so she rightfully thinks that everyone is just out to use her in some way...can't blame her, she's not wrong." He glanced over at her sleeping form with a small gloating smirk.

"So what's with the dark aura?"

Leviathan grimaced and sighed. "Tygarya is right, she could beat any soldier here with her unorthodox fighting style, so why am I not picking her as my champion if I want to secure the win?"

"Because she's a woman..." Antyn pointed out with a drawl.

"Why is that my problem, shouldn't it be theirs? They have made no specification that a woman can't be allowed to be chosen as my Champion..."

"Because it goes without saying, you're finding a loop hole, Leviathan."

"A loop hole would be that she's actually not human, so isn't technically a woman in their way of thinking..." Leviathan smirked.

Antyn sighed. "So what you're telling me is that you've decided to let Tyg fight this one?"

"Yes, I believe she is my best option..."

"How so?"

"She doesn't think normal, she's Elvian and trained as an assassin, she thinks not how to fight a person but how to effectively kill them within the shortest amount of time."

"That's abhorrently scary..." Antyn commented, grabbing a goblet off the table and pouring himself a drink of wine from the carafe Leviathan was using.

"Indeed, but effective in winning...no one can predict what she will do, she's impossible to fight against. That is our advantage and I would be stupid to ignore that. Any one of my men will fight the good fight, go toe to toe, and lose most likely. Ask yourself, can we take that risk?"

Antyn scratched at the stubble on his cheek. "Are you going to warn your Generals?"

"If they are good strategists they should be thinking the same thing."

Antyn chuckled. "But their pride will never allow them to speak those words to you."

Leviathan huffed in amusement. "They are so hung up on her being part Elvian they are blind to the potential having her possesses...luckily I don't care."

"Imagine if they found out her other side is possibly Jaeger."

Leviathan's expression cooled. "Quiet...there are many ears." He leaned back in his chair, taking up his goblet and sipping the contents. He lifted his fingers and flicked them almost imperceptibly causing an invisible ripple to go through the room checking if they were truly alone before he continued to talk. "It still doesn't make sense though..."

"What?"

"That excerpt from the Prophecies of A Godless Man, says she's born of three noble races and calls her an elemental...if she's Elvian and Jaeger like we assume then that's only two..."

Antyn nodded sagely. "And how would three even be possible..."

Leviathan breathed deeply for a moment. "The Elvians left were basically half breeds, that means she could be Elvian, human and Jaeger...but humans are not a noble race."

"No, I agree, it's not human...what other race could be deemed noble, aside from us?"

Leviathan's expression was dark as he stared into his cup. "Sorcerer, Elvian and Jaeger...that would certainly break the universe..."

Antyn sat up, his eyes intense. "I struggle with the concept of an Elvian and Jaeger together, Jaeger were created to hate Elvian by blood. Perhaps we are completely wrong and she's Elvian and Sorcerer."

"Perhaps...either way, it seems like the answer is staring me in the face and it's annoying." Leviathan stood up. "I'm going to bed."

Antyn couldn't help but feel like Leviathan knew exactly what he wanted to say but didn't want to say it and make the answer true. He wished he was in his library right now, he really felt like they were close to something just then...

51

The morning greeted them with a fanfare of activity as they prepared to move out from this southern most outpost and finally move down into Gua del Mar and the heat of the desert.

"Tyg, tonight once we enter the palace there will be a night of festivities, the Sabre will no doubt put on a demonstration, I want you there so you can watch them and learn their fighting techniques."

"Why?" She asked sullenly.

"Because I have decided to accept the challenge to a champion's duel and have you as my champion."

"Me? You want me to fight for you?" Her grin was vivacious.

"Yes." Leviathan smiled amused at her sudden exuberance. "Is that not what you wanted?"

"I get to finally fight?" Tyg jumped into his lap and curled her arms around his neck.

He placed his hands upon her hips holding her back. "Okay, don't be quite so happy about it, it's unnerving...so you're really fine with this?"

"Absolutely."

"Their Sabres are supposed to be the best..."

"Hmm, I'll let you know once I've seen them in action." Her eyes blazed with an excited glimmer as she bounced in his lap. "I'll get to finally bloody my new swords..."

"Okay, Tyg...settle down. " He grimaced, placing a hand on the top of her head.

LOYALTY BINDS YOU

"It's hard to now...I'm excited."

"Indeed, well you won't be with the next part..."

Tyg stilled and her eyes narrowed. "What?"

"You are going to have to wear a dress and let King Bahadur's wives take you away and make you up as their customs dictate and wear a head scarf to hide your hair colour and a veil for tonight's banquet."

"You are kidding me?"

"No, I'm deadly serious, Tygarya. Don't fuck this up for me, it's only one night and then you can dress how you like and stand by my side. We just need to adhere to their customs and protocols in this and that is how their women are expected to dress. Let me handle how I introduce you to them all, is that clear."

"Okay..."

"Good girl...I'm proud of you and once you beat his champion this whole kingdom will be mine, saving all those lives you care about so much."

Tyg scowled at that facetious comment, it wasn't that she cared about all the innocent lives, it just seemed a waste if there was a better way. "Good, then you can get rid of the stupid customs."

"It won't matter, Tygarya, we're not going to live here, just ruling over it. Oh, and another thing..."

"What?" She saw the dark look on his face and folded her arms. "I'm not going to like this, am I?"

"You're going to have to stay with the women at night and sit with them at the dinner."

"What the fuck...but there will be children there too...won't there?"

"I know, lots of children. King Bahadur has about twenty children to eight different women. Don't you like children?"

Tyg pursed her lips. "Not really, no. I don't like people in general...but I find children are unfiltered and tend to approach me unsolicited and ask annoying questions."

Leviathan couldn't help but smile. "You've never thought about children of your own one day?"

Tyg looked taken aback and gave Leviathan a strange expression. "The thought has never had the time to cross my mind."

Leviathan laughed, tightening his arms around her waist. "Mine neither, don't worry. Oh, and we aren't sleeping together as far as they're concerned. They have peculiar customs about their women. They marry as virgins and if they have sex outside of marriage they're stoned to death."

"What the...? I'd like to see them try."

Leviathan chuckled. "Let's just keep the peace for now and go along with their customs...so for appearances you are with me as my promised wife but still chaste, okay?"

Tyg grimaced. "Okay...I really feel like fighting them now."

Leviathan pulled her to him with a hand around her nape. "There's nothing saying kissing isn't allowed between people promised to each other."

He pulled her mouth to his and kissed her as she melted into his body and kissed him back.

As they entered the capital people stopped and stared at the procession. The people out on the streets were mostly men with only a few women, their faces and hair covered. Many men could be seen pulling their women away while others stood in front of their women and stared at the passing procession. It surprised Tyg how many children were out running around on the streets and playing in the dirt. She was more surprised to see young girls running around completely uncovered, their long hair completely unadorned and wearing short tunic style dresses. They were all very young and Tyg guessed the oldest girl she saw was maybe ten. She frowned with concern.

The avenue to the palace was lined with white buildings and palm trees. Tyg looked around the place with a sense of wonder…it looked so drastically different just traveling across the border and down one hundred miles to the edge of the continent where sandy white beach sand seemed to cover most of the terrain with large dunes and crystal clear water. It looked heavenly and the men walking around in long flowing robes seemed so exotic Tyg couldn't stop staring. She gasped when she saw a strange large animal being ridden like a horse.

"What the gods is that!?"

She was heavily cowled to hide she was a woman and Leviathan turned to her with his jaw clenched, his eyes blazing in warning.

"It is a camel." Antyn said on the other side of her, chuckling softly. "Gua del Mar is very dry, a desert really the further in you go…these beasts suit the conditions more than horses, especially for long travel. I'm glad the capital is quite close to the environmental change, I hear the further you go into this country it gets quite ghastly."

Tyg knew what he meant, she was literally sweltering under the cloak she was being made to wear, she couldn't imagine how the soldiers in their armour were faring.

The palace was expansive, a large white low lying building that stretched away far into the distance, the roof had four massive domes and from the outside it appeared that the palace was segmented into four specific parts.

They were greeted by King Bahadur on the wide steps leading up to a grand arched entrance from a vast paved area where many of his people had gathered to see Emperor Adramelech meet their beloved King.

The masses were being held back and although not outwardly hostile, they definitely weren't friendly. Leviathan dismounted and took Tyg's wrist as she dismounted and walked up the steps to the waiting King. He was a tall man himself about Antyn's height, with broad shoulders and a clipped black beard. His eyes glittered with intelligence and he wore a long flowing robe of white and gold that covered his girth.

"King Bahadur, I was pleased to receive your invitation." Leviathan said politely, holding out his hand.

Bahadur looked over Leviathan with a wary gaze which flicked to Tyg and then to where Leviathan was holding her wrist. His eyes went a little wide to realise that hand was feminine and looked back up. He beamed a huge smile and shook Leviathan's hand enthusiastically.

"Emperor Adramelech, it was my pleasure to invite you to my palace so that we may formally discuss my offer to you under peace treaty. I am glad to see you have decided to show your sincerity by bringing your woman with you."

Leviathan smirked, gripping Tyg's wrist tighter and stepping slightly more in front of her. "Of course..." Leviathan inclined his head. "This is my betrothed, Tygarya...I respect your traditions as I know you will respect mine."

"Indeed..." Bahadur clicked his fingers to a nearby servant who came running up and bowed low. "Escort Emperor Adramelech's woman to Silla, have her take good care of her until the banquet."

Leviathan glared at Bahadur for a second. "I know what you are offering, but allow me to escort my woman to the women's palace myself...I do not want her to be used as a hostage."

Bahadur's smile turned down slightly. "You do know our ways well...very well, let us walk and talk and I will get this attendant to go ahead and fetch Silla to meet us at the entrance, hmm?"

Leviathan nodded. "Very well."

"But first, who else do you have with you..." Bahadur leaned round and looked at Antyn then at Commander General Oltar and General Barrock flanking them protectively.

"Ah, this is my brother, Lord Antyn Adramelech and these fine gentlemen are my Generals, Commander General Oltar and General Barrock..."

Bahadur shook Antyn's hand but merely inclined his head at the General's as they did the same. "Excellent to meet you...I see you have indeed brought many important figures with you today. I shall arrange accommodations for you all in the south wing residence. However all weapons must be forfeited now."

A sabre came forward and held his arms out as everyone gave up their swords and daggers. Tyg didn't move, as Leviathan removed his sword and dagger and handed them over. She was bristling with weapons but knew no one was going to search her. In this country women didn't dare to wear a weapon, it was a man's honour.

"I shall have your soldiers stay camped where they are outside the city, your escort here I will allow to set up camp right here in the main grounds...surrounded by my guards of course."

Tyg knew that Corvyn and two of his officers had led five hundred men across the border and that Corvyn and his platoon of fifty had marched into the palace grounds with them. It seemed his promotion had gone down well with everyone, including General Oltar. She smiled to know Corvyn was close by.

"Let us see to the comfort of your lady, shall we...?" Bahadur indicated to follow him inside, sweeping his robe sleeve elegantly before pivoting around and walking off with his large retinue in tow.

Leviathan and Antyn, with the two generals followed along with guards and Sabres flowing behind them. Tyg flexed her wrist.

"It's starting to hurt can you ease up a bit?"

"Endure it, Tygarya." Leviathan grumbled under his breath. "And remember to behave once you're handed off."

"Handed off?" Tyg said a little worried. "I thought I wasn't going to be given as a hostage?"

"You're not...the woman's palace here in the main palace is where Bahadur's harem live, they never leave their quarters, unless given permission by the King, their husband...they are autonomous within their own walls, you will be safer with them than with me for the moment."

"Oh...okay..." Tyg pursed her lips and looked up at the marble interior of the palace and the large marble statues sitting in alcoves as they walked down the halls. They crossed a large garden space that was under glass with lush plant life growing. Tyg looked up and her hood slipped slightly. She grabbed at it quickly but she heard a gasp and looked over at a palace guard standing at attention against the wall. Leviathan squeezed her wrist making her wince.

"Keep alert!"

"Sorry...I was surprised at the atrium..." Tyg lowered her head to look at the floor for the rest of the way.

As they approached a set of large ornately carved and well-guarded doors they opened up to reveal a lovely woman wearing a flowing silk dress of a pale lavender with a matching headscarf covering her hair and a sheer veil across her face leaving only her eyes visible. Her eyes were made up with dark kohl and were chocolate brown. She lowered herself into a deep curtsey, looking at the floor as her husband approached.

He took her hands and lifted her back to her feet. "Silla, my Queen, let me introduce you to..." He looked back as Leviathan strode forward with Tyg. "Emperor Adramelech and his betrothed..." He frowned and looked up at Leviathan.

Leviathan smiled. "Lady Tygarya Essyndyl..." He announced as he pulled her forward and for the first time put her in front of himself and face to face with Queen Silla.

Bahadur smiled. "Please take care of her until the banquet."

Leviathan coughed delicately. "As a gesture of good faith I would like your wives to dress Tygarya in the appropriate way for such a banquet."

Silla clapped her hands together and smiled broadly up at Bahadur as he laughed. "Indeed, you have heard the man, Silla...I have every faith in you to make this woman of the Emperor, beautiful."

"Yes, of course, my husband and King." She looked up at Tyg and peeked under the hood. Her eyes went wide and she gave a strange little smile before holding out her hand.

"You are very young...please come with me..."

At those words Bahadur chuckled and wiped a thumb over his lips. "I look forward to meeting you once you are properly attired Lady Tygarya."

Leviathan snorted. "Behave." He ordered of her.

Tyg looked back at him once and he flicked his head at her to get going. She looked back, ghosting Silla's offered hand and walked through the doors into the women's quarters.

Silla dropped her hand almost apologetically and gave a nervous laugh. Leviathan clucked his tongue. "She doesn't like contact with people, forgive her insolence, like you said she is young and still being trained to be polite."

Silla gulped and dropped her head in a bow.

Bahadur laughed. "Ah, it makes sense, that is all good, your Imperial Majesty...I'm sure the girl is overwhelmed merely by your enigmatic presence at her side let alone all that goes along with it." He waved at the guards to shut the doors.

Leviathan huffed an amused chuckle. "Flattery, your Majesty?"

Bahadur shrugged as the doors to the women's palace closed with a resounding boom. "Shall we continue to your rooms so you may rest a while and bathe from your journey?"

"That would be wonderful, you are being very accommodating in the circumstances, I appreciate it." Leviathan inclined his head politely and they set off back the way they had come.

"I must confess I had received news of your betrothal..."

Leviathan frowned and glanced up at Bahadur as he clapped him on the shoulder and walked along the hall side by side. "Really, well it's not surprising I haven't hid it from anyone."

"I heard she came back with you from over the sea..."

Leviathan clucked his tongue at that. "Then you are very well informed, but still not a secret."

Bahadur laughed as he led him down another lengthy hallway tiled in marble and to a very opulent wing. His Generals and Antyn were shown to rooms that were lavishly furnished but when Leviathan was led into his room at the end of the hall he was more than surprised by the extravagance and wealth of the place. There was a lounge room and a bedroom both of opulent size and the lounge room led out to an enclosed courtyard atrium, a smaller version of the large central one that they had past through.

"I do hope you are comfortable within these rooms, Emperor..." Bahadur said almost smugly.

"I'm sure I will be..." Leviathan made a show of removing his coat and throwing it over the back of a chair. A small frail girl stepped out of a corner and grabbed it, scurrying away and hanging it up on a hook. Leviathan growled at the little mouse making Bahadur chuckle.

"Pay the servants no mind, let them know if you desire anything and they will see it done." His smile seemed to insinuate more than the words said and Leviathan scowled.

"It must be hard to keep your betrothed by your side without deflowering her..." Bahadur added with a salacious grin.

"I'm not going to fuck any servant girl..." Leviathan spat disgusted.

"Ah, I see you're above such things...fair enough, it's always hard to know what a man holds as his moral code." Bahadur commented. "Forgive me if I insulted you, it was not my intention. If you know anything of our customs and traditions you will understand I came from a place of offering what is clearly on offer here."

"Yeah, I get it." Leviathan said surly now that this King was acting so high and mighty about basically saying the servants were available to anyone who wanted them and they weren't allowed to refuse.

"I will leave you to relax then."

Leviathan sank down into a deep armchair and let out a hefty sigh, wiping a hand over his face once King Bahadur had finally left, closing his eyes.

He heard movement and opened one eye to see the waif girl had returned and was standing by the door timidly looking at the floor. His lip lifted on one side and he was just about to tell her to get out when someone knocked on the door and it opened.

"Lev?" Antyn's voice called out as his head poked in. He smiled to see Leviathan and opened the door up all the way, seeing the girl and grinning at her. "Hello...you're a pretty little thing, how about you go and get us some refreshments, hmm?"

She bobbed down into a curtsey then left and Antyn closed the door, turning back to Leviathan with a slow breath. "Well...it seems we are allowed to walk this hall between our rooms, and I suspect we will be allowed to go to the large entrance quad to see our troops...I've got General Barrock going to experiment with that soon." Leviathan huffed and sank a little more into his chair, dropping his chin into his hand. Antyn sat down in a chair in front of him with a concerned frown. "Are you sure Tyg is going to be okay?"

"She'll be fine, if anyone tries anything she'll just kill them."

"That's the part I'm worried about, we are in enemy territory, Lev."

"Don't fret...I'll sort it so that Tygarya gets returned to me and allowed to stay within this room with me while we are here."

Antyn gave him a speculative look. "Okay, so you have a plan, that makes me a little less apprehensive at having her locked away from us."

"Us?" Leviathan snorted, his eyes hardening a little.

Antyn sucked his teeth and shook his head. "Wow, you possessive jerk, you know what I meant."

52

Tyg heard the boom of the doors closing and stopped walking, turning around to see the woman, Silla walking towards her with a pleasant smile showing in her eyes. Tyg breathed out a slow determined breath and lowered her hood.

Silla stopped walking and stared at her with an open mouthed gasp before lifting her hands to her mouth. Tyg grimaced and looked away down the hall in the direction of where she could hear voices then back to Silla.

"Do you speak the common tongue?"

Silla smiled, recovering from her shock. "Yes, I do...sorry, you are such a rare beauty...and your hair, I have never seen this colour before."

"Is that why Leviathan wants me to keep it hidden?"

"I would say so, you would cause quite a riot amongst the men of Gua del Mar if they saw you."

Tyg frowned darkly. "Why is that?"

"You're quite angelic...and the men in this country like to think the women they own are the best looking women...even the King would desire to own such a rare beauty as you just to be able to have someone so strangely different to our people."

Tyg rolled her eyes. "Great..."

"Your Emperor did the right thing making sure you were brought within these walls, you will be safe here."

Tyg chuckled. "I'm safe anywhere...shall we go in?"

"Of course...let me show you to a room." Silla took the lead and walked briskly down the hall opening the doors at the end with a gracious bow of her head.

The first thing that hit Tyg was the sound of children's laughter then her senses were filled with a great many aromas of sweet flowers and perfumes then her vision was filled with a large open area filled with bright colours from tapestries to floor cushions and thick rugs.

The children all stopped playing to stare at the strange woman in black with the unusual silver hair and pale blue eyes. There were a couple of other women too, who stood up and appraised Tyg with a hard judgemental look.

Silla spoke quickly in their strange language and the women seemed to relax, they gathered the children to them however as Silla led Tyg through this large open space and to another hall and finally to a small room with a comfy bed.

"I will organise some clothes for you and then lead you to the baths." Silla said cheerfully. "Stay here and rest."

"Thank you." Tyg said, dropping her cloak from her shoulders and revealing the leather clothes and weapons underneath.

"Oh my!" Silla exclaimed, then muttered something in her language.

Tyg turned and grinned wickedly, taking a dagger off her belt and running her finger along the broad side of the blade. "I told you, I'm safe anywhere."

"You're a warrior? I've heard of other lands having women who are independent but..."

"I'm an assassin actually...but don't worry, I'm not here to kill your King."

Silla's eyes went wide and she started trembling. "Oh..."

Tyg dropped the dagger back in its sheath. "I assure you...you can take my knives if you want." Tyg started undoing the thigh straps then unbuckled her belt, threading it out of the sheaths loops and handing her daggers out to Silla.

Silla nervously stepped forward and took the knives with a little smile. "Thank you for that offer, but how did you get them inside the palace?"

"Your men don't search women." Tyg huffed.

"Of course..." Silla smiled slightly sardonic. "An oversight considering you are from a foreign country."

Tyg grinned as she saw the spark of intelligence in Silla's eyes. "So you are smart..."

Silla winked. "I run this palace, not just the women's quarters, but the whole palace...so yes."

"Wow, you're allowed that much power?" Tyg said sarcastically earning a little stiffening of Silla's back in response.

"I am Queen and am given this task as a sign of respect, although I still must relay my requests to men to carry out."

"Request...not order..." Tyg said sharply. She's delusional if she thinks she's in charge of anything trapped in here.

Tyg grit her teeth as she was woken from a doze while waiting for Silla to return. The knock on the door was timid and when she acknowledged hearing it the door opened and Silla stepped in with two young boys dragging Tyg's luggage trunk. The boys kept their eyes to the floor and left immediately.

"I have arranged the baths for you if you would like to follow me, Lady Tygarya."

Tyg sat up and put her feet on the floor then stood up, stretching. She was surprised to see Silla was no longer wearing her veil, she was quite a beautiful older woman, her skin an exotic golden colour. "Sure lead the way..."

As they entered the baths Tyg was shocked to see it was a large room similar to the baths at the castle. She grinned as she stripped off, it had been a month since leaving Kairo and she really wanted to be able to soak.

Silla seemed to see her excitement and smiled, pleased. "I will leave you to bathe...I have a selection of dresses I think may fit you, you are quite tall...I will come back in a short while to get you out."

"When is the banquet?"

"In about two hours..."

"Okay, how long does it take to get your eyes like that?"

Silla giggled. "We are very fast, having done this all our lives...we will wrap your hair too...that takes more time."

"Okay, should I not get my hair wet then?" Tyg flipped her braid up and around as Silla took a hairpin from holding her wrap in place and handed it over.

"Best not to wrap it wet." Silla confirmed. Tyg smiled in thanks for the hairpin, secured her hair on top of her head and stripped off her clothes then dipped into the water with a satisfied sigh.

Silla grinned widely and left.

Tyg closed her eyes and relaxed back. "This might not be so bad..."

53

Tyg looked at herself in the large mirror in the women's quarters astonished, she hardly recognised herself. The women had dressed her in a black and gold gauzy dress of many layers so it became impossible to see through, it had flowing sleeves that hung and drifted when she raised her arms and even covered down to her bare feet. Her hair had been wrapped in a black cloth then a mesh gold scarf with a matching gold veil along with a wide gold belt around her waist and gold hand and foot jewellery that jingled when she walked. Her eyes were piercing against the thick black kohl and looked extremely sultry yet intensely challenging at the same time.

Tyg smirked. "Amazing...I like it." Leviathan is going to lose himself!

"Oh, we're so glad!" Silla said, she was the only one who spoke the common tongue and the other women giggled and nodded along.

It hadn't been so bad with these women, they had pretty much kept Tyg away from the children, had fed her exotic fruits, nuts and cheese with a fruity sparkling water. It had been pleasant so when Silla led her and the wives back to the entrance doors of the women's quarters Tyg was feeling quite relaxed with everything.

When the doors opened an armed escort of King's Guard Sabres waited to take them to the banquet hall. Tyg noticed the women changed their personas instantly in the presence of men, becoming timid and keeping their heads bowed and their eyes on the floor as they scurried along.

Tyg saw that Silla was the only one that kept her head up.

Tyg did to, and looked over at the guards and met their eyes with a hard challenge. They had all looked at her appraisingly, saying things in their language that the other women clearly baulked at so Tyg guessed was either sexual or derogatory, either way Tyg looking them straight in the eye was obviously something they weren't used to as their expressions went flat after that.

Silla placed a gentle hand on Tyg's arm and leaned in. "Be careful, Lady Tygarya, please..."

"Fine..." Tyg huffed and looked away.

As they entered the hall it was bustling with the cacophony of voices greeting each other and merriment. Everyone was sitting on large floor cushions on thick patterned rugs with low tables in front of them full of wine carafes with woven grass around them. Tyg noticed instantly that the men all sat in an oval with King Bahadur at the apex slightly elevated with their women behind them, unless the woman was kneeling in front and pouring her husband's wine or feeding him some of the food that was already present, similar to what Tyg had been served. She wondered if the women weren't allowed to eat here and so had to eat before coming. These men were big and raucous, warriors all of them, some didn't even have robes on that concealed their torsos, wanting to show off their muscles, scars and tattoos. They all went quiet as Silla led the wives of King Bahadur in and they sat upon cushions behind King Bahadur.

Silla led Tyg over to where Leviathan was sitting on a large cushion just to the left of Bahadur and she curtsied low. Leviathan was staring in shock at Tyg, she met his gaze and saw his darken with pleasure. She sank into a low curtsey before him.

"My Liege, did you miss me?"

She heard Bahadur chuckle as Silla went to him and whispered something in his ear and then sat behind him.

Leviathan patted a cushion that was nestled beside him between him and Antyn. "Tyg, you look amazing, I knew this style would suit you, you like to cover your face it must take you back..." He chuckled. "Sit..."

Tyg huffed, making her veil lift slightly then sat down, curling her legs to the side like Silla had taught her. Antyn chuckled too and Tyg grimaced.

"Watch yourself." She muttered.

"Tygarya..." Leviathan called making her look back at him. He lifted a finger under her chin and leaned closer making her heart thump in her chest. "I hope you behaved for Bahadur's wives?"

"Of course I did, they made me very welcome."

Leviathan gave her a dazzling smile. "Very good."

Bahadur yelled out in a deep voice announcing the banquet. "Welcome Sabres, Ministers and wives. This is a momentous occasion to have the Emperor of Tylandria here with us this evening! I look forward to showing him your skills, my Sabre!"

A mighty roar of a cheer went up from the warriors as they fisted the air. Tyg rolled her eyes at the masculine strutting going on.

"They're like peacocks!" She muttered.

Leviathan's hand came down on her thigh. "Hush."

Antyn laughed behind his wine goblet. "She's not wrong...it will be interesting to see just how good these swordsmen are."

"Hmm..." Leviathan acknowledged while he raised his goblet to the crowd in acknowledgement of King Bahadurs introduction.

Some young girls came out with platters of food and Tyg noticed that they must be second wives and would actually leave the room to fetch their husbands' meal from the kitchens. Some other men were served by scantily clad servant girls who they groped and teased making Tyg grit her teeth.

King Bahadur leaned over to Leviathan. "I will get a servant girl to bring your meals to you and your Generals."

"No, thank you, not for me...Tygarya will serve me." Leviathan said and Tyg heard the amused lilt. Antyn coughed and chuckled beside her.

"What the fuck?" Tyg whispered.

"Ah, yes. A very good decision, I'm glad you wish to follow our customs while here." King Bahadur said smiling as he waved Silla over.

Leviathan turned to Tyg. "It is a custom here for a promised woman to spend time in the service of her husband to be, so he can see proof that she will be a good wife."

Tyg looked at him incredulously. "You must be kidding?" She squinted at his smirk. "You're lapping this up, aren't you?"

"It will be rather amusing for me, yes."

"I hate you!" She growled.

"Yes, we establish that fact at least once a day." Leviathan laughed it off in Bahadur's presence as he turned to look with a small frown at Tyg back chatting.

"Please show Lady Tygarya our customary ways, Silla, my dear." Bahadur said. She grovelled on the floor then bowed to Leviathan, making Tyg scowl even darker.

"With your permission, Imperial Majesty..." Silla said meekly. Tyg rolled her eyes.

"Of course..." Leviathan watched smiling as Silla held her hand out for Tyg to accompany her. Tyg stood and folded her arms. "Tygarya..." Leviathan growled. "...behave."

"You'll be lucky I don't poison your damn food!" Tyg hissed under her breath and stormed off behind the nervous Silla. Leviathan chuckled, wiping a thumb over his lips as he watched her hips swaying in that black dress.

"Are you sure you want to marry that one?" Bahadur asked, leaning close.

"Hmm..." Leviathan thrummed, his eyes still on Tyg walking away. He noticed the other eyes on her tracking her movements appreciatively.

"She appears quite head strong."

"Indeed she is." Leviathan murmured.

"Ah, you like that in your women?"

Leviathan turned and gazed at King Bahadur a moment. "Yes, our women are allowed to be independent and speak their minds to us."

"Strange customs, but you still refer to her as your property I hear..." Bahadur smirked widely as he grabbed his wine goblet.

Leviathan's mouth twerked in amusement. "Yes, she is."

"But you let her argue with you...and even wear weapons I'm told."

Leviathan clucked his tongue, Silla had obviously informed him about Tyg being armed when entering the palace. "She does, especially in foreign lands...she is a formidable warrior in her own right."

"Indeed!" Bahadur scoffed. "I find it hard to believe that a woman, as soft as they are, could be a warrior, but I have heard tales concerning this woman of yours."

"She's not soft."

"She looks soft...her skin that is..." Bahadur smirked.

Leviathan looked at him, his eyes glowing. Bahadur caught the look and swallowed hard. "I meant no offense."

"You wouldn't like anyone looking at your wives, Bah, so don't look at mine." Leviathan's tone was chilly making Antyn shuffle closer.

Bahadur grinned. "Yes, you are possessive to be sure but she is very beautiful, men will always look at her. Do you not worry about her when she fights?"

Leviathan judged that Bahadur was genuinely curious. "No."

"No?" He was shocked.

"You'll find out why I don't soon enough." He answered smugly, he heard Antyn cluck his tongue, annoyed at his decision.

Bahadur baulked and stared at Leviathan disbelieving. "You are not suggesting that she is your champion for tomorrow's battle?"

Leviathan returned his shocked look calmly. "What if I was?"

"A woman cannot fight!" Bahadur's fists clenched as he spat the words out making his wives behind him flinch.

"Calm yourself, your majesty, she's not a mere human woman..." Leviathan said nonchalantly.

"What do you mean by that?" Bahadur growled getting worked up.

Just then Silla and Tyg returned to the hall with the servants each carry a plate. Silla came up to her husband while the servants went to Antyn and the Generals. Silla put the plate on the small table in front of her husband, bowing deeply onto her knees then took the napkin that was draped over her arm and shuffled around to the side and placed it upon the King's lap. Tyg was watching her with complete distain and almost threw Leviathan's plate at his head, but then smiled wickedly. When she came around to the side and knelt next to Leviathan she purposely brushed his thigh with her hand heading inwards towards his groin as she placed the napkin on his lap provocatively. Leviathan grabbed her wrist lifting her hand up and growled at her, his eyes glowing. Tyg calmly blinked at him and smirked. He let her wrist go as Silla stood up, letting Tyg stand also. He looked up at her, his eyes dark. Tyg turned away and went to walk off behind Silla, but after a couple of steps she glanced back over her shoulder and winked at him.

Leviathan muttered under his breath.

"I think you had better hurry up with your wedding plans." Bahadur said amused.

"Perhaps I should just spank her." Leviathan growled.

"Oh, yes...quite." Bahadur laughed. "That would be most amusing...she would let you, this head strong woman?"

"No, but that's half the fun, isn't it?" Leviathan sipped his wine with a small smirk.

"Hmm...so explain to me how you can subdue her in such a way yet you claim she is a warrior?"

Leviathan chuckled. "I have my ways to tame her."

"Oh..." Bahadur's eyebrows rose as he understood. "Magic?"

"Hmm..."

Silla came back in looking startled and fast walked up to King Bahadur and Leviathan. Leviathan saw the look on her face.

"Oh shit..." Leviathan muttered. Antyn looked up from his food and his jaw clenched. Bahadur glanced at him as Silla came up, bowing low in front of him then came up and whispered in his ear.

Leviathan saw King Bahadur's eyes go wide and as he turned to look at Leviathan.

Leviathan growled. "What has she done?"

"You had better follow Silla to the kitchens..." Bahadur said sounding extremely concerned.

"What has she done?" Leviathan repeated his eyes starting to glow. Antyn scooted close and placed a hand on his arm.

"Ah...apparently one of the kitchen staff took it upon himself to instruct your woman on the finer etiquettes of being a serving girl." Bahadur said, choosing his words carefully.

"What does that mean?" Leviathan demanded, standing up and gaining the attention of others.

"A serving girl must genuflect to all men."

"And she didn't...but she's not a serving girl! She doesn't even look like one!"

"No, and Silla here explained as much but the man's dignity had probably been questioned when Lady Tygarya refused to do anything but look him in the eye and spoke to him rather rudely apparently."

"Fuck's sake." Leviathan cursed. "Take me to her."

"She is currently being held under custody..." Bahadur added cautiously, seeing Leviathan's rage building.

"What?" Leviathan growled. Antyn sucked his teeth and lifted a staying hand to the two Generals to stay seated.

Bahadur also stood up. "I will sort this out, but she stabbed the cook in question..."

"Fuck..." Leviathan wiped a hand over his face. "Of course she did."

"This happens often?" Bahadur looked shocked.

"Fairly often, yes." Leviathan admitted as Bahadur looked at him concerned. "It's not her fault though, you're Majesty. There will be more to it, I'm sure...there always is." Leviathan gave a derisive snort of dark amusement. "Lead the way..."

54

As they entered the kitchens they saw the kitchen staff all huddled down one end of the vast kitchen area, two wounded ones were being treated. On the other side of the kitchen Tyg was sitting on the bench, casually peeling and eating an orange looking calm and unperturbed while surrounded by four Sabre with their swords drawn. Beside Tyg was a couple of cook's knives, one covered in blood.

Tyg's veil was gone revealing her face making Bahadur gasp as he entered to see she had been insulted in this way.

Tyg smiled faintly at Leviathan when he entered, Bahadur ordered his Sabre to stand down and Leviathan stepped through them and up to Tyg.

"Well?"

"Well what?" Tyg asked popping an orange wedge into her mouth.

"Tygarya, don't push it...we are not on friendly soil remember."

"No, I can see that...especially back here in the kitchens." She sneered.

King Bahadur came up beside Leviathan his face clouded and unreadable.

"Get off the bench, Tygarya." Leviathan muttered. Tyg slid off the bench to stand as Bahadur appraised her. She smoothed her dress down, unperturbed.

"I don't normally deal with such matters, but as you are guests in my house and here under treaty I will step in, please tell me what happened, Lady Tygarya?"

"Well, perhaps you should take more notice of what's going on under your own roof, your Majesty." Tyg's tone of belligerent.

"Tygarya!" Leviathan warned.

Tyg glanced at him and lowered her gaze, sighing in resignation to him. Bahadur watched with increasing interest.

"That idiot over there thought I was a new serving girl, can you believe it, I think it's just an excuse...I mean...look at how I'm dressed...anyway, apparently new serving girls, or perhaps just any girls, are fair game around here and when I stood up to him he went to strike me...that's when I snapped his fingers."

Leviathan frowned listening to her words. "I was told you stabbed him..."

"Yes, I did...but that wasn't him...that one." Tyg pointed. "Is the one who tried to touch me and then strike me...that one..." Tyg pointed to the second injured man. "...is the one who tried to step in when I broke the other guy's fingers and pushed your wife over when she tried to step in and stop things by explaining who I was, he's the one I stabbed."

"What!?" King Bahadur exclaimed. "He pushed my wife, Silla? Why did she not say anything?"

"Because your society does not allow her to!" Tyg growled. Leviathan stepped up to her and put his arm around her shoulders.

"Calm down, Tygarya." Leviathan turned to King Bahadur with a small smirk. "See, what did I say?"

"Yes, yes..." Bahadur said enthralled, stroking his beard.

"So what are you going to do about the fact that man tried to touch my property?" Leviathan's eyes were blazing now. Tyg looked up at Leviathan's side profile with a dark scowl, but he squeezed her shoulder.

Bahadur turned to his Sabre, he noticed one was holding a gold veil and took it from him. "Arrest both men for touching the consort of royalty." He turned back to Leviathan as the Sabre bowed and went over grabbing the two men and dragging them off as they yelled for clemency. "They will be the warm up entertainment tomorrow, does that appease you?" He asked Leviathan as he held out the veil to Tyg who took it and put it back on.

"Very well. I think it best Tygarya returns to the feast seated next to me for the rest of the night."

Bahadur glanced at Tyg whose eyes were also blazing. "Yes, very well..."

As they walked back to the banquet hall Tyg looked up at Leviathan with a concerned frown.

"I'm really sorry, Lev...but I couldn't..."

"Shush, it's okay. I'm not mad at you." Leviathan gave her shoulder a gentle squeeze.

"Thank you, but have I stuffed things up for you now?"

"No, in fact you've given me a great spin on this to make you a hero...you stood up for his wife's honour."

"Well..." Tyg's mouth twisted dubiously.

"That's the story, Tyg." Leviathan insisted.

"Okay..." Tyg looked away as they entered the hall and Leviathan's arm dropped from her shoulders.

"I am a bit annoyed you got out of serving me dinner though..." Leviathan smirked at her.

"Yeah, cause that was my plan the whole time." Tyg rolled her eyes.

Leviathan chuckled. "It wouldn't surprise me if it was, but then again you did just roll your eyes so that's something for me to look forward to."

Tyg smiled then flinched and looked away. As they walked back to their seats Tyg stiffened as she looked over to the Champion of King Bahadur and saw a young girl serving him that he was touching inappropriately and laughing as she squirmed and blushed in humiliation.

"Tygarya." Leviathan warned again. "She's not a serving girl she's his promised wife."

"She doesn't look older than fourteen." Tyg muttered through gritted teeth.

"She's probably not, I explained this to you."

"You explained they marry as virgins not that they are virgins because they are so young!"

"Tyg, look at me." Leviathan ordered, his tone dropping.

Tyg looked up at him as they stopped by where they were seated. He hooked a finger under her chin. "Just focus on the job at hand, you can't save them all."

"I can save that one..." Tyg said with a glimmer in her eye. Leviathan raised an eyebrow at her. "By killing him tomorrow." She finished with a wicked grin.

He snorted with amusement as he could faintly see it. "Very well, that's focus for you I guess..."

Tyg's grin became a beautiful smile as he stroked her cheek through the veil and smiled back.

As they sat down Tyg looked across at the King's wives and saw them all looking at her with furtive glances. Tyg smiled to herself and looked away.

King Bahadur went up to Silla and Tyg watched as he spoke to her quietly, holding her tenderly by her shoulders. Silla's head was bowed and Tyg wondered what Bahadur was saying. Silla suddenly looked up startled as did the other wives and then Bahadur hugged Silla then went down on his knees and hugged all his wives in one big family hug.

"What's going on?" Tyg asked.

Leviathan looked at her with an eyebrow raised. "I would say you've managed to make a difference."

"Me?"

"Did you not say to Bah that he should take more notice of what's going on?"

"Yeah, but I didn't think a man like that would listen."

"He obviously cares for and loves his wives." Leviathan glanced at Tyg and raised his arm and reached for her. Tyg shuffled closer and Leviathan put his arm around her placing his hand on the side of her head pulling her head to his chest. He kissed the top of it, inhaling the strange scent of her from the exotic oils. "You again amaze me, Tyg."

As King Bahadur came over to take his seat he paused and looked down at Tyg. "Thank you for opening my eyes."

"Thank you for listening, your Majesty." Tyg said softly, surprising Leviathan yet again. He had expected her to say some sarcastic comment. He stroked her head wishing he could curl her hair around his fingers and smiled.

Bahadur sat down and turned to Leviathan. "I would ask that you seriously reconsider letting your woman fight Alta tomorrow, she is special and I would hate to have her lost to this world."

Leviathan stared at King Bahadur intensely as he felt Tyg tense against him. He gripped the back of her neck to keep her quiet.

"You ascertained that from a first meeting?" Leviathan asked.

King Bahadur smiled. "No, it is the request and opinion of my wives."

"Your wives?" Leviathan said startled as he felt Tyg actually flinch against him.

She shook her head against his chest. Leviathan grabbed harder around her neck and pulled her head up gently so he could see her face. Tyg's eyes were glowing faintly and were a pale sky blue. He smiled at her then turned to King Bahadur, loosening his grip on her neck.

"I'm afraid to say King Bahadur that that decision is not mine to make."

Tyg smiled and slid her eyes to King Bahadur with a glitter of smugness.

"Oh, you let her decide to fight for you?"

"Yes, it's completely her choice, I would normally fight as my own champion but you negated that in your conditions so Tyg has insisted to fight in my place."

Bahadur stared at Tyg. "But why?"

Tyg grinned savagely and glanced over at the King's Champion, Alta who was now staring at her with a mix of sexual predator and hostile hatred. Their eyes locked and Leviathan grinned just as savagely to himself to see Tyg's eyes change colour to ice blue.

"I want him dead at my feet." Tyg snarled loud enough for Alta to hear.

Bahadur quailed at the cold blooded sound to her voice. Alta stood up, clenching his fists. "King Bahadur, I will not fight a woman, how disgraceful to me to even have such a thing suggested, his Imperial Majesty should be ashamed."

Leviathan let Tyg's neck go.

Tyg stood up to face Alta across the dais as Lev placed a discreet hand on King Bahadur's arm to prevent him from rising and putting himself between them.

"You think fighting a woman in the arena disgraceful, but you don't mind fighting young girls in the bedroom, do you?" Tyg sneered at him. Leviathan curled an arm around Tyg's thigh to prevent her from launching herself at Alta.

Alta was enraged.

"What I do with my wives is my business!"

"Better make the most of tonight, Alta, it will be your last!" Tyg growled back causing Alta to take a step forward. His wives and the young girl were all quaking behind him.

"Stop!" King Bahadur shouted. "Alta, be seated! Now is not the time, but now I'm sure you are more than looking forward to tomorrow, yes?"

Alta sat down begrudgingly as Leviathan pulled Tyg back down. "Most definitely." He smiled viciously at Tyg. Tyg grinned back just as vicious but it went unseen under the veil. Leviathan pulled her back into him and held her firmly like he was holding back a wild animal.

"Good, now I think the wives should retire and leave the men to their drinking and fighting." King Bahadur said then.

Alta stood up again, bowing his head. "I will also retire, your Majesty, with your leave."

"Of course, Alta, rest up for tomorrow."

"Ha!" Tyg barked. "He's planning for losing tomorrow! Better say goodbye to all your wives, huh?"

The whole room looked at her indignantly as Alta's fists clenched and his face reddened with anger.

"Tygarya, that's enough now." Leviathan scolded under his breath.

Alta's jaw was clenching as he bit his tongue because Bahadur raised his hand up for silence. Alta bowed to his King and left with his two wives and the young girl promised to him in tow.

Bahadur turned to Leviathan and Tygarya. "I really hope you can control that woman from making too strong an impression on my Kingdom."

Leviathan laughed. "It won't be your Kingdom come tomorrow, Bahadur."

Bahadur looked startled a moment then his eyes narrowed in challenge. "We shall see....but I am going to break with tradition this once and allow your woman to stay in your rooms with you tonight and compete tomorrow."

"Really? That's a huge break with tradition...the staying in my rooms I mean, why?" Leviathan asked as Tyg heard Antyn chuckle behind her.

"Because he doesn't want my independence to rub off on his wives, he suddenly doesn't want me anywhere near them...am I correct?" Tyg answered with a smirk.

"Very much so..." Bahadur grimaced.

"Well, perhaps Tyg can do something to alleviate the awkwardness her actions have caused?" Leviathan said, his tone changing to a light-hearted one that made Tyg instantly nervous.

"What?" She looked up at him worried. "I thought you said you weren't mad?"

"Oh, I'm not..." Leviathan smiled. "Perhaps Tygarya could entertain everyone with a song?"

"You want me to sing...but?" Tyg went to protest but Leviathan put his hand up.

"She sings as well?" Bahadur asked surprised.

Once again Tyg heard Antyn chuckle behind her and grit her teeth, what were these two setting her up for?

"Yes, so before your wives leave perhaps a song to settle everyone's nerves, as part of our good will." Tyg could hear the underlining smarm in his voice, she had been frowning but suddenly smiled and stood up, she turned and curtsied to Leviathan.

"Of course, my Liege." She said in a purr of a voice causing Leviathan to shudder and frown. "I will just have to consult with the musicians." Tyg walked off to the far corner where the musicians were seated.

Leviathan smiled to himself as he saw all eyes in the room on her as she sauntered past them.

"Does she sing well?" Bahadur enquired.

"Like an angel, Bah, like a fucking angel."

"Okay, then the fighting can begin."

"Certainly, only I ask that Tygarya gets to stay and watch as a warrior and my Champion."

"You ask a lot...I will determine my answer on how well she sings."

"Agreed." Leviathan said grinning. He glanced over at Antyn as he popped a piece of fruit into his mouth. He already knew the outcome of that and smiled smugly as Antyn met his gaze and returned his smile.

Beyond Antyn he saw the grumpy sour looks on the faces of Commander General Oltar and General Barrock at Tyg being announced his Champion for tomorrow's duel.

After several minutes the music began, a sole lyre player stepped forward and took up a soulful swaying tune as Tyg stepped up and walked slowly forward. Leviathan's jaw clenched at seeing her dressed like that and made up like she was. The black kohl around her eyes made them stand out even more than usual and he had heard more than one person comment about them and the tall lithe body that hid under those gauzy layers of flowing fabric in such a teasing manner. Leviathan picked up two small wads of cloth out of his pocket and stuffed them into his ears. He had instructed Antyn and his Generals to do the same but make it discreet.

He could already see the power emanating from her like a magical aura. He glanced at the King's one and only warlock, more a witch doctor than any threat, and saw him staring wide eyed at Tyg. She started singing, a song about a boy determined to become a hero one day. It was a very inspirational song and had everyone completely enthralled.

"Where exactly did you find this woman?" King Bahadur asked as he stared at her and the way she commanded the room as she walked and swayed around the centre circle, twirling with a natural elegance.

"Across the sea." Leviathan said obscurely.

"Are you sure she didn't fall from the heavens?"

Leviathan laughed. "I told you..."

"Yes, like an angel, how can you risk her fighting?" Bahadur seemed agitated by the thought.

"That I have already told you as well, Bah...it's her choice, she has devoted herself to me and likes to prove her loyalty." He couldn't hide the smugness in his voice and didn't try to. He was proud of her in the moment, proud that she belonged to him.

"But she could die...I see now what my wives were trying to tell me."

"She won't die." Leviathan said with a confidence that astounded Bahadur, making him gape at the Emperor for a moment.

As Tyg finished her song everyone applauded as she walked back to Leviathan. He stood up and held his arm out and Tyg walked into him, wrapping her arms around his waist as he held her head to his chest and kissed the top of it. He looked up and surveyed the room over the top of her head. His eyes blazing azure blue as he took the power from her and settled her.

King Bahadur shook his head at the natural alpha male action to claim his woman so profoundly as his gaze challenged everyone, then clapped his hands.

"Let the fights begin...first blood rules apply!"

Leviathan took his seat, bringing Tyg down tight beside him. "Now watch carefully this is the only chance you will get to learn their techniques."

55

After the banquet Leviathan led Tyg back to his rooms. Tyg saw her chest had been delivered to Leviathan's rooms and she felt a little relief to know she wasn't going to have to keep up the pretence of amiability with Silla and the wives. Although she had found Silla rather intriguing...

Tyg stretched, tossed away the veil and started removing the head covering.

"Ah, I'm so glad I don't have to go back to the woman's wing."

Leviathan poured out some water from a large urn into a glass. "What was it like in there?"

Tyg thought about it. "Opulent, smelly."

"Smelly?" Leviathan laughed.

"Lots of perfumes and incense...gave me a funny light headed feeling."

"Hmm...and Silla, what of her?"

Tyg gave Leviathan a poignant stare. "Ah, I get why you sent me in there now...she thinks she has power but she doesn't, every decision that she is allowed to make regarding the running of the palace still must be approved by a man."

Leviathan nodded as he sipped his water. "Figured as much, but I had heard she is educated."

"Oh, she is...definitely. She has a smart mind, shame she's locked away like she is. Oh, that's something she told me..." Tyg saw Leviathan's eyebrow rise curiously. "Did you know that Gua del

Mar supply Kolastan with meat, blubber and skins from some large aquatic beasts that come close to shore for breeding and also salt for curing meats for winter. Kolastan was not going to starve in a siege."

Leviathan frowned deeply. "I knew they supplied such things but not in what sort of quantities. I guess it's lucky your plan worked in getting the gates open then." He gave her a little grin.

Tyg gave him a dark scrutiny. "Did you plan things that way?"

Leviathan chuckled. "How could I? I had no idea you felt like you wanted to show me your loyalty in these sorts of violent ways, Tygarya."

She sucked on her teeth and went over to a large basin and filled it with water then dipped a cloth in before going and sitting down upon Leviathan's bed in the next room. He followed her and leaned on the doorway, folding his arms in amusement at her actions.

"Is that not an accurate depiction of your feelings, Tyg?"

She looked at him with suspicion hearing him shorten her name and say it so deeply and inviting.

"I guess it's the only thing I can offer..."

Leviathan came in and sat down in an armchair by the open fire that kept the chill of the desert night out, and looked at Tyg sitting on the bed, her legs folded, her feet were bare and her long braid was over one shoulder.

"Well I'm all for it. So what did you learn from watching the Sabres fighting techniques?"

"Not much." Tyg shrugged with a scornful lift of her top lip.

Leviathan rubbed his forehead. "That's not helpful, Tygarya."

She was wiping her face with a cloth trying to remove the black kohl from her eyes. She lowered the cloth to her lap to give Leviathan a cool look.

Leviathan smiled in amusement at the smudged kohl on her face.

"Fine..." Tyg sighed. "They are flat-footed. They rely too much on their opponent coming at them head on."

"Is that so?" Leviathan pursed his lips, impressed at her critique.

"It seems they have spent too much time battling in arenas and not in a real life situation, they may look impressive and their movements are fast and accurate but stiff and posed, text book stuff which is way too formal and will not cope with my type of fighting. It will be easy to eliminate him. He'll never see my strike coming."

"Excellent." Leviathan stood up and wandered over to the bed and sat down sideways to her and grabbed her braid. He started undoing it as Tyg looked up at him. "Get the rest of that stuff off your eyes..." He ordered in that low commanding tone that made her insides do a flip.

"Oh, I thought you liked it." She teased back, lifting the cloth.

"I did...but it just looks a mess now you've smudged it all over the place." His smile was lop-sided and sexy.

"Well, sorry." Tyg muttered and started rubbing at her eyes again.

Once Leviathan had freed her hair and shook it out satisfied, he snatched the cloth from her hands and grabbed her chin. "Stay still." He ordered softly and started wiping her face gently with the cloth. "You've managed to smudge it off your eyes and all over your face."

Tyg said nothing and just watched him, he noticed her eyes went a strange mauve blue he hadn't seen before. He got up and went to the basin of water and rinsed the cloth out. "Maybe I should just send you to the baths?"

"It's late." Tyg said with a grumble.

"True..." Leviathan muttered and came back with the cloth and resumed cleaning her face. "You know..." He said after a couple of minutes of wiping and looking at those eyes. "...you really are beautiful." He said it with a smile and lowered the cloth. He stared in her eyes as he held her chin up. "And you know I'm not going to be able to lie in here with you without..."

Tyg suddenly crashed her lips into his cutting him off and pushed him down on the bed. He threaded his fingers into her hair holding her to his mouth and devoured her as he flipped them over taking control and pulling the dress from her shoulders.

56

Tyg followed Leviathan into the arena, followed by Corvyn and Antyn. As the fighter is allowed to be accompanied by three supporters Tyg had petitioned for Corvyn to be the third saying that in Leviathan's entire army Corvyn was the only one she knew and trusted to be there.

Tyg was cloaked and hooded as she entered and Leviathan had told her not to reveal herself until she was introduced. He wanted to keep her hair colour under wraps until the last possible moment as it was obvious that the wives had said nothing, but it was possible the wives didn't know what Tyg's hair colour represented.

"So here we are Emperor Adramelech." King Bahadur said formally, his champion Alta, standing at his left shoulder.

"As you have agreed the winner of this champion's fight will determine the fate of this Kingdom. Whether it remains independent and under my rule or if we must bow our heads and decree fealty to you as our new ruler and become part of your mighty and ever expanding Empire. Thereby we save thousands of lives in an unnecessary war of which both sides are no doubt very grateful."

"Yes, I have agreed to the terms." Leviathan announced.

"Excellent, I introduce my Champion, Alta Salda, General Supreme of the Sabres."

Alta stepped forward and removed his cloak, showing that he was going to fight shirtless. Leviathan heard Tyg scoff.

"I introduce my Champion, Tygarya Essyndyl, last known Elvian of the Royal Houses of Elvania now gone from this world." Leviathan announced with a smug smirk.

Tyg threw her cloak off to the gasps and shocked shouts of everyone present in the spectator stands.

"What is the meaning of this?" King Bahadur exclaimed, staring at Tyg with her silver hair tied up in a braid, who was standing calmly behind Leviathan's left shoulder, her head bowed and her eyes closed as she breathed slowly and measured in through her nose and out through her mouth.

"I told you, Bah, she was no mere human woman."

"She's not even human! You say Elvian but I see Jaeger!"

"No, she's not human, she is half Elvian, half unknown, but Elvian had the silver hair not white like Jaeger do." Leviathan said amused and turned to Alta who was standing with his arms folded. "Do we have a problem?"

"No, knowing she is Elvian and not human makes this easy. I do not see such a creature as a woman." Alta grunted.

"Why is she standing there like that?" King Bahadur asked a little rattled.

"Keeping her rage in check no doubt...shall we begin?" Leviathan answered smoothly.

King Bahadur swallowed hard and looked away, perturbed. Glancing at Alta who met his gaze and simply nodded confidently.

Tyg had been focusing on her surroundings, shutting out the chit chat and listening for any threat to come from outside, Leviathan had warned her that someone may try to end this match before it could even happen by underhanded tactics and to be very aware. Tyg heard a strange noise, this was what she had been listening for. Her eyes snapped open and she stepped up to

Leviathan pushing him in the back and using the momentum to launch herself in the air turning backwards and sending her hand out like she was swatting at a fly.

"Lev, look out!" She cried as she moved fast.

Leviathan clucked his tongue and stepped forward with her push then spun around and aimed his hand at a back corner of the large enclosed arena sending his power out in a stream of purple and black tendrils.

As Tyg landed on the ground she started cursing like an old sailor. Through the palm of her hand was an arrow. "Fuck that hurts!" Tyg snarled as Antyn ran forward just as someone started screaming caught in Leviathan's trap.

Antyn pulled the arrow out, examining the wound as Tyg grit her teeth.

"She caught an arrow using her own hand?" Bahadur exclaimed going pale.

Leviathan spun on him. "Was this your doing?"

"No, I assure you, Imperial Majesty, it has nothing to do with me." Bahadur shouted at his guards. "Get that man and bring him here at once!"

The guards ran off. "I'll go too." Corvyn muttered and took off after them.

"So does this mean she can't fight now?" Alta seemed disappointed as he spat the question out.

"Oh, no...I will be ready to fight by the time the other entertainment is done with." Tyg sneered at him.

"How is that going to be possible? Your hand will be shattered."

"Well, consider it an advantage to you...you're going to need every advantage you can get."

Alta growled and stepped forward, his hand going to his scimitar.

"Not now!" King Bahadur ordered. "We have more pressing matters..." He watched as the guards were hauling over the assassin, followed by Corvyn, his eyes glowing golden.

It was then that Tyg took a moment to look around at the crowd and the people gathered in the special seating area for the Royal family and the Champion's wives.

"What the fuck did you do?" Tyg yelled at Alta suddenly, stepping forward towards him. Leviathan dropped a hand on her shoulder.

"Tygarya!"

"Oh no, not this time...look at her face!" Tyg pointed to the seats where the wives of Alta had been seated. The young girl promised to him was cowering in a seat, her face black and blue from an obvious beating and assault.

Alta laughed, his hands on his hips, throwing his head back.

"Fucking hell..." Leviathan muttered and rubbed his forehead exasperated.

"Well, since you think I'm going to lose today I took it upon myself to take what's mine before our wedding." Alta gloated causing a gasp to ripple through the crowd of people already in the arena.

"You fucking bastard!" Tyg growled.

"So regardless she won't be saved by you." Alta laughed savagely. "Because if I win she's mine anyway but if I lose..." He paused for dramatic affect as Tyg glared at him. "...no one will have her now, and as she's not a virgin any longer and out of wedlock she'll have to be put to death."

Leviathan had wrapped his arms around Tyg's body and was holding her back. "You see, Tyg...that's a real asshole." Leviathan said in her ear. "But you're going to have to wait."

"Fine..." Tyg breathed through gritted teeth.

"Antyn take her, please, I don't trust she won't just slit his throat here and now."

"What? No way she could!" Alta laughed, puffing his chest out enjoying the fact he had managed to rattle the opposition.

"Okay, brother." Antyn came up and stood between Tyg and Alta and took Tyg's wrists. Leviathan turned to where King Bahadur had the assassin on his knees.

Leviathan strode over, placed a hand on top of the assassin's head and calmly sent his power into the man's head. He curled up into a ball on the ground, screaming as he pulled at his hair in pain. Tyg looked over and flinched.

"Gods, is that what I look like when he does that to me?"

"Hmm, but Tyg it's the only way to get your emotions in check when you lose control." Antyn said to her as he steered her away from Alta and to the other side of the arena floor.

"I want to find out who it is..." Tyg objected as she was dragged away.

"Just stay out of it, Tyg and focus on your own task. For all we know this was merely a diversionary tactic to throw you off."

"Hmm, still..." Tyg was looking over Antyn's shoulder, craning her neck to try and see.

Antyn backed Tyg up against the stone wall of the arena. "Stay here, please."

Tyg looked at his pitiful boyish face. "Fine." She huffed and folded her arms, leaning on the wall, even as several spectators leaned out from their seats above to peer down on them.

"Thank you, Tyg." Antyn smiled at her warmly.

"That King called me a Jaeger?"

"Ah, well...it's the hair, regardless Jaegers had white or ash blond hair...no one else does...but yours is distinctly silver, definitely Elvian."

"Huh, I get it, although to be honest it can sometimes look white..." Tyg said with a dubious frown, she felt like Antyn wasn't being a hundred percent truthful.

"Hmm..." Antyn shrugged and looked away, dismissing the conversation.

Leviathan and Corvyn stepped over after only a couple of minutes. Tyg knew that was all most people could endure of Leviathan's gift. Leviathan was not at all happy.

"Fucking Montrual sent an assassin, no doubt because they know they're next!" He growled.

"I guess that takes peaceful accords off the table for them then?" Antyn said mildly.

"Damn right!" Leviathan spat. "Come on, we need to sit down and watch these people get executed first..."

Tyg suddenly crashed into him, wrapping her arms around him and squeezing him tight. He stood shocked holding his arms out for a moment his eyes a little wide and wild as he looked down on her. Antyn shrugged as he looked up at him questioningly, Corvyn sighed and looked away, disturbed.

Leviathan smiled and wrapped his arms around her and kissed the top of her head.

"Thank you for that, Tyg..." She looked up as he shortened her name. "And thank you for saving my life, but it was okay, I would have been fine, I have wards you know."

Tyg blinked her large blue eyes and reached up on tip toes to kiss him on the lips, then smiled. "No problem, my Liege. I had forgotten about that fact."

Leviathan chuckled and hugged her tight and kissed her again.

"Ah...not the time love birds!" Antyn spat, smacking Leviathan on the back as he walked past and giving him a strange look. "Celebrate after the asshole is dead."

456

Tyg grinned. "Right after."

"Confident as always." Leviathan smiled as he kept his arm around Tyg and walked over to where the stairs led out of the arena circle and to some seats near the King but respectfully far enough away.

King Bahadur clapped his hands and several public spectators were then allowed into the higher seats. Once they were settled the prisoners were brought out for execution. There were six all together and were lined up on their knees and one by one their crimes were read out then they were beheaded by the Sabre with their large and very sharp scimitars. When the assassin was beheaded, his head was wrapped in a cloth, put into a crate and presented to Leviathan.

"What's this?" Tyg asked.

"I asked for his head so I can send it back to Jarl Revna." Leviathan explained.

"What? Revna sent the assassin?" Antyn asked surprised.

"What surprises you about that?" Leviathan turned to his brother with an eyebrow raised. "She is next in line to the throne, I guess she's protecting her assets."

"Revna is a girl?" Tyg asked surprised.

"Woman, actually..." Antyn replied full of innuendo.

"Oh, don't tell me...you?"

"Maybe..." He answered coyly. "...but that's only thanks to Lev rejecting her."

"Shut up, Antyn....now is not the time." Leviathan grumbled under his breath.

Tyg smirked and looked at Antyn, then quickly looked away when Leviathan glanced at her.

"Tygarya...focus, you're nearly up." Leviathan grabbed her hand to look at it and saw her wince slightly at his manipulation of it. "Antyn, help this heal."

Antyn got up and changed seats so he was sitting next to Tyg and took her hand in both of his. Tyg felt the same tingling sensation she had felt on the ship and grit her teeth as it got intense. As Antyn let her hand go he glanced at Leviathan.

"She is incredible...all nerve and tissue damage is already healed it was just the bones that needed a bit of help knitting."

"Hmm..." Leviathan grunted as he slid his gaze to Tyg who was testing her hand by squeezing it into a fist. "Better?" He asked her.

"Yeah, I forgot Antyn can do that...how come you can't?"

"Our powers manifest in different ways."

"Oh, okay...that's why only you can do the head thing, huh?"

"Yes." Leviathan smirked amused.

"Well, thank you, Antyn. It feels much better, it wouldn't have been completely healed on its own in time, bones seem to take a while."

"Well...you're up." Leviathan muttered.

57

"About time." Tyg said as she stood up, her eyes suddenly blazing. She watched Alta walk down the stairs to cheers from the crowd and go to the centre of the arena. Tyg walked to the edge of the wall and stood there with her hands on her hips looking down at Alta with a vicious taunting grin. He turned and folded his arms, smirking up at her.

"Hurry up, Elvian, I haven't got all day!" He called out.

"Ah, Tyg..." Antyn went to say something about the stairs but Leviathan put a hand up and stopped him.

Tyg suddenly launched off the edge of the pit, somersaulted and landed in the arena in a slight crouch. She straightened slowly, her head coming up last. Leviathan, Antyn and Corvyn all saw Alta's face when he saw Tyg's. Her eyes had dilated to black. Alta swallowed and grimaced.

Leviathan chuckled to himself.

"Well, she knows how to make an entrance." Antyn said as the crowd roared.

Corvyn's jaw clenched tight, he didn't like this one bit. He had seen how fast and how strong she was but had never seen her in a one on one prepared fight before and he knew assassins didn't generally get into face to face combat. He saw Generals' Oltar and Barrock in the crowd not far away, both with very serious expressions on their faces and their arms folded across their chests.

Neither one had been happy about Leviathan choosing Tyg as his champion but for completely different reasons, Corvyn doubted either one would care if Tyg died today.

Tyg walked slowly over to stand in front of Alta and drew her swords, flicking them around as she went down on one knee and jammed them both into the hard packed dirt in front of him. She stood up and cockily sauntered backwards ten steps then stood there smiling benignly at him, her focus unwavering upon him.

"What are you doing?" Alta growled. "Retrieve your swords!"

"Not yet, they're fine where they are." Tyg answered looking away bored at her fingernails with that smirk on her face turning condescending.

King Bahadur stood up and raised his hand. The crowd went silent.

"Is everyone ready?" He boomed down to the two combatants.

Alta drew his scimitars. "Yes, my King. I am ready." He declared in a loud clear voice.

Tyg rolled her shoulders and neck. "Just hurry up, already!" She muttered, annoyed.

Alta growled. "The insolence..."

King Bahadur dropped his hand.

In a flash Tyg was running and jumped up lightly onto the tip of her two swords and leapt up from them high into the air doing a twist pike and coming down to land behind Alta, she grabbed a dagger off her belt and deftly cut through the hamstring muscle of his left leg slicing deeply then rolled away as he went down onto his knee crying out in shock, pain and confusion.

Tyg stood up and walked back to her swords, holding the dagger that was dripping blood.

"How the fuck!?" Alta screamed at her. "This is not honourable fighting!"

Tyg laughed sarcastically. "Honourable? No one said anything to me about honourable..."

King Bahadur had gone deathly pale, the crowd silent in shock and awe.

Leviathan leaned over. "Is this a battle to the death or an honourable display, please clarify?"

Both Antyn and Corvyn were stunned and the Generals were horrified.

"Ah...yes...a battle to determine the best, by whatever means is what was agreed." King Bahadur quailed.

Tyg laughed and grabbed one of her swords, swinging it round in an arc, the noise of it slicing through the air almost musical. She swapped hands over with the dagger and held the sword up pointing it at Alta.

"Get up you son of a bitch!"

Alta struggled up onto one leg, he had lost a lot of blood and gritted his teeth against the pain. His leg was completely useless to him, the nerves severed. He balanced on his one good leg and held his swords up.

Tyg grinned and walked closer. "So you like to beat up and rape young girls, do you?"

Alta growled through bared teeth in a deep rage.

Tyg cocked her head to the side and brought the dagger up to her mouth, licking the blood off it in a gruesome display of savagery.

Antyn and Corvyn both heard Leviathan thrum a deep growl in his throat of satisfaction. Corvyn wondered who the actual monster was.

"Oh, shit." Antyn muttered. "She's not going to make this quick, is she?"

Alta's eyes had gone wide with shock at Tyg licking his blood off the blade. Now as she grinned at him all her teeth were red with it.

"People were right to exterminate your species from this earth, you're nothing but a monster!" Alta growled out fiercely drumming up his own courage. "Fight me, bitch!"

That was all Tyg was waiting for. She charged forward at astonishing speed, deflected Alta's first sword, and clashed her sword against his second as she turned her body away from him. She came inside his circle and pressed her back against his chest.

"Like this?" She purred at him, plunged the dagger back past herself and into his stomach, then crouched and rolled away again before he could get his first sword back around.

He staggered backwards, looking down at the dagger protruding from his stomach. As he did Tyg attacked again from the side, cutting through his left bicep, nearly severing his arm.

He staggered and fell, losing grip of his second sword as well. Tyg walked up and kicked both swords away. She stood over him, looking down with a feral grin. She crouched down over his chest, tilting her head to the side.

"Hello, Alta."

Alta screamed in his terror. "Get this devil off me!"

King Bahadur stood up, shaking and pale. "Enough, I surrender to you, Emperor Leviathan Adramelech of Tylandria, please call off your demon!"

Leviathan stood and walked over to King Bahadur. "Very well." He held out his hand but King Bahadur fell to his knees to a gasp of the shaken crowd.

"I swear fealty to you Emperor Adramelech."

"Take my hand, Bah." Leviathan muttered and hauled Bahadur to his feet. "There's plenty of time for that."

They were suddenly disturbed by an unearthly scream. They both looked down into the pit.

"Tygarya, enough...stop!" Leviathan yelled. "King Bahadur has yielded!"

Tyg looked up from where she was sitting on Alta's chest, she had cut his other arm up to disable it so he had no way to fight her off and she was taking delight in very slowly driving her dagger into his heart. She was shaking her head and muttering. "No, no, this one dies..."

"Tygarya!" Leviathan jumped into the arena pit.

Tyg growled up at him like a feral beast, baring her teeth. He could see she was lost to the bloodlust. Tyg grinned and leaned on the dagger, driving it home as a gush of blood erupted out of Alta's mouth.

Tyg's head exploded in pain as Leviathan walked towards her. She grabbed the sides of her head and screamed at him. "No! He has to die!"

Leviathan reached down and grabbed her by her braid, twisting it around his arm and grabbing her head with his hand at the base, he lifted her up and off Alta as she kicked and screamed.

"He's already dead, Tygarya." He said quietly and dragged her back a few steps as she continued to fight against him and the pain in her head.

Antyn and Corvyn had run around and down the steps. Corvyn retrieved Tyg's weapons and as he pulled the dagger from Alta's body he confirmed Leviathan's words.

Leviathan had pulled Tyg back into his chest, holding her around the waist with his other arm and was talking softly in her ear telling her to calm down, that it was all over. His eyes were blazing intensely as he syphoned off the power raging inside her. The crowd watching were stricken silent at the events unfolding, as they saw the power of the Emperor in full force to control the Elvian monster.

He felt her relax and submit so let her hair go and stopped his power and held her tightly and gently, undoing the braid releasing her wealth of glorious silver hair.

It took several minutes for Tyg to come around, time enough for the Sabre to clear the spectators out. She eventually sighed a heavy resigned sigh and looked up at Leviathan's face. He smiled to see her eyes were a pretty sky blue.

"Well done, Champion." He grabbed her chin and kissed her deeply.

Tyg wrapped her arms around his neck suddenly very aroused after the blood lust and kissed him back fervently.

"Ah, guys...again, not the time or place!" Antyn muttered.

Leviathan picked Tyg up as she wrapped her legs around his waist, turned and walked off up the stairs, past King Bahadur and out of the building.

"Typical, it's always left to me to tidy up." Antyn whined as he turned to walk back to where Bahadur was quaking. Corvyn's jaw ticked and he closed his eyes taking in a deep breath trying to calm himself, he didn't even understand why he was so angry, it was her life.

He turned and followed Antyn.

Leviathan carried Tyg all the way to his room in the palace, servants scattering out of their way. As he lay her on the bed Tyg looked at him and smiled.

"I get it now."

"Get what?" Leviathan asked, looking down on her with an eyebrow raised as he ran a hand through his hair.

"Why you did what you did to Palin."

Leviathan blinked stunned then smiled. "Good." He leaned over her and kissed her deeply as he started undoing the buckles on her leather jerkin.

She pulled her head away. "Aren't you worried about the blood?"

"Have I ever?" Leviathan grinned, his eyes glowing. "But I have to say, what possessed you to lick the blade?"

Tyg chuckled. "I thought you would like that touch." She looked up at him with a coy smirk.

"You did that purposely to get me?"

"Did it work?" Tyg looked into his eyes with mirth as he finally got her jerkin open and yanked it off, then he pulled her undershirt off over her head and locked eyes with her again as she settled back on her forearms.

"What do you think?" He growled causing Tyg to laugh, then she squealed as he lunged over her, biting and sucking at her neck.

58

When the couple finally emerged the next morning, bathed and dressed regally for Leviathan's inauguration they stepped out onto the dais in front of the palace.

Tyg noticed all the red livery flags had been removed and replaced with the black and gold pennons of the Adramelech Royal House. Large flags with the dragon symbol flying high and proud as his soldiers cheered from their lines surrounding the dais.

"That was quick work." Tyg muttered.

"It was all planned and ready to go as soon as you won."

"Who's the confident one now?" Tyg smiled at him.

"Of course, I never doubt you, Tygarya. If you say you can win I know you can." Leviathan took her hand and stepped forward to where King Bahadur was waiting to formally yield in front of the masses gathered within the courtyard square. Beside him stood Antyn looking pleased with proceedings.

As the ceremony was taking place Tyg was bored and looked around at the sea of faces below. Some were not happy, some seemed elated. Mostly the women, Tyg thought, as their eyes seemed fixed on her which was causing her all sorts of uncomfortable anxiety.

Leviathan's army had infiltrated the city now and there was a whole regiment inside the palace grounds standing watching the crowd.

As King Bahadur knelt in front of Leviathan and held his simple crown out to him he spoke in a clear loud voice. His speech in part was surrendering to Leviathan, but part was directed to his people telling them to not rise up against their new ruler. Tyg was surprised to hear that, but guessed it wasn't really necessary since Bahadur was going to be given his crown back and given governance of his country back under the guide of the Emperor. All that was really changing was the colour of the flags and uniforms. Tyg felt a little sorry for the women still locked into oppression.

As Leviathan started his speech Tyg turned to watch him. He was certainly in his element. Tyg could see why he was a leader every time he made these speeches. It was really the only time he spoke more than one sentence. Just as she had guessed Leviathan graciously gave back the running of the Kingdom to Bahadur in the Emperor's stead, only demoting him from King to Lord Bahadur as an Earl, allowing him to keep all his lands and women. As Leviathan's speech came to an end Tyg breathed a sigh of relief, that meant she could go and get changed. She loathed wearing dresses, they were cumbersome and restrictive. Tyg glanced up at Leviathan surprised suddenly as he added one more thing...

"I hereby abolish the laws of marriage in this country. No longer will a woman...or girl..." Leviathan snarled. "...be punished in anyway especially death for not being entire out of wedlock for reasons of rape and abuse. Neither will any woman be forced to marry another without her own consent, these laws are final and start now!"

With that Leviathan turned and walked away from the crowd as they all stared, stunned. Tyg looked at the crowd again. Her eyes fell on a young girl at the front, her face was bruised and she was staring at Tyg with eyes filled of tears. The young girl that had been promised to Alta that he had purposely abused and raped the night before the fight, because she had provoked him.

Tyg moved off the dais and down the steps towards the crowd making all the soldiers in the front bristle and tense up.

"Tygarya!" Leviathan spun around on his heels.

Tyg stopped, but reached her hand out and beckoned to the girl. She broke out of the crowd, the soldiers letting her through and ran at Tyg, dropping to her knees in front of her and hugging her arms around Tyg's knees as she bawled her eyes out.

"Thank you, princess! I owe you and the Emperor my life, how can I ever repay you for this?"

Tyg looked down at her stunned and flinched at her words. She didn't know what to do, she hated this close contact and wanted to kick the girl away, but the crowd were watching, having fallen silent.

Leviathan walked up and took the girl's hand gently. "Stand up." He said to her in a calm voice.

As she clambered back to her feet Leviathan looked down on her from his full height of nearly seven feet. She cowered underneath him barely even reaching five foot, her eyes fixed to the ground at his feet.

"You're scaring her..." Tyg muttered.

Leviathan grabbed Tyg's hand and put the girl's hand into it. Tyg looked up at him mortified.

"She's your problem now." He grinned amused then turned and walked off. Tyg blanched and looked down at the girl who looked up with large innocent eyes.

Antyn came over to help Tyg out, a small smirk of amusement on his lips. "Bring her inside so we can talk freely."

Tyg shook her hand free of the girl's clutches. "Alright...follow me then I guess..."

As Tyg walked inside Leviathan was waiting for her, smiling amused.

"In here..." He motioned to an empty reception room.

Tyg followed with Antyn and the girl behind her. It was a small antechamber off the main throne room where people waiting to see the King normally waited for their audience.

Leviathan sat down on a bench seat, leaning back on his elbow and bending a leg up putting his foot on the bench as he lay sideways across it. His other foot still on the ground he stretched his long leg out in a relaxed manner.

"You're enjoying this, aren't you?" Tyg said accusingly as the girl was still grovelling at Tyg's feet.

Leviathan just smirked as Antyn approached.

Tyg looked down at the girl. "Stop that!" She growled causing the girl to flinch away in fear, tears in her eyes. Tyg looked at Antyn with a pleading look.

Antyn took the girl once more by the shoulders and stood her up as Tyg stood there unmoving with her arms folded, scowling at Leviathan. "What the fuck am I supposed to do with her, I just wanted to see if she was okay?" Tyg asked frustrated.

"Take her into your service." Antyn suggested.

"My service? I don't have a service." Tyg growled at the preposterous remark. "You know I can't..." She flailed her hand around in the girl's direction with a detestable expression.

Antyn looked at the girl as she stood there wringing her hands with large frightened eyes. "I'll talk to Bahadur, maybe he can take her into his staff."

"No way!" Tyg scoffed. "I've seen first-hand how girls are treated by the staff here. Leviathan may have just revoked the law allowing them to kill her but she's still a non-virgin out of wedlock in a society that will probably take years to adapt to Lev's new law." She sucked on her teeth, annoyed and frustrated.

Antyn raked a hand through his hair and shrugged. "Well, I don't know..." He sat down in a chair.

Leviathan chuckled. "Leave it..." He said to Antyn. "It's up to Tyg to sort it out."

"Why do I have to sort it?" Tyg snarled at him. "You wanted me to kill him!"

"No, I wanted you to win, but Bah surrendered before you killed Alta, you killed him to keep him from hurting her." Leviathan admonished. "Take responsibility for your actions, Tygarya, I told you to leave it alone, but you had to provoke him and this is the result."

Tyg levelled a baleful glare at Leviathan. "How could I not kill him after he did that?" She flicked her hand towards the trembling girl.

Leviathan shrugged looking over the girl's bruises. "I've done worse to you..."

Antyn grimaced and looked away frowning as Tyg's eyes blazed into a cool ice. "I can handle it." Tyg said through gritted teeth.

Leviathan sat up. "Okay, Tygarya, I think you're getting carried away...you need to calm down."

Tyg glanced at the girl. "Would you just sit down?"

The girl quickly sat on the floor making Tyg's teeth grit together even harder.

Leviathan held his arm out. "Come here, Tygarya."

A servant entered the room silently and came up to Leviathan and prostrated on the floor at his feet. "My Liege, Lady Silla has requested a word with Lady Tygarya if you would be so kind as to give your permission."

Tyg pursed her lips together and folded her arms. "I'm right here, you could just tell me that directly."

Leviathan looked sharply at her. "Tygarya, give it a rest, this is protocol."

The servant stood and backed away to wait for instruction.

"It's ridiculous is what it is!" Tyg said as she went to walk off.

"Tygarya..." Leviathan hissed in that low commanding tone, causing Tyg to freeze and look back at him. "Where do you think you're going?"

"To see Silla." Tyg looked at him confused.

"I haven't given you permission to go." He said looking down at his hands obtusely, wiping them casually. Antyn groaned and raked a hand though his hair, slouching back in his chair.

Tyg rolled her eyes. "Fuck's sake...really?"

"Tygarya!" Leviathan's voice lowered into a menacing growl for rolling her eyes at him.

Antyn and the girl were both watching them carefully. Tyg's eyes flicked to the girl who hadn't moved an inch since Tyg had told her to sit. "Oh, is this for her benefit?" Tyg sneered at him.

Antyn clucked his tongue bitterly as he rubbed a hand over his eyes. "Shit..." He breathed out.

Leviathan stood up, he gave a quick glance to the waiting servant. "Get out!" He advanced on Tyg as the servant fled.

Tyg backed up as Leviathan advanced on her until her back was against the door that the servant had quickly closed behind him in his escape.

Leviathan stared at her, putting his hands in his pockets to contain his rage. They were only a foot apart and his height crowded in on her like it always did in these situations, almost like he got taller when he was angry or perhaps she shrank when she was afraid.

"Nothing I do is ever for the benefit of a nobody servant girl who shouldn't even fucking be here!" Leviathan spoke in that deep dangerous tone.

"So what then?" Tyg breathed out nervously.

"If a servant addresses me and not you directly it should tell you."

"I bloody hate all this macho male bullshit!" Tyg folded her arms defensively. "I was right there, I don't see why he couldn't have just spoken to me."

"We've been through this, Tygarya!" Leviathan suddenly yelled at her, making her flinch and stare at him wide-eyed, but they flashed with an icy fire. "Learn your fucking place! Everyone else in the whole damn fucking world gets it...why can't you?" He grabbed her chin forcefully with one hand and sighed a deep breath, then spoke deadly quietly. "I changed one law for you, Tygarya, I did what I can in the moment without rocking the boat too much."

Tyg stared at him, the light going out of her eyes. "Fine..." She sighed and looked away, unfolding her arms in defeat. "So can I go and see what Silla wants now?" She looked back up at him. "My Liege." She sneered derisively.

Leviathan's eyes went dark and he placed his other hand on the wooden door beside her head, leaning in closer to her face as he still held her jaw firmly. Tyg bit her lip, perhaps she had gone too far with that?

"Antyn..." Leviathan growled while staring closely into Tyg's eyes. "Get that girl and leave."

Antyn didn't have to be told twice. He sprang up and grabbed the girl's arm and left the room through the exit that led to an outside courtyard. Once the door was closed Leviathan crushed his lips against Tyg's forcing his tongue into her mouth as his hand slipped down to her throat then around the back of her neck holding her firmly in place by a fistful of hair. His other hand he dropped off the wall and grabbed the side of the split in her dress and swept it aside revealing her naked thighs. He trailed his hand up her inner thigh as he kicked her legs apart.

"Lev..." Tyg breathed, her hands pressed against his chest as she tried to stop him. "Not here."

"Why not?" Leviathan growled against her lips as his hand reached her sex. She gasped as his fingers breeched her panties.

"Protocol...decorum..." She breathed out in gasps.

Leviathan clucked his tongue and pressed his forehead on hers, dropping his hand from between her legs and taking a deep breath. "Practise what you preach, Tygarya." He snorted.

"You did say we're not supposed to be...you know."

Lev stood up away from her, raking his hands through his hair with a long intake of breath. "Come on then..." He indicated the door behind her.

"What?" Tyg looked confused.

Leviathan's eyes darkened again. "Well, I'm not finished with your punishment...so get that pretty little arse to my private chambers, now!"

"Oh...shit..." Tyg chewed her lip frantically as she turned and opened the door.

"And stop biting that fucking lip! That's my job..." Leviathan growled with a sexy chuckle as he grabbed her by her wrist and stalked off through the halls dragging her behind him.

59

When Tyg walked back into the antechamber half an hour later Antyn was still sitting there with the girl, waiting.

"Well, finally." Antyn said with a roll of his eyes as Tyg blushed and looked away awkwardly. Antyn's eyes narrowed as he looked her over. "Bloody hell, is that what's been going on? Honestly you two are so bloody right for each other...psychopaths!"

Tyg's eyes flashed. "Shut up, Antyn." She turned to the girl. "I don't even know your name?"

The girl looked at her shyly with a rosy blush of her own on her cheeks. "It's Allegra, my Lady."

"Allegra! Wow, that's actually a nice name." Tyg laughed with a relaxed smile.

"Thank you, my Lady...but people call me Ally."

"Okay, Ally, well you're coming with me to see Silla."

"Very well, my Lady." Ally stood up, smoothing her skirts down.

Tyg grit her teeth at all the 'my ladies'. Antyn chuckled.

"What's so funny?" Tyg asked rounded on him.

"You. You'll never get used to all the pomp and protocols of royal life, will you?"

Tyg sighed. "No, I hate them, I hate titles, I hate 'my ladies' and sirs and my lords."

"Such a wild one." Antyn said amused.

"Argh..." Tyg grumbled. "Shut up." She walked out the door and Ally ran to catch up.

Silla was sitting in a lovely little private courtyard having herbal tea when Tyg finally got around to seeing her after Leviathan's waylaying of her.

Silla smiled as the servant let Tyg in.

"Sorry I'm a bit late, Silla."

"No, you are not late, Tygarya, you get here whenever your Lord allows you to come."

Tyg grit her teeth. "Yeah, apparently."

"Please sit down...would you like tea?"

"No thanks." Tyg said as she sat cross-legged on a large pillow, pulling the skirt of her dress over herself.

"Perhaps something a little stronger for you, yes?" Silla grinned with a little mischievous glint in her eye.

Tyg smirked. "You're getting to know me quite well."

Silla indicated to a servant who approached. "A goblet of our finest wine, please."

The servant bowed her head and left. "I see you brought little Ally with you, good."

"Ah...yeah." Tyg glanced back at her awkwardly.

"I may be able to help you find a place for her."

"Really? That would be great, because she can't stay with me."

"No, you do not have any retinue."

"What? Oh, no..." Tyg said as the servant came back with the wine. Tyg tasted it and smiled appreciatively.

"It is strange for a woman to not surround herself with other women, do you not get lonely for female companionship?"

Tyg looked at her strangely. "No."

"You are a strange woman indeed, perhaps you would have been better suited to be born a man, no?"

Tyg laughed. "Don't let Leviathan hear you say that."

Silla giggled. "No, of course not, what we women talk about in the confines of our private chambers stays there."

"Oh, that's what you mean, about female companionship?" Tyg chuckled.

"Quite..." Silla's smile was appraising of Tyg's reactions.

"So, about Ally?" Tyg looked over her shoulder and saw the girl standing behind her. "Sit down." Tyg groaned, then looked back at Silla as Ally quickly sat. Silla smiled at Tyg congenially.

"Be kind, Tygarya, the poor girl has been through a lot."

"I know that, but..." Tyg sighed. "I can't stand this subservient grovelling behaviour." Tyg took a large mouthful of wine.

Silla's eyes went wide. "Indeed, you are certainly a strong character, especially for a woman."

Tyg's eyes narrowed. "You see that...right there...that 'for a woman' bullshit, that's what pisses me off the most. You women just accept it as your lot in life."

Silla quailed as Tyg's eyes blazed icy blue fire. Tyg saw her flinch and sighed again, calming herself down. "Sorry, it just makes me so..." She huffed.

"Mad?"

"Reckless." Tyg finished causing Silla to look at her in shock.

"Well perhaps you will change the world, my dear."

"Hmm...I doubt that, I can't even get Leviathan to change his stupid royal protocols." Tyg muttered.

Silla smiled at Tyg's almost child-like admission reminded of how young Tyg actually was. She turned to Ally, looking around Tyg's shoulder. "Come here, dear."

Ally scurried up next to Tyg on her knees.

"Tell me, do you have family?"

Ally looked at her and nodded. "But my father sold me into Lord Alta's service when I was only ten."

"Fucking hell..." Tyg muttered, pinching the bridge of her nose and closing her eyes against the rage that swelled up. "Are you telling me he's been grooming you up for this since that age?"

"It is not uncommon, Lady Tygarya." Silla said sadly.

Tyg frowned darkly. "We need to change that."

Silla smiled at the way Tyg seemed to show such coldness for the world but then strangely latch onto an ideal and was prepared to fight tooth and nail for it. She reached out and patted Tyg's knee. "If only you could..." Tyg scowled at her as she continued with Ally. "Was your family of any distinction?"

"My father had a small holding but he was penniless, that's why he sold me."

"Oh, that is a shame, dear...I could have helped if your family had at least some kind of title."

Tyg's eyes narrowed. "Explain that to me."

"I am allowed to choose my own servants that attend me, all females of course, but they must be of a certain social class to be allowed in the palace as a lady-in-waiting."

"Does that work everywhere? I think it's the same in Tylandria too."

"I believe so, queens are not allowed to be attended by anything less than titled Ladies. Snobbery I know, but it does come from a deep seated class system."

"So if I can get her some obscure title you can take her on?" Tyg asked, already trying to devise some sort of plan.

Both Ally and Silla looked at Tyg in wonder at the impossible task.

"Well, yes, but how would that be possible?"

"Leave it to me..." Tyg grinned and stood up. "Thank you, Silla, you've been very helpful."

Silla stared at Tyg as she left with Ally silently following her. "Yes, she is going to change the world."

60

Tyg was told Leviathan was in the Royal offices with Antyn, Bahadur and several officials and lords as they sorted out the changeover of rule and what changed and what didn't change within their laws and politics.

The guard at the door took one look at her in the dress she was still wearing and wasn't going to let her in.

"No women allowed within the council chambers." He said as he barred her way with his pike.

Tyg's eyes blazed as she stepped closer to him. "How would you like me to shove that pike down your throat?" She smiled insanely at him showing teeth.

The guard baulked as he realised this was the woman who had killed Alta and that meant she wasn't human.

"I'm sorry, milady but I can't let you in. It is forbidden." He stammered.

The door swung open and Leviathan was standing there. "Tygarya...I thought it was you being noisy."

Tyg looked at him and smiled facetiously. "So you can actually sense my presence? I don't know if that's endearing or creepy..."

Leviathan snorted, amused. "What do you want, I'm a bit busy?"

Tyg scowled. "Can I come in?"

Leviathan raised an eyebrow at her, his amusement clear. "No."

"Because I'm a woman?" Tyg's voice lowered into a snarl.

Leviathan's jaw clenched. "Cut it out, Tygarya, this is your only warning."

Tyg rolled her eyes and clucked her tongue annoyed. "Ah, fine."

Leviathan folded his arms and settled that vulture gaze on her. "Fine what?" His voice was level but leading.

Tyg stared at him, she could see the officials in the room beyond, some of them were watching with disapproval heavy in their eyes.

She grit her teeth and did a perfectly executed curtsey, lowering her head. "Fine, my Liege." She couldn't keep the sarcasm out of her voice though.

When she stood up and lifted her head everyone was looking at her. Antyn's face was filled with curious amusement but Leviathan's vulture gaze had darkened to an intense smoulder of dangerous desire.

Tyg held her breath.

Leviathan waved the pike that the soldier still held in front of Tyg out of the way and reached out to gently stroke Tyg's cheeks. He trailed his fingers around to the back of her neck and pulled her suddenly into him. As she crashed into his hard body she put her hands out to his chest and looked up at him startled.

"Lev?" She breathed.

He smirked at her. "What do you want, Tygarya, besides distracting me with your boorish behaviour and divine scent."

"A quick word is all."

"Regarding what?"

"Allegra."

Leviathan frowned at the name but Tyg lifted a hand off his chest and pointed to the girl cowering behind her. Leviathan's eyes flicked to the girl briefly then slid back to Tyg no longer amused but cold and dismissive. "Whatever it is, no."

"Leviathan..." Tyg protested.

He once again raised an eyebrow at her but said nothing as he still held her firmly round the neck. He lifted his other hand and grabbed a lock of her hair and brought it to his nose. Tyg took that as an invitation to continue. "I need you to give her some sort of obscure little title, anything will do."

Leviathan dropped his hands and stepped away from her. "No, Tygarya, I told you she is your problem to sort out, not mine."

"But..."

"No, Tygarya." Leviathan pointed a finger up to silence her and turned away, walking back towards the waiting officials.

"Do you not even want to know why?" Tyg yelled at him as the guard went to close the door.

"Go away, Tygarya." Leviathan growled without turning around as the door closed firmly.

"You'll regret turning your back on me!" She yelled at the closed door. Tyg stared at the guard who wouldn't meet her gaze.

"Damn it!" She muttered and stormed off with Ally in tow.

Antyn gave Leviathan a cautious glance conveying he didn't think that was wise to let an enraged Tyg roam the halls unchecked but Leviathan ignored him.

Later that evening Leviathan finally came to their rooms. Tyg smiled sweetly at him as she was sitting on his bed wearing nothing but a short black silk chemise, brushing her hair.

Leviathan smiled at her appreciatively then caught a slight movement out of the corner of his eye.

Ally was kneeling on the floor, with her head bowed low trying not to be noticed. Leviathan frowned and turned back to Tyg.

"What is the meaning of this?" He asked indignantly, indicating the girl.

Tyg looked over at Ally as she sat timidly on a cushion on the floor by the bed not looking at either of them.

"Well, you see, Mister Protocol and Law. I took it upon myself to do some research and found out the proper legal formalities and rankings of class into what Allegra actually is now I have taken up her care..."

Leviathan rubbed his forehead exhausted. "Fuck's sake, Tygarya, it's been a long day, do we have to do this now?"

"No, but you asked." Tyg pointed out with a pleasant smile.

Leviathan sighed and folded his arms. "Fine, but think long and hard about this before you proceed because I'm wound tighter than a violin string right now as it is."

Tyg looked down, glancing back at Ally for a second. "We don't need to discuss it then if my Liege is too exhausted from his long, hard day cooped up in a room full of stuffy old men arguing legal resolutions to rule."

Leviathan laughed in spite of himself. "Oh, my dearest...you are an incorrigible brat." Leviathan sat down on the divan and stretched his legs out along it as he rested his head back and closed his eyes for a moment, his hands on his stomach.

She sat watching him silently, chewing on her lip, waiting to see what he would do next.

"Okay, Tygarya..." He said without even opening his eyes after a silent minute feeling her eyes on him the whole time. "Let me have it."

Tyg smiled. "Well it seems this strange male misogynistic run country has this obscure law for something they like to call a pet."

Leviathan opened his eyes and glanced sideways at her with a dark warning gaze.

"It seems the only law that actually gives any woman any sort of power..." Tyg mused as she purposefully looked away and ignored his clear warning. "Anyway, since Ally here is not of any standing in society she is unable to be a lady-in-waiting to me or any kind of close attendant, as I am the consort of an Emperor."

Leviathan snorted. "Only when it's convenient for you. Get to the point."

Tyg stood up and went and poured Leviathan a glass of Arak, the spirit left in their room that was the locally made spirit of choice. It was strong with an aniseed flavour but had been distilled with figs making it slightly sweeter. She held it out to him as he frowned and sat up, taking the glass from her as she continued.

"I found some texts that allow me to take Ally on as a pet."

Leviathan's frown turned stormy. "What does that mean exactly?"

Tyg smiled with a beguiling pout to her lips. "I'm so glad you asked..."

Leviathan clucked his tongue and downed the drink in one go, placing the glass down on the side table. He knew by her belligerent attitude he was not going to like this.

"A pet is someone, usually of no worth, that a matriarch of a harem...that's usually the first wife, but in our case me, your consort...can take into her bedchamber and she has the right to place this pet..." Tyg saw Leviathan's eyes darkening as his vulture gaze settled on her, she decided it best to walk to the other side of the room again and sit on the bed. "...in her stead when her Lord comes calling." She looked up at him and slow blinked in her smugness.

"What the fuck, Tygarya!" Leviathan growled as he looked over at the quaking form of Ally. "What are you saying to me? That if I want to take you to bed you can present her to me instead?" He scoffed.

"Exactly, and by law here you have to accept it." Tyg's smile was benign.

Leviathan stood up. "You know that's not going to fucking happen! Why? Because I won't give her a fucking title or because I turned my back on you and had the door shut on you?"

"Well, if she had a title she would be able to go straight into Silla's court and attend her, she's more than willing to take her in."

Leviathan couldn't believe what he was hearing. "So you're more than happy to whore out this fourteen year old girl to me rather than lay with me yourself until I bestow her with a fucking title to get her out of your hair?"

"If that is what my Lord wishes to do with me, then yes, my pet will stand in for me." Tyg was being overly pleasant and it grated on Leviathan's nerves to see her acting so full of herself.

He lunged over to her, pushing her down on the bed with a hand around her throat before she could move. "You're trying to black mail me, Tygarya." His face was vicious.

"You left me no choice, Lev." Tyg said in a panicked tone as she gripped his wrist. "Seriously, I don't want her in my care! I shouldn't care for anyone, you know that. I'm too fucking damaged to care for anyone else I can hardly care for myself, look at how I keep stuffing that up!"

Leviathan stood up, his eyes wide as he raked a hand through his hair and expelled a calming breath. Tyg panted, looking up at him with fear and apprehension.

"By the fucking gods, Tygarya..." He muttered, glancing over to Ally looking petrified. "I will get her the title she needs to get into Lady Silla's court, now make her leave."

Tyg sat up and curtly inclined her head towards the door indicating for Ally to leave. The girl got up and frantically sprinted for the door fleeing in terror.

Tyg was looking at her lap, feeling Leviathan's gaze heavy upon her. "Thank you, Lev."

Leviathan stepped back up to the bed and knelt on the floor in front of her, she looked up in surprise.

"Is that truly how you feel about yourself, Tyg?" Leviathan brushed her hair away from her face and flicked it back over her shoulders.

Tyg shrugged. "I know I cannot be responsible for another life like Ally's, I would end up destroying her."

Leviathan trailed his fingers down the edge of the shoulder strap of Tyg's chemise then down along the edge of the bodice to her cleavage.

"Tygarya, you are so beautiful but truly so damaged. I don't know how to fix it...tell me how to fix it?" Leviathan raised his eyes to hers with a concerned look.

Tyg smiled and suddenly slipped forward off the bed and into his arms as she hugged him and buried her face into his chest. She curled her legs up onto his thighs as he knelt back on his heels and held her protectively.

He didn't know what was happening to him in this moment, he felt such strong emotions towards her right now it scared and confused him.

"You don't need to fix anything, Lev, I have quite accepted where I fit into this world, I am not human, so should not be with humans."

Leviathan closed his eyes as he heard those words it made him feel melancholy, but at the same time it sparked some primeval desire in him like this was meant to happen, another step closer to her being completely his. Another step closer to his ultimate plan of world domination.

"Tyg, let me protect you from them." He grimaced at his own controversial words knowing how Antyn would react to hearing him say them, but getting her completely loyal and complicit was the goal wasn't it. Leviathan smiled to himself as he pressed his lips to Tyg's hair. She was now as loyal as she was probably ever going to get. She had proved herself twice now, Kolastan and now here in

Gua del Mar, killing for him both times. She was completely under his control if still a little wild.

61

Tyg woke the next morning to find herself alone. She hated waking up alone.

She got up and dressed, deciding enough of the dress it was back to her leather gear. Leviathan was now in charge who was going to argue? She knew she would get more respect in this place wearing it and her weapons, she saw fear and respect in the eyes of all men she past when wearing her assassin's gear, she knew now they knew her as the monster that had killed Alta it wouldn't be any different here in Gua del Mar. She was what she was and was proud of it.

She noticed most of the guard were now in the black and gold of the Imperial house of the Dragon as she walked the halls and wondered where Corvyn had disappeared to.

As she approached the door to the Council chambers she noticed the same guard was there now wearing the black and gold livery. He baulked to see her in her battle gear and he did nothing to bar her way. She stopped in front of the doors and looked at him with a curious gaze.

She put a hand on the handle and turned it, still nothing.

The door opened a crack under her hand as she turned slightly to him. "What? I'm allowed in now?"

"Tygarya! Get in here!" Leviathan's voice boomed out causing Tyg to swing the door open with a push.

Leviathan frowned darkly when he saw the way she was dressed. Antyn was there and he paused in his reading of a large tome and regarded her with curiosity.

"How come I'm allowed in today?" Tyg asked facetiously, standing on the threshold of the room.

"Because the Lord's aren't in session." Leviathan muttered. "Why are you dressed for a fight?"

Tyg shrugged. "I get more respect around here if I do." She wandered in and the guard leaned in to grab the door handle and close the door.

Leviathan snorted and sat down on the edge of the desk, folding his arms. "No, you really don't, what you get is fear." He looked at her amused as she frowned. He ruled by fear, was she no better than him? Probably not.

"Whatever." Tyg shrugged. She took in all the large volumes of books that were stacked on the impressive desk. "What are you doing?"

Tyg noticed Antyn's sudden smirk as he slowly turned a page.

Leviathan rubbed a hand over his eyes. "I am hurriedly researching all the laws of this damn country."

Tyg smiled coyly, Leviathan caught it and his eyes darkened dangerously. "Yes, Tygarya, because of your little stunt last night."

Tyg glanced at Antyn as he chuckled and turned another page. "Yes, I told Antyn." Leviathan grumbled.

Antyn looked up and smiled at Tyg. "How did you find it? When you said it was obscure you were not wrong."

Tyg shrugged again. "I don't really know, I was in the library and was quite pissed off with Leviathan turning his back on me." Tyg glared at him.

"Move along, Tygarya." Leviathan muttered as he listened.

"Well, I was looking at some way I could twist Ally's father's small holding into some obscure title that sounded legit enough for Silla to take Ally and my anger was getting the better of me to the point I couldn't read the words on the pages of the stupid books."

"Tygarya..." Leviathan said in a low tone. He could see the power building around her as she relived her frustration. Gods, how did she not even know the power she held?

Tyg looked at him and sighed out a hefty breath. "Gods, I know...even thinking about it makes me angry again."

"I'm sorry, Tyg."

Antyn looked at Leviathan with surprise. It always amazed him how different he was with Tyg and no other, not even his own brother. He clenched his jaw as Leviathan raised his arm and Tyg habitually went to him.

Leviathan pulled Tyg in between his legs as they were stretched out and turned her around to lean back on him with her back against his chest, he put his arms around her waist and rested his chin down on her shoulder avoiding the handle of her sword. His eyes started to glow. "Please continue."

Tyg breathed in deeply, relaxing in his arms. "I don't know what happened, a whole lot of books fell off the shelves and the one I needed fell on top of the pile, open right to the page I needed to find."

Leviathan's head snapped up and so did Antyn's. Tyg heard Antyn whistle low as Leviathan grabbed her shoulders and turned her around to face him. He seemed to search her eyes for something but when he didn't find it he looked confused over at Antyn who had stood up.

"What is it?" Tyg asked. "Why have you both gone weird?"

"It's nothing..." Antyn answered as he walked around the desk. "You just seem to have the luck of the gods, Tyg."

Tyg scowled. "Well, fuck knows why."

Leviathan laughed and pulled her into his chest. "Because you are an angel, my dear."

They stood like that in each other's arms for a long moment as Leviathan and Antyn stared at each other, what was passing between them was vast.

"So about Ally's title?" Tyg softly enquired.

"It is all done, the paperwork is right here, signed by Bahadur. Quite happily, I might add...I think Silla may have already had a word with him." Leviathan explained. "It will be bestowed upon her this afternoon."

Tyg looked up with a beautiful smile and kissed Leviathan's lips softly. "So what are you doing with all these laws?" She asked curious.

"I'm abolishing the lot of them, all the stupid archaic laws putting their women in servitude...for you." He stroked down her hair, cupping the back of her head.

"For me?" Tyg's eyes widened as Antyn looked up in surprise, that's not the reason Leviathan had given him.

"Yes, for you. Although some I'm afraid may need to be filtered down and slowly changed over time."

"Like what?"

"The harems for a start."

Tyg shrugged. "Harems don't bother me...as long as everyone involved is happy and agrees to the situation."

Antyn muttered behind them as he pulled a book out of the pile. "Huh, says a woman in a monogamous relationship who scared her rival out of the palace on day one."

"Would you like a harem, Antyn?" Tyg asked as she looked over at him. He looked up startled then gave her a dashingly handsome smile.

"Absolutely."

Tyg's eyes narrowed. "Of course you would." She drawled facetiously.

Antyn laughed. "No, not really...to be honest."

"No, because he would still get bored of them and want to throw them in the trash after a few days." The tone that came from Leviathan's voice was frightening. Tyg stared at him in fear as Antyn flinched and stepped away slightly from the desk.

"Ah, okay...that turned dark quickly." Tyg said unsure what was happening.

Leviathan closed his eyes and pulled her further into him, hugging her strongly and dropping his head over her shoulder. "No mind." He said simply.

There was no apology for anyone but her, ever.

He relaxed his arms and leaned back, brushing a stray hair from her face. "I'm actually glad you came by..."

"Came by?" Tyg huffed. "Like I wasn't going to search you out when I woke up and found the bed empty beside me."

Leviathan's eyes widened slightly then darkened. "I'm sorry, baby...should I have woken you and said goodbye?" The change in tone made Tyg go weak and the way he held her shifted slightly suddenly feeling more sensual.

Antyn rolled his eyes and sat down back in his chair.

"Actually I would prefer it if you woke me and took me with you." Tyg confessed.

"Fuck, get a room." Antyn growled under his breath.

"We are in a room." Leviathan said back as he pulled Tyg's face to him and kissed her, his tongue pushing into her mouth as she kissed him back and ran her hands down his arms.

"One that is soon to be occupied by several Lords of State and you haven't even got to the point of what you were about to tell her." Antyn said without looking up from the book he had.

Leviathan growled and glanced at Antyn annoyed.

"What?" Tyg asked, suspicious.

"I just want to warn you that Alta's brother has commissioned a challenge."

"What...why?"

"Well, why do you think?" Leviathan gave her a strange confused look.

Tyg shrugged. "It's not a problem, Alta was supposed to be the best amongst them, wasn't he? So his brother won't be much of a problem."

"I refused it." Leviathan stated.

"Why?" Tyg demanded.

"Because in this time of turmoil and chaos through the changeover process it's not really a good idea."

"Oh, okay...that's fine by me."

"It's not, however, fine by him." Antyn said glancing up and closing the book. "Watch your back."

Tyg barked out a derisive laugh. "Are you serious?" She asked indignantly.

"Deadly." Leviathan said in her ear.

"Well, I am dressed for the occasion." Tyg smirked causing Leviathan to chuckle and rub his hands down her hips.

Antyn appraised her. "Were you planning to go somewhere dressed like that?"

"Actually, I was..."

"Really? Where exactly?" Leviathan asked, his tone intent.

Tyg suddenly thought better of answering catching something in his tone. "Ah, just for a walk."

Leviathan's eyes darkened instantly and Antyn scowled. "A walk where?"

"In the sunshine...just around the inner courtyard." Tyg answered evasively.

Both sorcerers didn't buy it. "Tyg..." Antyn rolled his eyes. "...why do you always do this?"

Tyg looked at Leviathan and saw his cold expression. She looked away, chewing her lip. "Exactly where, Tygarya?" Leviathan demanded.

"I just said." Tyg bit back.

Leviathan grabbed her braid and held her face inches from his own as he stared intensely into her eyes. "Going to visit a certain Colonel, perhaps?" His growling tone was deep in his throat.

"Well, I..." Tyg swallowed hard under that gaze, more than a little annoyed he had seen straight through her. Damn sorcerer! Her eyes blazed in response. "What's the problem with that? I just wanted to thank him for the other day...I haven't seen him since and..."

"There is no need to thank him, Tygarya." Leviathan spat, cutting her off.

"I think..."

"No, Tygarya! He was doing his fucking job." Leviathan stood up, still gripping hold of her hair as he twisted it around his hand and lifted it up so she was up on her tip toes and grabbing his wrist.

Antyn coughed and stood up in warning. The Lords had arrived and opened the door.

As they filed into the room they looked at Leviathan holding Tyg by her hair and they all froze.

Leviathan growled in a vicious rumble, dragged Tyg over to a chair and threw her into it. "You're not going anywhere!"

"Lev..."

"Shut the fuck up, Tygarya, I've heard enough! You will stay right there and not fucking move! I'll deal with you later."

Tyg pressed her mouth together and folded her arms, straightening in the chair with a snort of breath out her nose. Her eyes blazed ice blue fire at Leviathan as he stared back at her with his azure eyes glowing.

"She cannot stay in here during our meeting, Emperor."

Leviathan turned in a deadly slow pivot, glaring at the man who dared be brave enough to speak.

"She will and you will do exactly what I fucking say!" His eyes glowed with azure fire making them all shrink back.

They all bowed low in submission, quaking at the realisation that they were at his mercy.

"Lev." Antyn said calmly.

Leviathan glanced briefly at Antyn then took in a deep breath and rolled his shoulders, settling that calm repose back over himself. He turned and looked at Tyg, his vulture gaze intense.

Tyg lifted her gaze to meet him.

"Have you been put here just to torment me?"

Tyg frowned and looked away. "I hope I do more than just torment you, my Liege." She muttered under her breath.

Leviathan's eyes dulled back to a dark glare as he chuckled then turned to face the Lords. "I am leaving tomorrow morning, gentlemen, so it's going to be a long day."

"Leaving so soon?" Bahadur said surprised, but looked at Tyg sulking in the corner.

"Yes." Leviathan answered gruffly, watching Bahadur's gaze shift to Tyg. "Bahadur." He menaced.

Bahadur flicked his gaze back, startled and bowed his head.

Tyg rolled her eyes, it sure was going to be a long day for her. She tensed as Leviathan called her name in that deadly calm voice.

"Tygarya...please tell me you didn't just roll your fucking eyes again?"

"Ah...no." Tyg said meekly with a small frown, her eyes suddenly looking fearful and wild.

Antyn sucked his teeth and shook his head. Bahadur was seated next to him and looked his way. "I'm really quite glad he is able to control her, I would love to know exactly how..."

Antyn looked over at him with an eyebrow raised. "Wouldn't we all…" Antyn turned back to face Leviathan. "What do you do to her when she rolls her eyes at you, she looks positively petrified every time?"

Leviathan clucked his tongue. "None of your business, brother…unless you want me to do the same to you because I'm getting a little sick of seeing you do it to me as well?"

Everyone's gaze fell on Antyn. He swallowed hard under Leviathan's deadly gaze and looked away. "Sorry, my Liege." He said through gritted teeth. He hated calling his brother that, but he knew it appeased him and he was already in a very foul mood thanks to Tyg and her antics.

Leviathan rolled his shoulders and stretched his back giving a smooth dark chuckle before coolly regarding the Lords still standing in front of him.

"Sit down, gentlemen. Let us begin from where we left off yesterday…" He glanced at Tyg as he sat down. He wanted to pull her onto his lap and make her sleep, but he couldn't with all these people in the room.

He caught Tyg glance sideways at him and look quickly away when she saw he was staring at her. He smiled a little. "Tygarya…" He said it low and soft…enticing.

His mood lifted slightly as her eyes slid back to him on command. "You may as well lose the weaponry and make yourself comfortable. Read a book…" Leviathan picked up a volume that was on the desk in front of him and threw it over to her. It landed on the floor in front of her chair, she peered down over her knees at it then looked away with a sullen pout.

"Have you eaten?" He asked her.

Tyg grimaced. "No, not yet."

"So you came here as soon as you woke?"

Tyg looked back at him and her expression went flat when she saw his smug smirk. "Of course I did. I always do when I wake up alone these days."

The Lords had all settled themselves ready to begin the day's discussions and were watching the Emperor with his woman. Bahadur coughed and stood up.

"I can get some food sent in, my Liege, if you would like?"

Leviathan's gaze slid to Bahadur, then to the other Lords. He leaned back in his chair. "Yes." He said simply, Bahadur bowed his head and went and pulled on a bell-pull to call a servant.

"I'm not hungry." Tyg muttered as she stood up, unstrapped her swords from her back and stood them in the corner.

"No one cares, Tygarya." Leviathan rebutted. "When food arrives you will eat it."

Tyg swept the book off the floor and contemplated throwing it at him but his eyes swung up and locked with hers almost daring her to do it.

She smiled sweetly at him and sat down, opened the book and started reading it.

He smirked to himself satisfied that she was going to finally settle down and opened a large tome on his desk to where he had marked a certain page.

"Right..."

62

"So what are you going to do with Jarl Revna and Montrual?" Tyg asked Leviathan as they were packing up to leave the palace.

"It was always the plan after Gua del Mar to back off, regroup and let things settle down a bit before approaching Montrual and Petonia." Leviathan answered mildly. "My agenda will get to Jarl Revna all in good time."

"Huh? Can I ask why you don't just keep going from this side and around?"

Leviathan regarded her with an interested smirk. "Of course you can ask...come here." He patted his lap and his smirk widened.

Tyg's eyes narrowed in suspicion as she regarded him.

"It's a desert from here on around the peninsular...nothing but sand and soaring temperatures during the day down to freezing at night...we can't go that way...we could pull back a bit and go over the mountains but that would mean our forces would be susceptible to ambush and barricades...and we wouldn't want to get caught with autumn and winter coming in behind us...I need to pull the main force back to Enyana to weather the winter, I do not wish for them to be stranded on this side of the continent until spring thaw without my access to them."

"Ah...that makes sense."

"Besides, it will give the soldiers a good time to recuperate, they are exhausted after such a long campaign, for some of them they have been working since invading Enyana last year. Which was a long and hard battle as you've probably heard. They put up quite the resistance..."

Tyg saw the look in Leviathan's eye and smiled at him. "So you do give them a chance to rest and see their families."

Leviathan snorted. "Of course I do, why would I not, I'm not the tyrant you seem to think I am."

"You clearly rule by fear."

"Fear and respect. I'm a sorcerer, a very powerful one...I am destined to rule, Tygarya, just like my father before me except better. I am merely filling my rightful place in this world to rule absolutely."

Tyg stared at him for a moment and felt a cold tingle up her spine.

"Besides, I have another thing on my agenda I must do now Kolastan is subdued..."

"What's that?"

"Hunt the sorcerers who live in these mountains...now that King Davalos has given up their locations." The smirk on his face was terrifying.

"Why?"

He regarded her for a moment. "Because they stand in my way." He said it like it was obvious. "Now, come here." His voice dropped low making Tyg grit her teeth.

She moved over to him and he ran his hands around her hips as she lowered herself down onto his thigh. He buried his face into her neck and breathed in deeply.

"I love the way you smell."

Arriving back into Kolastan's capital city Tyg noticed two large black monoliths being transported through by large draft horse pulled wagons.

They had to stop and pull to the side to allow the huge monoliths to pass.

"What the hell are those?"

Leviathan glanced at her. "A symbol of my ultimate rule over city and country. I am having them erected everywhere as a constant reminder to the people that I rule."

"Oh, that's not egotistical at all..." Tyg muttered, earning a glare.

"Not egotistical, Tygarya, a necessity, you will one day see and understand."

Tyg frowned at him a little perplexed by the glib statement but didn't press the issue. What did she care if he put up monuments to himself?

As they neared the castle of King Davalos Tyg saw another monolith being erected in the large town square outside the castle gates.

"So were those other two heading for Gua del Mar?"

"Of course." Leviathan stated.

King Davalos was on the steps to welcome them in as they circled around into the front courtyard. He still seemed a little unsure of everything and the man Leviathan had left to assist the King in his stead and to monitor him, General Kloine, gave Leviathan a sly grin just before bowing his head.

"Davalos! Things are progressing well I hope?"

"Ah, yes, your Majesty..."

Leviathan noticed how Davalos hadn't changed to 'my liege' and nodded solemnly. "Good, I would like a word with you on a matter of urgency, please lets go inside and get refreshments, no need to stand on protocols for this as it is of a somewhat personal matter..."

Davalos straightened his back with surprise. "Of course...this way..." He clapped his hands to the servants as he walked inside ordering refreshments be sent to the back parlour room.

Leviathan took Tyg by the arm and stopped walking, pulling her to a stop. "Go with Antyn and get settled into our room. We are only staying a couple of days to refresh the horses then we'll be leaving, I don't want Davalos spending any time with you and realising that you and Duchess Targatha are the same person."

"Okay..." Tyg glanced at Antyn, he was talking to the castle steward and a couple of servants outlaying their requirements for their stay.

"Good girl...and behave, I will be with you shortly." Leviathan pinched her chin affectionately before walking off after Davalos.

Tyg sighed and looked around the cold grey stoned castle. She wondered why anyone would want to live in such a dreary cold place.

"Tyg..." Antyn called out.

She made her way to him and they followed the servant together to their respective rooms. She wondered what the personal thing was that Leviathan had to talk to Davalos about alone.

Antyn followed her into the room she was shown for her and Leviathan to stay, it was warmer than the rest of the castle as a large fireplace burned brightly with coal. The bed looked stuffy with thick velvet drapes hung around it and she noticed there was no balcony, only two small windows that didn't let a lot of light in.

She sat down in an armchair that was hard under her bottom and let out a little unsatisfied groan.

Antyn looked around the room and rubbed his cheek. "Well, Davalos certainly isn't giving up his rooms for us, is he?"

"I think I've become too spoilt in my time with you, even though on the road is hard and lacking of most comforts I still find this room underwhelming...I should be grateful."

Antyn laughed. "It's easy to get used to comfort and riches, eh?"

"Easier than I thought...am I getting soft?" Tyg mused. "So what's the personal thing Leviathan wanted to talk to Davalos about?"

"Wouldn't that be personal?" Antyn quipped.

"Hmm." Tyg snorted. She spied a carafe of wine on a side board and stood up, going to it and pouring herself a glass. As she sipped it she caught Antyn's disapproval. "What?"

"Nothing..." He commented, looking away.

"Clearly there is..." Tyg retorted. "If it's my drinking habits, blame my upbringing around hard alcoholics and gamblers."

Antyn gave a wry smirk. "Well I guess we should be grateful you don't gamble then?"

"Who says I don't?" Tyg smirked over the rim of her glass and took another deliberate sip.

"When would you dare to have the time?" Antyn said facetiously smug and made his way to the door.

Tyg felt like throwing the glass at his head, but she remembered she had tried that once and he just used his magic to stop it.

"Don't get yourself too incapacitated before Lev gets here..." He said with a little sarcastic tone before leaving. "Oh, and he's talking to Davalos about those sorcerers hiding in these mountains, he's hoping to try and flush them out."

Tyg sucked on her teeth and put the glass down, glaring at the door. He was getting cockier every day regarding her relationship with Leviathan and she wasn't sure if he was jealous or disgusted by it. Either way that had been a jibe about being under Leviathan's control and influence and Leviathan hated her drinking too much.

She left the wine where it was and moved to the window to stare up at the mountainous terrain. So Leviathan was planning to take action against the sorcerers as well?

As they headed out across the flat land after descending from the steep ravine to cross the border back into Enyana, Tyg looked back over her shoulder with a frown up at the mountains of Kolastan they were leaving behind. She had thought they would return to the camp that was still set up there and plan a new campaign to search for the sorcerers, instead they moved east heading back to the coastal highway with only a thousand troops as the rest stayed behind to clean up and rest or guard and protect Leviathan's interest, right through to Gua del Mar. Leviathan was having a huge permanent barracks built in Enyana for his army.

"Aren't we going in the wrong direction?"

"Whatever do you mean, Tygarya?" Leviathan gave her a strange, amused look.

"Well, I understand coming all the way back to this location from Gua del Mar as it's flat and plentiful, but why are we heading home? I thought you wanted to hunt sorcerers in the mountains of Kolastan?"

Leviathan chuckled as Antyn gave her a long, concerned sideways glance. "Oh, I am...I also have an empire to run, and other various tasks that need to be completed...I'm a busy man, Tygarya."

"What do you mean, you are? Do you have someone else searching them out for you?" She sounded disappointed. She had hoped to be able to do some hunting herself.

"Exactly, see you can figure these things out for yourself." Leviathan looked almost smug about it and Tyg felt the prickles of suspicion.

"No need to be rude, I was only asking...so who did you send?"

"I put together a rather special group of people..." He replied vaguely.

Tyg's suspicion grew as she glanced at Antyn, seeing his worried face she knew the news wasn't something she was going to react well to. "Who?"

Leviathan turned in his saddle and gave her that vulture glare. "Why is it so important?"

"Why are you so vague?" Tyg retorted with a hiss.

He chuckled and looked forward again. "It is of some renown that the ones I search are formidable old men, I had to send people skilled enough to hunt them without detection..."

"Warlocks?" Tyg grimaced as she felt her skin crawl with an ominous feeling.

"Of course, as well as some other special men I have at my disposal..."

"You sent Corvyn, didn't you?" She breathed, realising now why she hadn't been able to find him in the crowds the last few days since leaving Kolastan.

"Colonel Corvyn has been given this task, yes...this could put him on the road to becoming a General if he succeeds. I have put him in charge of a very select group of warlocks and I expect great things from him."

Tyg looked away back to the mountains, chewing her bottom lip.

"Don't even think about it." Leviathan said firmly. "It's a reconnaissance mission, nothing more...do you truly have feelings for that man?"

Tyg looked up and met Leviathan's intense gaze. "No, not the feelings you're thinking..."

"Good, I would hate for him to go missing up in those mountains..." Leviathan snarled, put heel to his horse and cantered forward.

Tyg glared at his back, seething. "You knew about this?" She asked Antyn.

Antyn shrugged and nodded. "Of course, and you know not to show emotional attachment towards other people, if that man dies it will be on your head, Tyg."

"But, I don't..."

"It doesn't matter, don't you get it?"

Tyg grimaced, pulling a bitter face. "I belong to him." She spat dejectedly.

"Indeed you do, and you've just spent the better part of this whole campaign proving your loyalty to him, so well done." Antyn's tone was savage.

"So why won't he let Corvyn off the proverbial hook, the man is completely innocent of anything, if I had to call my feelings towards him something, it would be like a brother?"

Antyn adjusted his seat, the leather of his saddle creaking, as he sighed. "That man's destiny is unclear...it rattles him."

Tyg jolted in surprise. "Unclear, what does that mean?"

Antyn sucked his teeth. "He is strangely unreadable...and therefore important in some way, so Leviathan likes to test his loyalty just as much as he likes to test yours."

Tyg chewed her lip and looked away with a bad feeling in her stomach that fate wasn't going to be kind to either one of them and wished Corvyn all the luck. For all the times he pissed her off he was one of the genuine ones. Someone Tyg called a friend, the only one she had here. She felt a little bitter he was once again not going to be able to be that needed friend for her back at the castle.

63

Returning to Estafeld and Leviathan's monstrous castle seemed satisfactory to Tyg. It felt like she was returning home as she entered her rooms and trailed her fingers over the large desk she had procured for her small business. She smiled at the pile of order forms and decided the business was going well enough to possibly expand a little...

She intended to hire two botany druids and a metallurgy druid, after discussing what other products they could invent before leaving for the campaign and she had plans to purchase a warehouse and workers in which to start full time manufacture. Tyg felt life was going to go well from now on.

She was walking back from the training grounds with the intention of bathing before she had a meeting with the owner of an apothecary store in the city she wanted to rent, even though she had only been back for two days she didn't want to waste a single opportunity. She stopped when she saw Ra'chek walking her way.

"Oh, you're back..." Ra'chek said somewhat facetiously.

Tyg sucked on her teeth her mouth twisting derisively, he knew damn well she was back and as her training schedule of three times a week had been reinstated yesterday, what was his deal?

"I hear the Emperor used you rather than the army to make two Kings concede to his superior rule." His expression was hard to read. "What an absolutely terrifying monster you are."

"So?" Tyg spat back at him.

Ra'chek shrugged. "No, no, it's a good thing. Why waste all those soldiers' lives when he has a loyal Elvian pet to do his bidding? Makes perfect strategy from an economical and human life casualty perspective." His droll sarcasm was perfectly clear now.

Tyg bared her teeth snidely. "Are you jealous?"

Ra'chek laughed. "Ha! Hardly, I have far too much self-esteem for that."

"What do you mean?" Tyg frowned, feeling the insult.

He merely shrugged again and scratched absently at the stubble growing on his rough cheek.

"What the fuck do you mean?" Tyg asked more forcefully, stepping up in front of Ra'chek and glaring at him eye to eye, intimidatingly.

Ra'chek's eyes narrowed slyly. "I really shouldn't say...I hear his Imperial Majesty cursed a lot of soldiers for speaking out about you."

Tyg grinned viciously, a hand going to the hilt of her dagger on her hip. "You really should..."

He smirked and folded his arms. "How do you think the Emperor would react if you killed me?"

Tyg's mouth twisted as her eyes intently turned to ice. "Would he really care, you're not that good at your job as I pointed out last time..."

Ra'chek rolled his eyes. "You really don't see how everyone here sees you, do you?"

Tyg's face clouded and she grit her teeth as she stepped back slightly. "Just spit it out, it's quite clear that you're dying to say something to me."

"You've been tamed, like a wild animal. It's really quite astounding to see." Ra'chek revelled in Tyg's shocked expression. "Elvian's were always seen as prideful rabid dogs, both male and

female, war mongering, rutting, psychopaths, but look at you..."
His tone was clearly condescending and Tyg was holding herself in
check wanting to hear the rest of what he was daring to say to her
face.

"Everyone's quite astonished by the fact that our Emperor has
actually managed to tame and control such a demon as you. You're
nothing but a monster with the Emperor's collar around your
neck."

"You think I do what I do for him because he orders me to?
Don't make me laugh, Ra'chek, you're deluded if you think I'm
taking orders from him to do his bidding."

"So you do them because you're a puppy in love, is that it?"
Ra'chek chuckled sinisterly. "Or because you think he loves you?
You're nothing but a pathetic collared dog."

"I am not." Tyg seethed as her eyes blazed with her fury.

"You're being manipulated and you can't even see it, you're
strangely naïve and innocent, yet you strut around this place like
you own it, flexing how dangerous you are meanwhile the Emperor
shows you off like a pet lying on his lap asleep while he pets your
head." He snorted amused. "Tells you to be a good girl and to
behave...are you truly blind, or do you like having a master?"

Tyg stared at him blankly, feeling a little stunned. Lying on his
lap asleep while he pets her head? Was he serious?

He scoffed at her inability to answer him. "Question more, why
you are really here?"

He walked off leaving her watching his back in silent repose,
frowning at his harsh words but feeling enough shock by them to
reflect seriously on them.

She scowled as her fists clenched and wanted to scream. She
closed her eyes and breathed in deeply to try and calm down.

"He was just goading you..." She muttered to herself. "It can't
be true..."

Still, the words had hurt as she knew there was a sparse amount of truth to them. She had been brought back by Leviathan claiming she was his and important to his rule...was this why? Or was there still some other reason yet to be revealed. Enough of this, she needed to get to the bottom of it once and for all.

She opened her eyes and scanned the hall as she heard footsteps approaching. She looked up and saw the tall figure of Leviathan come around the far corner.

He stopped as he saw her, his vulture gaze studying her tense posture. "Tygarya? What are you doing?" He lifted his arm, beckoning her.

She rolled her shoulders as she relaxed her body and walked towards him. "Heading to the baths after training, so I'm all sweaty at the moment." She said calmly.

He curled his arm around her and pulled her into his chest, bending down to nuzzle into her neck and inhaled deeply. "I care not, you always smell divine to me."

"That's weird..." Tyg commented a little surly, still rattled by Ra'chek's words.

Leviathan lifted his head and his eyes bore into her. "What's wrong?"

Tyg looked up at his intense expression. He was extremely good at reading people, her included and it was something that irked her. "Nothing is wrong...will you join me in the baths?" She gave him a beautiful smile hoping to distract his attention.

"Hmm...perhaps I will."

64

Tyg was coming back from a visit with the botany Druids through a bottom level of the castle when she overheard two courtiers talking out on a bench seat in a small courtyard garden. She froze when she heard one particular sentence, then melted into the shadows.

"Do you really believe Lord Coulter could have that sort of power and influence?" One of the men was saying in a hushed voice.

"I don't know, but if the Emperor finds out..."

"Yeah, it wouldn't just be a quick death as a traitor..."

"I can't believe he thinks he could go up against the Emperor and win..." The other chortled in bemusement.

"That's the thing...he's not planning on that...he's planning on divine intervention. He's been preaching something about the Emperor's planning on killing every sorcerer that is alive today to make himself stronger, and if he does he will be unstoppable. "

"You have got to be kidding me?"

"No, he travels to Temple Island every week to hear the priests sermons on it...they say the Emperor is insane and trying to become a God, that in itself is heretic and he should be stopped...he's fanatical about this."

"Really?" The amazed breath made Tyg grit her teeth.

"It's also said he plans to leave all his worldly possessions to those priests and that he gives them large donations and wants others to do the same, to support them."

"How large?" He sounded completely enthralled.

"Large enough that he thinks they are going to kill the Emperor for the sake of the world, apparently there's a prophecy. He says they are training for it, it's their life's work."

"He's the insane one...we should say something..."

"Are you crazy!? The Emperor would kill us just for knowing about this..."

"Yeah, your right...what do we do?"

"Keep our heads down, say nothing..."

"But Coulter wants an answer..."

"Hmm...and if we say no? Does he have us killed for knowing too much?"

"Argh..." The other made a strangled noise in his throat. "We're in a real bind..."

"Let's just say yes, but then not participate..."

"How can we do that? He wants our money!"

"I don't know, when's the meeting?"

"Tirsdag..."

Tyg had heard enough. What the hell was going on inside the castle? Was this espionage? Mutiny? She had to find out how serious this was...and who the hell were the Temple Priests?

She had to decide what to do with this information. She was going to need help and she certainly wasn't going to trust anyone in the castle. She wished Corvyn was here...although he wouldn't agree to go along with any of her schemes...would he?

No, the pain in the ass would probably sell her out to the Emperor again...

She needed to find some people that could be made completely devoted to her and do everything she needed them to do, which was going to be a lot of planning, she realised. She wasn't going to be able to do much of it herself, not with Leviathan always keeping one eye on what she was up to.

He really didn't trust her.

The only time she could really guarantee Leviathan was completely busy and wouldn't be able to come looking for her was the two hours every afternoon that he spent sitting on his throne listening to the 'Petitions of the People'.

Tyg smiled to herself as she wandered through the halls deep in thought. Yes, that could work...she just had to find the right people to trust...

She stopped walking as it came to her.

Of course, it was so simple...how could she forget her own upbringing? How long had it been already? Eight months? Eight months of living in the company of an Emperor living and breathing only for him, being loyal to him and she had forgotten her life from the streets and what she actually was.

No, she hadn't or she wouldn't be scheming now, would she?

Tyg laughed to herself. Yes, it was time to go and meet the other King of the City...the one who ruled the underworld that she was sure was there. Thieves, pickpockets, brigands...she knew they were there, they were always there and whether or not they were run with the efficiency they were back in Arial or not, she knew there would be someone claiming the top spot, and that top spot she had set her sights upon. If nothing came of this information at least she would then be in a position to start looking into the claims that Ra'chek had made. For the moment she would put that aside and focus on the threat.

She had noticed the young children the day Leviathan took her to the market soon after arriving in the castle, would they remember her? They definitely saw her that day as she had seen them, standing staring at the Emperor and his consort. She hoped they wouldn't put the woman in the fancy dress months ago together with the killer in black leather with the crazy ice eyes that they were about to meet face to face.

End of Book Two
continued in
Tygarya Saga Book 3
Betrayal Frees You

GLOSSARY OF TERMS AND PRONUNCIATIONS

Tygarya – *Ti-gar-ya*
Vanarya – *Van-ar-ya*
Essyndyl – *Es-sin-dal*
Tylandria – *Ty-lan-dree-a (roll r)*
Antyn - *An-tin*
Adramelech – *A-dram-e-lek*
Corvyn – *Kor-vin*
Enyana – *En-yarn-a*
Arial – *Air-re-al*
Landau – *Lan-dau*
Annul – *An-nule*
Barion – *Ba-re-on*
Karon – *Kar-ron*
Irion – *I-ri-on*
Palin – *Pay-lin*
Enyana – *En-yarn-a*
Gua del Mar – *Gu-a-del-mar*
Kolastan – *Kol-a-stan*
R-hyan – *Ri-hy-an*
Barrock – *Bar-rock*
Migel – *Me-gell*
Ra'chek – *Ra-check*

LOYALTY BINDS YOU

Tiagratis – *Ti-a-grat-is*
Frameur – *Fram-e-ur*
Morphun – *More-fune*
Kairo – *Ki-ro*
Silla – *Sil-a*
Bahadur – *Ba-ha-dure*
Montrual – *Mon-true-al*
Severn – *Sev-urn*
Gravelle – *Grav-al*
Marcuis – *Marc-ess*
R-Hurin – *Ri-hu-rin*
DePerin – *De-pe-rin*
Allegra – *Al-egg-ra*
Coulter – *Coal-ter*
Days of the Week in Tylandria
Monday – Mandag
Tuesday – Tirsdag
Wednesday – Onsdag
Thursday – Torsdag
Friday – Fredag
Saturday – Lordag
Sunday – Sudag

History of the Races

E lvian
      Very tall muscular people, women from 6ft, men from 7ft onwards, with golden to white and silver hair. Blue, green or golden eyes, high cheek bones and flawless complexions and golden skin. A beautiful race said to be descendants of the Gods. Their life spans ranged up to 2500yrs, being the oldest living Elvian recorded. They had the extraordinary ability of accelerated healing, only decapitation or a solid blow to the heart could kill them.

A very arrogant warrior race. Men and women both fought side by side and they fought for the glory of the Elvia motherland (now the wastelands). They lived for their strength and prowess in battle, stronger than humans by tenfold. They were always practising and perfecting, holding tournaments and glory was always with the winners held in the highest esteem, having innate abilities to fight with any weapon with undefeated skill. Their Royal families bred only amongst themselves and harboured other magic, said to be from the Gods themselves. They were an unbeatable race that ruled the world through fear and subjugation. They kept humans as slaves, seeing them as lesser beings, forcing them to fight on the front line of tribal wars, starving them, treating them no better than dogs. The Elvian's gathered insurmountable riches and lived in splendor and luxury. The greater the warrior the more prestigious the position. They did not put a lot of importance on education and their written language was primitive. They were constantly warring with the Trolls of the North and the Goblins of the North-East, but would turn their attentions towards the humans that lived to the south, reaping the land, and retrieving slaves every spring.

Morphun Adramelech was the Sorcerer that finally rallied the scattered human tribes to fight back against imposing odds. Banding together the few sorcerers that existed and building an army of warlocks the war with the Elvians started in 1610. After a decade long war he created the Jaeger along with Viktor Wolfstein to help in the war, after another long and savage ten years of the Elvians finally meeting their match, the Elvian's were finally defeated, slaughtered by the decree of genocide and fled back to the far east where they went into hiding in the great Elvian forests of Redwoods, now hunted. They disappeared from the world in 1640, the remnants of the once glorious race said to have sailed East into the unknown to their demise.

Mages/Sorcerers

Born originally from humans with special talents of magic, they look just like humans. A very rare species of man, there was a fable told that the first ever sorcerer was born from a woman that had slept with a dragon. At their most prolific they were only twenty in number and it is not actually known how they came to be. They have a special ability to absorb the power of other sorcerers when they die, retaining the memories of that person and that is how their knowledge is past on, so not many books exist about them. They are a monk-like race seen as non-human and preferred to stay out of human society and keep the knowledge of their power secret.

Generally of average to tall stature they also vary in looks as humans do. Being able to store magic within themselves in what is known as a power core, they are able to wield magic without spell casting, weaving or ritual. Their magic is beyond the scope of warlocks and is past down through generations through bloodlines making each generation stronger with selective breeding. Their life spans range depending on their ability to slow the aging process but it is said any powerful enough could live for a millennia or more. A very secular people they mostly chose to stay to themselves and not interfere in what was going on around them until the Elvian race started coveting more and more land and decimating humanity into slavery, starvation, poverty and disease.

Morphun united the Sorcerers to the common cause against the Elvian race, with his friend Tiagratis Sindal volunteering to be the first Jaeger and undergo the genetic transformations to become the one to rule the new Jaeger race that was the turning point against the Elvians.

After the war with the Elvians the Sorcerers that were left wanted to return to their solitude, except for Morphun. He made them see that as they were superior one of their ranks should remain with the humans and monitor them to keep the peace. Now that a new race had been created in the Jaeger, the humans were nervous they would just become the new overlords. It was agreed, as Morphun was the most powerful and he had led everyone to victory, that it should be him. Morphun later made them all agree to not reproduce without the agreement of them all as any offspring could be seen as a potential risk to the balance he had created. He had already had his two sons in secret and decreed later that his line only should continue as the overseers of peace. He decided the humans needed to be kept under guidance and declared himself King over a large part of the land that was left after the Elvians, naming the land Tylandria after the castle that stood on the Eastern cliffs, even as many humans that had been Generals and leaders during the war dispersed with Elvian gold and were stepping up and declaring lordship on their own causing land wars. Morphun started the building of Estafeld and Adramelech Castle.

Tiagratis stood against Morphun, wishing to make that same fertile land a place for the Jaeger to settle.

Morphun betrayed his promises to Tiagratis and made his people appear as a new threat and that they also should not be allowed to live and breed, being genetic mutations.

A war between Tiagratis and Morphun started in 1643. Morphun died in battle in 1645, his son Leviathan Adramelech, the most powerful sorcerer of all time already, emerged from secrecy and became King at twenty two years of age and led the war against the Jaeger finally winning and a treaty was signed, the Jaeger forced to live in exile in Tylandria Castle to the East on a barren spit of land.

Leviathan then created the Hunters based on documents he found left behind by the disappeared Wolfstein (2nd Generation Jaegers from normal humans) to maintain a guard over the exiled Jaeger and to hunt down all those with Elvian blood, no matter how diluted it was. He sought to get rid of anyone powerful enough to oppose him and the other sorcerers feared he would come for them and take their power so fled into hiding. At this time only eight remained, not including Leviathan and his brother Antyn.

It was also made a decree after the devastation of the twenty year wars left Elvia as a wasteland due to the sorcerer-type and elemental magics that were used poisoned and killed the earth, that any subsequent wars should label anyone using such magic against another kingdom as a criminal and shall be brought to justice by the other sorcerers as a measure against one going rogue. The remaining sorcerers were shocked to find out Morphun had been experimenting on people to create a new race, saying it was blasphemous. They were horrified to learn of Leviathan's existance and what the prophecies had to say about him, making their decree all the more important as they fully realised the betrayal of Morphun Adramelech and his intentions from the start to manipulate the continent under his rule.

In 1655 Leviathan declared himself Emperor, after several of those documented prophecies came to light and he moved against Gardonia pushing them back and giving Tylandria a huge parcel of land right through the middle of the continent, handing him many of the continents sought after resources, agriculture and shipping, also giving him the biggest population of people to rule, therefore the biggest army, and access to the west coast, building the city of Asbel over the next few years. Gardonia built the massive wall during this time which isolated the northern kingdoms from the rest of the Tylan continent.

In 1660 Leviathan was challenged by Tiagratis, but he failed and was killed by Leviathan, the Jaeger retreated and placed a barrier over the forbidden forest for their own protection and once again self-exiled.

Leviathan's kingdom became powerful, rich and well under his control over the next decade of peace.

In 1674 Leviathan moved against Enyana laying seige to their capital for a year before destroying it and slaying their King. Enyana fought bravely but were unable to match the strength, size and magical power of Tylandria.

To date there are only nine sorcerers believed to be alive.

Jaeger

Tiagratis Sindal was the first Jaeger, volunteering with his sorcerer blood to enable the creation of more using warlocks and his blood to turn them into Jaeger. He started with his own extended family that had several warlocks and witches, first, making them all powerful Jaeger with magical abilities, fierce, strong and able to stand against the formidable Elvians. Other warlocks were used to gain a number of 500 Jaeger to bolster the human troops led by Morphun and fight against the enemy Elvians, this number was expanded to 2000 over the next ten years, but then decimated in the decade long war as well as the later wars against Morphun and then Leviathan.

Genetic manipulation and splicing, using transfiguration magic and the outlawed blood magic using wolf blood and Tiagratis's sorcerer blood was used in developing the Jaeger. Viktor Wolfstein, a genius warlock scientist is recognised as the one who developed the science behind it and subsequent experiments that have for a long time been hidden and denied, fetal experimentation and blood manipulation amongst them. It took him several years to perfect the Jaeger resulting in many unrecorded deaths from the brutal experiments done in secret, with only Morphun knowing. Many more warlocks were also killed as their bodies rejected the deadly mutations even after it had been perfected.

Going through the genetic changes was a horrific and painful process, taking days to complete, sometimes up to a month. Leaving the person completely changed in looks. All Jaeger appear white-haired with pale complexion and ice blue eyes. Their lean muscular physique is accentuated and their strength was tripled. They have an ability to change into the form of a wolf, larger and stronger than actual wolves, their hearing, eyesight and appetites are also changed.

Carrying the blood of the original Jaeger, Tiagratis, their magical abilities also grew to sorcerer status, able to wield magic without the use of casting or rituals due to developing a magical core.

The curses that Morphun had Viktor intergrate into the change as a precursor for control, ignited when Tiagratis stood against Morphun, they were the inability to withstand sunlight, blistering leading to severe skin disintergration occurs leading to death. A restriction on distance from Tylandria Castle, resulting in instant heart failure and the inability for the female Jaegers to reproduce. Some were also trapped within their wolf forms after being in the form for too long becoming wild and roaming the forbidden forest. These measures guaranteed the slow decline and non-threat of the Jaeger race once exiled.

Apart from the curses causing death or death through battle injury the Jaeger were believed to be immortal as they had outstanding regeneration abilities similar to the Elvian purebloods and did not seem to age.

Warlocks, Witches and Druids

The start of the human orthodox calendar co-insided with the birth of humans able to harness the magic of the world around them, nearly two thousand years ago. Magical births are completely random and do not follow bloodlines or breeding. These humans were given the names Warlocks and Druids, for males and Witches for females. They were persecuted and slaughtered by Elvian overlords as soon as they were discovered as children and a lot of them over time would flee to the far north-west or deep south until called up by Morphun to help in his war against the Elvians.

Witches are very rare and seldom born, often being quite pretty they are sought after by nobles for marriage to try and birth warlocks into their bloodline. This, however, is not guaranteed as magic ability is not past down by genetics yet many nobles still try.

After the war Warlocks and Druids were becoming more and more prevalent with most being taken in by certain institutions to learn their gift and learn how to serve their country with it, namely into the service of Tylandria and its army, the Warlock Brotherhood in the North, or some other similar armies or smaller kingdoms.

Warlocks are generally quite tall and known for their handsome youthful looks, being able to slow the aging process. Most living on average for two to three hundred years. Warlocks were put on the front lines of attack and consequently not many survived the twenty year wars.

Druids are generally more normal in looks and personality, not having the same magic abilities as Warlocks but still showing a connection to the magic that made them excellent botanists, metallurgist and healers. Warlocks and Druids now take up approximately 0.1% of the population, heavier concentrations do exist in some places, where others ban warlocks all together, like Gua del Mar, the King keeps only one as an advisor.

Witches are only about 0.004% of the population and also include natural healers, seers and herbalists.

Humans

The most base of the species, showing no predisposition to magic at all, they are the back bone of civilisation, infrastructure and agriculture. Population for the continent is estimated to be about four million people, with the highest concentration of two million in Tylandria. Most Kingdoms have there own beliefs and customs, the oldest being Gua del Mar – a nomadic people that have lived in the desert for as long as anyone can remember, they were never reached by the Elvians and are a secular people with a strong male dominated class system.

Hunters

Created by Leviathan Adramelech after the exile of the Jaeger in 1650, to hunt down any Elvians remaining in hiding, half-breeds and their families. Created from base humans they received only half the mutations of the Jaegers, avoiding going through the transformation and not having any magic. They stayed relatively human but twice as strong, more agile and with heightened senses, their hair would still turn white or a whiteish grey like they had aged through the process but their faces stayed youthful, aging normally over time. They were sent out by Leviathan with no restraint to hunt down every Elvian they could find, resulting in a lot of them being reckless and arrogant in their exulted station making many townsfolk and villagers fear and distrust them until

Leviathan finally called them all back and enlisted them into his army.

Other

Also found on the Tylan Continent are;

Trolls, live in the far northern reaches near the polar ice cap, cut off from the rest of the continent by the large desert wasteland where the Elvian's used to live.

Goblins, live to the East of Troll country on a narrow strip of land forced there by the Elvian race many centuries ago.

Dragons, mainly fallen into myth, have not been seen on the continent for a millenium.

BOOKS BY THIS AUTHOR

Unwanted Attention

The Vampire in my Mirror

Caught in the Middle

Tygarya Saga
Book 1 – Destiny Finds You
Book 2 – Loyalty Binds You
Book 3 – Betrayal Frees You
Book 4 – Destiny's Shadow Defines You

To Love A Vampire Queen
Book 1 – Houses of Shadow and Wolf
releases Feb 2026

ABOUT THE AUTHOR

ANNETTA LINCOLN

Annetta lives in New Zealand with her son in the lovely rural community of North Canterbury.

She loves walks on the local beaches and through the natural native bush that surrounds her little piece of paradise.

In 2019 Annetta was diagnosed with a rare SCC cancer and has battled with ongoing treatments, operations and scans. In 2023 she was told it had now traveled to her lungs at Stage 2, palliative care and more chemotherapy treatment would be needed.

Currently Annetta is living comfortably in a stable remission.

Annetta loves animals and owns two cats at present, barn rescue kittens they are gray tabby, brother and sister, Roman and Lily.

Annetta spends the rest of her spare time enjoying Anime and K-dramas, she is a great reader of fantasy and horror genres and loves listening to her son playing the guitar.

Annetta likes to spend her days writing in the hopes she brings a little joy to those who discover and read her books and leave a comment.

LOYALTY BINDS YOU

Instagram - annettalincolnauthor